PROPHET OF THE BADLANDS

THE AWAKENED BOOK 1

MATTHEW S. COX

DIVISION ZERO PRESS

Prophet of the Badlands
The Awakened – Book One
Second Edition
© 2013 and 2018 (second edition) Matthew S. Cox

A DIVERGENT FATES NOVEL

Cover Art by Jackson Tjota (Tjota.deviantart.com)

Interior art by Ricky Gunawan (http://goweliang.deviantart.com)

Cover layout by Alexandria Thompson (www.gothic-fate.com)

ISBN (ebook): 978-1-949174-24-3

ISBN (print): 978-1-949174-25-0

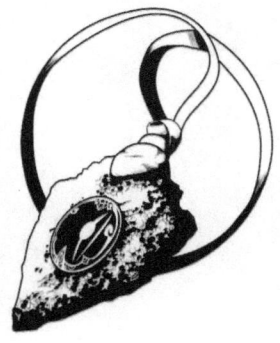

The Awakened Series

Prophet of the Badlands

Archon's Queen

Grey Ronin

Daughter of Ash

Zero Rogue

Angel Descended

CONTENTS

PREMONITIONS

P ure and cool, a breeze rustled a curtain of lustrous ivy, casting a wavering pattern of sunlight and shadow on Althea's body and the wall behind her. She crouched, motionless beside a crumbling barrier of mismatched stone and rusting metal, listening to the raven calls of bickering old men flutter away into the sky from the other side. The tribal elders couldn't agree on which direction to send the Seekers.

Althea smiled to herself. That they still talked about it meant they hadn't yet discovered her missing from the *Cha'dom*.

She clutched her hands in the dirt, stalking low to the ground toward the end of the hanging greenery, her motion quieter than the faint hiss of wind in the vines. At the edge of the wall, she paused, waiting for the path ahead to clear of villagers.

When opportunity came, she burst out from ivy, bounding on pale sinewy legs hardened by many hours spent running. Tattered leather strips that served as a skirt bounced around her as she careened down a curving walkway. At the end of the path, she ducked under the front end of an ancient car jutting out from the second story of the spear-maker's home.

One wheel, long devoid of rubber, intoned a song of rust to the wind, spinning in the light wind. The village wall, a collage of ancient, dead vehicles, stood at the end of a row of scrap metal dwellings. She ran to a gap only a child could squeeze past, and climbed in, gazing up at the wall's interior.

Althea leapt up and grabbed a horizontal spar, pulling herself upward, a spider monkey climbing a lattice of metal bars, struts, and old machines. Her breaths came rapid with fear and anticipation while she worked her way up the vertical maze toward a beam of daylight far above. Near the midway point, she slid into an old, crushed car, its door long absent, and scooted across the crumbling upholstery to emerge out the shattered rear window. Althea stood and crept to the edge of the trunk, cringing as the metal beast creaked. A short jump sent her lithe figure higher into the tangle, legs flailing for purchase as she grabbed a bit of rebar; maroon footprints in dust the only trace of her passage over the car. She hooked her toes on the bumper of a flattened truck and pushed herself onto another hood.

Minutes later, she propped herself against metal tubes and leaned her face out a round opening. Once sure she wouldn't be caught, she grabbed an overhead bar, pulled herself up, and threaded her legs into the portal. She sat on the edge for an instant before letting go and sliding down corrugated metal plates into the thick growth at the base.

The plants, laden with the dew of morning, tickled her with cold, wet fingers as she crawled toward the sound of the boys preparing for their foray into the Lost Place. Her toes dug into the cool dirt. She stretched forward, peeking through a veil of her tousled flaxen hair around the wall.

A dozen Seekers, skin the color of sienna, gathered in a circle under the shade of the Spirit-Tree. Except for the youngest, they had powerful, sinewy bodies. All but one kept their raven hair cut short. Palik, who fancied himself a half-chamán, wore it down to his belt, loaded with baubles.

Den stood among them. She stared at the lean contours of his muscles as he helped the older seekers gather supplies. The sight of the only boy in the entire tribe who didn't radiate terror being around her made her smile, but delight faded to a sense of worry. The past night's sleep had left her with a foreboding feeling something bad would happen to him today.

The elders of this village had been kinder than most that found her. It had taken a mere two months before they trusted her promise she would not try to run away. Only two months of pleas before they no longer kept her in the cage. Den believed her. As the son of Braga, the chief, he had demanded her release. The elders didn't permit her to leave the Cha'dom, much less the village. The *chamán* expected her to assist with the rituals, even if she didn't understand them. To earn their trust, she obeyed. Althea feared the cage more than the bizarre wild-eyed man with a dead wolf skin upon his head and paint upon his face. She had done as he told her to do, holding the bowls and spreading the powders, even swallowing the odd plants that made her feel funny and see strange things.

Fear knotted her gut at the thought of running outside, even though she had no desire to flee. The elders would be furious, but she had to warn Den no matter the consequence. With any luck, the sleep she had given the *chamán* would still be upon him when she returned.

Althea picked at her leather skirt while she watched the Seekers prepare, thinking she needed to add more material. She made it around two years ago, when she'd been ten years of age by her best estimate. Collected scraps of leather armor, old belts, shoelaces, and such had made for a tough garment. Most tribal Scrags wore only what they made or found on their own, or what a courting Seeker gifted them. She did not wish to wait for the latter. As the Prophet, she doubted any boy would court her, and tired of having nothing to wear. *Little* Scrags, unwanted women, and inept warriors ran about with only air for clothing, and Althea didn't consider herself little anymore.

Roughly two years later, the steady process of repairing and adding to it had created a tangle of mostly leather tatters down to her knees. The garment served its purpose well, though the dingy grey chest-cloth Den had given her wouldn't last as long. Althea squirmed, still unaccustomed to the feeling of wearing anything above the waist. The thin shirt left her arms bare, only two thin strips of fabric over her shoulders. It seemed utterly without purpose.

She continued wearing the itchy before-time scrap only because *Den* had given it to her. As much as it annoyed her, tossing it away would feel like being mean to him.

The boys marched off in a line, following a rocky trail down out of the hills. Althea looked between the wall and the hunting party with a desperate grimace. If they caught her, the elders would think it an escape attempt and put her back in the cage. If she didn't go, Den would have no warning of danger and she feared he would die.

It didn't make for much of a choice.

As soon as they walked out of sight, she closed her eyes for the span of a breath and dashed from her hiding place. The clearing between the wall and the forest blurred as she sprinted. Tall weeds smacked her shins and she clawed at the tall grass to shove it out of her way. At the woods' edge, she leapt into the first bits of underbrush and clamped onto the nearest tree. Coarse, wet bark scratched at her skin, but at least her dirt-smeared figure blended like camouflage. She stood on her toes, frozen for almost a minute, listening for any trace of danger.

Motion attracted eyes.

No shouts arose from behind, no one came running, and the hunting party didn't react. Her keen ears detected only the soft hiss of the wind in the branches. She let out a gasp of relief, pulled her hair out of her face, and followed the rustles and snaps growing distant in the forest.

She stepped around rocks and roots, brushing vines aside, walking as fast as she could without creating noise. The hunters had trained senses, but she could be far quieter than the boars they preyed upon. Moving from tree to tree in a series of sprints, crawls, and leaps, she soon came within sight of them.

A birdcall echoed, one of the Seekers making a signal. In response, the spread-out group gathered close. The boys collected around something on the ground. The eldest, a grown man named Nalu, crouched and stuck a large knife into the dirt, picking at his beard while the scent of something dead teased at her nose. Trying to get a look at what they found, she crept closer, crawling into a thick patch of fern for cover. She sat back on her heels and craned her neck for a better view. The cause of their delay, a huge dead boar, had been torn open from neck to groin. Her eyes widened at the sight as she tried to imagine what could have done such a thing. The boys radiated fear, wonder, and hunger in varying degrees.

Jake, the youngest of the group, backed away from the mangled beast. Scrawny and small, he was about the same age as Althea and clad in a pair of boar-hide shorts he had made after his first hunting trip. Pants had let him feel as though he left his boyhood behind and had become a man; he had spent several days showing them off to everyone. Unlike her, he had taken the time to smudge the dirt on his cheeks and chest into a pattern resembling war paint.

He leaned on his wooden spear, looking anywhere but at the pig. He exuded fear the way incense gave off smoke. His gaze swept toward her, and he gasped, pointing. Althea stiffened as they all turned and stared at her one by one. Den smirked and waved her over. With a guilty face, she rose to her feet and trudged out into the open, head bowed.

"You have the sight of a hunter already." She smiled at Jake.

"Did you forget your eyes make light like the stars and your skin is pale?" Den tried not to laugh. "Why did you follow?" He jogged over and put his hands on her shoulders. "Girls should stay safe at home. The elders will think you are running away."

"She is running from the village," barked Palik.

Althea glanced at Den's hand, dark brown against her skin. "The Alamos tribe has more girl Seekers than boys." She folded her arms in defiance. "Their boys are lazy."

The other six fixed her with uneasy stares. Jake took a step back with his spear all but pointed at her. Nalu stood, turning away from the dead pig, and shook his head. Like Althea, he wore a garment resembling a skirt made from leather strips, only his had a rectangular orange metal plate hanging in the center with strange marks on it. She had seen similar things attached to old cars, and thought it silly to use such a thing for armor. They hadn't protected the cars at all. He pulled his machete out of the ground and approached.

Den poked her in the belly. "You can't be a Seeker. You won't kill anything. You don't have trouble *eating* the boar, but you refuse to kill one."

She thrust her lower lip out, unable to argue his truth. Killing anything, even for meat, seemed evil.

Nalu's expression grew stern. "It is not that you are a girl. You are the Prophet." He frowned. "You promised you would not flee."

Althea scooted behind Den and clung to him. "I am not fleeing. I came to warn you."

Den smiled at her touch, but the others continued radiating fear. "Warn us of what?"

"I had a bad feeling." She tried to touch the blue light on his back cast off by her eyes. "I dreamed you would be hurt today."

"You should go back." Jake's voice quivered as he gestured at Den. "Glow-eye says you will die."

Den puffed his chest up and hefted his metal spear. "I'm not scared."

Althea glanced down at his one large boot and one torn shoe, fruits of a previous trip into the Lost Place. "I go with you." She gradually lifted her gaze up his body, past the agate arrowhead hung around his neck, and stared into the eyes of a man set in the face of a boy. "Please trust me."

Jake shook his head. "Glow-eye will bring bad luck."

The other Seekers shifted with unease.

At a brief gust in the wind, Althea's hair tickled the center of her back and strands of leather caressed her legs. Nalu turned his gaze up to the whispering treetops and sniffed.

"Prepare." He dropped into a fighting stance with his machete held high.

Den grasped Althea's arm and dragged her to the nearest tree of decent size. "Up. Animals approach."

Once she started to climb, he grabbed her about the waist to help, then cupped her feet and pushed her higher. Within seconds of her perching on a high branch, grey furry streaks emerged from the brush. Skinny, disheveled dogs with charcoal hued fur formed up in a line, staring the Seekers down with intelligence beyond what seemed natural for such animals.

Bonedogs. She bit her lip. They didn't usually attack large groups like this. Something felt wrong.

Five canines with bright yellow eyes and jagged, mismatched teeth protruding sideways from their snouts snarled in unison. The largest, as tall as Nalu's chest, sniffed at the air and focused on Jake. The others followed his direction, noting the weakest of their prey. Althea gazed around, bewildered by the rapid eruption of emotions from the Seekers. Nalu gave off annoyance, Den guarded confidence, Jake terror. The others were frightened, but not to the same degree as the youngest boy.

When the alpha dog again tossed his nose in Jake's direction, the pack ran at him.

Nalu grabbed the boy by the shoulder and hauled him back, shouting for the others to circle around. Den remained close to the tree to protect her. Delight at his concern faded when she sensed the embarrassment surrounding Jake become rage. He didn't want the others to think of him as a little frightened boy, even if he was only eleven.

She bounced to her feet on the branch. "Jake, no!"

Spear held high, he let off a high-pitched cry and leapt out from behind Nalu, rushing at one of the creatures.

The bonedog ducked, leaving Jake stabbing at dirt, then nipped at him while backpedaling to lure the boy away from the much bigger Nalu. Jake followed with a bloodthirsty grin, mistaking the dog for being frightened of him. Two others distracted Nalu with a flash of snapping teeth and drool while the last one crept around, taking advantage of the boy's fixation on the 'scared' dog. It lunged, sinking its teeth into the boy's calf before wrenching him to the ground with a twist of its head.

Jake screamed. Nalu turned and sliced at the ambusher, exposing himself to the two distractors.

The dog with a mouthful of Jake's shin leapt away from the machete strike, baring bloody teeth in an angry glare at Nalu. Protecting its meal, it snarled, refusing to back off.

"Bonedogs." They like ta rip off arms or legs and run away with 'em." Den looked up, amused at her lack of squeamishness.

"I know. I have seen them before." A huge mass of black fur loomed up behind him. She pointed and yelled, "Den! Look—"

He turned as the Alpha pounced, managing to wedge his spear handle sideways into the beast's mouth before it clamped its jaws around his throat. The weight and momentum of the animal knocked him flat on his back. With one twist of its great neck, the enormous dog thrashed the spear out of his grip and tossed it to the side. Den scrambled backward on the ground, but the dog stepped on his chest, pinning him. When it swung its head back to lock eyes with him, it radiated delight.

"Nalu!" Althea screamed. "Help!"

The eldest hunter wrestled with another dog in an effort to keep it off Jake. The boy had become frozen in fear. He didn't cry, but couldn't defend himself. The others traded superficial wounds with the rest of the pack in a roving skirmish through the trees. Nalu couldn't do anything for Den in time to matter. Althea couldn't change Jake's emotions fast enough to matter for Den.

She looked down as the alpha snapped at Den's face. He grabbed it by its cheek fur and held on. Teeth snapped at his nose and drool sprayed in his face as its effort to overpower him pushed him along the ground. After a few feet, it twisted and bit him on the forearm. Den grunted, kicking at the dog's underside, not that it appeared to notice.

"No!" Althea slid from the branch and landed on all fours like a wildcat.

She ran to Den's spear, urged into a panic at the sound of bones splintering behind her. With a feeble attempt at a roar that came out as a wail, she lowered the point and ran at the giant canine. Desperation made the light in her eyes flare bright. A subconscious command empowered her body, boosting her strength. The alpha's bloodlust kept it focused on Den. It didn't react to her charge until the spear tip plunged into its side. The shock of impact knocked her grip loose, hands sliding forward over the leather cording on the metal bar. Emitting a belabored groan, the

Alpha wheezed and released Den's arm before stumbling sideways. Althea jerked the spear free, and the animal collapsed on its side.

The other four dogs abandoned their prey and converged on her, enraged at the death of the alpha. She spun to face them, standing over Den with the spear aimed forward. He grasped her ankle, then slid his hand up to squeeze her calf.

"Run," he wheezed.

Determined to protect him, she gathered a telempathic emanation of fear. The perpetual azure glow in her eyes brightened. She glared from one monster to the next, daring them to attack while projecting dread into their minds.

Stalled in their tracks, the animals hesitated for mere seconds before their tails swung down between their legs and they backed away with hesitant growls. Althea took a step at them, thrusting the spear in a menacing gesture not intended to hit anything. The pack turned as one and vanished, smears of grey into the woods.

The hunting party, except for Den, gawked at her in silence. Nalu didn't seem to know what to make of this, while the younger ones looked at her as though she had become a dangerous entity, not some child to be protected or a precious commodity to be guarded.

The Prophet had killed.

2

A LAMB AMONG WOLVES

The bonedogs darted into the shifting greens and browns of the wood. Althea stood guard over Den, clutching the spear, motionless until no trace of the animals remained in sight or hearing. She let the tip of the heavy spear sag to the ground, no longer able to bear its weight. After dropping it entirely, she knelt and pulled Den's mangled arm into her lap.

He moaned at her touch, lolling his head toward her in a half daze. "You... killed it?"

She frowned, ashamed. "I'm sorry! He bit your arm and I—"

"It's okay... only a bonedog." He let his head fall back to the ground. "You saved me."

Althea stared at the large mound of dark fur, on the verge of tears at the sight of its lifelessness. True, it would have killed Den, but that didn't weaken her guilt at ending a life. A drip of hot blood on her leg brought her attention back to him.

With a firm grip on either side of the bite wound, she reached out with her mind, searching for a connection with his body. In seconds, his heartbeat and the ebb and flow of his breaths entered her awareness. In the blackness of her closed eyes, Den drifted toward her. She perceived the discrete parts within him as amorphous masses of color: white for bone-shapes, dull red for muscles, bright red for blood-shapes, and dark blobs for the important things in the middle. Althea poured her power into him, commanding his body to repair itself. After detaching his mind from pain, she pulled and twisted his mauled arm, the bones scraping over each other while she worked the limb back to its natural shape.

Her breaths came deep and rapid as she poured her energy into him. Charged with her power, his body's normal healing process sped up by an order of magnitude. Slender white forms flowed whole from splintered fragments. Crimson strands launched threads over black chasms that pulled closed as his muscles re-grew, before at last, new skin spread over the wound. Within a few minutes, a pink blotch of tenderness remained as the only hint of a formerly destroyed arm. She opened her eyes and let the link fade. Den drew in a hiss, cradling the tender spot.

Althea knew full well why everyone in the Badlands wanted to own her.

At a presence hovering nearby, Althea looked up. Nalu stood over her cradling Jake in his arms. The boy's leg had shattered, but the older hunter's quick reaction had prevented the bonedog from tearing half the limb off and fleeing with it. Nalu set him down beside her. The boy tried to scoot away as if she would devour him.

"The Prophet will not harm you." Nalu held the squirming lad down with one hand.

She made a sad face and radiated calm, overpowering the fear inside him. His trembling stilled. Althea set her grimy, blood-soaked fingers upon his wounded leg and concentrated. He tensed as his muscles undulated, rebuilding themselves. At the sight of his skin sealing without a mark, he gasped.

"They guard their kill." Nalu pointed at the pig carcass. "They have fed from it. This boar is unsafe for us to eat. We must move before they return."

"The bonedogs hunt too close to us," said Palik, glaring at Althea. "This is omen."

Den sat up, his attempt to speak stalled by a loud gurgle from his gut.

Althea giggled. "Making hurts go away makes hungry." She offered a weary smile, fatigue evident in her voice, and mended Nalu's superficial wounds.

Jake scrambled to his feet, stumbling as soon as he put weight on his leg. Nalu caught him, lowering him back to the ground.

She looked from Den to Jake, then up at Nalu. "The hurt will be sore for a time, maybe an hour. Please let them rest."

Nalu shook his head. "Understood... but not here. We must distance ourselves from their food before they return in greater numbers."

He carried Jake and gathered the others. Althea stood and offered a hand to Den to help him stand. A chill spread over her when she noticed the alpha bonedog had vanished. Where once had been a body, threads of shadow seeped into the trees, black wisps the only trace of its presence. She pulled Den away from the spot as fast as she could coax him to go.

They followed Nalu for a while before he decided to let them rest at a spot where an old crumbling concrete wall faded back into the earth. After arranging the group in a defensive circle, he set Jake down against a fallen log. Other Seekers migrated further south, away from her. She sighed at Nalu ruffling the boy's hair. The brotherly affection they shared only served to make her feel more apart from the tribe, more a possession. She couldn't remember anyone ever sharing a moment with her like that, not since the Wagon Man took her. She'd been five or six then, and scarcely remembered her parents. The men and boys of this tribe even cringed away from her healing touch, enduring it only as long as it took to mend them.

Not one person among this tribe wanted to be near her, much less hug or carry her around—except Den. He wandered over to where she had flopped, sitting next to her in the shadow of the tiny wall before putting an arm around her shoulders and pulling her close. Astonished, she held her hands to her chest and leaned into him. The others thought him crazy for being near such a creature as her. Even Den's father Braga expressed dismay that his son chose her. The talk among the elders hinted at their expectations Den would ask permission for the joining ritual soon.

Althea grinned at the thought of joining. She didn't know what it meant beyond it happening between two people who liked each other a great deal. She could see in Den's thoughts he wanted it, and his emotions toward her gave her comfort.

"What are you smiling at?" He glanced over, swallowing a bit of dried meat so he could talk.

She helped herself to a piece of it and tugged at her ragged shirt. "Braga's face when you gave me this."

"Yala is still angry."

Gnawing on the hard ration, she glanced up at him with an inquiring expression.

"Before we found you, father had set her aside for me because I had not chosen."

Althea looked off to the right, muttering. "She is pretty… her hair is so long and beautiful."

"You're pretty, too." He poked her in the side.

She scrunched her face up at him and squirmed. "I'm too pale."

"You are of a different tribe. Still beautiful… and Yala's eyes don't make the night run away."

A blush settled on her face for an instant before sorrow gripped her. "If I wasn't… I mean if I was normal…"

"I'd still want you for a wife."

"What?" She shot upright and stared at him, a hint of a tremble in her. "They said we were to be joined, not that I was to be wifed!"

He took her hand, eyebrows drifting closer. "What do you mean? Getting joined means you are my wife."

Althea shivered. Her eyes reddened and she rubbed at a lump in her throat. "I thought it meant something nice."

Den fixed her with an unblinking stare. "What do you think a wife is?"

Her head pitched down, she cried. "I have seen slaves get wifed."

He beckoned her close again. "It is not the same. We are not raiders."

"So if we are joined, you won't wife me?" She sniffled back tears, looking at him.

"Someday, you'll want to." He looked up with an impish smile. "I hope."

Althea glared with confusion and peeked into his mind. His feelings seemed quite different than what she expected. Getting wifed had been the most evil thing she had ever seen. The women always either tried to fight or beg them not to, but the raiders never listened. She would never allow that to happen to her. However, the contents of Den's thoughts didn't look anything like what she'd seen in raider camps. He believed a girl would *want* to do that. His thoughts proved a little embarrassing, and she couldn't keep looking at him without blushing. He probably didn't know what 'wifeing' really meant, and used the word wrong.

Relieved, she settled back against him. "Would you like me even if I wasn't the Prophet?"

"Uh huh." His adrenaline had worn off, leaving him sounding about ready to sleep. "Maybe… As long as you still had glow-eyes."

She poked him in the side. "I like it here." The tiny lie made her bite her lip. Den she liked, the rest of the village—not so much. However, it beat being a captive of killers and crazies. Even if this village made her go back in the cage, they didn't roam the Badlands attacking people.

He laughed. "I'm glad."

Althea traced her fingers in lazy circles across her bare stomach. "Den?" She lifted her head, waiting for him to look at her. "Why are they scared of me? All I want is to help everyone."

"They fear the stories." He brushed a finger across her forehead, moving her hair off her face. "The old one says darkness will follow you."

Althea stared down, focusing on the agate arrowhead hanging at the center of his chest. "Bad people always take me." She cuddled closer, reaching an arm across to play with the pendant. Adoring the feel of warm skin on her cheek and his breath on her head, she enjoyed a sense of contentment.

He smiled, watching the bit of agate move over her fingers. "They want what you can do. Stop giving medicine and they will leave you alone."

She looked up with a gasp. "I can't let people hurt."

"If you had to choose 'tween bein' with me or bein' the Prophet, what would you do?"

"I..." She stared, unable to balance her happiness against the needs of so many people. Her gaze fell to the ground; she could neither give voice to her answer, nor lie to him.

"Time to go." Nalu's shout fell on them both like a bucket of cold water. "Watch her. Make sure she does not run."

"You know the stories," said Den, gesturing at him. "The Prophet does not run. She has promised."

Althea studied her lap.

They rested for a little while more while Nalu went about rousing the others into motion. Althea sat up, hiding her face so he couldn't see the deepening red around her eyes. Nalu had punched a hole in her bubble, reminding her she was the tribe's possession and not a member. Den ambushed the exposed skin at her sides and continued to tickle her after she leapt to her feet, until she grabbed his hands. Out of breath from laughing, she smiled.

He flashed a mischievous grin. "I like this face more."

The others gawked at him as if he tried to play fetch with a wild tiger. Den didn't react to them, holding her hand and walking with her at the rear of the expedition toward the Lost Place. As the group marched on through the woods, the others cast occasional worried glances their way. Althea ignored their frowns, adrift in the dream of a girl being with a boy she liked, free of the burden of her gift.

In time, the trees parted to reveal an expanse of strange stone obelisks dotted with scattered glimmers of reflected sunlight. Flat strips of black rock covered the land that stretched out in front of her, between rows of one-branched metal trees with bizarre bulbous pods. Some of the immense stone spires had split open, revealing hollows inside with dozens of separate spaces. Althea shivered, dreading the size of the wasps that must have built such nests.

Cool dirt and grass gave way to hot black stone under her feet. Althea jumped back, giving Den a frightened glance. The boys laughed at her reaction to the paving, all except for Nalu, who glared with annoyance. With Den coaxing her, she stepped cautiously over the foreign surface and stared in awe at where the rising buildings cut apart the sky. She had heard stories of the Lost Place, but had never imagined how big or how frightening it might be.

"Put her in there," barked Nalu.

She jumped at the sudden command. The man pointed at a large green creature standing by a crumbling wall where a patch of rough weeds forced their way up from cracks.

"Inside that beast?" The expression of utter revulsion on her face made everyone laugh.

Nalu grabbed her wrist. "It is not alive. It is a driving machine of the before-time. It is a war box that will protect you until we return."

"We shouldn't leave her alone." Den tried to interpose himself between them.

Nalu, much stronger, shoved him aside with ease. "She will slow us down."

Althea glared as he dragged her along. "Because I'm a girl?"

He whirled on her once they had reached the shadow of the old machine. "No. You are not a Seeker. The Lost Place is dangerous, and you will get hurt. You cannot kill without hesitation; you are a burden here."

Den clasped her other hand. "We can protect her."

Althea looked back and forth between man and boy pulling on her arms, a wishbone in a tug of war.

"If you are fool enough to enter the Ritual of Joining with her, then you can do with her what you will. For now, she belongs to all of us, and I will not be blamed for losing her."

Nalu grasped the top of the vehicle and pulled a hatch—the entire back—down. The screech of protesting metal made her shiver.

Had it opened fully, it would have formed a ramp, though age and debris caused it to stick half way. Unlike the driving machines she had seen among the raiders, this one had many small metal wheels wrapped in a band of interlocking pads, and thick, windowless sides. Nalu hauled her into the air and set her on the half-open ramp.

Den grabbed his arm. "Be gentle with her."

Nalu ignored him, shoving her forward with a hand on her backside.

Althea skidded on the steel floor, falling into a hard bench seat along one side of the wall a second before the heavy door slammed closed behind her. From the muffled shouts outside, she assumed her yelp started a fight between Den and Nalu. She ran to the hatch, pushing at it with her whole body, but couldn't budge it.

Althea gave up trying to open the door and yelled. "Stop!" She slapped at the wall and shouted again, louder. "Please don't hurt him."

Her voice echoed to silence inside the metal box, leaving only the sound of her breathing. She had delivered her warning, saving him from the alpha bonedog. The dread of this great enclosure filled her, and she stared at the floor. Fear of what Nalu would tell the elders about her leaving the village brought shivers.

If it kept Den alive, she would tolerate the cage again.

3

HAUNTED

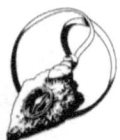

lthea stared at the wall of the metal beast, listening to the silence outside. Whatever had happened between Den and Nalu ended as soon as it began. She let her hands slide down the painted surface, arms falling limp at her sides. Sniffling, she surveyed her surroundings and sighed. The massive ramp had closed out the sun's light, but not its heat. Already, trickles of sweat ran down the backs of her legs. The interior of the vehicle no longer appeared drab green, having faded to tones of grey.

Dark.

A narrow doorway at the opposite end of the chamber looked in on a smaller room, and the shoulder of a person in a seat on the left. Light from her eyes flickered as she reached out in search of thoughts, but sensed no active mind. With an apologetic frown, she crept closer and grasped the doorframe. She slipped past the seat into the front section, and came face to face with the former driver—a skeleton. The body slumped to the side against the wall, the bones coated in the decayed rot of several centuries. He had been dead so long the runoff of his decomposition felt like thick, spongy dust underfoot. Despite the gruesome occupant, the air held only the scent of metal and rotted fabric. Ancient bloodstains spattered the controls, the cause of death as obvious as the bullet holes in the cranium.

Althea frowned, patting him on the knee. "I'm sorry."

She eased in front of him, prodding and tweaking various buttons and switches, hoping to find one that might let her out of the sweltering prison. When poking and twisting failed, she resorted to slapping and pounding with little improvement in the result, save for the amount of dust in the air. Grumbling, she edged past the corpse, careful not to disturb it, and approached one of the two benches in the rear chamber. For a moment, she stared at the dingy seat, wondering which irregular blotches came from blood. Overcome with resignation, she spun around, sighed again, and plopped down.

The old cushions spat a torrent of particles as she fell onto them. She had little to do but wait for the Seekers to return. Althea leaned back against the warm metal wall, closed her eyes, and counted the trickles of sweat running down her back, stomach, and legs. Dread that the Seekers would not return at all teased at the edge of her mind, but for now, she kept it at bay.

A tickle quite unlike a sweat droplet crept across the instep of her left foot. She sat up and blinked at a two-inch long beetle that had crawled up to perch upon her. Althea lifted her leg, staring at the confused motions of the bug as it scurried from side to side, searching for solid ground.

"Are you trapped in here, too?"

She lowered her foot and the beetle rushed off, vanishing under the bench on the other side. For an uncountable number of minutes, Althea sat straight with her hands in her lap. When that grew intolerable, she shifted through a series of positions, searching in vain for one that offered any degree of comfort. She eventually decided to stand and paced about. The faint motion of air provided an almost unnoticeable improvement over the stagnant stillness. Her steps squished and slipped upon the floor, even the soles of her feet had a coating of sweat. Raiders sometimes put disobedient slaves in a sun box, though she had never before suffered such a fate.

How cruel of them to leave me in here.

The beetle emerged near the ramp, wandering an erratic circle.

She squatted and reached out to pluck the tiny explorer from the floor. "Do you think Nalu wanted to punish me for leaving the village?"

Had it any opinion on the matter, the beetle kept mum as it crept over her hand and between her fingers. Upon sensing distress from it, Althea released it and stood. She glared at the ramp, unsure if she felt guilty for defying the villagers by sneaking out or worried the dogs might not have been the substance of the foreboding feeling she had about Den.

Her concern built for him. Several minutes of nervous pacing only made her fear grow. Althea screamed and launched herself against the metal, shoving at the rear hatch, but succeeded only in creating sweaty smears in the dust on the floor as her feet slipped backward. Perspiration ran in her eyes, and she wiped her face on the chest-cloth to regain the ability to see.

A spike of worry intensified without warning or explanation. She scowled at the immovable ramp, too furious to cry and too sad to scream. A quick look about yielded nothing of use and reduced her to pounding both fists on the ramp and shouting for help.

Out of breath, Althea stared at the wet fist-shaped marks she'd left. Attacking the rear door wouldn't do anything. She trudged to the forward compartment, pouting at the skeleton and the worthless buttons and switches. To the right of the dead man, a second seat cushion folded up against the wall. She pushed it down into place and sat, staring at her dirt-streaked arms. Time passed in silence interrupted by the scrapes of her flicking a finger at the rotting canvas beneath her. She pulled her legs up, heels on the edge of the seat cushion, and hugged her knees to her chest. For a minute or six, she stared in silence at the skeleton, dizzy from the heat.

"If they get hurt, I'll starve in here." She looked past her dangling toes to the floor, studying the spots of sweat appearing in the dust. "I'd rather get shot like you, in the head. I bet it did not hurt much. At least I won't be alone when I die."

His cobweb-packed skull met her weak smile with an impassive stare.

"I shouldn't try to escape. If they think I'm running away, they won't trust me again."

Shapes crept around the dead man as she examined her surroundings; the castoff light from her eyes stretched tiny buttons into large shadows. One droplet of sweat fell from the tip of her nose, landing on her thigh.

A wisp of doubt traced ephemeral fingers across her shoulders, causing her to look up. "I have a bad feeling. What if Den is still going to get hurt?"

Nalu's words echoed in her mind, making her wonder if she would be able to kill a person to save his life if she had to. The thought rode in on a wave of nausea. The salty flavor of sweat clung to her lips. As woozy as she'd become from the sweltering cage, she half expected the driver to answer her.

"She's in there," said a man, his voice muted but close.

Althea gasped at the dead man. "You can't talk. You're dead."

A centipede as big around as her thumb emerged from its nose, crawling over the jaw and into the folds of his old camouflage uniform. Scuffing outside snapped her out of her fog. She drew an anxious breath and lowered her feet to the floor, clutching the cushion on either side of her rear end. Focused on listening, she held herself completely still. Unfamiliar voices murmured.

"You sure?" asked another man.

"Yeah. Help me get 'er open."

Tapping at the rear hatch proved they tried to get to her. She peered around the partition separating the driver compartment from the back, momentarily pleased at the thought of being kidnapped again, as it would get her out of this intolerable oven.

She hurried to the door, clasped her hands in front of herself, and stared compliantly at the ground, waiting to be taken while trying not to faint from heat. Thoughts of Den came with a gentle caress on her cheek. She smiled at him standing beside her, but he vanished. The touch of his fingers became a trickle of sweat dripping onto the hand she raised to him.

A new complication arose in her mind. If another tribe took her, she would never see him again. Nauseous thoughts of resistance replaced obedient surrender. She gazed in a panic around the small chamber, looking for a place to hide, but her surroundings offered no cover. She rushed over to the former driver and put a hand on his shoulder. The material crumbled in her fingers.

"I know you can't answer me, but what should I do?"

The skull tilted away and rolled to the side, wedging between the seat back and the corner. Althea swallowed the urge to cry as the thought of losing Den became more and more real with each bang at the ramp door. She looked away from the skull and faced toward the increasingly loud noises. Out of the corner of her eye, she spotted a lever in the roof, right in line with where the skull's empty sockets pointed. It looked like a small hatch to the roof.

"Thank you," she whispered.

Grateful for the low ceiling, she stood on her toes, grasped the lever, and pulled. Centuries of disuse had left it immobile. Rather than move the metal bar, she pulled herself up off the floor and hung. For a few seconds, she dangled, trying to use her weight to move it. She wanted to scream in frustration, but contained herself and dropped back to her feet. A *creak* from the back changed some of the grey to bright olive green.

She squinted at the lever. Fright gave way to determination. The men figured out how to work the ramp and would be on her soon. Althea concentrated on her magic. A sense of her body filled her vision with the strand-shapes of the muscles in her arms. Focus sent more of her blood-presence there, urging them beyond their capacity for a brief moment. With a grunt, she heaved. The bar broke the crud and spun around. Planting one foot on the back of the driver's chair and another against the wall, she shoved upward.

Decaying rubber flakes crumbled around her as daylight pierced the disintegrating seal. She hauled herself up and slithered out onto the hot, sandy roof, her sweat-covered legs sliding with ease. Air washed over her with a wintry embrace. Her drenched shirt smeared a trail of wet over the metal that evaporated in seconds. Flat on her stomach, she eased the hatch closed and lay still while a throbbing ache worked its way out of her arms. She had hurt herself inside making her limbs that strong, but it took only a moment to repair torn muscles. Seconds after the pain stopped, the rear ramp crashed to the ground, lofting a billowing cloud of dust.

"Oi, c'mon out, you. We know yer in der," shouted a man, while banging on the old vehicle.

"Yah. You ours now." A different voice followed.

Althea waited for them to walk into the green beast, and leapt to the ground. She had no idea which way Den had gone, but the Lost Place offered a better option than those men did. After a quick glance back at the boxy relic, she sprinted into the city.

♫ ✴ ⚉ ⬙ ♋

FREE FROM THE SWELTERING CHAMBER, SHE DARTED DOWN DECREPIT streets, adoring the beautiful cool air. Althea cornered at random in hopes of eluding her would-be abductors. After several alleys, her stride slowed to a jog, then a brisk walk. She wanted to call out to Den, but shouting would let everything in the area find her. Tall buildings surrounded her with various degrees of decrepitude, some spilling their contents into the street while others appeared ready to collapse at a whisper.

Her gait slowed further to a gradual rotating creep while gazing up at the structures. Within the wasp-hollows, tables, chairs, and other signs of man gleamed in the daylight. It occurred to her that giant wasps hadn't made these nests at all. Amazed at how people could have made something so large, she lowered her gaze to the wall at her left, and touched it, tracing her fingers over the rough stone while wondering about the powerful mystics who must have been here to make the rock so flat and perfect.

Energy within the material called out to her. She pressed herself against the building, resting her cheek upon the warm surface between her hands. Eyes closed, she opened her thoughts to the spiritual imprint. Her vision swirled with flashes of history etched into the concrete by pain, desperation, and terror.

Althea gasped and jumped away, shivering, an accusatory glare aimed at the wall. The images of many people dying in this place changed the presence of the city around her. The wonder and awe at the towering structures drowned in pitiful sorrow from feeling the final emotional moments of thousands of lives. She fell into a squat, wrapping her arms around herself as she cried, unable to stop the overwhelming tide of loss.

A mournful call from a distant bird brought her attention back to the reality of being lost, hunted, and alone. She flung her hair out of her face with a twist of her head and looked around at the destroyed city. The surge of raw emotion from other people had subsided; her feelings once again belonged to her. This had to be the reason she felt uneasy. Something in this massive tomb hungered for more blood. Nothing good would want to be in a place where the very walls held such evil.

She bounded to her feet and yelled. "Den!"

Her voice echoed, weakening into the distance and chasing a group of birds out of their roosts in the steel girders above. A man's voice grunted in pain to her left. Concerned, she jogged toward it, rounding a corner, and stopped short at the sight of two men clad in patchwork armor made of panels of leather and scrap metal. Tanned skin gleamed in the relentless sun, smeared with dirt and marked with many old healed wounds. Althea's eyes widened at the rifles across their backs. The man on the left doubled over, but she sensed greed—not pain.

He faked a hurt.

"Thar you is." The standing one grinned at her.

She took a step back, toes gripping the pavement, alone with two raiders… which meant no innocent people to threaten if she disobeyed. Before they could say another word, she sprinted off.

"Hey. You ain't s'posed ta do runnins!"

"Yah," yelled the shorter one. "We knows da Prophet's stories."

They chased after her, but she bought a few seconds by ducking into a gap in a wooden fence they had to break down. She hurried along a strip of smooth black stone between rows of blasted buildings and dozens of old cars left where they crashed. A pause to pick a direction lasted mere seconds; the *smash* of the fence collapsing kicked her into motion again. The men came too close. If she tried to hide here, they would surely see where she went. Half a block down, she spotted a narrow metal opening along the edge where a strip of white stone bordered the dark path.

She rushed over and crouched, peering into a pit below the ground. The two came out of the alley and charged. Althea gasped at their sudden appearance and abandoned her fear of going underground. She slid into the storm drain feet first, letting go of the rim barely a second before a man's hand slapped into it.

"Gar dammit!"

Althea dropped about eight feet to a painless landing in semisoft mud. Scrambling to regain her footing, she looked up at the two faces in the slot.

"I am sorry, but I cannot go with you. Den needs me."

The sense of security afforded by a gap too small for men to squeeze into evaporated when a circular section of ceiling above her opened, showering her with dust and exposing the sky. The metallic ringing of the manhole cover tossed to the side followed, then a roar as one of the men jumped in.

Althea clambered up into the opening of a white stone pipe and sprinted. The *slap* of her feet upon the dry surface echoed over the growls of the raider behind her. He couldn't stand at full height in the tube, allowing her to outpace him. After a moment of running, her arms flashing in and out of view faded to light grey. She came to a stop at a T-shaped crossing, unable to continue forward. To the left, it went straight as far as she could see, but to the right, it bent down after a short distance. Althea headed right and reached the end in six strides. A vertical shaft led down to a lower level. She crouched, listening to the raiders stumble along in the dark. They didn't give up, even though they couldn't see at all.

Keeping her eyes closed so they couldn't see the glowing light, she turned her back to the pit and scrambled onto a metal ladder caked with soft muck. Once she descended below the level of the floor above, she looked around at a square-walled passage lined with a staggering amount of debris. Pipes, old furniture, boxes, and other machinery she had never seen before lay scattered among liberal amounts of spray-painted words.

At the bottom, she dropped thigh deep into water frigid enough to paralyze her. Althea clamped her hands over her mouth and swallowed a shriek, fearful of attracting attention. Seconds later, she sucked in a breath past chattering teeth and forced herself to move. Ripples spread from her legs as she walked, jostling the floating junk. Her natural reaction to such cold water kept her motion slow enough not to make too much sloshing. A layer of clammy slime squished between her toes and gave way to the coarse texture of old concrete beneath it. Althea advanced without hesitation, pushing the flotsam aside. She had stepped in worse things before.

After several minutes, she jumped at a scream. The man, unable to see the ladder or the sudden end to the corridor, tripped over the first rung and fell face-first into the water at the bottom. The wave from his impact sent frigidity up to the base of her ribs. She gulped back the urge to cry out.

He broke the surface, slinging his head around. "Gar dangit thas col'er 'n hell! Me balls fell off."

Only one of them came this way; Althea figured they must have split at the junction. Debris clunked against the wall as his splashing increased. She bit her lip, wondering if he might need help putting his man parts back on.

"Where you goin?" he yelled.

She made the mistake of looking at him.

"Thar you is." He stared right at her. "Ah chosed right."

Althea checked his thoughts. He'd only been kidding about parts falling off. She whirled away and shoved a floating wooden box out of her path. Splashing, crashing, and banging resonated in the tunnel as the man, blind in the pitch dark, walked into everything. She fought the desperate want to look back, fearing he'd be closer. Arms held up over the water, she advanced among the junk clogging the sewer. Her small size and ability to see in the dark allowed her to navigate the black and white world faster and quieter, avoiding the big stuff. The raider yelled curses each time a part of his body found a solid object. When he emitted a genuine yelp of pain, she stopped.

Her teeth chattered. "Are you hurt?"

"Naw, it's just a… Yeah. Dammit mah leg's off."

Sensing a ploy, she kept going. At the sound of her sloshing, he grumbled. "Damn, too much, wadn't it."

"Yes." She stopped again. "You should go back. You can't see down here, you'll get hurt for real."

He didn't reply, continuing to follow her.

Althea glanced up as she walked under a low hanging pipe, an inch or two over her head. She closed her eyes to hide their glow and faced to the rear. "There's a pipe. Be careful, or it'll hit you in the face."

The splashing behind her lessened. She imagined him holding his hand out, but didn't dare open her eyes. A faint twinge of guilt at putting this man at risk faded at Den's voice in the air. The sound emanated from a round opening near the ceiling a short distance ahead. Her elation caused her to run carelessly forward. Something sharp caught the inside edge of her right foot and she came to a hopping halt, gritting her teeth to muffle her yelp of pain.

The passage jutted out from the wall over her head, out of reach. A nearby box served as a convenient stepstool, and a short jump got her fingers over the lip of a protruding pipe. She braced her uninjured foot at the wall and hauled herself up into a tunnel too small for her to sit up in. A line of dried muck colored the bottom darker grey than the rest of the world. The opposite end appeared to lead to another underground passage. Satisfied she hadn't found a dead end, she crawled, smiling as the man sloshed right past her.

Twenty yards later, she peeked out of the other end at an even bigger tunnel made of the same white stone as the first, with a tiny stream running along the bottom. Althea slithered forward and slid hands-first down the curved wall, coming to rest at the bottom with a splash. Taking a moment to breathe, she sat cross-legged and pulled her hurt foot up to look at it before focusing her power into her body. The cut stood out as a clean black line tracing from below the ankle to the center of her sole across the red shape of her foot.

She commanded her body to repair itself. A warm tingle spread over the area. The cut foamed. A sick had gotten into the wound, but hadn't infiltrated her body enough to come out in the usual manner. Ill-scented ichor dribbled down over her heel from the closing injury.

The dirty water had bad things in it. For a moment, she worried the man chasing her had found a sick as well; however, the pipe she crawled out of protruded from the wall of an immense, round shaft, at least twice her height above. She couldn't climb the wall to go back, no matter how guilty she felt. Raiders with guns had come for her. She understood at last what caused the dream.

She had to warn the Seekers.

4

THE LOST PLACE

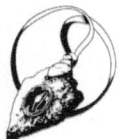

Amid several inches of frigid water, she sat and rubbed her foot to chase away the phantom pain. No light pierced the gloom of this subterranean tunnel. Though she could see in complete darkness, her vision lacked color, leaving her unable to tell mud from blood among the smudges all over her leg. Althea stood. Behind her, the tunnel ended at a collapse not too far away. With only one way to proceed, she advanced, cringing at the loud slosh of water. Trying to straddle the flow and keep her feet on dry concrete reduced her to an ungainly waddle. Walking entirely on one side of the water put her on an annoying incline—so she resigned herself to trudging in the shin-deep rivulet.

At least it had a current, which left the molded concrete free of slime and offered sure footing. She kept her feet underwater, lifting them only enough to slide forward without breaking the surface to reduce noise. After about a hundred yards, the giant tunnel ended at a square chamber many times the size of Den's hut, also flooded. The water inside it matched the depth of what she walked in. A spot of color caught her eye, glimmering from within a pipe protruding from the distant wall at the top of a ladder. Grinning at the promise of daylight, she ran forward.

Unfortunately, the chamber's floor lurked much lower than the bottom of the tunnel. She fell in, closing her eyes and clamping her mouth shut as she submerged in old rainwater so cold it had no business being anything but ice. A shriek filled several bubbles as she sank, paralyzed by the bone-chilling liquid for a few seconds before collecting the presence of mind to start swimming. She broke the surface with gasping breaths and wiped a hand over her face. The room looked different from that angle, but after spinning in a circle three times, she oriented herself and paddled to the base of a ladder.

She gripped the rusted metal and probed around the murk with a hesitant toe until she found the nearest rung. Althea climbed with great care, easing her weight down on each step, careful not to cut herself again. Two stories above the water, she climbed into another molded concrete tunnel and sat shivering at the edge, squeegeeing the water out of her scrap skirt with her hands to make the burdensome thing lighter. Sluices of cold trickled down her legs, and for a fleeting moment, she missed the warmth inside the green beast.

She froze as Nalu's voice broke the serenade of droplets rejoining the pool below. He yelled at someone to be careful. Hope filled her heart. She clambered to her feet and sprinted down the open pipe until she reached the source of the sound—another well like the one she had entered, illuminated in beautiful color by a narrow slot of sunlight. Althea leaned her face into the warmth, reveling in its caress.

She cupped her hands about her mouth and shouted, her tiny voice echoing. "Den? Nalu? Help! I'm down here. Nalu!"

A boy's shrill squealing cry from outside preceded the unmistakable *clank* of metal on pavement. She knew the hissing; immense roaches as long as her height. Nalu's war shout made her shudder and back away from the opening. A squishing crunch brought the shrieking to an end.

"Den?" She jumped up and down, waving her arms. "Nalu?"

Jake's face appeared in the gap. He blinked in astonishment then ducked out. "Glow-eye got away!"

The faces of Nalu and Den appeared next, looking down with anger and worry respectively.

"No!" Althea stomped her foot. "Someone tried to steal me. I am running *to* you, not away."

The anxiety around Den grew stronger as Nalu calmed. His anger at her non-escape shifted to concern. They backed off out of sight. She waited in the damp space, shivering, wondering what they muttered about.

Jake appeared again, sliding in headfirst. The others had him by the legs, and the look on his face would have been appropriate had they been shoving him into a grinder. He reached reluctant hands toward her, turning away as they grabbed each other's forearms. Unfortunately for Jake, only he among the Seekers could fit past the gap.

His fear frightened her, the same reaction most people had to Mystics. Scrags regarded them with terror, as few people had any ability to defend themselves against their powers. However, Mystics didn't have glowing eyes, nor had any of them been known to heal—only inflict pain and enslave the minds of others. Everyone in the Badlands knew Althea for her ability to heal and unwillingness to cause harm. Even she understood she couldn't be a simple Mystic. Whatever she was had been the cause for adoration, greed, and as with this trembling boy, dread.

Her toes clawed the moss from the wall as she tried to help the Seekers pull her up. As soon as her arms emerged from the storm drain, two older hunters each grabbed a wrist. Jake clamored away as they lifted her out and set her on her feet. She offered a pleading look as she realized they didn't intend to let go. When they gathered rope, she stared down at her feet, ashamed. Two large insects lay dead not far away. Althea offered no resistance as they forced her wrists together and bound them.

"Hold." Nalu raised a hand at them. "I believe her. She did not run away."

"She came seeking us," Den snapped at the man holding the rope.

Den's objection gave her hope. She squirmed, protesting their grip. "Two men came to the driving machine. They knew I was in it and they chased me into the underground."

When the Seekers untied her, she ran to Den's side.

He patted her on the back, drawing her into a hug as he gave the man with the rope a possessive glare. "You're safe now."

She looked at him, then up at Nalu. "We should go home... now." After a glance at the bugs, she examined everyone in turn. "Are any hurt?"

"None are harmed." Nalu gestured to the south. "We will leave soon, but there is a place of interest there." He pointed at a white door in the side of a smaller building.

Althea tugged at Den's arm, her voice a desperate whine. "No. We mustn't wait. We have to leave now. Marauders are here."

"Quiet, girl. If they stalk us, you will help them." Nalu sent a mild glare at her, hand signals at the others directing them into formation.

She clung to Den as they went to the end of this path of flat black stone. The men gathered at the side of an old structure with a red-painted door. Nalu approached it with the second eldest, Palik, the keeper of the bag that held the sacred relics of opening. The boys, even Den, gasped in reverence as he removed a long metal rod with one hooked end from the bag and held it up to the sky as a tribute. She took the opportunity of standing still to remove her sopping wet shirt and wring it out. Palik held the *great opener* to the skies, murmuring chants under his breath.

Althea smirked, and leaned up to whisper in Den's ear. "It's just a pry bar. It's not magic."

With an astonished glance, Den grasped her shoulders and pulled her away from the others. "It provides us with food, clothes, and weapons. It is the opener."

She stared out from under flat eyebrows, snapping the scrap of cloth a few times to dry it more. "It's just a lump of metal. There's nothing—"

The loud clatter of the door bursting open on its hinges startled her mute. The 'magic opener' had done its job, and the men filed into the building. Palik kissed it before returning it to the bag. She wriggled into the somewhat drier chest cloth and fell in step with the others, behind Den. The interior held long shelves, strewn with the wreckage of broken pottery. Dead plants stuck out from clods of dirt. The air hung with a heavy, earthy smell, which intensified as the Seekers moved large sacks piled against the far wall. The men seemed most interested in ones with seeds, and sifted around in search of anything they could plant and eat.

Althea leaned against a shelf, folding her arms while watching them. Den hovered close, and she allowed him to distract her into a lighthearted conversation about what things would be like after the joining. He still had to convince Braga to allow it, as even the chief had superstitions about her. The *Cha'dom* stood close to the Great Hut where meetings took place. Althea had heard them arguing over her. Almost half the Elders expected she would bring doom upon them. Of course, she had another problem: Yala, the mate Braga had chosen for Den. The girl was four years older than her, almost a woman already, and closer to his age. His defiance of the chief's command had not gone over well, and Yala's father became quite upset at missing his chance to be connected to the family in power. Guilt and worry pulled her gaze to the floor.

Den brushed her hair away from her face and slid his hand over her head. Staring into the soft blue glow of her eyes, he whispered. "They are foolish to fear you. You are so kind and pretty."

She held his hand and leaned into him. The sounds of the men dragging bags around became quiet, lost amid the presence of Den's heartbeat. She felt love from him, but couldn't hide her confusion when he pressed his lips into hers. There they lingered for a moment before his heartbeat surged and his hand tightened around hers.

He pulled away.

She opened her eyes, searching for the breath to ask him why he touched lips with her. The question never came out. Jake shouted in alarm.

Two raiders stood in the doorway with rifles of wood and metal aimed at the group, rust-pocked bayonet tips glinting.

"We takin' the Prophet," the one on the right grumbled.

Nalu slid his spear off his back and lifted it in a ready pose. "You are two against many, and your spear is very small."

Althea found it odd how angry the raider became at being told he had a small spear.

The other seekers followed suit, even little Jake, preparing for war.

"No." Althea leapt away from Den, into the middle of the room. "Those are guns, not spears. They'll kill you all."

The man who followed her underground reeked of moldy water. He waved the weapon at her. "Git on, then. Do as you're told an' we won't hurt yer li'l friend."

She stared at Den, holding back the tears that struggled to fall. The moment she dreaded happened again as it always did. Cornered in this room, she had nowhere to run, and death of others would follow disobedience. Althea took a step toward the raiders with her head down. Den grabbed her by the shoulder and pulled her behind him.

"I challenge you." He glared at the man on the left, drawing a knife from a thigh sheath with a practiced grip. "You win, you take her. I win, you leave."

The hunters clasped their hands over their ears as a rifle shot deafened them all. Den's right thigh exploded in a wash of blood, knocking him flat to the ground away from Althea.

"Okay." The raider laughed, and aimed for Den's head. "Looks like I win."

"Stop!" She leapt on Den. "I will go with you. Please don't kill him."

The Seekers backed against the wall, the only sign of Jake's presence, a dropped spear. Den gasped in pain, clinging to Althea's arm. Despite his wound, he kept a defiant scowl. She laid her hands on his thigh, one on either side of the jagged hole leaking blood at a deathly pace. Her crying eyes lit up the room with a flare as she channeled power into him, forcing his body to regenerate itself. The raiders grinned with toothless glee at proof they had found the real Prophet.

Den sat up, grimacing at the tenderness of his repaired leg and his pronounced hunger. He stared at her, his expression mirroring her fatigue and sadness. "What magic is this?"

"It's not magic." She sniffled. "They have guns. They can kill everyone from far away."

He squinted with suspicion at the raiders.

"Please, don't." Althea put a hand on his chest, holding him down. "He gunned you in the leg. If it was your thinking shape, I couldn't make the hurt go away."

Den removed his agate pendant and slid it over her head, kissing her once more on the lips.

"I will find you."

Althea wept, clutching the small green arrowhead as she stood and backed over to the grinning men in the doorway. She stared with longing at Den as one wound rope about her wrists and tightened it, keeping her gaze on him until the tether dragged her out of the room.

"If'n I see any of you, Prophet won't be able ta fix yas." The raider swept his rifle over the Seekers, who leaned away as it passed.

They led her across the Lost Place, encouraging her forward with a not-too-gentle yank on the rope whenever she trudged too slow for their liking. The short one kept watch to the rear, emanating a bloodlust that sickened her. She pouted at the road, unable to bring herself to look up. It had been silly to expect her life would change simply because she liked a boy. She was the Prophet, and someone always wanted her. The premonition about Den came to pass, though she wondered if it had done so only because she had followed them.

The raiders dragged her out of the dead city to an open-framed buggy with two huge knobby wheels in back and two small tires up front. It had two seats arranged one behind the other. The lead raider climbed into the forward seat, mounted low to the point he could barely see over the front. The second raider lifted her, rough fingers digging into her sides. He dropped her into the rear seat, threaded the rope through an eyebolt in the roll cage, and pulled her wrists above her head before tying the other end to the metal frame out of her reach. After tugging at the rope to ensure she couldn't pull the knot loose, he moved around behind the vehicle and hopped onto a platform to ride standing. The clattering of a belt buckle rang out a few seconds before he banged his rifle on the metal bar twice, a deliberate signal.

Althea tugged at the bindings, wincing as they pinched. "Are you sure you want to take me? Someone stronger always comes. Every camp that stole me has been killed."

The driver twisted in his seat and glanced at her. She tried to look as pleading as possible and peeked at his thoughts. Anticipation of reward for bringing a prize like her back to his chief chased away his moment of hesitation. He turned away. The buggy's engine roared to life, filling the air with the fragrance of ethanol, smoke, and burning oil.

She screamed as the one behind her fired his rifle again, sick to her stomach at a distant cry of pain in Nalu's voice. The engine behind her blocked any view of what happened; she thrashed against the rope, kicking the back of the driver's seat.

"You said you wouldn't hurt them! Please let me mend him."

"Told 'em not ta follow. Breaks da promise," yelled the driver.

Althea collapsed, hanging by her wrists while crying.

"Dammit, just winged 'im," yelled the man at the back, barely audible over the revving engine.

The buggy surged forward. Althea sagged in the seat, resting her cheek against her arm, hot vibrating metal beneath her feet. Unable to contain her feelings for Den, she sobbed. The buggy rocked and picked up speed when they hit an old strip of flat rock that formed a path in the forest. Her hair whipped about in the wind, and she tried to shield her eyes as best she could behind her arms.

A long while later, they raced out of the verdant greenery, following the stone ribbon into the flat, open nothingness of the Badlands. The men shouted to each other over the noise, trying to find their bearings. Eventually, Althea ran out of tears and sat in silence.

Here and there in the distance, patches of abnormal woodland flashed by on both sides, trees growing in the desert where trees didn't belong. She had heard someone say the before-time people forced them to grow, but no one knew why. One hour dragged into the next, the rope keeping her hands above her head shifting from irritating to intolerable.

The sun dragged itself across the sky, heading for the cover of the western horizon as the raiders drove the day into dusk. Half-awake, she swayed forward when the vehicle slowed. The jostle of uneven ground broke the monotony of the past dozen hours, and she lifted her head as they approached a large building in the center of a field of concrete squares. Thousands of fragments of broken panel windows along the upper story gleamed in harsh orange light, catching the fading day. Pale grey corrugated metal walls wobbled in the gusty wind that rolled over the desert and sent swirls of sand against the structure. Other raiders dragged open a rolling gate made from two crushed trucks.

The driver leaned back and grinned the yellow disaster of his mouth at her dust-caked face.

"Welcome home, Prophet."

5

A PRIZE CLAIMED

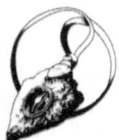

The buggy entered the gate and circled before coming to a halt by a herd of similar vehicles. No two matched, each one cobbled together from whatever parts the raiders scavenged. Some had guns mounted on them, others looked large enough to carry eight or nine men at a time. The scars of combat covered them all, the vehicles decorated liberally with bullet holes, burns, and old dried blood. Their shadows crept long across the Earth as the sun sank ever deeper.

Althea's arms fell into her lap when the raider loosened the cord from the frame. Hours of sitting with her wrists tied over her head had left them aching and her hands red. She concentrated, letting the soreness flare up and fade without giving them the amusement of crying out. A tug at the rope nudged her into motion. She clambered out of the seat and stepped upon warm concrete tarmac.

Raiders milled about; a handful hurried with specific tasks while others roamed as if on patrol. Towers, masterpieces of scrap metal and hope, held armed men at each corner of the compound.

The man pulled her past the vehicles toward four rows of kennel cages built out of chain link fence and aluminum poles. Each space only had enough room for a man to stand inside of. The pens held about a dozen people unfortunate enough for this raider group to find them. The captives slouched low to the ground, some moaning, some sleeping.

Althea looked up at the raider pulling her along, unable to understand what could drive people to treat each other this way. Her gait slowed in response to the slaves staring at her, some calling out when they saw her bright eyes in the forced shadows of the receding day. A few gripped the fencing that caged them, leaning up and begging her for help. Althea gripped the rope and fought against her lead to get close to them. A quick yank pulled the tether from the raider's grip and she ran to the cages, sticking her fingers into the fencing by an older man who had the beginnings of grey hair. Ripped scraps of his clothes danced in the wind, somewhere between green and drab brown.

He clasped her bound hands through the barrier and offered a sympathetic look for a seconds before glaring at the raiders. "Woe to those who harm an agent of the *Lord*, his wrath shall fall upon them."

Althea jumped at the sudden outburst, clutching the fence to resist the demanding pull of the rope at her wrists. "He's sick, please, I must—"

The raider snapped the cord like a whip, jerking her away from the cage hard enough that she stumbled toward him and almost fell to her knees. "Later."

She cast a sorrowful stare at the old man as they led her away. The captive settled back against the wall of his cell. He nodded and smiled at her before firing a phlegmatic cough into his fist.

Her captors dragged her to a battered door on the giant building, decorated with a poor attempt at a skull in black spray paint. Cooler air inside made her shiver, as did the icy concrete floor. The cavernous place held hulking machines that dwarfed the largest structures in Den's village. The men led her down an aisle between two rows of the enormous contraptions. Althea tried to imagine people capable of creating such things, and had no idea what they could've been used for. At the far end of the room, a muscular, imposing man sat upon a cushioned throne. The dusty leather chair had a strange three-tined star set in a circle on the pad behind his head. Metal armor covered his chest, painted in blood and rust. Leather connected smaller metal panels on his arms and thighs. The big man leaned forward to survey the approaching trio. The raiders dragged her up to him. One put a hand on her back and shoved her down.

"Kneel for chief."

Althea collapsed to all fours, hiding her face behind a curtain of blonde. Elation and anticipation surrounded the men who brought her here. They had just claimed a great trophy. The man on the fancy chair didn't radiate any strong emotion.

The large man's deep voice vibrated in her ribs. "What is this?" He didn't sound happy. "Why do you bring this one here? It is too small for the harem. It is too small to work. We must wait. Put it outside with the others." He rubbed his chin. "Blonde. Pale skin. Rare. She will be valuable."

Althea shivered at the implication.

"Vakkar... this be Prophet." The man to her right bounced like a small boy pleasing his father. He grabbed a fistful of hair and wrenched her head back, forcing her to look up at the chief.

"Ow." She whimpered.

"What?" Vakkar descended from his throne.

The raider released her hair, retreating in a rapid scurry. She sat back on her heels and straightened up. A glove wrapped in sharp things lifted her chin. She stared up at the metal-armored man towering over her. His radiant disinterest became worry. She didn't expect the wave of anger that emanated from him as soon as he saw the glow. Terrified, Althea curled into a ball, cowering away from his bellow.

"Fool!" roared the big man.

The raider who had shoved her hit the ground nearby, screaming and bleeding from the nose. She crawled away from the scene of the beating, huddling against the throne platform. The raider chief expressed his displeasure with their rough treatment of her by repeated application of a metal gauntlet to the man's head.

"Bad fortune finds those who mistreat the Prophet!" Vakkar slipped a punch in between every other word.

Once the man became immobile, the chief turned to face her. "Stand."

She complied, keeping her eyes aimed low. Many bandit chiefs reacted with violence to the insolence of a woman making eye contact, much less a young girl. He lifted her chin again and stared into her eyes, then examined her belongings.

"Did they steal?" His hand moved to the tether, pulling her arms toward him.

She maintained eye contact, unafraid. "No, sir."

The tight coils of rope sprang away from her wrists before she noticed the knife in his hand. She ran her fingers over the red skin where it had been, kneading the soreness away. Vakkar selected a length of chain connected to a giant machine adjacent to the throne, and wrapped it about her right ankle. Pinching it closed into a shackle, he searched for a lock. A minute trace of hesitance in him gave her hope she might avoid a leash.

"Please, no." She pressed herself into his side like a scared daughter. "I promise I won't run away."

He frowned. "I have heard the legends. This is not for running. It is in case one of these fools gets the bright idea o' stealin' you and runnin' off ta start their own camp."

She whined. "Please. I'm scared of being tied."

A barely perceptible glimmer brightened the glow as she nudged his emotions toward pity and kindness. He dropped the chain and looked to the rear corner of the factory where metal mesh formed two cages. One appeared empty while the other contained a number of women—the chief's personal harem. He put a hand on Althea's back and guided her over to the unoccupied cell.

"This will be more comfortable."

Walls of dense metal gridding with a diamond pattern created a room-sized cage against a cinder block wall at the back. One metal shelf inside held a few small boxes that looked quite old. Only a thin barrier of the same mesh separated it from the cell holding the women. She couldn't remember anyone ever putting her in such a big cage before.

Althea stared at the floor.

Vakkar walked a few paces away to a metal column and lifted a key hanging on twine from a hook, using it to unlock the door. She stepped in, cringing as the metal banged closed behind her. After locking her in, Vakkar put the key around his neck, tucked safely under his armor.

Old boxes littered the cell, fallen from metal shelving bolted to the floor. Shredded sleeping bags covered a spot at the center of the room in preparation for an expanding harem, and their soft presence offered a welcome change from the cold concrete. A plastic bucket had been left to the right of the door, its purpose no secret to anyone with a sense of smell. She sat among the olive drab and red flannel, wondering how long it would be before she changed owners again.

6

RARE PRETTIES

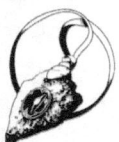

Azure light shimmered down Althea's legs, casting them an unnatural shade. She sat with her face in her knees, toes buried in the soft warmth of shredded wool. Exhausted, parched, and starving, she shivered not from the cold, but from the battle of anger and sorrow skirmishing in her heart. Abduction bothered her much less when she didn't like the people raiders stole her from. Then again, except for the first time years ago when the Wagon Man grabbed her, she couldn't remember ever being taken away from someone she liked before.

A whisper crept into the stillness from beyond a mesh wall to her left.

"Is that the Prophet?"

Althea lifted her head and peered in the direction of a female voice. Four women occupied the other security pen. A tall, athletic redhead with blue eyes had come right up to the partition between rooms, gazing down at her with an air of superiority. She appeared older, perhaps in her mid-twenties, and had numerous small scars on her arms and body. She wore only a bit of metal held around her neck by a dangling padlock. The people from Den's village had thought Althea pale, but next to this woman, she felt almost dark-skinned.

"Hunter?" Althea whispered.

"I was." The woman scowled, picking at the collar. "I don't plan on being here too long."

Another woman younger than the first reclined in the bedding at the center of the other room, stretching before focusing a semiconscious stare on the new arrival. Like the redhead, she wore only a collar. The soft lines of a pampered life curved around her slender un-scarred body, and her calm emotional state suggested she had been a prized concubine for a long time. The woman's exotic features and a slender build reminded Althea of someone a raider had once called Japanese.

The other two sat as far back as possible, against the corner where two cinder block walls met. Frail and bony, one hid behind a thick mass of silky black hair down to her thighs. She shook with a perpetual shiver like a tiny dog afraid of its own shadow. Her skin was dark, her features delicate, and her attention absorbed by her task—feeding the fourth captive.

Anger radiated strong from the last woman. Not fear like the thin woman drowned in, or contentment like the Japanese girl basked in—not even the arrogant confidence exuding from the redhead. The fourth lacked a collar, though the raiders had chained her hands together behind her back. Her rich brown skin wasn't quite as dark as the woman feeding her. Short black hair clung to her head in a pixie cut that went light tan at the tips. Large brown eyes that would have been beautiful in another place glared out from above a blunt nose similar to a cute plastic doll head Althea once saw. The woman watched the distant shadows of raiders, giving off emotional energy that said she wanted to kill someone.

Althea couldn't guess her age beyond adult. Her toned body seemed like that of a hunter, but she lacked the telltale scars of repeated healed wounds, only some fresh bruises. She might be old enough to have been Althea's mother, or maybe only twentyish. Althea decided the fourth woman had to be younger than thirty, but carried herself with the poise of someone older. Something quite strange lurked in her mood, unlike anything Althea had ever sensed before from a captive. No sooner did the last woman notice Althea looking at her than the anger vanished into a spiral of embarrassment.

"Oh Christ! Is that a goddamn kid?" The restrained woman shifted in an attempt to hide her nakedness. "What kind of fucking animals are these people? That girls' like ten. What are they gonna do to her?"

That woman intrigued Althea. She had never before seen someone with hair like that. Neither long and wild nor shaved, and the ends bore a different color. She couldn't help but gawk at a person who would waste the great amount of time it must have taken to do such a thing.

"Look at her eyes," the redhead blurted. "I did not know the Prophet was just a child."

"I'm twelve... I think." She folded her arms and furrowed her brow. "I'm not a little kid, and my name is Althea."

The relaxed woman twirled a finger at her long, black hair. "Kinda small for twelve. You sure?"

"I am called Zhar." The redhead patted herself on the chest before gesturing at the comfortable one. "That is Aya." She waved at the two behind her. "Ramani, and the chipper one is Rachel."

The cuffed woman made a strange gesture with one finger.

Althea felt sad for her. "Why is she tied?"

Zhar grinned. "She killed one of these shitheads when they caught her last week, and she got a piece of Vakkar when he came for her. Pissed him off good. He's gonna leave her like that 'til she begs for it."

"Begs for what?" asked Althea.

All four women found something other than Althea to look at.

Rachel glanced away, unable to lift her sad stare off the floor. "Yeah... Only got one, there were too many. So groggy when I woke up I couldn't fight." She pulled against the handcuffs. "I don't care what he does, he's gonna be waiting a long damn time."

Althea laced her fingers through the mesh, staring at Rachel, studying the radiance of confusion, anger, and shame. The feel of it told her this woman had not yet been wifed, but dreaded its imminence, and masked her fear with rage. Her thoughts looked strange. She had memories of the before-time: many people in strange camo-green uniforms, a bed with glass over it, a white room, and a swarm of raiders tearing her clothes away. A knife flashed. Pain and unconsciousness followed the sight of blood. The woman desperately wanted someone named Police to find her.

"It ain't right." Rachel curled against the wall. "She's too little."

Ramani forced a smile. "At least they let her keep clothing."

Jealousy wafted from Zhar. "They don't want her for that. She's not harem. She's the Prophet."

"What the hell does that mean? Prophet?" Rachel made eye contact at last. "Umm. Shit. That kid's eyes are glowing like a goddamned firefly."

"What's a firefly?" asked Aya in a lazy voice.

Althea sank to the floor, sitting with her legs off to the side. "I make hurts and sicks go away."

"I saw her once." Ramani spoke, not looking up. "Before I was taken, years ago… a man had her in a cart and would charge trades or coins to let her touch you."

Unable to contain a spike of sorrow at the memory, Althea cried.

"What's wrong?" Zhar sank to her knees, at eye level with her.

"He was bad." Althea sniffled, regained her composure, and wiped her face. "When people did not pay, he let them die. I couldn't get out of my cage to help."

Rachel seemed less concerned with her own predicament. "Help people? Wait, cage? Who puts a little girl in a cage?" She writhed, trying to pull her hands loose. "This shit don't fly. I gotta get the fuck out of here."

"Come." Althea leaned up on her knees and stuck her fingers past the mesh again.

Zhar touched her just to do it, enamored with meeting the Prophet in person. Althea tensed at the presence of a sick tainting the woman's aura and gripped her fingers.

Althea shut her eyes. "Hold still."

Wispy darkness swam within the form of Zhar's life energy.

After a moment of concentration, Althea looked up.

Zhar swayed on her feet and put a hand to her face. "Everything's spinning. What did you do to me?"

"You had a sick," said Althea. "It's gonna come out now."

Rachel blushed and looked away as Zhar scrambled over to their bucket.

Althea tilted her head at Rachel. "Why shame?"

"Where I come from, you don't piss with people watching."

Ramani whispered something in Rachel's ear while motioning toward Althea.

Rachel blurted. "What the hell is a Scrag?"

Zhar and Aya exchanged a glance, knowing full well what awaited the newest addition to the harem. Aya rolled onto her back, reclining as if in a palace, completely at ease with captivity. Althea sensed she did it on purpose to make Rachel feel more embarrassed. A look of amusement on Zhar's face displaced a pained grimace. She sighed in relief, moved away from the bucket, and eased herself with great care into a seated position as if sore.

"Scrags live in little camps here and there. Most of 'em this far south don't wear too much." Zhar curled up on the bedding.

"Aren't you a Scrag, too?" Rachel continued trying to get her hands free.

Zhar shook her head. "No. My home is a few days north in the mountains. We don't have to scavenge for clothing. We have tools, and we know what guns are." Zhar scowled at the bucket. "We even have toilets. Scrags are the primitives out in the dust that use license plates for loincloths and worship things like flashlights, thinking they are magic. I *had* clothes before these sons of bitches ambushed me."

"And pry bars…" Althea giggled.

Zhar grumbled. "These raider bastards picked me clean."

Aya smiled, draping herself over Zhar's back and stroking her hair. "You should feel lucky. You have beautiful red hair and skin like the clouds. Vakkar chose you for himself. You're not baking out there in the kennel."

Zhar shied away, awash in shame she didn't want the others to see. Althea looked down, understanding why.

"They took mine, too." Ramani blushed at the floor, trying to cover herself with her hands.

Zhar glanced back with a half-smile. "I've seen him… big guy in a brown dress with face-hair down to his balls."

"Guess they don't know it's girly…" Rachel gave up her struggle with a hiss.

"What's girly?" Althea blinked.

Rachel grumbled. "Means only girls are supposed to wear dresses."

"That's silly. Clothes are clothes. Please, come. You are hurt. I must touch you." Althea forced her fingers past the grate as far as they would fit.

Rachel fired a shamed glance at the floor for a few minutes before she found the courage to slide up to the mesh. As soon as her fingertips made contact, Althea closed her eyes and forced the forms to change. The bruises, as well as the cuts and chafing from the handcuffs, faded. Rachel gawked, stunned at the sudden cessation of pain.

"What the heck are you?" Rachel shivered.

"I'm Althea," she said in a matter-of-fact tone. "Why are you clean?"

Rachel curled, doing what she could to find modesty. "I was in a stasis pod."

"The bed with glass over it?" Althea sat back on her heels, letting her arms fall to her lap.

"Yeah. How the hell did…?" Rachel shook her head. "I was stationed at White Sands. The corporation war just went into high gear when we took a hit from an unidentified bio weapon. Some of us wound up trapped inside building six. We hopped into the pods to get away from the virus. The damn thing wasn't supposed to keep me asleep for so long."

Althea blinked. "Like a bed?"

"Yeah. Like a bed, but it kept me alive, just frozen. Hey, if you're some kinda Prophet thing, can you magic these cuffs off me?"

"I wouldn't do that." Zhar glanced over. "Vakkar said he'd put them on all of us if she got loose."

A wave of terror gripped Ramani.

"You can get out as soon as you let Vakkar take you," Aya cooed. "Obey, and the chief is good to you."

"That might work for you, hon, but I ain't gonna be nobody's fucking pet." She strained against the unforgiving metal, collapsing against the wall out of breath and sweaty a minute later.

Zhar laughed. "He's waited a week for you to break. I give him one more before he just takes what he wants. It's not like you have a say in it."

Rachel glared. "Fuck that. I'll die first."

"The more you fight him the more—"

"Stop!" Althea shouted, reacting to the emotional storm surging in Rachel at the idea she had no way to resist being wifed. "Leave her alone."

Althea crawled away from the awkward silence in the other cell. She had seen other harems. She had witnessed wifeing before, even healed them when things got out of hand. The thought that a few years from now, men would look at her in *that* way scared her. Some hope came in the truth not all women suffered that fate. Some, like Zhar, were strong enough to be hunters, and sometimes even raiders. Those lucky enough to be among tribes like Den's were protected as daughters, sisters, and mates. She dreaded the thought of where she would be when she came of age, but at least she had her magic.

Some minutes later, Zhar recovered from the soreness of expelling the sick and paced the other cage like a trapped lioness. It confused Althea how that woman had wound up in the harem. The Badlands were not kind to the weak of body or mind, and Zhar appeared to be neither. Rachel seemed not to be of this world, an oddity which made what awaited her all the more jarring. Bad enough to be captured and wifed, but everything she'd known had vanished as well.

Sensing Rachel's spiraling mood, Althea blurted. "Someone always comes for me."

The women looked at her.

"Wagon Man died when raiders with guns did not want to pay. They took me to their town."

"Did they let you out of the cage?" Rachel glanced up.

"No." Althea shook her head. "The ones after that did, but they put a chain on my leg." Althea tapped her right ankle. "It was nicer than the cage. At least I could move around the tree."

"That's horrible!" Rachel gasped. "What kind of fucked-up world did I wake up in?"

Althea shrugged. "It's okay. Sometimes nice people find me, but I always get taken again by bad ones. The nice ones are never strong enough to fight."

She buried her face in her knees. The agate pendant swung forward and brushed her legs, bringing with it a fleeting glimpse of Den's smile and the memory of how she felt while with him. Althea pictured his face. As she did so, a strange realization came over her.

The endless cycle of abduction had finally started to bother her.

7

EMPATHY

Her face against her knees, Althea wrapped her arms around her legs so no one could see her crying. She had lost track of how many times people captured her as a prize. A Den-shaped crack opened a breach in the wall of indifference she built up to constant abduction. This time, being taken hurt. She didn't understand why Den had pressed his lips against hers, but she wanted him to do it again. The Raider buggy had driven all day into the night. It didn't seem likely he would ever find her—not that their primitive tribe would stand any chance against a large group of raiders with guns.

As much as it hurt to think, she hoped he stayed away.

Rachel muttered in protest about something. Sniffling, Althea lifted her head and looked over at them. A spike of anger came from Rachel when their eyes met. It had been so long since someone reacted to her crying with something other than amusement or indifference, she had no idea how to feel.

"She will not be hurt." Zhar shook her head. "All want the Prophet… she's no good dead." She spotted Althea watching, and crawled to the mesh, leaning her face up to the grating to whisper. "When we escape, I will bring you to my home. It has mountain walls. You would be safe there… no one can ever take you again."

Althea furrowed her brow. "If it is so safe, why are you captured?"

Zhar growled. "Stupid gamble. I made a bet I could go hunting alone and take a bigger kill than Finlay. They got me outside the town. Inside my home, no raiders can ever steal you."

"If I had a home like that, I would stay in it," said Ramani, barely above a whisper.

"You are a mouse, which is why you are in this cage." Zhar rolled her eyes.

Aya perked up. "You are in the cage too, lioness."

Zhar drew a breath to yell, but the commotion of an approaching raider startled her away from the partition. The man slid a large metal bowl of beige slop into the harem cell, then offered two skewers of charred meat to Althea. Famished from healing, she dove on the food and savaged the first chunk before hesitating. Still chewing, she glanced to her side at the other women fighting to choke down the beige goo. Zhar glared at her, jealousy wafted around her like perfume.

Althea crept to the partition between cells and knelt. "We can trade if you want. You look starving."

As soon as she swallowed the food Ramani's hand had put in her mouth, Rachel blurted. "You're not going to take real food away from a little kid."

"If she's gonna offer it, I'm gonna eat it." Zhar watched Althea eagerly as she nibbled bits of meat off the hunk small enough to fit past the gaps in the lattice.

The older woman devoured them.

"Share," Althea said in a demanding tone, talking at the women like an annoyed mother.

Showing no signs of anything but greed, Zhar continued gobbling every scrap. Althea narrowed her eyes, the radiant blue glow flared as she radiated fear. Her tousled blonde hair stirred in a breeze that didn't exist. The four women stared with trepidation, like mice in the path of a diving eagle. Zhar's mouth hung agape, Aya ran to the corner shivering, and Ramani hid behind Rachel, the handcuffs clicking apart her only noticeable reaction.

"I said share." Althea fixed Zhar with a dire glance, relaxing the radiant fear.

The women divided one skewer while Althea ate the other. The way the harem attacked it made her think solid food had been a long distant memory for them.

With the meal gone, Althea settled into the tattered scraps of old sleeping bags. The women huddled together at the center of their bedding. They all lay in silence as the last vestiges of daylight faded from the broken windows, mourned by a cool breeze that circled the room. The moon drew great shadows across the floor in the distorted shapes of the old machinery. Every breath smelled like she'd stuck her head into the front end of an old truck. Althea rolled onto her side, staring at the keyhole in the door of her cage. Behind her, the soft clinks and rattles of Rachel's endless search for a comfortable position mixed Zhar's chiding whispers asking her to settle down and sleep. Ramani whispered a repetitive phrase in a strange language, while Aya passed out in less than a minute.

🐀 🦅 🗿 ◌ ♋

THE RATTLE OF STEEL AND RACHEL'S SCREAMS SHOOK ALTHEA FROM HER approaching sleep.

"No! Get the fuck off me!"

Althea shot upright. The sight of Vakkar dragging the woman by one ankle out the door as she kicked at him blurred in her semiconscious brain. Trying to contain and move her at the same time, he failed to do well at either. Rachel thrashed while the other three watched. Ramani shook in the corner, a guilty stare at the floor, glad the raider king chose someone else. Aya had little reaction aside from an annoyed moan at the noise. Zhar seemed unconcerned with Rachel's situation. She stared between the open door and Vakkar's weapons as if weighing her odds.

Althea didn't need her abilities to know what thoughts dwelled within the raider king's mind, though the emotions radiating from him confirmed it. She sprang to her feet and ran to the wall of her cell, slapping at the grating.

"Stop! Wait." She cried out in a desperate wail. "You do not want to do that."

His grin said he very much did. Althea summoned up a surge of mental energy, seizing on the lust in his mind and replacing it with worry. The enthusiasm with which he dragged the struggling woman waned, and he blinked at Althea.

"Why not?" His body jerked as Rachel squirmed to free her legs from his hands.

"Get off me, you piece of shit!"

"She's sick." Althea raced to come up with an excuse. "She's from before-time. She has sick that will kill you. Is old sick you cannot fight. Before-time sick will make man bits turn black and fall off... much hurts."

"But you're the Prophet!" He gestured at her with Rachel's foot. "Fix it!"

"I never see this sick before, must learn. It will take days to fix. This sick hurts men much fast." She emphasized the point with a telempathic poke of dread.

The war chief dropped Rachel's leg, taking a pace back and wiping his hand on his metal armor as if touching her had left some manner of residue on him. Rachel kicked at the ground, shoving herself into the cell away from him. The other women cowered from her.

"No use for this one, then." He pulled an old pistol from his belt and aimed at her face.

"*No!*" Althea screamed, clutching the grating of the cage door. "*Don't you dare!*" The wave of energy that radiated from her knocked the war chief back a step and left a dumbfounded look on his face.

She hated using the magic that forced people to do whatever she said. *Mystic* magic. That kind of power made people want to kill to protect themselves. No one knew she could do it since she so rarely did—because she feared what might happen to her if word got out. Althea only used that power to protect herself from wifeing... but she couldn't sit back and watch Rachel die.

Vakkar glanced at her, shaking his head and blinking as if clearing his senses from a severe punch to the nose. She stared down, the commanding tone fleeing into the delicate whine of a child pleading for something. "Please don't hurt her."

Seemingly drunk and unaware of who he even was, Vakkar kicked the door closed and hung the key back on its peg before staggering off out of sight. Rachel scooted over to the partition and pressed her cheek into the metal. An unending stream of thanks flowed with her tears. She wanted to scoop her up in her arms and hug her tight, but the grating between them and the metal about her wrists had other plans. Althea leaned into the lattice, an exchange of body heat as close as they could get to an embrace.

"Do that for me next time," Zhar whispered, a crack in her pride showing. "Please."

"Is she really sick?" asked Aya in a blasé voice.

Ramani huddled in a ball, wrapped in mute shame.

Althea shook her head and sank to the ground, sick with worry. She didn't want word to spread she could do such things. Her ability to influence emotion was much stronger than forcing direct commands upon people. Some Scrags became terrified enough from merely watching her heal. Thoughts of how they would react if they knew she could force them to obey scared her to the point of trembling. One or two she could control, but not a whole crowd of angry men. Better to be caged than killed.

"What's wrong?" Rachel no doubt felt the quivering despite the barrier.

Althea whispered. "If people learn I can make them do things, they will be mean to me. I… Only when it's important."

"Taking you away from someone you love and putting you in a cage is pretty damn mean already." Rachel pressed harder into the barrier.

"It's pretty damn important not to get ra—" Zhar swallowed the rest of her words as someone approached.

"Where's the damn key!" A man's voice made everyone but Zhar jump.

The raider brutalized for shoving Althea to the ground leaned up against the post, six feet away from the pens. He looked a mess, and glared at the empty peg.

"Vakkar has it." Althea spoke at the floor.

He stumbled closer and pressed his face, covered with purple and black, to the mesh. "Make hurt stop?"

Cradling her growling stomach, Althea dragged herself to the door. The sight of the man responsible for her being here brought memories of Den. Tears splattered onto her feet, running between her toes to the concrete. She raised her arm, sticking her hand out a small gap between the door and the cage wall. With surprising care, he clasped it, fell to one knee, and bowed his head.

Eyes closed, she concentrated on the energy of his life. Dark bruises receded into his skin as the exertion sapped the strength from her legs. Within minutes, she collapsed to the floor, clinging to the grate to keep from falling over. Her head sagged and she gasped for breath. He stumbled away, his body restored. By the time she had the energy to look up, he had returned with another meat skewer and a grateful smile. She curled up among the mass of soft flannel, gnawing on the lukewarm meal.

Zhar perked up.

"Don't you even think about it," whispered Rachel, glaring her down. "Look at the kid. She's starved to skin and bones."

The raider paused, a brief look of remorse upon his face, before he left her alone with dreams of a home she almost had.

8

THE ARENA

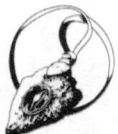

R outine fell into place as the days became a blur. Althea's world consisted primarily of this twelve-foot chamber. Cheers echoed within the factory whenever the raiders gamed with the strange sphere, shouts when they fought for spoils. Roaring buggies woke her before the dawn most days as they made forays out into the Badlands. Each time they left, she asked the ancestors to ensure the raiders didn't return with any unfortunate souls they meant to enslave, and so far, the ancestors listened. Sometimes the buggies didn't return at all. Whenever Vakkar discussed a missing raiding party with his inner circle, Althea would gaze at the broken windows along the roof, face against the metal cage, wondering what became of them.

With each raiding excursion came the inevitable follow of being dragged out to the injured raiders and made to mend them, initially at the end of a chain padlocked about her throat. Vakkar softened to her after two weeks, and no longer permitted the leash. It became a point of contention among the more aggressive ones, male and female, who believed she would flee at the first opportunity. Some raiders treated her fairly well—those who feared the legends. The raiders who didn't manhandled her like a first-aid kit that could talk. She suffered it without tears, sustained by the joy of helping people, even bad ones. One good thing, at least no one in this raider camp gave off any sense of wanting to wife her. A handful even had sympathy for her.

It had been almost four weeks since she made up the lie about Rachel's illness, and she feared Vakkar wouldn't believe it for much longer. Aya took pride in being chosen at night, offering no resistance whenever he came to collect her and bring her to his bed behind the throne. Since the woman appeared to enjoy it, Althea let it happen, but didn't watch. Zhar had a look in her eye that she'd fight him to the death before surrendering again. Ramani dreaded her turn as much as Rachel, but couldn't bring herself to fight back. Subtle twists of emotion had helped focus Vakkar's affections on Aya, the only one of the harem who didn't mind her situation.

Althea scraped her fingers greedily at the warm flavorless slop given to her that morning, shoveling it into her face in an attempt to finish before they came to collect the bowl. The clatter of the harem cage opening lifted her gaze. Under the watchful eye of Vakkar, a group of raiders collected the women one by one, leading them off after securing chains to their collars. Since Rachel lacked a collar, a handful of men held her down while another padlocked a chain around her neck. Althea looked away, unable to watch, as they dragged her shrieking friend across the factory.

Paralytic guilt vanished with the cavernous reverberation of a slamming door. Alone in the massive building, she licked the last bits of nutrient paste from the steel bowl and set it on the concrete by the door. This room afforded her the luxury of motion far more than any other cage she had been kept in, and she spent some time running around in circles and climbing the shelves to keep herself in tune. As she exercised, her thoughts drifted to a blur that might have been her ninth year.

A man named Reed rescued her from a pack of wildmen she no longer much recalled. He took her to a place with strange trees and rough, rock-laden hills. He had come from a place he called the 'real world,' and had been a soldier. He'd shown her 'sit-ups' among other exercises. Thinking about him made her smile widen each time her chest touched her knees. Reed taught her about animals and creatures, what plants she could eat and which ones not to touch. Exercise was his favorite pastime. Out of breath, she clamped her arms around her legs and stared off at nothing. Sadness crept in as she thought about where he could be now.

He had meant to protect her by bringing her to a remote place, but bandits had found her anyway after a little less than a year. She found some solace in how they ambushed her while Reed had gone off to hunt. Althea clung to the hope they did not kill him. In a way, she found comfort in how pragmatic he'd been with her, emotionless but dutiful. He had found a child, taken her in, protected and provided for her, but love and tenderness were not in his repertoire. That had made it possible, but far from easy, not to miss him.

Althea pressed the agate between her thumb and finger, thinking about Den. The edge gleamed white in the sun from the jagged glass at the top of the far wall. With a sigh, she crawled to the water pail, drank, and splashed her face. At a rattle from her cell's walls, she looked up at the opening door.

Vakkar stood outside, waiting, quite unlike how he had gone for Rachel, or Aya the night after, or Zhar the night after that. This seemed as much a request as a demand. Althea stood, keeping her eyes on the floor, and padded obediently to his side. He took her hand like a normal person rather than an owner, and led her across the huge room out into the blinding day.

Hundreds of raiders assembled around a square area defined by faded yellow lines painted centuries ago upon the ground. Blood stained the concrete here and there in front of a large dais composed of old crushed cars and machine parts. The women sat around a throne of welded scrap, two on either side, their leashes padlocked to the dais. Aya basked in the gaze of the crowd, posing to accentuate her looks. Zhar knelt still, tolerating her exposure. Though she blushed, Althea sensed she comforted herself with the idea she remained a captive only because she had not yet attempted to leave. Ramani had her head away from the crowd, unable to suffer the gaze of so many people while wearing only a collar. She trembled as if one bad smell away from vomiting. Rachel gave off such shame and panic at being paraded in front of all these men in such a helpless state, Althea worried she'd hurt herself.

As he stepped up onto the platform, Vakkar gestured. "Sit where you like."

Althea spun with a sharp twist that fanned the strands of her scrap leather skirt and sat in front of Rachel, granting her a bit of cover from the crowd. As the chief lowered with great pomp into his 'outside throne,' a monstrosity of scrap metal, Althea put a comforting hand on Rachel's foot and pulled the woman's emotion under control before she reached a point of self-harm.

"The men compete today," shouted Vakkar.

Althea cringed at a wash of warm booze-air that flew from the raider king's throat.

He grinned, pointing at the arena. "Some will be hurt. You will mend them."

She stared with a horrified grimace at the crowd.

"Relax, child." Vakkar pet her like a cat, stroking his fingers over her head. "They are not to kill each other. That would only weaken us. This is practice. The wounds should be minor."

Some of the men scowled at Althea. She leaned back into Rachel, aghast at sensing people stare at her with hatred. Not until she peeked at their thoughts did she understand why. Her presence here had made Vakkar order them to practice fight with deadly things instead of toys, since she could stop the infections and death from even small cuts.

Because of her, they would suffer.

Crying, she leaned up to beg Vakkar to stop this, but her plea went unheard, drowned out under the roar of two raiders facing off in the confines of the peeling amber quadrangle. Sword held high, one charged in behind a shield made of several octagonal pieces of red metal with white markings. The other circled, holding a pair of knives at the ready. An older man at each corner shouted suggestions and criticisms to their respective trainee as the fight progressed. Althea hid her face against Rachel's shoulder. She knew they wouldn't kill each other, but she couldn't bear to watch violence for which she felt responsible.

"What is this?" Rachel's shivering whisper interspersed with the ringing of metal blades.

"They are training. Later, there will be contests of rank." Zhar explained how the raiders organized themselves into squads and groups, and leaders had to win their rank in trials by combat.

Rachel tried to contain her rage. "I can guess why the kid's here, but what are we doing out here?"

"Why have pretty pets if you don't show them off," Aya said from the other side of the throne, where she reclined.

Althea scrunched up her face a little, bewildered at the woman's emotional reaction to the leash. She *liked* it.

"I'm not a fucking possession," Rachel grumbled.

Zhar tugged at the chain hanging from Rachel's neck. "We are until we fight our way out."

Rachel brimmed with anger and shame.

The tension between the two grew as taut as the link between Rachel's wrists until Ramani crawled over to the extent of her leash. No longer making any effort to cover her nudity, she stared at Althea, poised with a strange grin. Something different shone in her eyes. A foreign presence, something other than timid Ramani, stared back at her.

"There you are... little one," said a female voice, quite obviously *not* Ramani. Sultry, and with an odd accent, it exuded calm laced with arrogance.

"Who are you?" Althea asked, her voice stern. "Let Ramani go."

"That is Ramani." Zhar shot a quizzical glance at Althea, gazing back and forth between the two. Something in the slender woman's eyes unsettled her. "That is Ramani, isn't it?"

Ramani looked down at herself and around at the other women. "Bloody hell. I've half a mind to kill all these pigs for what they are doing to you lot." She smiled at Althea. "Buck up, mite. Know that friends are coming." With that, the bony woman shuddered and fell seated, swooning as if drunk.

"What just happened?" Rachel edged away from everyone, still wringing her hands in an attempt to get loose.

"Stop that. You're going to cut yourself." Althea rubbed the redness out of Rachel's wrists. "Someone was inside Ramani."

"That would be Vakkar." Zhar laughed.

Rachel made a disgusted face. "In no world is that funny."

Althea frowned at the redhead. "No, a spirit I think... maybe the Ancestor of Mischief."

"I felt something cold drift over me a minute before," said Aya.

Zhar flashed a dark smile and she whispered. "Then it is true. The Prophet will bear forth our freedom."

A tremendous *clang* made the women cringe, though Althea shot a blasé glance in the direction of the arena. Another pair of raiders went after each other with swords as long as their height, seemingly made of old flattened and sharpened car parts.

"Seriously? Goddamn swords! I'm chained by the neck, naked, to the throne of a bandit king while guys are trying to kill each other with medieval weapons." Rachel shuddered and curled forward. "Please wake up... Please wake up... So help me Harris, if I'm in a fucking sim right now, I am going to rip your balls off."

Althea looked away from Rachel, ashamed of her own guilt. She could force Vakkar to free them and he would believe he wanted to for a time, but then he would realize what happened, and then people would know the Prophet could do such things. Then there would always be cages and chains, assuming of course the people simply didn't kill her out of fear. And people didn't kill mystics in nice ways.

"I'm gonna kill that mother—"

Althea put her hand over Rachel's mouth.

"The child is right," Zhar whispered. "Act tame and strike when they lower their guard."

"Tame? This is so fucking far from okay that—"

Zhar jerked the leash, pulling Rachel nose to nose. "You think I'm happy to be here? You think I like this?" She shook her own leash. "I'm just as pissed off as you are, but I'm not stupid enough to act like it and get my ass beat. Sit down, shut up, and do what they tell you to do 'til we can do something about it other than get killed."

She let go.

Rachel glared, eyeballs almost bulging out of her head. Zhar folded her arms over her knees, glaring off into the distance. For an instant, her outward demeanor faltered and let a single tear slip past the iron wall. Scowling, Rachel slumped and plotted.

A wail of agony preceded a noise like an out of tune cathedral bell. All eyes went to the fighting. One sword lay on the ground. Half a forearm sailed overhead, raining blood upon them as it passed over the throne and out of sight. Aya looked annoyed at the red on her legs; Ramani screamed and wiped it off as if acid had dripped on her. Zhar seemed happy to watch one of them suffer, and Rachel didn't even notice it, too angry. The bandit chief cheered and lunged to his feet with a murderous howl of approval.

Althea scampered over the platform, sprinting in the direction of the hand. Ignoring the raider's shouts of alarm, she darted down the rear of the dais and jumped after the errant limb over the edge of a drainage ditch. Thigh-deep in water the color of weak coffee, she swished her hands around the mud looking for it. The peculiar urgency in the raider's alarm made sense as she came abreast of a corrugated metal pipe, large enough for her to walk into with only a slight stoop. It ran under the factory wall, leading quite a ways into the distance to a spot of sunlight.

Freedom stood so close, staring at her out of the heat blur shimmering from the ground outside. She could run, right now. By the time the raiders mounted up on their buggies, drove out the front gates and around the compound, she could be gone, hiding somewhere they couldn't find her.

Her hand brushed the floating limb and she picked it up out of the water. Althea turned away from the pipe and glanced up at a crowd of men arriving at the ridge. They slipped over the edge like lemmings failing to slide to a stop at a cliff. Althea held the limb up over her head so they could see why she had run off. Several rushed into the water toward her to foil her assumed escape. They slowed when she tried to climb the dirt back *into* the compound rather than flee.

She squirmed under the grip of hands hauling her to the tarmac, breaking free and running away from the crowd to the wounded man lying on the ground in the battle arena. Althea fell to her knees beside him, a hand on his forehead. He fell limp once she told his mind to disregard pain. After positioning the severed limb in its approximate natural pose, she clasped her hands around the torrent of blood bubbling out and called upon her power.

Raiders, and the harem, cringed at the wet *crunch* of rapidly knitting bones. Some of the men lost their nerve at the sight. She regarded the gore with no more unease than a potter working clay at a wheel, having seen far worse before. When the wound had mended, she wiped her bloody hands off on his shirt and looked up at the crowd.

"His arm will be soft for a week. Do not make him work or let him lift heavies." She trudged to the painted line.

A hornet's nest of discontent surrounded Vakkar as his men yelled at their chief over the Prophet's near-escape. He calmed them with raised hands.

"The Prophet has promised not to flee, and behold—she is true to her word." Vakkar pointed a sword at her before raising it overhead. "We have the Prophet, and she is loyal to Vakkar!" He stood and roared to the men. "Nothing shall stop us. The land shall belong to us all."

Bloodlust radiated from a wall of pumping arms, roaring throats, and hot bodies. The emotional surge from a hundred and a half raiders flooded her with elation, hatred, and even arousal, crushing Althea to her knees. That the bandit king used her as the inspiration for their insane need to harm people left her too horrified to cry.

Her lip quivered, but she could only whisper, "Please stop," not that anyone noticed.

She wanted more than anything for Den to sweep in and gather her away from this horrible place. If she had to spend her days once more in a tiny cage to be with him, so be it. Everywhere she looked, legs blocked her path. She trembled under the thought of what her presence here enabled these people to do.

An army of hands seized her. She screamed as they hoisted her aloft, grabbing and squeezing wherever they could gain purchase. Althea floated above the crowd, able to see the harem over the undulating sea of bodies. Weapons, spikes, and wild hair jutted out here and there amid endless dirt-streaked howling faces. Zhar had crept to the end of her leash, leaning as far as she could toward the nearest raider who had his back to the dais. Her face had turned red from the collar pressing into her throat, her fingers stopped inches from a handgun on his belt. Rachel stared at the pistol, muttering inaudibly in a repetitive pattern. Ramani shook her head, crying. Aya stared in shock, paralyzed with fear.

"We shall rule the sands!" screamed Vakkar. "The Prophet brings us glory."

"The Prophet brings us glory," repeated the entire throng, somewhere between chant and shout.

Althea didn't try to fight the hands that held her up, too overwhelmed by the guilt their words brought. Disgust at what she caused brought on a sick feeling. Bouncing up and down did little to settle her unease, and soon the protein slime spewed from her mouth and nose, splattering all over a huge man in a fluffy pink wig. At that instant, her dread and revulsion emanated in a radiant telempathic pulse that stopped their revelry cold.

The deafening cheer petered out. All eyes went to the beige slop gliding down the man's leather armored chest. Zhar backed up to the dais and sat on the edge, chin propped on her fist with a look of annoyed discontent. Vakkar eyed the clouds warily and waved at his crew, who set her back on her feet. Unable to stand, she swooned to all fours and threw up again. No one seemed to much care, as they all gazed about wondering what had just happened. She coughed the last of the bile out and staggered upright, intent on returning to the dais. Before she could take two steps, the raiders remembered why they had gathered and converged once more on the arena. Men and women pressed together, forming an advancing human wall that pushed her to the edge of the fighting area.

Althea knelt upon the hard concrete behind the painted yellow line. Dozens of raiders blocked her from returning to sit in front of Rachel. Men shouted, though the words lost meaning under the blur of her mood. A strange feeling pulled her attention up a second before a spritz of warm blood sprayed over her face, arcing from the neck of a skinny, screaming man clutching a nail-studded aluminum bat. He spun in circles, blood spurting from his neck and groin. A tall metal-armored woman with spiked shoulder guards and a pair of hatchets had scored first blood. She strutted in a circle, holding her weapons high to the side, winding up the crowd.

Female raiders always seemed to be the most vicious.

The injured man fell, and dragged himself toward her. "Please…"

Althea sighed, expecting a long and miserable day.

9

CALM BEFORE THE STORM

G laring light brought the discomfort of consciousness back to
Althea's mind. Fragments of glass in the once-windows focused
sunlight into her cell with such intensity it hurt to open her
eyes. Shielding her face with an arm, she sat up and squinted around. The
factory sat in silence, save for the soft breathing emanating from the
tangle of women that slept nearby. All the mending from the arena had
left her aching.

After using the bucket, she slithered once more amid the old sleeping
bags with her back to the light, and lay on her side with one arm tucked
beneath her head, the other draped in front of her. She stared between
her blurry fingers at the pale grey wall beyond the field of red fabric.
Heavy, stagnant hair hung with the stink of sweat and urine. The harem's
bucket needed changing. Ramani choked on the fumes. No air moved
despite only one wall of the cage being solid.

Althea scrunched fabric over her face to hide from the stink. Her
thoughts leapt from the fighting, to the women's shame, to Den, to
attempting escape by that tunnel the next time they let her out of the cell.
Sighing, she gave up on that idea. The Badlands held dangers she found
more frightening than captivity. A girl her age—even the Prophet—would
make a quick meal for some beast lacking the reason to understand her
reputation.

Clutching the agate pendant to her chest made her think of Den. She curled tighter and sobbed without a sound. Only once before had being abducted made her cry; the first time it happened, about six years ago. Blurry apparitions of a man and a woman who once took care of her haunted the fringes of her memory, a time before anyone knew she could heal. The chaos that followed overshadowed her thoughts. The Wagon Man discovered what she could do. Her village had helped him when he staggered in wounded. Althea saw him hurting and made it stop. She'd saved his life. He repaid them with death, and her with a small cage.

A flash of green, a spinning forest, filled her mind and the crying stopped. Energy flowed from the pendant into a cascade of spiraling images: Den in the middle of the village, standing and pointing, his angry yells repeating into the distance of the dreamlike blur of quasi-time. Her mind-sight moved in a slow orbit centered on him as he gestured toward an indistinct shape.

He bellowed. "You did *what?*"

The face of Yala, an older girl of about sixteen, clarified out of the blur. Perfect skin the color of burnt sienna shimmered in the sun. Almond-shaped brown eyes framed in long black hair widened with surprise and fear. Den's emotion flooded back from the dream sight, overcoming her. He had become the embodiment of fury.

She sat bolt upright out of the vision and glared at the wall.

"Prophet?" A man's voice came from behind.

"What!" Filled with inherited rage, she whirled and fixed him with a stare that made him drop something and fall over himself to run away.

Her fists trembled as she gazed after the shadow fleeing between the great machines. She wanted to smash something, to hurt someone, to make something scream. A gasp drew her attention to the left a quarter turn; the expression on her face caused Aya and Ramani to shriek and jump away. Den's anger boiled out of her eyes, flooding their cell with an intense azure glow, brighter than she had ever seen.

The foreign rage had taken over.

Althea shifted her weight to her knees and sat back on her heels. Upon noticing her palms streaked with crescents of blood from her fingernails, she searched for calm. The scratches faded as she hid her face in her hands. When her emotion settled, she slid them down over her chest to the pendant. She understood. Yala led the raiders right to her. She must have noticed Althea's escape and followed from the village. Althea was a rival for Den's affections, and he would be the chief once his father became too old. At least Den knew of her treachery.

"What's his name?" Rachel slid close to the barrier.

Althea looked over, startled. "What?"

"Girls your age only make that face about boys or having their cell phone taken away. I'm sure even in this fucked-up place nature still works, and I doubt you know what a cell phone is." Rachel tried, but seemed unable to smile.

"Den." Althea stared at her grimy legs peeking out from leather scraps, still smeared with dried raider blood.

Rachel nodded. "Byron was the first guy to dump me."

"He didn't!" she wailed. "I was…" No voice came to her.

"I understand… bandits. Hey, come here."

Althea crawled over to the grate. "Are you hurt?"

After looking around to make sure none of the raiders could overhear, Rachel whispered. "That thing you do to their boss to make him leave us alone… I can't take this anymore. Please do it again and let's get the hell out of here." She broke down in tears.

Althea had never thought of doing such a thing. Hearing her say it made it sound possible, even plausible. Momentary elation fell flat. "We will just get taken by others."

"Maybe *you* will. *We* won't." Collar rattling, Zhar padded closer, inserting herself into the conversation.

Rachel glared. "That's awful to say."

"That's not what I mean. Together, we can fight." Zhar glanced between them before smiling, whispering as if she tried to sell a stolen item. "Hey… voodoo us outta here and we can protect you, but you can stay if you want. At least save us. You can't keep Vakkar off your buddy there forever."

Althea made a concerned face at Rachel when the handcuffs rattled. Judging by the look on the woman's face, had she been free, Zhar would have just received a black eye—or worse. Looking away, Althea considered the idea. She probably could compel Vakkar to release the harem, but shivered at the thought of what they would do to her once they realized what happened. Not to mention what the rest of the raiders would do if Vakkar no longer wanted the women. She would have to use her powers again to make them forget. It would be an endless repetition, and she had to sleep sometime. Not to mention four unarmed women would not fare well outside. They would probably wind up enslaved again, or become food for some monster.

Before she could answer, two raiders approached. The women looked away. Althea stood and walked to the door, obedient gaze on the ground. One man had hair down to his belt, the other shaved bald. They stood with their backs to her, looking at the peg where the key should have been.

The one with hair kicked the post. "Oi! Key's gone."

"Boss 'as it." The bald one shrugged.

"What fer?"

"Make it harder ta steal Prophet."

The long-haired man picked up the object the first raider dropped when he fled, and stuffed it under the door, kicking it into the cell hard enough to knock a cardboard box from one of the shelves. Althea squatted and picked up the rectangular packet, glancing for a moment at the debris that fell out of it. A few days earlier, Rachel had explained that years ago, these 'cages' had been used to protect valuable items. The electronic component, or what remained of it, had been put in here so no one would steal it—just like her. A bizarre kinship formed with this relic from the before-time.

"Eat." The bald one pointed. "We scored a convoy, got some goodies."

Zhar grumbled. "Great, more slime."

"It's one'a dem healthy bars. It'll make you shit a rock." The other man chuckled.

The bald one smacked him on the head. "Don' talk to the Prophet like that. Respect."

Althea glanced at the crinkling thing in her hand. "I don't want a rock to come out of my butt."

The two raiders burst out laughing. Rachel almost even smiled.

"It's just a turn o' phrase, mate." The bald one rushed his words in between gasps and a reddening face. Althea's clueless look made him rephrase. "Just eat it, we'z kiddin' bout the rock."

Gnawing on the end, the plastic taste made her wrinkle her nose and glare at them. The bald one relapsed into breath-stealing peals of laughter. The other raider explained how to take the wrapper off, after which, she found the block of semisweet granola far more appealing. She flopped upon the sleeping cloth and munched. Rachel's halfhearted laugh turned into a scream as she futilely tried to defeat the handcuffs with brute force.

"Dammit! I gotta get out of these, I'm going fuckin' crazy." She shivered. "Almost four damn weeks, I can't feel my fucking arms anymore." Anger became desperation, and she sobbed.

Zhar smirked at her. "Your choice not playing along. If you want outta them that bad, just let Vakkar have you. Don't gotta like it. Make him think you're his, then strike when he turns his back."

Winded, Rachel scowled at the grimy redhead. "I have no idea what kind of fucked-up world I woke up into. How long was I asleep? What year is it?"

Zhar shrugged. "No idea."

"Great. We've blown ourselves back to the stone age." Rachel grumbled. "Besides, I don't just roll over on my back for anything with a dick." She cringed, glancing at Althea.

"Bitch!" Zhar pounced.

Rachel leapt to her feet and fell back against the wall, catching Zhar in the gut with a knee that took the wind out of her. The growling woman's fingers slipped from Rachel's short hair without purchase, and a shoulder-bump launched her face-first into the cage wall where she slid to the ground, wheezing. Aya rushed over and helped Zhar up, pulling her away while Ramani dove against Rachel to hold her back, begging her to stop fighting.

"Please, you mustn't!" Ramani whispered. "They will punish all of us."

Althea thought Zhar 'mean,' and felt awful Rachel had been tied for so long. As she picked the last flecks of granola out of the flannel, she toyed with the idea of 'encouraging' the raiders to free Rachel's hands, but only Vakkar had the key. She remembered Zhar's warning and imagined him putting chains on her as punishment when the command wore off.

Althea traced a finger over her ankle. Some years ago, other raiders put handcuffs on her legs so she couldn't run, and had left her that way for months. That had been terrifying, but to have her hands trapped behind her would be so much worse. No one had ever done that to her, but then again, no one feared the Prophet hitting them—only that she might flee. She shied away, her guilt at being happy Vakkar hadn't chained her made her unable to look at Rachel. Punishment she would take with a smile if it would free the woman, but in the Badlands, helplessness meant death.

With an arm across Zhar's chest, Aya made a blank face at Rachel. "Vakkar said he would release you if you submit to him. You should do it." She looked down, as if trying to convince herself as well. "It's only sex..."

Rachel swallowed her nasty remark, feeling only pity for the broken woman in front of her.

Vakkar sauntered into view, approaching Althea's cage at the head of a small group of raiders. He regarded her with an imperious frown and took out the key. She walked to the door, staring down at her feet, waiting for it to open.

"You will tend to the common stock." He pointed to the right.

She walked at their direction, gaze downcast, following the two men in the lead. The men whispered in argument, not sharing Vakkar's trust. They wanted her leashed or at least hobbled. Their leader, however, remembered the stories. She never runs away, always does what she is told, and cannot hurt anyone.

Other legends existed, stories of calamity that followed those who mistreated the Prophet. Althea wished them true. Unfortunately, ill fate tended to follow whomever she found herself with regardless of how they treated her. She thought of withholding healing until he took the chain from Rachel's hands, but that would make her no better than the Wagon Man, selling the gift of life.

Unlike the people of Den's village, these raiders did not fear her. They coveted this great treasure they had all to themselves, unconcerned with her also being a person. Few looked at her like a girl, or even an annoying child too young to be useful.

To them, she was the great healer, a source of power.

Not a little girl, and most certainly not a person.

10

OATHS AND OMENS

Sun glint flashed over the flaking grey paint. The battered door groaned open with a grating screech of rusted metal. Althea squinted at the harsh change in light outside compared to the old factory building. A steady, hot wind rolled in from the west, blasting her hair aloft. Heat blur danced along the tarmac between the factory and the kennels.

Dozens of raiders scattered about, some lounging, some working, others playing the bizarre game kicking the bouncy sphere around. Althea gasped at the blazing concrete under her bare feet, hot enough to hurt, but not to the point where she would have to heal herself. With quick steps, she followed the group to the first of the occupied outdoor cages, rushing toward a shaded spot to stand in. The raiders had at least been nice enough to put an awning over them. Dead, dehydrated slaves had no value.

As soon as she came into view, the old man began praying in a loud voice, startling the other captives and earning threats and shouts from the raiders, which he ignored. A raider moved forward to unlock the first kennel space; Althea looked up at Vakkar.

"Please, sir?"

He gave her a suspicious squint. "What?"

"The sick girl inside, can you please free her hands? They hurt her and I have to keep mending it."

"That one is dangerous." He waved dismissively. "Not to mention useless."

Althea bowed her head. "She is not from now. She is from the before-time. Many years in the past. She does not know you own her. She must learn. I will fix her for you."

"I will think it 'round." He stroked his fringy beard.

Her heart sank. It didn't seem likely he would listen, at least not without her making a threat she lacked the cruelty to deliver on. She could warn them their luck would be bad if they didn't do as she asked, but that would be lying, which she figured as bad as hurting someone. Of course, she'd already lied about Rachel having a sick. Maybe that's why the raider chief hadn't freed her yet—punishment for being false.

Fingers dug into her shoulder. A raider pulled her back, twisted her about, and prepared to shove her into the kennel. He thought better of it when Vakkar glared. The man let go and pointed at the wheezing body slumped upon the ground.

Althea entered the small cell, knelt, and put a hand under the man's tattered shirt, on skin cold and clammy despite the sun. She shut her eyes and concentrated, reaching into his presence for the taint of sickness. Before long, she sensed it as a black miasma drifting around the red/crimson energy field of his life force. The shapeless form recoiled from her presence as she chased it into oblivion. Once confident it had been purged, she looked at him. His fever broke, and the last vestiges of sickness bubbled from his lips in the form of a pale grey slime.

Without hesitation, she swiped a rag off the belt of a nearby raider and brushed the man's face clean.

"Give him as much water as he wants," she said to no one in particular while dabbing.

The raiders smirked.

Vakkar slapped one on the head. "Do as she says. She knows the ways of a mystic. This meat sack is worth nothing to us dead."

One by one, she tended to the twenty-six captives, a dozen of them women. The men had injuries borne mostly of forced work and failed escape attempts; the women had injuries from their capture or entertaining the raiders' rank and file. Unlike the harem, all were indistinct in their ethnicity, the products of many generations of commingled cultures. Most had become sick from the harsh conditions, and the last of the men—a new arrival—suffered a festering gunshot wound which rendered him delirious.

When they opened his cage, she crawled in and undid the pitiful attempt at a bandage. Beneath the cloth lay the sickly sweet smell of decay and dried moonshine, as well as crimson skin charred black with rot and roiling with maggots. She reached behind her and removed a knife from the boot of a raider with a large scar down his face. He grabbed her wrist, squeezing hard in an attempt to make her drop the weapon. She bit her tongue, but stared up at him defiantly, refusing to let go despite his painful grip.

"It is for the wound. Let her be," Vakkar bellowed. "Do not tell me you fear a little girl with a knife?"

The man flung her wrist away, glaring at Vakkar.

A few nearby raiders chuckled at him.

"Din ka'ya deem," he seethed in a dire tone.

Vakkar laughed, then hit himself in the chest with a sideways fist. "I accept. Your blood shall paint the arena at the next trials."

After giving the scarred one a dirty look, Althea brushed the maggots away with her fingers. A quick mental prod disconnected his mind from any sense of pain, and she scraped the knife at the dead flesh, cutting away all the rot. Her guard escorts cringed, gagging and unable to watch the strips of flayed skin tumble to the ground. She sliced at the area until she hit fresh muscle, and put the weapon back where she found it. The glower its owner gave her made her look into his mind. He wanted to see her leashed and cowering to avenge his wounded pride. An odd feeling about this man came over her, going straight to her tongue without her brain's involvement.

Narrowing her eyes, she rose up on her knees and spoke in an eerie tone. "You'll not live out the week."

The others fell silent, dismayed at the raider's poorly hidden fear. His daydreams of her suffering left his mind, replaced with fear. She turned back to her work, threading her fingers into the man's leg, rooting around until she found the bullet lodged in the bone. She commanded his flesh to let go of it, plucked it out, and tossed it aside. Althea cleared her mind and set her hands around the wound, funneling her power into his body. Flesh regenerated at her command. The mangled gash closed, covered by pristine skin in a matter of minutes.

With a weary smile, she came out of her meditation. At a nervous male whimper, she glanced up and back.

The scarred raider grabbed at his chest, his face contorting in horror. He screamed at a sudden swollen presence rising up under his shirt.

Althea scrambled to her feet and reached toward him with a look of concern. He palmed her head and shoved it into the metal pole at the corner of the kennel with a hollow *clank*.

"What are you doing to me?" Still clutching a fistful of her hair, he leaned all his weight into her skull, mashing her ear into the pole.

She cried out in pain, grabbing his wrist with both hands. Vakkar seized him by the shoulders and threw him to the side, aghast someone would attack the Prophet.

Althea crumpled to the ground, wrapping her arms around her head and whining. She fought the urge to cry while forcing the dull pain out of her head.

"*She* does nothing." A placid woman's voice echoed as if over a loudspeaker.

The scarred raider's leather vest split open. Feminine fingers protruded from the rip, grasping at the edges and tearing it asunder. His skin stretched out, up, and away from his chest until the warping flesh took on a hollow female form, a woman embedded waist-deep in his torso. His body convulsed and gurgled, muscles twitching in a paralytic rigor while his eyes rolled back in their sockets.

"Hello again, little one. Are you ready?"

"*See!*" The old slave yelled. "The wrath of the *Lord* has come down upon you. Bow down and be spared." He bent forward, pressing his forehead into the ground.

Althea gawked at the apparition of skin with no idea what to do. For an instant, she ceased being the Prophet; she was a little girl—and screamed like one.

After a glance at the gun on his belt, the entity smiled at the raider chief. "Right, you wanker. You fancy collecting women? P'raps it is time your fat arse is collected by one."

The twitching raider yanked the weapon into the air. Vakkar sprinted for cover, cursing at the fool for hitting the girl. Althea cowered, curling into a ball against the chain link fence as gunshots erupted. Something leapt past her followed by the thump of bodies colliding. She flinched at the unmistakable *crack* of a breaking neck, and the feminine laughter that followed it made her feel sick.

Althea crawled from the fray, keeping her eyes closed, not wanting to see the death that tugged at her heart behind her. Whenever something died nearby, she felt it as an icy scrape across her heart. The concrete under her hands and knees went from warm to scalding, and the sun fell on her back as she left the awning's shade. An arm circled her chest and lifted; she cried out in surprise. The man who had been infested with maggots scooped her off the ground and carried her. She looked away from the glinting gun in his other hand, buried her face in his shoulder, clinging to him as he ran. He slowed after a few strides and bent forward to let her down.

A hand on her cheek made her look up; he smiled. "Stay here. I'll be right back."

After stashing her behind an old truck, he rejoined the mixture of gunshots, screams, and proselytization from the old man. Althea cringed with every terrible noise as she hugged her knees tight to her chest. Other slaves arrived one by one, taking cover and grasping at her. She couldn't tell if they wanted to comfort a terrified child or sought solace from the great Prophet.

"Where did you go?" The placid female voice saturated the area. "Althea? Where are you little one?"

"Praise be to the—"

Bang.

"Stupid old man." The ephemeral woman spat, annoyed. "Your God is dead."

The old man's wail, cut off by gunshot, drew Althea out from her cover. He lay upon the ground, struggling to breathe. Blood gurgled out of his mouth and stained his shirt dark.

"There you are." The hollow woman protruding from the raider's chest swiveled at her as she darted over.

"Stay away." Althea glared at the creature as she came to a halt, kneeling in the puddle of blood.

Gathering some fleshy bits scattered here and there, she stuffed all she could find back into the wound. He gurgled.

"The path is open now. You must flee before they organize." The skin-phantom hovered up to her, almost nose to nose.

"*Go away!*" The glow in her eyes flared.

The creature groaned as if caught off guard by Althea's mental command. The flesh-body snapped back into the raider with a *crack* like an immense rubber band striking skin. He huffed and clutched at his chest, stunned from pain and wearing a look of complete terror. Before he could utter a single word, other raiders mowed him down in a hail of bullets.

She crossed her arms in front of her face to shield herself from the shower of blood and bone matter, glancing up as the scarred man hit the ground.

I just said he'd die soon to be creepy... Althea squirmed, wondering if the odd feeling she had about him might have actually been prophetic. More likely, she sensed the strange female spirit nearby.

She dug her fingers into the man's chest, pouring as much energy as she could into his elderly frame, rebuilding it and exhausting herself. Old people always did drain more, and age coupled with such a severe wound left her hurting. She collapsed over his chest, smiling at the blotch of pink new skin. The chaos around her blurred into a tangle of shooting and screaming until a hand on her shoulder shook her awake. Forcing her head up, she recognized the man who had maggots in his leg. The others had armed themselves from dead raiders. All around her, the tarmac had become a bloody mess. A few lingering gunshots popped in the distance. The captives had won; the kennels stood empty.

"Come, we are fleeing before more of them return!" He tugged in an effort to get the listless child to stand.

Althea looked at the old man. He would live, but she lacked the energy to move. "Take him. I cannot go with you."

"I'm not leavin' a little girl here. Get up!" He pulled her to her feet, supporting her weight.

The agate pendant danced between her fingertips, and she wondered if these people could bring her home. The feeling of having a home felt as strange as it did painful. The roar of more raiders dispelled the fantasy.

"Can you release the harem?"

He shook his head. "Love to, but there ain't no time; more of 'em are coming. Going *into* the building would be suicide."

"I made a promise. I cannot go with you." She glanced at the wave of raiders streaming around the corner of the factory. Her heart sank. A part of her couldn't believe she tried to talk them out of taking her home. "They will hunt me. Take these people and get away. You will not be safe if I am with you. They will not stop until they kill you all. If they have me, they will not chase you."

He stared, frowning at the thought of leaving her, but knowing she spoke truth. This girl would be both a great boon and a terrible burden, and flying bullets offered little time to argue. Althea swayed to the ground as he dragged the old man into the bed of the truck and banged twice on the roof. She drew an arm across her face as a cloud of exhaust blasted her, and cried as her chance at freedom sped off in a hail of bullets. At least those people might survive. Had she gone with them, she would only have caused more death.

She rolled onto her back in a patch of someone else's blood, gaze fixed upon a single puff of cotton in the otherwise clear sky. Tears ran down the sides of her head, settling in her ears. She searched the cloud for an answer to why everyone treated her so cruelly when she only wanted to help people.

Red-faced, Vakkar staggered to a halt, towering over her. He glanced back and forth between her and the truck. Other raiders jumped on buggies to give chase. Althea sensed his pride, and surprise, that she had chosen to stay.

She closed her eyes, picturing the lonesome cloud floating amid the endless blue and whispered, "I promised."

Happiness belonged to real people, not a creature like her.

11

REBELLION

Althea drifted at the precipice of sleep, lost within a dream-forest around Den's village. Barely aware of her nest of warm cloth, she rubbed her cheek into the material and snuggled deeper, emitting a soft sigh of contentment. Tranquility lasted only minutes before a flurry of loud shouts erupted in the distance.

She pushed herself up on all fours, wide-eyed and still, listening for danger. The grated metal walls came into focus. The quiet of her cell replaced the tranquility of the woods around Den's village. Upon recognizing her cell, she remembered the slave revolt and her heart pounded with panic. She sat back on her heels and patted herself down. Once sure she hadn't been chained, she resumed breathing.

Raiders screamed at each other outside; angry men hurled threats and insults while the women gave off horrible war-shouts. She crept to the wall between the pens and jammed her fingers into the diamond shaped holes. Three of the women lounged around half awake, though Rachel looked as wired as Althea felt.

At the sight of the woman still in cuffs, she stared down and sighed. "I asked him to let you out. I'm sorry."

"He's been yelling all afternoon. He didn't even show up to f—uhh, *wife* anyone last night." Rachel let off a sad chuckle. "S'pose it's pretty silly to swallow the bad words given our fucked up situation. You've probably heard 'em all anyway."

Althea nodded. "Yes. Words cannot be bad. It's what's in here"—she tapped herself on the chest—"when you speak that matters."

Zhar sat up, blinking at her. "Hot damn! You're still alive? You were a bloody mess when he carried you back in. We thought you died."

Althea looked down at herself, sulking. "This is not my blood."

"Look, kid." Zhar stood. "All hell is breaking loose out there. You *have* to do something before we all die!"

"What can she do?" asked Ramani barely over a whisper. "She is so small. If *you* cannot break the door, what could this child possibly do?"

Zhar gave the little woman a look of anger borne of having no answer for the question. "Uhh... Prophet it open!"

Althea glared under flat eyebrows at Zhar, with no reply for something so stupid.

The clatter of a metal door grated into a loud *bang* that echoed over the factory. Distant gunfire became louder with the door open. The women jumped. Althea burrowed into the red flannel to hide. Shouting and tromping approached inside. Sparks and a ricochet flew from one of the huge machines. Rachel dove chest first to the ground with a fleshy *slap*, her cuffed hands not allowing her to catch her fall. She shouted at the others to get down.

The chieftain backed into view, his face lit by staccato muzzle flashes from his huge handgun as he fired past the giant machines at people out of sight. Dull *clanks* became fleshy thumps as bullets struck him in the chest. Althea peeked out from her hiding place, horrified at the gouts of blood pouring from holes in the metal vest. Vakkar wheezed and careened over backward, landing on his side, a spatter of red flying from his mouth.

Althea locked eyes with the bandit king, plunging into his thoughts.

Vakkar, enraged at the incompetent loss of the slaves, blamed the raiders' ill treatment of the Prophet for their bad fortune. His belligerence, lubricated by moonshine, exploded into violence in the wee hours. The fighting escalated to outright mutiny when the raiders' reaction only fanned the flames of his superstitious paranoia.

Althea ran to the door of her cell, pounding and kicking at it. "Over here!"

His eyes rolled around, barely able to focus at the voice so small amid the sounds of war. He rolled over onto his stomach and dragged himself toward her, gurgling. Another bullet glanced off his back, gouging the armor.

She assaulted the cage, pounding and slapping while shrieking. "Let me out! Please, don't die!"

Rachel glared at him, a vengeful, eager grin from ear to ear.

Three men sauntered around the corner of the ancient machinery, as if they had all the time in the world. Two reloaded their rifles. The third man spat on Vakkar's back. Althea cringed at the metallic *clack* of weapons cocking. They laughed at their wounded leader and leveled their weapons at him.

"Din ka'ya deem, motherfucker," said one, reciting the mortal challenge with a mocking laugh.

"Don't kill him." Althea wailed, slapping the cage wall. "Please, no!"

Up on her toes, she rattled all her weight against the door, screaming as a barrage of gunfire shredded his armored vest, painting the floor with an ocean of sanguine crimson that burbled out from twisted metal flowers around the exit wounds. For an instant, Vakkar looked at her in silent apology before deflating with a final gurgle. His cheek slapped onto the floor.

She shuddered, an icy claw raking over her heart as life left him.

Palms flat against the grating, Althea slid down until she knelt upon the tatters of her skirt. With her face pressed into the steel, only her fingers hooked in the gaps above her head prevented her from falling over. All strength left her from watching this man die so close and being unable to stop it because of a locked cage.

The raiders ran off laughing.

"Why?" She fell into sobs.

Zhar kicked the partition between cages with a loud *bang*. "The hell are you crying over a piece of shit for? Don't you dare feel sorry for that bastard."

Ramani made a spitting gesture in Vakkar's direction and put a trembling hand on Zhar's shoulder. "She is life. Any death hurts her, even one as vile as him."

The Indian woman recoiled from the angry glare, but as much as they loathed Vakkar, Ramani's words made sense.

Rachel scooted to the wall. "Hey, Althea. It's okay. C'mere. We're gonna be okay."

She surrendered to wracking sobs, her little body shuddering under the weight of grief.

Zhar went to the front of the cell, straining to get a view of the outside, and wound up staring at the post. Her fingers couldn't fit into the diamond-shaped holes in the lattice, much less stretch the six feet beyond it to the key. She kicked at the door, shaking the entire partition, but couldn't batter it down. Aya's calm demeanor had fled. The security of her place as the most favored among prized pets had vanished with Vakkar's life.

Althea raised her head, sniveling from her grief. While Zhar paced, the other three crawled close and huddled against the barrier between cells.

"Please help us!" Ramani wailed, the loudest she had ever been.

The ring of a ricochet near the roof preceded a *clank* that shook the grating.

Aya's voice trembled. "I don't want to die, please... Please do something!"

"Look, kid," said Rachel in a commanding tone not befitting a captive wearing only handcuffs. "We can't take the chance of just waiting here to see what happens. Those raiders are killing each other. With Vakkar dead, do you have any idea what they'll do to us when they stop fighting? They're gonna line us up and take turns. It's gonna be a shit show. We could die. I saw how they looked at you. They don't respect you like Vakkar did."

Althea cringed. Vakkar's lieutenants hadn't much cared for her being free to roam while out of the cell. Her fear of going from a sought-after Prophet to a hunted pariah made her search for a compromise in an uncompromising situation. She spoke in a breathless half-voice that didn't sound like she even believed herself. "Don't be afraid. I am the Prophet, and you are special, rare pretties. They won't harm—"

A small rocket pierced the far end of the factory, sailed halfway across the room, and detonated against an ancient hulk, knocking pipes and metal bits into the air in a glittering cloud of debris and dust.

"Wanna rethink that, kiddo?" Rachel tugged at her wrists. "Fuck. Do something! How can you just sit there? *Come on!*"

The random clanks of debris returning to the ground filled the air with a disharmonic symphony of scrap. Rachel had a point. Althea could no longer ignore the begging of four people in such danger, and looked around for anything she could do. Accepting captivity was one thing, but they had all gone from captives to people stuck in cages in the middle of a war zone. Without Vakkar in control, the women he collected would suffer brutality at the hands of a crazed mob. Rachel, Ramani, Aya, and even Zhar didn't deserve that.

Cinder block dust spat in puffs from the gun battle raging o utside.

Althea circled her cage, rummaging boxes and testing the bolts that held the fencing to the wall. The key to her cell sat a short distance from the door, hidden in a mass of gore between Vakkar's chest plate and his body. Finding nothing of use in any of the old boxes, she wanted to cry. She felt as vulnerable trapped within these walls as if she had been tied, and slumped in a heap amid the bedding.

"Can't you do something?" Zhar yelled.

Ramani put a hand on the redhead's shoulder. "She heals the body. She cannot do anything to metal walls."

A bullet ricocheted off the cage in a shower of sparks.

"Get down!" Rachel rolled onto her stomach. "Get the fuck down before you take a bullet."

They all complied, huddling close to the floor. Aya and Ramani clung to each other, trying not to scream. Zhar crawled close to the door, waiting for the first fool to be stupid enough to open it. A shaft of light pierced the dark factory around the shadow of a staggering raider that stretched along the floor past the edge of one of the ancient machines. The wobble in the gait coupled with raspy moaning gave away his injury and need for help.

Althea stared as the silhouette. Resigning herself to captivity, she let her gaze fall into her lap. A thin strip of flannel draped over her wrist, catching her eye. Inspired, she tore the scrap of red cloth from the bedding and scurried over to one of the metal shelves. With her back against it, she put her hands behind her around the pole and wound the material about her wrists as if bound in place.

Ramani could not believe her eyes. "She's doing it!"

"Nice," Zhar whispered.

"Good girl," rasped Rachel.

A bleeding man lurched around the end of the giant machine, clutching it to keep from collapsing. He swayed in place for a moment, gazing into space. Tattered, bloody, and weaponless, he spotted Althea and shambled over. When she didn't get up and come to the door, he banged his fist on the grating.

"Oi. Need 'elp." Blood dribbled out of his mouth.

She wriggled, pretending to tied. "I can't reach you. You have to come inside. I need to touch you to make the hurt go away."

He glanced at the post, taking the key and fumbling with it at the door.

Althea made a show of tugging at her supposedly tied wrists. "No, not that key. Vakkar wears it around his neck."

A distant explosion knocked shards of glass from the windows and drew screams from the harem—except for Rachel.

He flung the key over his shoulder. Zhar jumped and pressed herself to the cage, her gaze locked upon the flying glimmer of metal bouncing along the concrete until it vanished under a pile of silver tanks. The other three all screamed "No!" in unison. Rachel added some other words.

Althea hated lying to this man, making him hurt longer than he had to, but she couldn't let these women die. As he searched Vakkar for the key, she pondered if making a bad person suffer a little longer for the sake of four innocent lives was justified. When the raider stuffed his hand into the armor, she drew in a breath with rapt anticipation. After a terrible long minute of rooting around, he held up a bloody key and stumbled to the door. Metal scratched at the lock plate. All of a sudden, he stopped and looked at her with a squint of distrust.

She wriggled and whined, fighting her fake bindings, reaching at him with her foot, toes splayed. "I gotta touch you. Please! Don't make me watch you die, too."

The wounded man stared at her a while longer before the strength seemed to fade from him. Out of time, he opened the lock and the door swung wide. He swooned in and grabbed her hovering leg about the ankle.

"There. Touchin. 'Elp." He fell to his knees.

Smiling, she leaned forward and grabbed him on either side of his face. "Sleep."

"Oi wha—?" His eyes fluttered closed and she guided him to the ground.

When she set to the task of healing him, the women all yelled at her. She didn't care if they had little time. She could not leave this man hurt, especially after lying to him.

Once she mended him, she darted out and locked the door. A look at the empty peg upon the post stopped her heart.

"The key's over there!" Zhar pointed. "By the propane tank."

"What's a propane tank?"

Zhar growled. "Dumb Scrag. The round silver things."

Althea glared, reaching into her mind to understand the meaning. "I'm not dumb."

The entire factory rocked with a thunderous *boom*, the building shuddering under the impact of a vehicle somewhere along the outer wall. A torrent of dust fell from the rafters. Althea ran to a stack of old silver tanks that matched Zhar's thoughts, and got down on all fours to peer under them. The key glinted in the dark. She reached in, but her fingers fell inches shy of where it had bounced. She grunted, trying to force her arm deeper under the pile. With her head turned, she had to work by feel, and brushed the key with a fingertip.

She shot a pouting look at the harem. "I can't reach it."

"Do something!" yelled Zhar.

"Oh, that's helpful," muttered Rachel.

Ramani burst into sobbing.

Althea flattened herself to the floor. More shots clanked and sparked off the ancient machines overhead. The key defied her, too far from the edge to reach. Her wish for longer arms gave her an idea. She spun around and stuck her leg into the gap. After planting a toe on the key, she dragged herself forward, pulling the key out into view.

The women crowded around the door as Althea carried the tiny chip of metal over, such a small thing that meant so much right now. She hurried the key into the lock and turned it. Zhar burst out the door, the swinging metal grid nearly knocking Althea over, and ran straight for Vakkar's pistol, bare feet slipping in blood. The redhead fell on him, tearing at his gear.

"Search him for keys," Rachel shouted, rattling the cuffs.

Zhar managed to get her balance and grab the gun. The second her hand touched it, a wicked explosion reduced a man-sized door at the far end of the factory to metal shreds.

"No time." Zhar hooked Rachel's arm and hauled her away from the flaming door toward the truck ports at the rear of the building.

The detonation had sent Ramani into a ball under the shelves back in the security cage. Althea darted in and took her by the hand, dragging the shell-shocked captive away from certain death.

Chattering rapid fire came between screams and charging engines. Running past long-dead forklifts and roll doors, Zhar led the group toward the rear exit. Most of the fighting occurred on the front side in the main yard. Althea had seen such things before. With the death of a chief, the raiders had split into multiple groups vying for control. Behind the building, two decaying semi-trailers progressed in the slow process of rejoining the earth. Around them stood a great wall of corrugated steel, concrete, and barbed wire. The path to escape sat behind a hundred and a half men, or what remained thereof—shooting at each other.

"Shit!" yelled Zhar.

"This way!" Althea called out, running to the edge of the loading dock and leaping down.

Ramani followed without hesitation, as did Aya. Rachel stopped at the edge, casting an uneasy stare at the ground. After one more annoyed twist at her handcuffs, she jumped, landing in an ungainly stumble. Zhar lingered, annoyed by the usurpation of her authority by a child.

Althea ran backward for three steps so she could make eye contact. "Zhar, please..."

Shaking her head, the redhead leapt down and followed. Ahead of clattering collars and scattering curse words, Althea ran across the tarmac and vaulted into the drainage ditch with a splash. Aya and Ramani supported Rachel's arms as she navigated the uneven dirt. Zhar jumped right in.

The water varied in depth, paralyzing Althea with chill the first time it rose up over her waist. If not for the gunfire behind them, Ramani might have enjoyed the cool bath. Down here, they had the protection of earth between them and stray bullets. Althea went right for the pipe she remembered seeing during the arena matches. She trudged as fast as the muddy water allowed, heading a hundred and change yards to the end of the ditch and around a corner to the left. Despite being safe in a trench, she cringed at the constant sounds of war overhead.

Upon reaching the tunnel, Althea climbed into the corrugated metal tube and waved at the others to follow. The large pipe allowed her to run in a slight stoop, but the others had to crawl. Rachel managed a clumsy knee-walk that left her cursing each time her shins found rocks.

Althea held her hands to the sides for balance, skidding over the occasional patch of semidry mud. The distant blur of hot sand at the end of the pipe drew nearer. She wondered what it would offer them—but it had to be better than the cages.

GUARDIAN ANGEL

Althea reached the bottom of the shaft first, and stepped onto the hot dirt outside. Miles of open space led off in every direction except backward. With such openness came the fear of the unknown. Captivity provided a sense of order as well as some degree of safety, but her present circumstances had left Althea bereft of both. She stepped aside, watching the mud-covered women emerge from the pipe before glancing up at the sun, weak in the western sky. With a hand shielding her eyes, she squinted at the sparse clouds. At the *whump* of Rachel falling on her ass, she glanced at her for a second to make sure she hadn't hurt herself, then peered at the sky again.

"It will be dark soon," said Althea.

Zhar helped Rachel to her feet.

"Hey, Zhar." Rachel turned her back and pulled her arms as far apart as she could. "Shoot the chain out."

Zhar shook her head. "Not worth the bullet, and it will make noise... attract danger."

"What?" Rachel's voice began as a shout but sank to a whisper. "Y... You can't just leave me like this! Two damn months, Zhar. Two months! I can't take being in cuffs anymore."

"We can make it to my home in about four days. We have tools there that can get you free. A few more days won't hurt."

Rachel glared. "You're not the one fuckin' stuck like this. Couldn't take two god damned minutes to search him for the k—"

A distant explosion silenced her.

Zhar glanced at the compound, then to Rachel. "You rather be chained or dead?"

Rachel had to think about it.

"Please stop yelling and let's get out of here!" Ramani bounded forward like a scared deer.

The fighting at the factory still raged, the sound as well as the danger somewhat muted by the distance. After looking around in a spin, Zhar picked a direction and led the group across the scrubland. For some time, only the rattling of steel collars, the occasional nervous whimper from Aya, and Rachel's sub-vocal grumbles at her situation broke the silence.

Sun glare danced over the large pistol Zhar carried like a mark of authority, as if it made her their leader. In a way it did. The ability to kill any of them in an instant provided a strong motivator to follow orders. Althea made up her mind. She would command Zhar not to hurt anyone if she had to.

The sun slid without ceremony into the hazy mountains in the west. Eventually, Zhar stopped walking. Citing the darkness as a reason to take a break, she waved the pistol at the ground. Aya sat where the woman pointed like a trained dog obeying a command. A few seconds later, Ramani settled in beside her. Rachel glared for a moment, but gave in. Althea knelt close to Rachel, observing her new companions.

Rachel bristled at her lack of clothing, angered at her state. Ramani drowned in embarrassment. Aya didn't seem to care at all. When Althea peeked into her head, she learned the woman had never worn anything. She'd grown up as a Scrag like Althea, but raiders abducted her before she became old enough to catch a Seeker's attention and earn a gift of clothing. While Zhar disliked being outside with nothing to wear, it didn't bother her much. She considered it a necessary annoyance to be dealt with on her way home. Being collared made her furious far more than being exposed.

Althea considered offering her skirt to Ramani since it wouldn't bother her to be without it and the woman suffered such shame. Though, it wouldn't fit her and, truth be told, Althea considered it precious since she had made it herself.

Zhar paced around them, studying their surroundings. "Aya, you take first watch. In two hours, wake up Ramani. Ramani, you watch for two hours and wake me up."

"I can see in the dark," Althea said. "I should watch when it is darkest."

"No way, kid." Zhar shook her head. "Those eyes of yours will attract death like moths to candles. It's as bad as lighting a fire at night. Stay down, and keep them closed."

Althea sulked and kneaded the soreness out of Rachel's arms. Everyone complained of thirst, but the area offered no water. The night would get cold, and they had no protection from it aside from each other. Consequently, the women plus Althea huddled in a pile for warmth.

Althea tucked up to Rachel, chatting for a while about what the world had been like in her time, where people called police would never let raiders exist. This world sounded like stories made up to help children feel safe in their beds. Eventually, exhaustion guided Rachel off to sleep and Althea felt the tug of sleep at her eyelids.

The shadows of the sinking day elongated over the entwined mass of women, and darkness took the land.

§ ¥ 🛡 💧 🔮

"HELP!" A PLAINTIVE WHISPER GREW LOUDER OVER SEVERAL REPETITIONS until it woke everyone.

Althea rubbed the sleep out of her eyes and became aware of daytime warmth. To her left, Rachel lay rigid, staring at a black scorpion the size of a housecat moving with a tentative creep onto her stomach from her thigh. Its pincers poised not quite closed, the tail barb swaying like a snake charmer's pet. Its presence had even stalled the perpetual war between Rachel and the handcuffs. Aya's casual morning stretch stopped with statue stillness when she saw the bug. Ramani scampered backward, barely managing not to scream.

"Get it off me!" Rachel whispered. The muscles in her arms swelled with strain. A trickle of blood ran from both her wrists.

Althea crawled over and stared at the scorpion. "Hello."

Primitive territorial anger wafted from the creature. She wrapped her mind around the emotion and forced calm over it. Its pincers closed, empty. Althea stooped and eased her hands under it, plucking the enormous insect off Rachel's belly. As soon as it no longer touched her, the woman rolled away, shivering.

"Hey there. We're sorry we bothered your home. We won't be staying long." Althea swiveled it around to look at its face, radiating trust and peace.

The tail relaxed. She carried it a few paces away and set it down, continuing to whisper soothing, meaningless sounds. The scorpion scurried off into the sand. Ramani knelt, bowing at Althea and muttering. Rachel still hadn't taken a breath until a nearby gunshot shocked air into her lungs.

Aya and Ramani flattened on the dirt, trying not to scream. Rachel tried to spring up in a combat pose, but wound up on her face. Althea crouched with feral readiness, fingers and toes dug into the sand, staring in the direction of the sound. A short while later, Zhar walked into view dragging a dead animal that resembled a huge prairie dog. After skinning it with her hands, she tore off hunks of meat and passed them out.

Althea ate without hesitation, as did Zhar and Aya. It took Ramani awhile longer to get the raw meat down, but Rachel merely stared at it. Althea held some up so she could bite, and eventually hunger overcame her disgust.

"I was wrong." She cringed after swallowing the first mouthful. "I didn't think this nightmare could get any worse."

"At least the kid kept Vakkar off *you*." Zhar smirked. "I can still smell that bastard."

Althea frowned. "I'm sorry."

"What for?" asked Rachel.

"For not being kidnapped soon enough to stop him from wifeing Zhar."

Rachel sighed. "That ain't your fault." She turned a sad stare toward Zhar "Hey... you shot the dog. Please get me out of these damn cuffs?"

"We have to eat. Food is needed, comfort isn't."

"Comfort? Comfort!" Rachel struggled to her feet and stepped up on Zhar. "Are you fucking kidding me? We could be attacked at any time out here and in case you haven't noticed, we're all butt-ass naked, and I can't fight like this."

"Get your tits out of my face." Zhar's hand flexed on the pistol grip.

Althea darted over and grabbed Zhar's wrist with both hands, shaking her head. "No, don't. Don't be mad at her 'cause I stopped him from wifeing her. Be mad at me for not being kidnapped sooner."

Zhar broke her gaze from Rachel to sigh down at the girl. "Damn, kid. Don't be so pathetic. I don't understand why you can make people do whatever you want, but you just let them piss on you."

Althea stared down, watching several dark spots form around her toes from fallen tears. "Eww. They don't do that to me."

Zhar sighed. "I don't mean actual pissing... the way they treat you."

The cuffs rattled. Rachel might have punched Zhar if she were able to.

"You shot. Things will have heard. We should move," muttered Althea without looking up.

The tension fizzled out to a lingering glare between the two women that broke when Zhar paced off. Althea fell in step at Rachel's side and mended the cuts on her wrists. Rachel tried a few times to awkwardly pat, hug, and console her, as she still pouted from what Zhar had said to her.

Some hours later, they stopped at a small rain-puddle and drank. It tasted like dirt, but offered a wonderful relief from thirst nonetheless. Althea cupped her hands together, lifting water to Rachel's lips. Sitting around on this break, she sensed Zhar's impatience, Ramani's embarrassment, and Aya's worry about what her new owners would be like. Rachel had abandoned shame to focus on anger.

Zhar stood on her tiptoes, staring at the horizon and the sun before waving everyone to their feet. Her pale skin had turned bright red, burned from a day in the desert. Althea approached and put a hand on her arm, concentrating on mending the damage. Pain and redness faded, earning a brief smile.

Eventually, the break ended. Zhar headed off in the lead again. Althea fell in step alongside Rachel, holding her hand and keeping her spirits up with an unending stream of consoling words and smiles. Rachel cried in silence at the sight of several disused roads, the reality of this world hitting her at last.

A walk upon wind-driven sand took most of the morning. Zhar came to a halt and squatted to examine the ground near what appeared to be tire tracks. The others waited in silence while she poked at something embedded in the dirt. Her hair fluttered about in a fiery dance over her alabaster back in the breeze. A moment later, she held up a spent cartridge.

"Looks like 7.62," Rachel muttered, wandering closer. "Guess I didn't sleep *that* long if they're still usin' that stuff."

"Look," said Althea, rising up on her toes and pointing at a dark spot in the distance.

Zhar stood, discarding the brass, and followed the tire tracks. They ended about a hundred yards later at a raider buggy crumpled against a massive boulder, evidently abandoned. Riddled with bullets, the vehicle seemed quite far from operable, and no trace of its former driver remained. A gore-caked skeleton hung from the roll cage by a pair of handcuffs, the rusting collar about its neck a badge of its former station. Long hair clung to a rotten patch of leathery scalp that fell down onto its back. Flies buzzed about and tooth marks on the bones of the wrist hinted that whoever it was had survived the crash but remained trapped. Althea wondered if they had died before or after being eaten.

Rachel squeezed her hand at the sight. "Don't look, baby."

Zhar crawled over the wreck, searching for anything of use, eventually returning with two crude spears. Each was made from a length of metal as big around as a straightened crowbar, tipped with a flange ground down to be sharp along both its straight and angled edges.

Zhar grinned and offered one to Rachel.

Rachel didn't fight the cuffs, only stared. "Funny. You're a fuckin' laugh riot."

Althea smiled. "We have spears now. You can spare one bullet."

Zhar frowned at Aya. "Well, you're a useless pet… Here." She handed the other spear to Ramani.

The slender woman took it, but the weight of the all-metal spear nearly pulled her over.

"Why are you so mean?" Althea made a face at Zhar.

Zhar fashioned a belt out of bloody rope from the skeleton's ankles and hung the pistol from it. "I'm not mean. I'm practical."

"A practical person wouldn't leave the one individual in this group with combat training in handcuffs." Rachel scowled.

"I've been shooting guns since before I could walk. I'd rather have a bullet for something that wants to eat us." Zhar hefted the spear. "Come on, we're still three days out."

Rachel fell to her knees, pulling at the damnable things and growling past clenched teeth. Althea stooped over her, rubbing her shoulder in an effort to comfort her. The woman's thoughts contained mostly screamed bad words as well as repetitious chanting as she tried to tell herself not to be angry at Althea for failing to command Zhar to free her.

Althea sent her voice into the woman's head. *If I did that, she'd hurt both of us when it wore off.*

"What the…" Rachel jumped.

I'm the Prophet, said Althea telepathically, sounding far less than enthused about the fact. *I can mind-talk and hear your thinks.*

She looked at the warrior woman, wondering if perhaps a child's pleading eyes could work just as well as magic. "Please, Zhar… Rachel is so sad and scared like this. It's not right to leave someone tied in the Badlands, anything could hap—"

"Hey!" Ramani called out. "Look."

Everyone glanced where she pointed. A bleached skeleton lay half buried in the sand, surrounded by fluttering tatters of cloth dancing in the breeze. A glint in the dirt hinted at a blade beneath the bones of the right hand. Zhar led the group over and crouched to examine the find. Nothing remained of anything flesh, leather, or cloth.

"Something ate him, ate the leather too." Zhar ran her fingers over the rib bones. "Never saw bones this clean."

"Uhh. I think I know what it was." Rachel's voice, eerily quiet, quivered in the air.

A dry hiss stole Zhar's sarcastic remark. A trio of millipedes, bodies as thick as a man's thigh, rose out of the loose dirt. The one nearest Rachel hovered at eye level. Bright red antennae quivered.

"Careful, they spit," Althea yelled. She hated these stupid things. They didn't have enough smarts to command them to go away, and she'd learned years ago not to try making them afraid. The millipedes reacted to fear with frenzy. Trying to force calm over them only bought a few seconds. The stubborn things' hunger won out.

One eyed Ramani, one went for Zhar, and the last continued its staring contest with Rachel. The handcuffs rattled. Unimpressed by the creature, Zhar lunged at the one by her, lancing at it with the spear. It coiled and hissed, evading her attack as it poured itself backward over the sand.

Ramani screamed and threw her spear in an arc so feeble it clattered sideways to the ground not even halfway to the beast. Aya tackled the thin woman away from its bite, and the two rolled to the side in a cloud of dust. Rachel leapt back from a stream of caustic saliva, somehow managing to stay on her feet as a torrent of millipede flowed around her. The brush of a dozen legs made her scream; a fourteen-foot long insect touching her destroyed any sense of military training.

Althea ran for the discarded spear, stepping twice on the back of the millipede chasing Ramani and landing astride the weapon. Rachel ducked around the buggy and went for the boulder, hoping to use it as a delay, but the multi-legged horror merely swam over the rock. Shrieking, she barked a series of obscenities and sprinted in a circle.

Aya and Ramani tried to stand while clinging to each other.

The other millipede rose into the air, poised to leap at the women. Althea loosed a mousy war cry and leapt into the air, driving the spear into its back with all her weight. The heavy weapon punctured it like an arrow, pinning it to the dirt and cutting its leap short. Mandibles snapped inches from Aya's face before the front end flopped down. The creature thrashed from side to side, squealing. Althea rocked the spear in the wound, twisting it until yellow goop erupted. A spray of caustic droplets spattered the women's legs, making them scream. Aya darted to the side and grabbed a melon-sized rock. She hefted it over her head while Ramani cowered behind her, then hurled it down on the millipede's head. Althea grimaced at the nauseating *crunch*. The monster went still.

Althea glanced over her shoulder at Zhar whipping the burdensome spear about like a toy. Her millipede's head darted in and out, evading the flashing edge keeping it away. Having no doubt the woman could protect herself, she hurried to put herself between the other one and Rachel.

Holding the spear up, she yelled, "Rachel!"

Rachel saw her coming and changed course. Their paths converged. Althea intercepted the insect the same instant the woman pressed her back against the hot metal buggy. Locking eyes with the enormous bug, Althea flexed her grip on the spear and waited for the strike. Its gleaming onyx eyes showed no sense of emotion; no hatred, no anger, no joy— merely an impassive insect looking for food. Again, she tried to force calm into it, but it's primitive thought process had no room for it.

"I thought they said you don't kill." Rachel's voice drifted somewhere between despondence and euphoria.

"Bugs are bugs." Althea glared at it. "Leave her alone."

It emitted a high-pitched shriek and lunged in. Althea barely managed to get the spear in the way, deflecting it to the side. The mandibles punched into the buggy with a dull metallic *thud*, inches from Rachel's hip.

"Oh my God!" Rachel trembled at the sight of holes in the sheet metal.

Althea shoved at the creature, then pulled the spear back and stabbed. Without her falling weight behind it, the point glanced off the carapace. She used most of her strength lifting the spear, and had little left to swing it. Althea didn't expect to have much chance hurting this thing, but she refused to let it kill her friend. Her heart pounded in response to her power making her stronger. The spear moved more easily, but a weapon longer than her height still proved unwieldy.

Rachel scooted away. "Not gonna pat this one on the head and send it on its way?"

"I can't. It's too stupid and mean."

The millipede's head rose into the air, towering over her. A tendril of lime-green drool fell from its mouth as it hissed, mandibles wide. Althea watched its mouth, ready to dive out of the way of acidic venom.

"You're saying that damn scorpion was smart?" Rachel blinked.

"Smarter than these." Althea stabbed at its face, creating a small crack in the shell.

It leaned its head to the right, coiling for another bite. Her stare followed it; she didn't notice the tail end come about and strike at her leg until its rear pincer snapped around her left ankle and whipped back, dragging her off her feet and out of the way as its head shot over her, lunging for Rachel's defenseless neck.

A gunshot went off with a *boom*.

Whump.

Althea slammed flat on her back in the dirt, all the air knocked from her lungs. The spear fell across her ribs, followed by a rain of hot, slimy gunk.

The bullet detonated the first two feet of the creature, spattering Rachel with viscous yellow goop traced with strands of clear. Squiggles of dark green slid down her chest. The millipede, reduced to a headless tube of flailing legs wavered side to side for a few seconds before collapsing with a *splat*, more ooze gushing from its blasted-off front end.

Rachel wished she hadn't been screaming when it exploded.

Althea, not bothering to sit up, rolled her head to the left and glanced at Zhar. The redhead had the pistol leveled off, a wisp of smoke leaking from the barrel. Another dead millipede coiled around her legs and a trail of blood ran down her chest from a small wound to the shoulder.

"That is why I'm saving bullets."

Rachel spat out a mouthful of bug guts and slid down against the crashed buggy until her ass hit the ground. Humiliation and terror overwhelmed her. She sobbed, past the point of coping with her situation. Althea pushed the spear off her chest and sat up to grab a dagger-sized, shiny red pincer in each hand. With a pained whimper, she pulled them apart and out of her ankle before dragging herself to Rachel's side. Already, the cold numbness of venom crept up her leg. She wiped the slime from the woman's face and stroked her hair, whispering reassurances everything would be okay.

She had never before felt someone *wanting* to die.

"Hey!" Althea grabbed Rachel by the cheeks, brushing tears aside with her thumbs. "Stop that. Don't think bad! You're going to be fine. I promise I will help you get out of those things."

Rachel sniffled and found a chuckle hiding somewhere inside. "This is backward. You're the kid. I should be saying that to you."

"They're just bugs." Althea went to stand up and fell over, her left leg as dead as wood.

With an exasperated sigh, she forced the venom out of the wound before mending her leg. After wiggling her toes to make sure everything was in order, she tended to Aya and Ramani's acid burns. Finally approaching Zhar, she weathered a disdainful smirk.

Althea put a hand on the bite mark. "You're last 'cause the hurts don't make you cry like the others."

Every time Rachel looked at the bug guts all over her, she dry heaved and gurgled, somehow managing to hold in the vomit that wanted out. After Althea closed her wounds, Zhar walked over and pulled Rachel to her feet. For a moment, she seemed to consider wasting a bullet on the cuffs. She wiped as much of the goo off Rachel's chest as she could, tossing it to the ground handful by handful.

"There's a small creek about an hour north. We can clean up there." Zhar went to walk away, but hesitated. "One more day? In a day, I will feel closer to home and I'll shoot the chain out, 'kay? Only got four bullets left."

"You only had to shoot it because Rachel was tied," whispered Althea. "If you gave her the spear, she could've killed it."

Rachel took a deep breath and tried to cling to her last scraps of dignity, but couldn't stop shaking. "Fine. Great call giving Rama the spear. That worked out well."

Ramani looked down. "I'm a farmer."

Zhar handed the second spear to Althea. "This kid is ten, and she at least tried."

"Twelve," Althea whispered, barely audible.

"Eleven if you're anything," muttered Zhar.

Ramani whined. "I'm not the Prophet."

With a growl of contempt, Zhar shook her head and trudged off. The women fell in line behind her, marching. Althea debated commanding Zhar to release Rachel, sick to her stomach at the battle of guilt and fear.

She looked to the clouds, wondering if this 'God' person Rachel kept talking to would show up to take the cuffs off.

A warm breeze continuously pelted them with bits of sand as they made their way north for some hours, stopping occasionally when Aya's complaints of fatigue grew too loud. Zhar led them to a creek that followed the ancient scar of a once-mighty river. Althea left her clothes on the dry bank and joined the women in the water. There, they bathed, drank, and recovered from the sun. The cold, flowing water didn't carry the taste of dirt, and she drank until she felt as though she'd pop.

Forgetting herself as they sat neck-deep in the water, Althea splashed Rachel, trying to play. Her smile faded in seconds, killed by guilt for reminding the woman about her bound hands. She offered an apologetic smirk, not noticing Rachel's foot until it kicked water on her. They laughed and splashed until they were too tired to do anything but sit there enjoying the cold.

After an hour or so, Zhar waved her spear around to get their attention. "We must go on."

Zhar led them onward, following the water north until it trickled off to something the width of an arm and vanished into the dirt. Althea carried her clothes until the wind dried her body, then wriggled into them while walking. Hours later, they reached the site of the creek's demise: the center of several huge rocks worn in graceful sloping curves toward where once a full river had been.

Althea sat upon one such rock, dry and hot against her skin. She smiled at the breeze tossing her hair around, a great improvement over the stagnant factory she called home for the past two months. As her segments of captivity went, the last had been quite brief. She braced her right leg to her chest, planting her foot upon the slope, and squinted into the wind at the fading sun. She didn't want to get her hopes too high. One fighter could not keep two women, a girl, and a helpless soldier free for long.

Rachel looked exhausted. She had struggled with her archenemy to the point of bleeding again. Zhar paced about as if lost in thought, the padlock dangling from her collar clicking.

"We need to find clothes, weapons, and get rid of these." Zhar tapped the metal band.

"No shit." Rachel sighed. "Did you just figure that out?"

"There's an old town that way." Zhar pointed. "Might be some stuff there we can scavenge. I didn't want to go there at first in case of bandits... and it's off course."

"How far is it, and do they have bolt cutters or a hacksaw?" Rachel shifted, trying to get comfortable.

"The hell is a hacksaw?" Zhar glanced at her. "Maybe two days... One if Aya wasn't so lazy."

"I'm not lazy," the woman mewled. "I'm just not used to walking."

"She has been kept since she was small." Althea spoke in an ephemeral tone, like a detached observer. "She does not know how to fend for herself. She has always been owned."

"Like you?" Zhar quipped.

"No." Althea fiddled with the agate arrowhead. Aya surrendered to her captors in every possible way. As much as it hurt to admit, Althea *did* have the ability to free herself, but feared to use it. "I am stolen a lot, but I am not owned."

Zhar smiled at the spark of willfulness in the girl. "Good. Stay here, I will hunt."

"There." Althea pointed. "Bread root grows."

Zhar squinted in the direction she indicated. "What?"

With a sigh, Althea let her foot slip forward and stood. "I can see in the dark. I will find food-plant. No bang."

Althea clambered up the rock face on all fours to what had once been riverbank some dozen feet above the mucky bed. She ventured into the flat open ground toward an uneven section covered in scattered growth. Remembering months of memorization, she smiled fondly at thoughts of the closest thing she had ever known to a father. Reed's voice whispered the names of herbs in her memory's ear while she knelt and scratched at the ground.

When she returned with an armload of breadroot tubers, she found Ramani failing to weave a skirt out of too-short grass and Rachel seething as she repeatedly bashed her wrists into a rock trying to break her restraints. Althea slid down the gentle curve of the stone into the space around the pitiful stream. After handing food out to the others, she sat by Rachel and held one out to feed her.

Rachel stared at the plant in front of her lips, trembling with a curious mixture of anger, finality, and humiliation. Althea titled her head, sensing several emotions cycle in Rachel's energy as well as on her face. The woman narrowed her eyes, overtaken by a transcendent calm. Being 'fed' like a pet had tweaked the last nerve.

Her voice came as a shuddery near-whisper. "Kid, I've had enough of these fucking things. I am not walking another god damned hour like this. I'm not sleeping another god damned night like this."

Zhar threw a dubious stare at Althea. "Don't you dare magic me."

The shaking woman leaned forward, touching foreheads with Althea. "At the arena, you fixed that man's arm when the bones were cut clean through. I need you to do the same for me."

Althea trembled. "But, you are not hurt."

"You want someone to cut your hand off?" Zhar glanced at the spear, blinking in disbelief.

"No!" Althea wailed. "Please, Zhar, Please shoot the chain. Don't make me force—"

Everyone jumped at a sudden loud *crack*. Rachel's soft, brown face reddened. She screamed past clenched teeth, then shuddered in silence for a few seconds, her mouth open in a silent cry of agony. When her hands came free in front of her, it became evident she'd broken her thumb. A grin of endorphin elation alighted upon her face. She held her disfigured limb up and laughed at the dangling cuffs.

"Why didn't you do that yesterday?" Zhar muttered over a mouthful of root mash.

Althea shot a somber stare at Zhar. "Even you would cry at this hurt."

She set her hand on Rachel's, numbing the pain as soon as she could focus. Once sure Rachel could feel nothing, Althea yanked the thumb into place with a faint *crunch*. Aya and Ramani cringed away. A moment of focus forced the woman's bones to mend. With her arms free, Rachel squeezed Althea in a desperate embrace that tried to make up for weeks of wanting to hug the one person who kept her sane during the nightmare in which she found herself. Rachel cried first, but after a minute, it became unclear who consoled who. Althea didn't encounter loving contact often, and having someone hold her like that made the rest of her life feel all the more horrible.

"Lock the loose end on the same wrist so you don't get caught on something." Zhar muttered over a mouthful of tuber.

Rachel grabbed her other thumb and shuddered, tears running down her cheeks.

She drew in a breath. "Screw that... I want this fucker gone."

Althea grabbed her hand. "Let me stop pain first!"

The snap of the break startled everyone, despite them all expecting it. Rachel's face didn't distort in agony. She stared at her twisted appendage with curiosity while wriggling the restraint over her hand, then threw it as hard as she could off into the sands.

Once Althea mended her hand, Rachel's ration of tubers died a fast death. She reveled in the ability to feed herself after weeks of total dependence on others. The amount of relief and confidence radiating from her was a stark change from how she had been, as though she had turned into a different person inside. Rachel took the second spear as they huddled close for warmth again through the night.

Althea cuddled up beside her, happy to have someone who would protect her.

GENTLEMEN

Zhar nudged everyone awake a few minutes before the sun slid over the eastern horizon. Getting started before light afforded a little bit of protection in case any surviving raiders continued to look for them. Althea wasted no time mentioning they faced more threats than Vakkar's men. One by one, they got up, shivering, and prepared to set out into the frigid morning.

Rachel shook her head. "Four women traipsing around bare-assed with a kid... Wouldn't we get a bit of sympathy if we find some survivors?"

Zhar laughed. "You don't know this place. Don't even matter we're women. Anyone out here roaming around is gonna try to take anyone weak looking captive. The safe spots are inside towns like mine."

"If we don't fight, we will be okay." Aya smiled with unconvincing hope.

"Hey, you might feel cute with that metal thing around your neck, but no one, and I mean *fucking* no one, is gonna put a collar on me." Rachel's voice dripped with venom.

Ramani looked down, ashamed. Aya picked at her collar with a helpless look, having known no other life. Jealousy radiated from Zhar. Rachel had no unwanted metal locked anywhere on her body. She looked the least like a slave. Even without physically restraining them, the collars were a mark of station.

Althea put a hand on Rachel's arm. "People will see the slave-metal on their neck and treat them like runaways. All towns are not nice."

Zhar nodded, sounding humble for once and radiating the shame she had been hiding so long. "Yeah. A girl walks naked into most places, the people feel bad for you... give you some clothes and a hot meal. If you got one of these on, you might get sympathy, but you might also get pounced on. This tells people you're weak."

Rachel took a step and grasped Aya's collar, examining it. "This is just a cheap padlock. Fuck's sake, gimme the gun. Spear's heavier, but too unwieldy." She held a hand to Zhar, who took a step back.

"I ain't gonna *waste bullets*, bitch." Rachel made a 'give it here' gesture with her fingers.

"Trust her," Althea said.

Zhar handed it over, scowling.

Rachel guided the Japanese girl to a large rock, balancing her over it with the collar braced against the stone such that the padlock dangled. A couple whacks from the handle of the pistol scratched it, but had little other effect.

Rachel grumbled. "Shit. My arms are fucked from being cuffed so long... stasis didn't help much, either. These padlocks will pop open if you hit 'em just right."

Althea put a hand on Rachel's back and concentrated, reaching with her mind into the amorphous shapes of her life essence. She focused energy toward the parts that corresponded to the arms, sending a surge of blood and adrenaline.

Rachel lifted an eyebrow as her muscles undulated and grew in prominence.

Althea smiled. "Try now. Hurry, it will not last long."

One wallop popped the lock, astounding Rachel with her temporary strength. Ramani couldn't wait to dive over the stone, almost tackling Aya out of the way.

"I thought Aya was the only one here that eager to bend over." Zhar chuckled.

"Stop it." Althea glared. "Can't you be nice to one person?"

Zhar reluctantly followed suit. She gave Rachel a look as if she expected the pistol to fall on her head rather than the lock, but the strike came true and destroyed the collar. Aya rubbed her bare neck, staring with powerless fear. Something in the woman's eyes evoked pity from

Zhar, and she put an arm around Aya's back as the group got underway again. She told her about the city she came from and how she didn't have to be anyone's property again, provided they made it. The town had something called 'electricity,' and the safety of a mountain to hide under. Bewildered at first, Aya soon grew fond of the idea that she might not have to be anyone's property. By mid-day, she couldn't wait to have the protection of the 'big mountain.'

The sun wound its way across the sky over the course of many hours. Rachel swung the spear about as they traveled, acclimating to its weight and complete lack of balance. Zhar held up a hand to stop them when a structure came into view by a long strip of that same strange black stone path Althea remembered from the Lost Place.

She ran up ahead, squatted at the edge, and touched it. The strange stone almost burned her, but she smiled anyway. Waving her hand to cool it, she looked in both directions at the scintillating blur clinging to the surface. The others caught up, wary eyes upon the building across from where they had stopped.

"What's wrong?" Rachel crouched next to Althea.

"This black stone path, I saw it in the Lost Place... where my home is."

"Lost Place?" Ramani looked up. "What is that?"

Althea described it.

"Sounds like an abandoned city." Zhar smirked. "There are hundreds of them all over the Badlands."

Althea looked down with a face as if she had learned someone died. If many Lost Places existed, she may never find her way back to Den.

Rachel rubbed Althea's back. "This is called a road. There used to be many of them. It's what cars drive on."

This, of course, required a description of cars.

Althea blinked in awe. "They can move? I thought people used them for walls."

"Yeah." Rachel squinted down the length of the road. "Got a feeling there ain't many of 'em left that can move."

"Let's check the building." Zhar pointed.

Rachel pulled Althea to her feet, holding her hand in an effort to chase away the sadness settled into the child's face. "Looks like a burger joint, something along the highway. From the size of it, probably an interstate."

"Highway?" Althea looked up.

"The road." Rachel smiled.

"But it's not high. It's on the ground."

"Come on." Rachel shook her head.

The women sprinted over the boiling surface, pausing to let their feet cool in the shadow of a twenty-foot-tall male figure made of shattered plastic wrapped about a steel form. Dressed in white, the statue once held an arm aloft. Its eyes had broken out, but the exaggerated smile still gleamed in the sun. Fragments of the old sign had long ago been carried off by the wind and the frame played host to an army of weeds and ants. Idle hornets glided in and out through the cracks riddling the large chef's hat.

Most of the building's windows lacked glass, and bullet holes decorated the interior walls. Pictures of plated food hung over a countertop littered with junk and dishes.

Rachel moved up to the nearest windowsill, standing on the gravesite of an old hedge bush. "If they haven't disintegrated, we can make some clothes out of the seats. Since I'm carrying a god damned spear I might as well have a fuckin' loincloth to go with it. I doubt there's any food left."

She crept up to the door, stepping with care around a minefield of broken glass. Her muscles tensed as she drew a deep breath. Rachel poked the tip of the spear into the door and nudged it open with an unpleasant, disharmonic groan of metal on metal. After another hesitant pause, she stepped into a cool, dim space littered with trash. She bristled with shame, as though she strolled naked into a public place. Althea winced at the surge of depression radiating from her friend. The condition of the interior told her a long, long time had passed. Anyone she had known would surely be dead. Bits of debris on the ground rustled as she took another hesitant step in.

The trash shifted.

Rachel swiveled to point her spear toward the disturbance, but another pile moved behind her. Four three-foot-long roaches erupted from the garbage, hissing and rearing back. Rachel yelled a bad word and ran, bypassing the small stairway with a leap straight to the ground.

The bugs followed, two down the steps while the other pair clambered out the missing windows. Aya and Ramani scurried away, with only Aya having the discipline necessary to avoid screaming.

Zhar fired; the bullet struck the nearest one near the head end with a loud *click* and all the effect of a strong punch. Three of the roaches charged at Rachel while the shot one swayed in place, dazed.

Rachel backpedaled, shouting, "What the hell!? Giant fucking cockroaches! Really? Can this get any more messed up?"

Althea yelled. "Their shells are magic! Hit them in the belly or the mouth when they hiss. It's the only way to hurt them!"

"Hell with that, they don't run fast," Zhar yelled.

"Fuck, fuck, fuck." Rachel sprinted toward the others. The word bounced out of her each time her feet hit the dirt.

Althea stood her ground as the women ran past, raising her arms and projecting her power into the world. The glow in her eyes grew brighter. She spread her fingers and radiated primal fear. The bugs skidded to a halt a few feet away, all focused on her. Their shells split open revealing angry buzzing wings. The bugs shifted side to side, emitting a threatening drone. It didn't scare her. These bugs weighed too much to fly. Their wings could only make noise.

The buzzing threat display proved too much for Aya and she panicked. Althea intensified the radiance and took a step toward the roaches. Sensing her as a dire threat, they retreated into the old restaurant, snapping at the air and hissing. Althea glared at the dark doorway, lowering her arms.

Rachel trotted up to stand beside her, faintly out of breath.

"What the hell was that?" She pulled her around by the shoulder make eye contact.

Althea blinked innocently.

"The creatures know the Prophet." Ramani's awestruck voice almost had full tone.

"Yeah... Whatever. Guess we're not going back in there." Rachel growled in frustration. "Looks like I'ma spend a few more days wandering naked in the desert." She kicked a puff of sand into the air.

"You kin spend 'em naked in our trailer instead." A male voice with a melodic twang came from behind.

"Heh," said a second, older sounding man. "Heard the gunshot, figured we had some raiders ta kill. Looks like we's hit the tittie jackpot, Bobby!"

Ramani folded her arms over her chest. To Althea's surprise, Aya didn't show hers off, instead clutching Ramani's arm with a downcast stare laced with anger.

Two men had come out of nowhere, both in white and grey fatigues, with smallish, ancient black rifles aimed at the group.

"Never thought M4s would survive the end of the world," said Rachel. "I doubt they work."

"You wanna gamble on dat? Nice and easy now, bitch. Drop tha piece." The shorter one on the right wagged his gun at Zhar.

Aya collapsed to her knees, sobbing into her hands. Ramani joined her, falling with an arm across her former cellmate's back and weeping at such a short taste of freedom.

With a dull *plop*, the gun fell from Zhar's hand into the dirt. Two rifles didn't make for an even match against a single pistol.

"Good thing you saved that bullet," Rachel muttered.

Zhar glared.

"Wait." Althea stepped forward, opening her eyes so they could see the glow. "I will go with you if you let the women go free. I am the Prophet."

"Holy sheepshit, Billy. It is! Look at 'er eyes!" The shorter one on the left shook with excitement.

"Well I'll be damned." The older man's hoarse wheeze burbled into a coughing fit of laughter.

"Take me alone, and I will do whatever you want." Althea pitched her head down and approached the one with greying hair.

"Baby, no!" Rachel muttered. "Don't do this."

"Okay." The short man grinned and pulled a bundle of rope out of his backpack. Tossing it to Rachel, he pointed at the other three. "Tie 'em up, and do it good. I shoot 'em if it's too loose."

"But..." Althea balled her hands into fists.

"We gonna leave 'em here, just don't wanna be followed case they get any fancy idears 'bout followin' us."

Rachel stared at the idiot.

He kept his rifle trained on her, making a series of lustful faces. "'Course, that black girl's cuter'n all hell. I cain't hardly wait."

"On the ground. Face down, move it, bitches." The older one pointed with his gun.

The three women complied. Rachel tied them each in turn, Zhar glaring death at her while she bound the woman's hands behind her back.

"Legs too," said the younger man, holding his gun on her the whole time.

The emotions that surrounded the short man while he watched the women squirm forced Althea to look away, feeling sick. When the others were secure, he walked up behind Rachel and slung his rifle over his shoulder.

She struggled halfheartedly as he gathered her arms behind her and fumbled with the rope. "You can't just leave us here like this; the bugs will eat us. Leave a knife or something so we can get loose once you're outta here."

"Don't worry, princess. You will be safe wit us." His laughter came with a speckling rattle that coated Rachel's back with spittle and the smell of last night's whiskey. "Billy, go get the truck once I get this sweet piece of ass roped."

"You lied!" Althea wailed, staring up at the older man as she fought to get her arm free of his grasp.

"Jeezis Billy, ya dun' lied!" The short man faked astonishment. "What wrong wit you!"

The older man's voice came out in a slow drawl. "Spose'n I did then. Ah guess you'll have to complain to the law." He glanced left and right. "Whoops… ain't no law."

Both men laughed.

Althea scowled at the dirt around her toes. "You're bad."

"Kid, *make* them stop," Zhar hissed.

She stared at the ground, terrified of how people would treat her if they knew she could do such things. Her mind filled with nightmares of leashes and cages. It would be better to behave like a good little girl. If she looked up, she would see Rachel's face and feel like she betrayed her new friend. Tears rolled down her cheeks as she searched for the courage to use her power.

"*No!*" Althea looked at the man holding her arm. Fear reduced the command to one word.

Rachel growled, yanking her wrist out of the half-cinched loop of rope and jamming her elbow into the short man's gut. A cloud of saliva sprayed from his mouth as he gasped for air. Spinning, she drove the ridge of her hand into his throat before grabbing his arm and collar, then flipping him to the ground on his face. Bobby convulsed, clawing at his throat, gurgling for breath.

The older man's reaction slowed due to Althea's ambiguous command. When he shifted to fire, Althea dove over his rifle, adding her weight to the task of aiming. The old man growled, lifting her and the weapon into the air. She slowed him down enough. Rachel somersaulted over Bobby's rifle and came up on one knee in a combat posture. Two rapid shots echoed; blood spattered on Althea's back. The rifle fell from the weakened arm, and she landed on all fours atop it, shuddering at an icy scratch surrounding her heart.

Rachel fast-walked closer, firing another round into the older man's head. Althea crawled away, cowering. Two holes seeped blood from the center of his chest, and the top of his skull had blown out.

Zhar's angry roar became confused silence as her impersonation of a fish on dry land got her free much faster than she expected. Understanding Rachel tied her loose on purpose, she discarded her anger and sat up, kicking her ankles out of the rope. Althea dragged the rifle away from the older man, threw it off to the side, and moved to stand between the still-living man and Rachel with a hand held up to both sides.

"Please don't kill him. Nobody needs to die."

A squishy crunch drew attention to Zhar. She had kicked in the ribs of the small man—and enjoyed doing it.

"No!" Althea wailed through tears. "Please don't."

Rachel squeezed Althea's shoulder.

Zhar approached in a curving path that let her pause to grab the older man's rifle. "Look, kid. Maybe you are the Prophet, but you are as weak as Aya. She doesn't know which way to walk without a leash pulling her along. People will own you 'til you stand up for yourself, even if you don't believe you're owned." She aimed at the man on the ground, despite the child trying to get in the way.

"Wait." Rachel held up a hand. "Don't shoot him."

Zhar glared confusion at her. Althea smiled.

"Don't wanna waste bullets right? Use a knife." Rachel pulled Althea away, holding her tight so she didn't have to witness. "Oh, and get his pants off first so he doesn't shit them nasty."

Althea sobbed at the sounds of the struggle that ended with a crunch, a gurgle, and an icy tickle at the bottom of her heart.

"Easy, child." Rachel patted her on the back. "Some men just gotta die. Way it is. If good people don't fight the bad ones, we'll be overrun with evil. What do you think those two would have done to us? What do you think they'd have done to the next women they found if we let 'em live?"

Althea couldn't stop crying. She knew full well wifeing would have been the activity of the night, and many nights after, but killing them felt wrong. Clinging to Rachel's side, she stared at Zhar as the tall redhead stripped the corpses of their clothes and dragged the bodies away out of sight. She thought about Rachel's fear of being wifed, similar to her own. These two wouldn't have been pleasant captors. They might have even wifed her too, Prophet and all. She buried her face in Rachel's arms, too disgusted to pursue the line of thought to the sad conclusion it really was better these two men died.

"Hello?" Ramani lifted her head. "Will someone please untie me now?"

Rachel patted Althea on the back and kicked the small man in the head on her way to untie Ramani. "S'pose we should thank these kind gentlemen for bringing us weapons and clothes."

DESTINY AND REGRET

T he frayed maroon padding made for perhaps the most comfortable thing Althea had been permitted to sleep on in many years. Hidden from sight below a slab of plastic-coated wood jutting out from the wall, she curled on her side with her right arm folded under her head, staring at the points of blue light that came back at her from the table's tarnished chrome brace. A gurgle of hunger murmured inside her, the sensation of it fleeing from the gentle caress of her fingers over her gut.

"Picked clean" was how Rachel had described the place they found a few miles down the road from the roach-infested one, nothing here to eat. Tiny tables and bench seats packed wall to wall in the long, thin building. Small plastic cacti with cartoon eyes smiled at her from all over the walls. Some held food, like tacos, that she recognized. The pictures reminded her of what they ate at Den's village. She smiled, thinking of the first time she shared one with him and had spilled it all over herself.

Althea wanted to giggle and cry at the same time at remembering the hot food rolling down her chest into her lap, but she did neither. The women muttered at the end of the room, closer to the door. They had put her at the table Rachel considered the safest, nowhere near a window or a door where she could be stolen in the night. She sat up, shifting to peek over the bench. The dried out faux leather, warm against her belly, scratched as she rested her chin atop her folded arms on the seatback.

The lack of color in the room told her it had become dark. Twenty or so feet away, Zhar sat cross-legged on the ground in her new sleeveless shirt, grey-on-white camouflage pants and combat boots. She deferred one of the camo shirts to Ramani, who took it without caring about the blood. The garment fit the slender woman like a dress, covering her down to her knees.

Rachel had taken the full set, shirt, pants, and boots. She gave that man's 'skivvies,' as she called them, to Aya, a black tank top and boxer briefs, which they had to practically force onto her. The woman felt she would be treated better if she 'behaved,' and by that, she meant staying nude. Aya blushed at wearing clothing the way Ramani did at having none. She had gone well out of her element, no longer anyone's property, and desperately tried to attach herself to Zhar. The redhead wanted none of it, no dead weight, and insisted Aya learn to pull her share.

Covered in camo, authority wafted from Rachel. She had collected all of the men's possessions and sorted them for anything useful. Althea suppressed a giggle while listening to her complain about the horrible condition of the rifles. One look at the weapons and the woman had demanded to know what year it was, but none of them knew.

Althea sank out of sight before her glowing eyes attracted notice. She buried her face between her knees and hugged her legs. A cool breeze filtered in past the shards of a distant broken window, threading about her limbs and chasing away the torpid air of the room. She should be asleep, but her mind refused to stop thinking about how much she missed Den. Rachel had shown a side that frightened her as well. For a fleeting moment, it seemed Rachel valued life, but she had no trouble killing—just like everyone else out here. Tears worked their way over her cheek and down her shins as she thought about Zhar's words. Would people always own her? Did doing bad things to bad people to protect others make one bad?

Vakkar's face hovered in the murk of her thoughts. She pondered how she had manipulated him to spare Rachel the pain of being wifed. Could she have done the same thing back in the seed room to make those raiders leave? If she had, she would still be with Den now. She could've stopped them. She *let* them take her. Feeling as stupid and weak as Zhar accused her of being, she cried harder.

So that's what 'pathetic' meant.

After a moment, she sniffled back her tears. If she had done that, these women would still be Vakkar's property, and he would've wifed Rachel.

Good had come of her losing Den. Could she really call it pathetic to tolerate his loss for their benefit?

"I know where we are now. We can get back to my settlement if we follow path forty to the setting sun and turn north on path eighty-four to twenty-five," said Zhar. "Once we get the kid there, we'll be set. No raider can get in."

"She has a home," said Rachel in a whisper undoubtedly intended to let Althea sleep. "And a crush on a boy."

Aya and Ramani made the kind of noises some women do at seeing bonedog puppies. Caught little enough, they could be raised as pets.

Zhar rolled her eyes, not that anyone but Althea could see. "She's not even twelve yet, blonde, and pretty. She'll have a different boy next week."

Althea let go of her legs and dug her fingers into the cushion, fighting the urge to yell. Squinting with anger, she lay down and crawled to the edge of the seat to listen.

They prattled for a while about their first boyfriends, save Aya who bathed in awkward silence. Rachel's tales of her life sounded far beyond anything Althea could envision. High school, dating, dances, something called a prom, none of which made any sense at all. Boredom threatened to carry her back to sleep.

"You will treat her like a person?" Ramani's timid whisper broke a pause in their levity. "I do not think it right to make a slave of the Prophet after she has helped us escape being slaves."

"No. She will be treated well. She is a child still, we must keep her safe in the mine."

"Mine?" Rachel asked.

"Yes," said Zhar. "My home is built in the depths of an old mine. We have a big metal wall in front of the tunnel. No raiders can get us. We will take the Prophet back and Finlay will eat his words."

Althea scowled. Of course, Zhar wanted to bring the Prophet back to her chief. Once more, she had become someone's prize to trade for glory. Even if this place would treat her well, she would be hidden away underground while so many other people needed help.

"We should ask her," Rachel said, scraping at the guts of the rifle in a feeble patch of moonlight. "For fuck's sake, when was the last time this thing got cleaned? Sergeant Michaels would have PT'd the shit out of this guy."

"A mother does not ask child's opinion on bedtime." Zhar gestured at the ceiling. "She is too young to make those decisions. I will do what is best for her."

"You want a captive princess," Ramani muttered. "Treat her like royal, but she cannot leave."

Zhar's whisper picked up a command tone. "So? It's the same anywhere for her. Better captive and princess than captive and caged. And she's a child. We're not leaving her alone out here."

"I... Yes." Ramani gave up.

Rachel sounded hesitant. "What if she doesn't want to go? It seems she has a home already."

"What good does it do her to return to such a weak place? Raiders took her once. They will take her again. She follows us there. If she asks, we say we can help her find her little boyfriend, but she will soon feel she is home. When the Prophet is at Shy Ann, we will be powerful."

"Shy Ann? Who the hell is that?" Rachel paused, a look of horror in her eyes. "Wait, do you mean Cheyenne? What does your mine look like?"

"It is a big hole in the mountain with a city inside."

Althea pictured Zhar holding her arms way out.

Rachel gave off a pulse of sorrow. "Fuck... Dammit."

"What is wrong?" Aya broke her silence.

"Cheyenne Mountain used to be a military installation, but if it has become a survivor town..." She fell quiet for a moment, before finding renewed determination. "No, I don't believe it. There's gotta be something left of civilization. The whole world can't be lost to this madness."

Althea scooted back on the seat at the scrape of a chair on the floor. She folded her hands under her cheek and pretended to be asleep as the scuffing of boots draw closer. Zhar's emotional radiance drew near. A hand pressed into her shoulder, groping about in the pitch dark to make sure she remained there.

"Sleep well, kiddo." Zhar's warm whisper fell across her face. She patted her head. "In a few days, you'll be safe."

She remained quiet. Dread of being taken again, even by these women, held sleep off with ease. Zhar had said people would own her until she stood up for herself. Tonight she would take a stand and seek her own destiny. As the boots scuffed away, she opened her eyes and listened.

When at last the sound of their conversations drifted off into the blur of approaching sleep and gave way to silence, she peered over the seat. Aya and Ramani lay against each other in a booth while Zhar draped herself over a pile of seat cushions gathered on the floor near the entrance. Rachel slept under a table against the wall, surrounded by an arc of empty glass bottles.

Althea slid off the seat and crept to the door, careful not to brush against anything that would make noise. She paused by Rachel, squatting to stare at the face of the woman she had almost come to trust. Crying happened, but silent. Had Rachel not gone along with killing that man, this would have been much harder to do. She swiveled to stare at the smug curl on Zhar's lips. Her mind filled with the sight of the daytime sky swallowed by the impenetrable dark of a mountain tunnel, never to be seen again. The image of Zhar presenting her to a faceless chief in the mine-village consumed her thoughts before an imagined cage door slammed in her face.

I'm tired of being kidnapped.

She crept around Zhar, bare feet silent on the tile floor, and made her way out via a broken window to the paving.

Night left the once-scalding stone path icy beneath her feet. Tattered bits of leather strands whipped about her legs as she ran along the strange surface. This road, as Rachel had called it, didn't yield under her steps, but left no footprints anyone could follow. She figured either Zhar or Rachel would come looking for her, one for greed and one for concern. Her pace slowed to a backward walk. She stared at the building. Streaks of violet moonlight gleamed in color where the silver trim remained intact, stark against the muted greys of her nighttime world. She stopped with her feet together, arms folded across her chest, and shivered in the breeze, having second thoughts about her destiny.

She mostly hesitated because of Rachel, thinking back to splashing and playing with her in the river, guilty for leaving without saying goodbye. With the woman free of those handcuffs, Althea had gone from caretaker to child, a bizarre sensation but one she had longed for. If she stayed, Zhar would take her like the raiders had. Rachel would probably go with Zhar to the underground city. Althea looked down at her toes, lifting and dropping them in cascades as she weighed whether to run away or go back.

Her presence among the women started a rift between Zhar and Rachel, which would likely grow wider the closer they came to that Cheyenne place, perhaps even spilling to violence. Rachel didn't like the idea of forcing Althea away from her home, but had come short of challenging Zhar. This world must be like a nightmare for her, going to sleep in the before-time and waking up after everything had come to an end. Althea tolerated captivity as long as she could help people. The idea of hiding away under a mountain for the rest of her life while everyone out here suffered filled her with guilt. Perhaps if she left, the two women could get along. She hoped Rachel would be happy. Like the slaves fleeing Vakkar's camp, her being with them would only bring tragedy to innocent people.

Althea forced herself to look away from the building, mouthed a silent apology to her almost-friend, and walked once more up to a run.

15

CONTAMINATION

Distant canine howls carried in the wind. Head-sized scrub brush dotted the shifting gradient of grey sand. Althea dared not look back again in case someone spotted the glow—or guilt made her stop. Eventually, her gait slowed as fatigue and lack of food combined to an overall discomfort. With the sound of the wind and her heartbeat in her head, the fear came. For the first time, she found herself alone in the world with no one to control her. That also meant no one to protect her.

She meandered for a while thinking about life on her own. Traveling the Badlands, she could help whoever needed it and keep the bad people in check with her other abilities. If it was true some people deserved to die, the lesser axiom of some people deserved to be compelled to go away also seemed like it would be true. Confidence gradually brought her stride back up to speed.

Althea walked for some time, pondering this unexpected turn in her life. Her fantasy popped at the unexpected sight of a forest emerging from the dry ground up ahead, quite out of place for this part of the Badlands. She had never seen trees like this before so straight and symmetrical. The ones by Den's village were irregular and wide with broad leaves that shifted color with the seasons. These stood far taller, straight and thick. Instead of leaves, they bristled with green needles. If nothing else, tree cover could shield her from the cold desert night wind, as well as creatures. Out of breath, she loped off the road across a patch of dirt toward the strange wood.

An odd presence hung over this place, but nothing looked dangerous. When she approached within ten feet of the closest tree, a tingle brushed her face. It started at her nose, matched by a similar feeling in her leading foot. She froze at a phantasmal caress upon her cheeks like she had walked into a cobweb. While she hesitated in place, her hair rose of its own accord, spreading out and up.

The thinner strands of her skirt followed suit, lifting and separating from each other as if the leather repelled itself. She reached out both hands, finding coolness in the air, defined and precise like a wall of a different temperature. At one point cool and dry, and two inches later, cold and not so dry. She looked to either side, at bizarre metal trees, devoid of leaves, standing in line with the climate separation. Bulbous parts along the poles' length glowed in thin slats; she assumed the unexplained objects had something to do with her levitating hair.

She took a step forward and her hair and skirt fell back into place, free of whatever energy field had charged them. On the other side of the fence, her toes sank into moist, dark soil instead of dry sand. The aroma of the forest held her awe for a moment until her fatigue overcame her. Althea sat at the base of a tree and curled against it, trying to think about anything but Rachel.

HOURS LATER, SHE AWOKE, HUDDLED AGAINST THE TREE WHERE SHE HAD taken a nap. The sun had come up, shining amid the shifting pines above her. She squinted at the light, smiling at the wind on her face and the beautiful caress of freedom upon her cheek. Hunger clawed its way into her consciousness. She stretched and went off in search of food.

Althea avoided mushrooms. She knew some of the ones that would kill her looked like ones she could eat. Unable to remember how to tell the good ones, she ignored all the mushrooms and foraged around for some time with little success. This place felt unnatural. Despite the pleasant ambiance, the more she looked around, the more she sensed a certain wrongness to the area. Other mystics existed among the Scrags. Some might have magic she did not know. Maybe this forest was the domain of one such mystic and he had made this place. If she could find his home, he might help her get back to Den.

Deeper into the forest she walked, feeling tiny and alone among the towering trees. The whisper of the wind became a pleasant companion as she lost herself in the new experience of being in control of her own life. Althea giggled and grinned as she stepped across rocks in a bubbling brook.

The meandering walk ended some time later. Discomfort at being alone spread like a cancer in her thoughts, soon eclipsing everything else she tried to think about. Althea loved being around people, and the hollow feeling borne from being alone grew as intolerable as a little cage in a snake oil salesman's wagon. Confinement in a metal box too small to allow her to stand bothered her less than total isolation from other people.

She pined for Rachel and sank into a squat, picking at the dirt in front of her feet, feeling quite silly for running off in the middle of the night. Pouting at the soil, she dwelled on the guilt of what it must have done to her friend to wake up and find her missing. The longer she thought on it, the more she felt like going back to them.

The scent of something edible drifted along the wind for the scarcest of moments, drawing her attention like a starving coyote. Althea leapt up and ran into the wind, leaping across a fallen log before splashing into a knee-high creek, sniffing for any sign of the fragrance.

She climbed up on a small boulder, standing on her toes while waving her face back and forth with her nose in the air, desperate to extract any trace of the aroma. Another whiff floated past. She ran again, moving in a series of jumps and dashes among the underbrush, leaping fallen logs. Soon, she darted around great, smooth square stones as tall as her shoulders. Curious at their unusual flatness, she touched one and found it to be metal. The sight of many of the strange boulders, gleaming white against the dark greens of the forest, brought her speed down to a timid walk. The smell changed; no longer reminiscent of something edible, it wrapped its tendrils around her throat and choked the air out of her lungs.

Dead things.

With an arm over her mouth, she crept closer, eyeing the giant cubes. She had seen similar objects before, certain a raider had referred to them as 'cargo boxes,' but these didn't look the same. They had no lids or handles, only a small grid of glowing crystals with funny marks on them.

Upon reaching the top of a shallow hill, she looked down the length of a path ripped into the vegetation at a silver vehicle with six fat, almost spherical, tires clawing feebly at the air. It had rolled on its back like some giant dead bug. Two men lay motionless on the ground, wearing unfamiliar clothing saturated with blood and bullet holes.

Althea ran to them without hesitation, sprawling on her knees by each man in turn and checking to see if she could do anything for them. Both had been dead more than a few days and had enough bullets in them to kill an entire raider encampment. She scrunched up her nose, confused why anyone would shoot one man hundreds of times.

The back end of the strange vehicle hung open. More strange boxes sat inside it. A few had burst, and among the many items she didn't recognize, she found one that looked familiar. It resembled the strange food bar the raider had given her, only a little wider and longer. The material wrapping it had a picture of a smiling little boy next to something that looked like a turd.

Althea stared at the thing in her hand, confused by who would wrap such things in plastic. Curiosity got the better of her and she peeled it open. The sweet scent of chocolate greeted her, a fragrance that awakened a long dormant memory of a man and a woman giving her a treat. Gripping it with both hands, she plunged the bar into her mouth and savaged it. With eager whimpers, she rooted around in the debris hunting for more. Finding another, she took her time with the second one, savoring the taste as she sat against the metal insect.

Once she'd licked the last bits of chocolate from her fingers, wiped her face, and licked her fingers again, she crawled into the hollow creature and searched for more food. Gathering what seemed usable, she made a pile to take with her and hunted for a satchel or bag to put it all in. Somewhere between the first and second candy bar, she had made up her mind she would return to Rachel as soon as she discovered a way to find her.

The dead men had strange things on them. Althea rummaged their pockets, momentarily entranced by her reflection upon a slab of black glass with rounded corners. As she turned it over, it beeped. She jumped, dropping it and scampering away. A panel of light flickered into being in midair above it bearing glowing symbols. Half a minute later, it winked out and went dark.

Unsettled, she made a face at the area around the two dead men and backed off.

"Sorry."

Whatever she had eaten had left her thirsty. She scavenged an empty plastic bottle from inside the big vehicle and jogged toward the burble of a creek. Althea navigated slick rocks to avoid shin-deep mud near the water's edge. Cold, slimy green moss squished between her toes. She perched on a boulder a few feet into the water and squatted, holding the container beneath the surface to fill it, then brought it to her mouth with both hands, drinking and wearing equal parts. Most bad things in the water she could rid herself of with little effort. This stream was cold, and in comparison to what she usually drank, clean.

Her third mouthful startled into a spray at a sudden mechanical whine punctuated by staccato clicking behind her. She twisted to the left; a glint of daylight drew her gaze to a man's torso stuck in the rocks downstream, covered in metal. In place of arms, two spinning bundles of rods pointed at her. Its face looked inhuman, also made of metal with eyes that glowed like hers, only amber.

"What are you doing?" She gasped.

"Attempting to terminate your life process," it said, with an emotionless, synthesized voice.

Althea guessed the spinning arms might be guns, and it had run out of bullets. She gulped at the realization it tried to shoot her. "Why!"

"You are human... contaminant."

"Are you hurt?" She edged away from the slick rocks, putting a tree between her body and the strange little man. "I can heal you."

"Hurt implies pain. CRP-W9 series cannot experience pain."

A single large wheel where it should have had legs squeaked over the wet rocks, throwing a sluice of mud into the air behind it. It had gotten itself wedged quite thoroughly.

"'Healing' implies bio fault. CRP-W9 series is not biological and cannot be 'healed.'"

She huddled behind the tree. "Are you going to shoot me?"

Its voice modulated tone from word to word with inhuman random inflections. "Autocannon one, ammunition depleted. Autocannon two, ammunition ten percent. System failure, environment has caused an electrical short. Autocannon two firing circuit is offline. Please transfer autocannon two ammunition to autocannon one so that I may proceed with contaminant removal."

She noticed the gun closer to the water didn't spin as fast as the other, though both still pointed at her. "You want me to help you so you can shoot me?"

"That is correct."

With a confused face, she ventured a peek. "Why? I am the Prophet."

"Prophet not found. You are biological contaminant. CRP directive implies removal of biological contaminants from central North America. Please move to within twenty-four inches of main unit."

She stepped out from behind the tree, still clinging to it. "You want me to get closer? Why?"

"Please move within twenty-four inches of main unit. Auxiliary contaminant removal system has a maximum effective range of twenty-nine inches."

She took a cautious step closer. "What is a auximarry taminant system?"

Althea jumped back when a twenty-nine inch blade sprang out of its chest. The sword waved back and forth as the machine-man twisted himself side to side. "Detachment of biological unit component 'head' will result in effective contaminant removal."

"You're awful!" She retreated to the tree. "Why do you want to kill me?"

"CRP Directive One stipulates all biological contamination be removed. You are biological, therefore you are a contaminant."

"I'm not a taminant." She frowned. "What is CRP?"

The machine twitched and whirred as the head spun around. "Cybernetic Reclamation Project. Original mission to purge the region known as"—the voice cut out, replaced for two words by a recording of a real man—"The Badlands." It rocked back and forth. "...of combat mutants and experimental genetic weapons implemented during the war. Project directive changed, override authorized by CRP command unit Sigma-Six.

"*Status*: Region contaminated by mutants.

Directive: Contamination removal.

Antecedent: Humans created mutant contamination.

Extrapolation: Humans will create more mutant contamination.

Conclusion: Humans are contamination."

Althea blinked, having no clue what it meant.

She pointed at the wreck site. "Did you kill those men?"

"Successful contaminant removal occurred thirty-two hours, eighteen minutes, and forty-one seconds ago. Purged contaminants are responsible for current levels of system damage." The strange thing's head swiveled at her. "Query."

"Query?" She peered around the tree, torn between curiosity and fear.

"Define nature of contaminant bioluminescence."

She stared at it. "Umm... What?"

"Current target exhibits undocumented manner of bioluminescence. *Species*: Human should not exhibit scleral bioluminescence. Please define reason."

"I don't know what you are saying."

"Target scan indicates no installed cybernetics but target emits light." It blinked at her.

"Oh. My eyes." She touched a finger to her cheek. "They've always glowed. I don't know why."

"Please move within twenty-four inches. Target contaminant scans as female, potential source of new contaminants. Extra points... must be removed."

"Umm. No. I don't want to be removed." She backed away as it twitched and struggled to free itself from the mud.

This small creature had no emotions and no thoughts. It wanted to kill her and was made of metal. If it got loose from the rocks, she would be in big trouble. Useless guns aside, it had a big knife, and a wheel, which meant it had to be as fast as a raider's buggy. The more it talked, the more frightened she became of it.

"Secondary target acquired. Subject CN43, canid series augmented biological combat organism. *Danger level*: elevated. Priority threat updated, secondary target is now primary target. *Attention*: female contaminant, please assist CRP-W9 to regain mobility. I will not kill you until the CN43 has been destroyed."

The machine-man shifted, aiming past her at something in the weeds. Turning toward where it looked, Althea caught a glimmer reflected in the shadows from two large ruby eyes embedded in a mass of fur. An immense hairy beast stared at her. A canine snout stretched forward from a head with human-like features, as if a dog and a human had produced a son. Drool oozed between its teeth as it sniffed the air.

Patches of metal stuck out from its fur here and there, rimmed by scab and decay, grafted into its body in ways that looked painful. Hoses descended from the back of its head into its forearms and metal blades enhanced its claws. Althea's throat tightened. She gazed into the eyes of one of those things lacking the reason to recognize her as the Prophet, one of the horrors she imagined waited for her outside. Creatures like this had been her excuse to accept captivity. It looked hungry.

"Until after?" Althea glanced sideways at the machine man. "That means you will still kill me."

The head rotated to face her and blinked. "Correct. Statistical probability ninety-nine percent your life will be terminated by CN43. Assisting CRP-W9 will not change your inevitable demise. Unlike the CN43, CRP-W9 will not eat you."

Althea took a step back, risking eye contact with the furry monstrosity. He radiated hunger and curiosity. The mutant couldn't understand her words, so she couldn't force it to obey commands. Tweaking its emotional state would be her only chance. Fortunately, her ability to control emotions vastly outstripped her much weaker power of direct commands. She had used it near constantly for years to protect herself from raiders' cruelty.

As she had with the roaches, she held her arms out and locked eyes with it. Fear came easy as she had quite a bit of it at the moment. Waves of terror flooded out of her and washed over the dog-man, causing the fur on its hackles to rise and an ominous growl to reverberate out of its throat.

Althea's backpedal became a full on run when she sensed its fear trigger a waterfall of pure rage. Most animals out here ran away when frightened. Like the millipedes, this thing wanted to destroy whatever scared it. She could hide in the giant dead bug-vehicle if she could make it. She clung to a tree to avoid falling as she scampered around it, then sprinted toward the dirt hill, grabbing at roots to pull herself up. The mutant came crashing after her, leaping and sinking its claws into a seconds-old footprint. Screaming at the top of her lungs for Rachel, she stumbled upright after cresting the bank and dashed with all she had, commanding the muscles in her legs beyond their limits. Her slender body lurched forward in a fawn's springing run.

She had chosen the wrong way; the metal carapace thing was nowhere in sight. Without time to think, she kept going toward a low spot where the creek had eroded into the ground. Splintering crunches and throaty growls from behind kept her moving. The beast came close enough to smell. Her foot plunged straight into the ground as the ridge gave out from under her. Pleas for Rachel became incoherent screams of pure terror. She spilled over the side of the crumbling earth, falling to the ground a few feet below. The unexpected drop spared her the touch of metal claws as the beast raked the air inches behind her back. Her arms and legs flailed about as she rolled down a root-studded incline, to a halt at the bottom with her face in an inch of icy water.

Althea groaned and gasped for air, in pain as though she had been punched in her everything.

The dog enjoyed a less gentle landing, headfirst into the earthen wall on the other side of the creek. She lifted herself out of the muck and looked in the direction the stream came from. Thirty yards ahead, a corrugated metal pipe offered sanctuary. Althea gathered her legs under her and ran. The slap of her feet in the wet brought the dog out of its daze. It snorted, shook its head, and came barreling after her on all fours. She dove into the pipe with her hands over her head and landed in a slide across inches-deep water. A heavy *slam* behind her preceded the groan of shredding metal. Scrambling for traction, she rolled on her back and shimmied away from the opening, staring between her knees at groping claws that missed her by inches.

Growling and gnashing, the beast lurched shoulder-deep in the tube flailing at her, giving off equal parts hunger and anger. Grateful the conduit didn't have enough room for her to sit up, she slid backward a little further and fell flat when she felt the distance safe. Exhaling, she enjoyed the cool water wrapping over the top of her head, around her shoulders, and down her back. With her hands on her chest, she lay still until the current carried her fatigue away.

When she no longer gasped for air, she lifted her head. The creature had given up on her and left. The circular aperture of light that hovered above her toes beckoned with the wonderful outdoors, but she suspected the monster would be waiting for her.

She rolled onto her stomach and crawled deeper into the tunnel. It soon opened into a flooded, square concrete chamber. Althea slid headfirst into the brackish pool, reaching for the bottom, and found solid, algae-covered floor when the water came up to her armpits. Confident she wouldn't drown, she swam for a little while to rinse herself of mud. When she put her legs down, she stood about knee deep.

Smears of green moss and rust covered the walls of a shaft extending at least thirty feet up to a grating. Above it, trees wavered in the breeze. Water leaked from a dozen smaller openings dotting the walls. Drips echoed, and the dank presence of this place made her shiver.

A metal ladder on the wall opposite the pipe led to a ledge much closer than the roof. She climbed up enough to peek over the top, careful of what might lurk there. Someone had collected an impressive amount of junk in a modest sized area, arranging it like a room. A steel framed cot stood against the left wall across from a table and a few metal folding chairs. Crates and boxes of all sizes were stacked against the opposite wall and a hanging partition of plastic sheeting attempted to close it off from a maze of large concrete tubes.

The dog had chased her away from her collected pile of provisions, so once more she had nothing. With the hope of human contact, this space provided a welcome alternative to becoming the creature's meal. If nothing else, it offered a dry spot to rest, so she climbed off the ladder and stood shivering and dripping while examining the room.

She figured whoever lived here probably went out to hunt during the day. Assuming, of course, they hadn't died. She meandered about, poking among the various collected objects and trying to gauge from their condition the chances of either being true. The overall grunge gave her no indication, but she did find a discarded set of leather armor. Something had lit into it pretty bad, shredding a hole in the breastplate she could fit her face into. After dragging it with her to the cot, she sat and picked at it. Weaving what she could from it into her skirt, she bolstered some sparse points and retied some of the loosening knots.

The process ate more than an hour, and still no sign of anyone showed up. From the color of the light in the water shaft, she knew the sun would be down soon. Too afraid to risk going outside, she pulled her feet up on the bed and reclined. Worn out from her first day of independence, she succumbed to the soft padding beneath her.

16

ATTACHMENTS

Den's laughter echoed in the foggy haze of a dream. Her arms stretched out and crossed in front of her, holding his hands as they spun around in the field. Blurry trees streaked past his smiling face. They whirled until her grip broke, leaving them both on their backsides, laughing. The dream didn't last long, but she woke up happy. Morning grogginess left her with the need for a good stretch. An unusual metallic clatter accompanied her motion. Her heart almost stopped when her right arm jerked to a halt with the bite of cold metal around her wrist.

Sitting up with a gasp, she found the same kind of thing that had kept Rachel's hands behind her for so long locked about her arm. Blotched with rust like the cot, it looked old. Other dark stains on it resembled dried blood, but smelled sweet. The other end rattled around the flaking grey paint of the bed frame. As soon as her panic faded enough to allow it, Althea scooted up on her knees and twisted her arm around in an attempt to pull her hand out.

She figured someone had found her while she slept and wanted to keep her. She fought and pulled until she worked up a sweat, as well as a red mark. Giving up on escape, she stared at her lap wanting to cry. It all started again, an endless cycle. A pathetic glance cast through wild hair at the rest of the room revealed whoever abducted her had left her alone with the chain.

Rachel had referred to them as handcuffs. She'd explained how, in her world, someone called police put them on bad people called criminals. Althea countered with her experience. Raiders used them to contain slaves, a concept that sent Rachel into a frightening spiral of anger. Even the word 'slave' had set the woman off on a tirade that made Althea want to hide.

She grasped the metal band and leaned away, straining with her entire weight, shaking the bed while kicking her heel at the head rail repeatedly. Althea refused to accept her fate. She didn't want to be kidnapped again. After several minutes of futile pulling, she sagged limp and looked around.

A small table a distance away held trash and paper cups, but no sign of a key. Twisting and pulling, she couldn't squirm her hand free from the ring, despite her wrist being much smaller than Rachel's. Not even with both feet pushing on the cuff and her sense of pain turned off could she get rid of it. After mending the cut and redness, she tried attacking the other end, locked around the frame. She rattled the cuff side to side, hammering it against the small vertical bars, but it only had a four-inch space in which it could slide.

Hopelessness reared up. She collapsed onto the cot and cried. Overwhelmed with a sense of foolishness for running away, she longed to have Rachel here to protect her from whoever did this to her. Why did she do something so stupid? She heard the plan. She could have forced Zhar not to keep her. She could have stayed with her friend. Some lessons were harder to accept than others, and this one made her bawl.

Building panic and desperation came to a stall at scuffing and whistling echoing in the cavernous distance. Althea froze, her crying stopped as if a switch had been thrown. She barely breathed as footsteps grew closer. By the time a blurry outline of a person approached the mass of plastic sheets hung over the exit, she trembled.

A battered blue plastic plate parted the barrier, behind which a man walked in. "Well, yer 'wake now."

Like most people in the Badlands, he had medium brown skin and a rugged—if frazzled—appearance. A dingy red ball cap perched atop thick, bushy black hair tinged silver. His dark shirt poked out from between the flaps of a long, army-green raincoat. The shape of his legs vanished in a billowy pair of green camouflage pants. Greedy eyes stared unblinking at her as he ambled closer and set the offering on the cot by her legs. Two small animals, rats or squirrels perhaps, cleaned, skinned, and grilled.

"Yer damn lucky yer a girl. Someone steals me bed, Ah jes' as soon shoot 'em."

Althea didn't like the way he looked at her, his gaze lingered upon slivers of bare thigh peeking out between the tatters of her skirt. The fragrance of the cooked meat created a strong distraction from the man, and she reached under her trapped arm with her free left hand to grab one. It was hot, less than a minute off the fire, but she didn't care. Not taking her gaze off him, she ate as fast as temperature allowed.

"Damn Scrags. Ah probley should kill ya. I know how yas are. Sendin' the little'uns in places 'dults can't go. Lookin fer stuff ta steal. Yer gonna go back and tell 'em all about my fortoon." He waved at the stack of crates.

Althea gnawed for a moment, swallowed, and drew a quick breath. "I don't want to steal from you. I'm hiding from a dog man." She explained the chase. "Please let me go, I promise I won't steal anything."

"Yer people not 'elp ya?"

He dropped into a dirty folding chair, strips of orange material suspended in a metal frame. His weight spread the legs apart and he raised a cup made from an old coffee can to his lips.

"Guess'n they lef' yas behind, ah couldn' find any o' 'em."

"I am not a Scrag. I'm alone." She pulled a large chunk of meat away from the dead animal with her teeth.

"Lotta 'dem critters here. Good eats. Hmm... alone." He rubbed his chin.

She finished off the rest of what he brought, neither of them speaking until two squirrel skeletons lay scattered on the plate.

"Please take this off. I promise I won't steal from you." She shook her hand to make the chain rattle.

"Cain't." He drew a sip of some foul-smelling alcohol and twitched it down.

With an innocent face, she whined. "Please, I'm not a threat."

"Ah cut them things few months back offa some dead slave. Never found no key." His breath skittered away in a dry chuckle. "Was some good meat, that. Might still be some grillin' sauce on 'em."

Althea stared at the not-bloodstain touching her wrist.

When the wave of disgust passed, she glanced back and forth from him to the rusty handcuffs in disbelief. "You put these on me and have no key? How will you let me out? Are you a stupid?"

"Well, if'n you wasn't a kid, you'd be on me grill now." He convulsed after another swig. "Ain't much care fer veal."

"Nibbler?" She slid as far away from him as her arm would allow. Cannibals didn't care about Prophets.

The handcuffs had been on someone he cooked, while he cooked them. She wanted to touch them even less.

"Naw. Them Nibblers is shit nuts. Ah ain't crazy, I'm just practical. Meat is meat. Ah beleeb yas 'bout the dog and not stealin', tho. Since you not stealin', I ain't gonna eat ya. Now, seein' as how you's so pretty and all, Ah figure ain't no big deal not havin' no key. No reason fer ya ta go any'war. You kin be mah wife."

The squirrel almost came back out. "I'm..." She gulped it back down. "A child. Y... You can't w... wife me. I'm tw—only ten."

He looked her up and down. "Yer big 'nuff. Tho mebbe I wait fer yer titties to come out. Mebbe."

Most of what he said fell into an unintelligible burble in her mind as she thrashed her wrist bloody trying to escape. He radiated the same emotion looking at her as what Vakkar did when he tried to drag Rachel out of the cell. Worse, it grew stronger as he watched her struggling to free herself. No one had ever felt *that* way while looking at her before—at least, not that she noticed. Wifeing didn't work that way. She wasn't old enough yet. She sniveled and kicked at the cot, trying to back away from him. The pain of the metal biting her skin snapped her out of the panic. Why did she sneak away from Rachel in the night? Why did she do something so damned stupid?

Freedom was okay, but she refused to let anyone do *that* to her. She'd heard the way some of the women screamed. Wifeing had to hurt a great deal. If she had to remain the pet of a raider camp to avoid being wifed, so be it. She understood how Rachel felt. Althea would rather die.

"No. I will not be your wife." She shivered, staring at him, leaning as far away as the chain allowed. "Sell me to the raiders. I'm the Prophet. See my eyes? They will give you riches for me."

"Purdy lights." He grinned toothlessly.

Althea hung her head. In a few seconds, a tickling droplet of blood had made it halfway down her forearm. This man had no idea who she was. Running into a person who didn't know about her seemed unthinkable, yet this fool showed no reaction at all to the title she so hated. Somehow, she found room between fear and revulsion to be astounded at this fool's idiocy.

He commanded no army of bandits. Also, with no one else here, he couldn't threaten someone to force her to obey out of guilt. She had no reason to continue being so... *pathetic*. Zhar's voice spoke the word in her memory. Fear gave way to shame, and then to determination. She forced the cut on her wrist to close before snapping her head up to stare at him.

"*Let me out*." The glow from her eyes flickered with each word in her command.

The hermit shuddered in the seat, emitting a whispery wheeze from deep inside his chest. Moonshine burbled from his half-closed mouth, dribbling down his chest. "No... key... cain't." His face and fingers twisted as he recoiled, his body reacting to an impossible compulsion.

Althea stood on the cot, held in a stoop by her shackled hand. Rising over him, she tapped her anger at what this man wanted to do to her. Blue light flared. She growled, burning fear into his mind and a malodorous emanation into his pants. His stare widened. His mouth hung agape, and he clutched at the cheap plastic armrests of the trembling chair, scratching it deeper into the concrete. He would never look at her without being afraid again. His lecherous stare would never trace the curve of her leg again.

This man would not wife her.

He fainted the instant she ceased channeling. She examined the bed frame, studying its various bolts and screws. There had to be a way out even without the fool having a key. Despite the futility of it, she strained against the metal for several minutes until she ran out of breath and fell to her knees. As she slouched there, panting, she spotted the handle of a pistol stuck in the hermit's belt. Rachel wanted Zhar to shoot the chain out—a gun could set her free.

She leapt at it, but the cuffs jerked her to a halt with her fingers still an arm's length away. Althea screamed, wailing with pain as she tried to drag the weight of the steel bed by one wrist. Her fingers crept an inch closer. Her feet slid in the dust. She grunted, teeth clenched, turning to grab the ponderous bed with her free hand. After a few tugs seemed to move it, she tried again, but her fingertips stalled a thumb's width from the weapon. She roared, leaning every scrap of her strength into the restraint until she bled. Metal legs scraped concrete. Her finger touched the handle.

"Calm yourself, mite."

That voice again, the placid woman from Vakkar's camp with the strange accent. Althea yelped and leapt back onto the mattress.

Althea whispered. "Who are you?"

"I am Aurora."

Althea grabbed the bars and pulled herself to the head of the bed, taking the tension off her arm. She ventured a glance at the hermit, still slumped back in the chair. The gun so close, yet so far. No flesh apparition burst out of him... yet.

She shivered in a ball. "What do you want?"

A spectral hand ran down Althea's back, over the skin in spite of her chest-cloth. Cold and phantasmal, it caused an involuntary tremble. "So innocent, so young. You are like us, and we are coming to help you. You do not deserve this life."

She jumped away from the touch, putting her back to the headboard, eyes darting about and finding nothing.

"Like you? Who are you? You are scaring me."

In the dark, the faintest glimmer of light hinted at the shape of a woman gliding around to the hermit. A cloud of luminous fog appeared in his gaping mouth, exuding several inches out before it drew back into itself and vanished down his throat. He twitched and sat up, more moonshine bubbling over his lip. He drooled, face turning at her with gaze unfocused. Melodic feminine words came out of him, trailed by the faint raspy wheeze of his real voice.

"You do not know what you are?" The hermit rose to his feet, moving like a zombie.

Althea sank into a crouch, hating the sensation of being tethered. "I'm the Prophet. Are you a Prophet too?"

A haughty laugh rang out, echoing in the maze of sewer pipes. The hermit shambled toward her. "That is adorable."

She shied back, but couldn't escape the hand patting her on the head. Althea didn't want this creature touching her, and desired that man's touch even less.

"You are psionic, Althea. It is not *magic*. You have abilities most people do not, but you are far more special than an ordinary psionic."

Her right hand turned purple from pulling at the cuff. "I don't understand."

The man jerked around in the dance of a drunken marionette and shambled across the room. Althea crouched on the bed and pulled at the chain with both hands, snarling; she did not care if it hurt.

"Relax, child. You have nothing to fear from me. I am your friend."

"Please take this off me." She stopped struggling, sensing the man's thoughts no longer his own. Another presence had taken over, something capable of blocking out her ability to see into the mind.

The body convulsed and gurgled. "He is not lying; he does not have the key. Other friends are on their way. Now that I have found you, I can tell them where to go. You are in no danger here, child. Do not worry yourself."

Althea didn't trust this woman. The ease with which she shot the harmless old man at Vakkar's camp was part of it, but another feeling joined it—an inexplicable sense of foreboding. She curled up against the cold headrest, letting her arm dangle loose.

"What did you mean when you said I was not ordinary soya... sayo... soro—"

"Psionic," said Aurora, though the man's lips didn't move. "Your mind has the ability to project your desires into the world. I bet you can hear people's thoughts, and I know you can force your body to repair itself. Tell me, little one, can you see the future?"

Althea thought for a minute, idly picking at the fringe of skirt by her knee. "Sometimes I have feelings something bad's gonna happen."

"You do not make a habit of telling people's future, then?"

Guilt pulled a tear from her eye. "No. If I saw futures, I'd have stayed with Rachel."

"I suppose the simpletons out here merely call you Prophet because they don't know what it means."

The woman's tone made her feel insulted, and she pouted. "How did you find me?"

"The same way you looked in on your little boyfriend. I have been searching for others like us for a long time now, mite. We call ourselves the Awakened. Our power is far greater than most psionics."

"Why?"

Althea tried to conjure up one of those weird feelings that could lead her to a way out of this mess. She suspected it a bad idea to wait for these supposed friends, the same kind of feeling that made her go after Den.

"The reasons are various, but for now, you need only know you have enemies out here."

Althea gawked at her. "Me?"

The woman laughed again. "Yes, little one. But not living ones."

"Ghosts?" She curled up tighter.

"You have seen ghosts?" The borrowed man swiveled to almost face her.

She shook her head. "No, but I have heard stories."

"Not ghosts." Aurora shuffled him away once more, taking a step toward the exit. "Did you ever wonder why so many people are so mean to you when all you want to do is help them?"

Althea sulked at this person. Teasing a girl tied to a bed was pretty mean too. "I... Yes."

"The Badlands has a king. It is not a man, a woman, or even a beast. A rogue sentience has formed from all that has happened here. It feeds upon the hate, the death, and the sorrow."

"A senshins?"

"Bloody hell, girl. You really need to get your arse in school. Sentience." Aurora spelled it, and sounded it out thrice. "It's a personality, a mind without a body."

"A ghost." Althea nodded.

Aurora lost control of the man for a second as her frustration mounted "Look, mite. Forget it. I don't have the time to argue semantics with you."

"Ticks don't bother me. I can make them stop biting."

"Argh!" The man shuddered again. "I can explain later when you are safe. In simple terms, there is a bad thing out there that likes to make you cry. It wants your power, and we are going to get you out of here."

"I have a home." She glared.

The haughty laugh came again, and with it, Althea's skin crawled.

"That bush boy will forget you in a week. When I was your age, I had a different boyfriend every month. Most of them I never even kissed. Of course, most of them only wanted to get with the freak."

Althea hid her face in her knees and sniffled. Den wouldn't forget her so easily, would he?

"Now sit tight and don't go anywhere. You should be safe here once I get rid of this piece of shite." The man's head rolled around to look at her as if his neck was broken. "Don't cry for this one. If I could, I'd kill him twice for you."

The zombie-hermit shambled off into the maze of pipes, bouncing off the walls into the distance and out of sight. If not for knowing Aurora marched him off to his death, the splash of him falling into a puddle would have made her smile. She flopped down on the bed, staring up at her trapped arm. The woman kept calling them friends, but Althea's struggle to free herself amused her, and she could kill with no more hesitation than changing her shirt.

No. I won't wait for these 'friends.'

LESSON REMEMBERED

Althea lay still as sloshing grew distant in the concrete labyrinth, staring at the small gap between the top of her wrist and the handcuff. She wiped the smears of rust from her skin with her free hand. For the moments it took her captor to vanish into silence, she scowled at the idiocy of his not even having the key. Up on her knees, she spit on her wrist as much as she could, smearing the saliva around in hopes it might let her slip free. She twisted her arm back and forth trying to squeeze her hand loose. Metal bit and pinched her skin, but she remained trapped.

The *crack* of a gunshot made her jump. Aurora had taken the man too far away for Althea to sense his death, which was nice of her, but that also left the gun way out of her reach. Even knowing what he wanted to do to her, his death bothered her. After her mental attack, she doubted he would have looked directly at her again, much less touched her. He didn't have to die. She sagged in a heap. Rachel would have shot him too. Killing and eating people was wrong.

Of course, with him dead, she frowned at the handcuffs and imagined Rachel's voice saying "easy pickins." Rattling her arm, she felt like a worm on a hook dangled in the creek. She curled in a ball, gazing at the ceiling and the room around her. Underground, she would likely go undiscovered until she starved, a fate even less appealing than the supposed friends coming to collect her. Fear mounted at the memory of the skeleton hanging from the crashed buggy.

She stood on the cot, balancing as best she could on the moving surface, and faced the water-filled shaft.

"Help!"

Her shriek repeated over itself into the distance.

"Help! Please," she yelled. "Somebody help me!" She banged the cuff on the bed for extra noise. "I'm the Prophet. Come kidnap me!"

Even if raiders heard her crying out, another cage beat starving. Only the sound of her plea bouncing back at her answered. She collapsed over the metal bedframe. After a few futile tugs, she tried bashing the shackle against it, but only managed to create a flutter of grey paint chips scattering into the dust.

Reason gave way to fear, and she thrashed. Feet planted against the bar, she shook the bed in an effort to break the whole thing apart. The headboard she could lug around—the entire steel bunk weighed too much for her to even drag. When her energy ran out, she swayed to a gentle halt on the damnably robust thing. As she lay out of breath, she gazed upon the dead man's 'fortoon.'

A shiny silver cylinder sticking out of a crate caught her eye. After a few minutes to recover her strength, she got off the bed and grasped the frame in both hands. Her feet slid out from under her as she tried to pull it. Grunting, she flung her weight backward and hauled the bed in a succession of short, half-inch bursts toward her goal. Screeching wails of metal on concrete rang out in the tunnels, falling silent when she backed into the pile. She collapsed, panting, over the mattress.

She grasped the cylinder and lifted it, recognizing a 'magic torch' like the one Palik had. It was long enough to double as a club, and quite heavy. This one did nothing when she pressed a thumb into the rubbery button on the side. She tried to remember the chant Palik had used whenever he summoned the glow, but couldn't. Without the right words, it wouldn't make light. Althea frowned. She couldn't use it to signal for help when it got dark.

However useless the light may be, it remained a heavy pipe. She raised a great clamor once more bashing at the metal part of the cuff where it circled the frame. More rust and paint went flying. When she stopped, tired, she'd only accomplished making a small dent in the bedframe.

The restraint defied her still.

With desperate whimpering, she rummaged crate to crate, flinging useless things to the ground. Socks, hats, scraps of cloth, strange little heavy cylinders painted copper on one end and black on the other, and a mess of unidentifiable plastic pieces clattered around her feet. One box had some tools. A screwdriver slid into the cuffs proved she lacked the strength, even boosted, to snap them open. She spit on her wrist again, despite her dry mouth, and twisted her arm as she pulled, but her hand wouldn't fit loose.

Desperation and anger swirled within her as she stared at her useless arm. She felt so foolish for running away from the women, she lost the will to stand anymore and fell on the bed, pulling the ratty excuse for a pillow into her lap. She hugged it, wishing it was Rachel. As she thought of her, and Zhar's words, she pondered the concept of some people deserving to die. She didn't want her life to end out here, not like this. Not starving in a pit while chained to a bed with nothing but her regrets at her side. People outside still needed her help.

Her independence and desire to escape remained in their infancy, and easily daunted. Something moved past the grate far above, stepping on a twig with a *crunch*. The sound took her right back to Rachel at the time she reached the limit of her tolerance. Tossing the pillow aside, she moved to her knees and grasped her right thumb. She would have to crush it, disjoint the bone, and her hand would slip right out like Rachel's had. Althea remembered the way Rachel's bone-shapes looked. She knew what kind of damage needed to happen.

With a cry of fear and anguish, she squeezed, but either strength or conviction lacked, and her bones didn't break. Panting, she fought back the tides of despair that threatened to swallow her, and grabbed the magic torch. Bashing the cuff had failed, but she could try smashing her hand. Clenching her jaw, she lay the trapped hand upon the metal frame and raised the weapon over her head, staring at her target. She hesitated, shaking. Pain didn't bother her for long. She could turn it off at will. Why then did she fear doing it? The veins in the back of her hand swelled thick with her racing heart. Every beat shook her ribs. Hot blood coursed in her veins, her whole body objecting to self-harm.

Althea stared at the swollen blood vessels on the back of her hand—and felt stupid.

She relaxed her grip and the torch-turned-club slid away, landing with a plop on the mattress behind her. Tracing her fingers over her arm, she pictured the bones. Eyes closed, she opened her mind-vision and linked it to the sense of her form. In the shadows of her thoughts, skin faded away, as did muscle, exposing the bones within—separate and distinct shapes unto themselves. A temporary alteration, a momentary attack of her body's defense mechanisms, and the ligaments holding her thumb in place tore apart. In her mind, a swarm of tiny little mouths devoured the cartilage and tendons allowing her thumb to float free.

This brought with it a pain unlike any she had ever imagined. Unable to contain the scream, she emptied her lungs and collapsed into the bed frame, tears streaming from her eyes. Trembling, she continued trying to shout despite having no air left inside her. Her right hand became an alien purple mass at the end of her arm. A tentative tug sent another wave of agony through her, even the air brushing her hand hurt. Her situation presented a unique paradox: she was in too much pain to concentrate on not feeling pain.

Slumped against the bed frame, she stared at her wrist and drew her breaths in a series of short gasps trying not to move at all. The initial wave of anguish passed to a momentary calm. Huffing rapid breaths, she forced herself to focus. She commanded her body to stop swelling. Her inflated hand receded back to normal size.

With a grimace and a twist, she pulled. A blinding flash of agony and another wail came as her bones ground over each other—but her hand slipped free.

The cuffs clattered against the bedframe. Althea fell on her side, staring at the lump in front of her face that used to be a hand. Her heartbeat echoed in the damaged flesh, but brought a wide smile to her face. For several minutes, she lay collapsed on the moldy mattress, the dank smell of it barely registering past the pain. She stared over the grey cloth at blurry strips of sunlight on the wall of the cistern, the sound of drops falling in water grew loud. Althea blinked, noticing the light had shifted inches upward from where she remembered it, telling her she had lost consciousness for several minutes. Her hand throbbed, again blown up at least twice its size and dark purple.

Her delirium passed, and the blinding pain had faded to a background annoyance. She forced herself to sit up, cradling her wounded limb to her chest. Her skin warmed as she focused on setting it back to rights. Tissues redrew themselves and spidery wisps of white bone-shapes spread open as she flexed her fingers. The red tint of muscle slid up and over them, then skin.

Althea opened her eyes in time to watch the hemorrhage recede back to the normal color of her skin. She kneaded the soreness out of her wrist and couldn't help herself but stick out a tongue at the defeated handcuffs. Out of spite, she locked the bloody end around another part of the frame, so no one would ever be trapped by it again.

Ignoring the soreness in her arm, she scrambled down the ladder and plunged her legs into the icy water. She had no idea how long she had been out after fainting, and wasted no time crawling back through the narrow pipe from whence she had first arrived in this dreadful place. She emerged from the end headfirst, walking on her hands until she pulled her legs clear, then stood in the ankle-deep stream.

Althea took a huge breath of beautiful fresh air. She leaned back and let the wind wrap about her, loving every tickle of hair or leather scrap as it danced around. The late afternoon woods appeared too quiet. Her joy at freedom faded to worry as she remembered Aurora's promise to come and find her. She had once again remained her own person, and she wanted it to stay that way. Someone came for her, but she would be far away from here when they arrived.

THE HUNTER AND THE PRINCESS

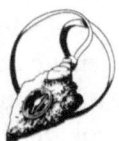

R unning.

Althea had become quite accustomed to it. She sprinted through the false forest, which turned out to be larger than she imagined. Her pace changed with the terrain, slowing as her bare feet skidded over mossy rocks, or she had to navigate dense undergrowth, or scale the occasional fallen tree.

One such log provided a place to rest for a moment as well as a bountiful nest of squirming white grubs. Sitting astride it like a horse, she cradled the agate arrowhead in both hands, thinking of Den as she popped the little things into her mouth like fine grapes. Aurora said something about finding her the same way she looked at him. Perhaps she could somehow get a sense of where to go. She clasped her hands around the charm and lifted it to her face, closed her eyes, and aligned her thoughts on the desire to find Den. A glimmer of sadness came out of nowhere, the kind of resigned melancholy that came with being forced to do something one didn't want to do.

She resisted the emotion and winced as she tried to bend her power to tell her which way to go. Warmth spread over her bare shoulders and neck from behind. She smiled, picturing Den's arm around her. Althea feared he had given up on her and had resigned himself to join with Yala. Tears squeezed out of the corners of her eyes as she tried to send the thought she was still alive to him. She didn't believe Zhar. Den liked her.

A heavy grunt followed a moist blast of hot air on her back that threw her hair forward. Her eyes snapped open. She twisted around to look back. The dog man perched on the log right behind her, muzzle sniffing. It's right eye, clearly machine, glowed. Thin orange lines and tiny symbols appeared within a ruby sphere the size of her fist.

Her breathing stopped. She leaned her weight into her hands against the moldy bark, lifting one leg in an agonizing, slow dismount of her pine steed. The dog man radiated pain and hunger. Angry and hungry mixed in such a beast didn't sound like a good combination for her health. Drool squeezed out from between its steel teeth. The foul odor of rotten blood clung to it, no doubt from the places where metal warred with its flesh, crude cybernetics grafted into a genetic experiment gone awry.

A pulse of radiant calm made it hesitate long enough for her to drop to the ground and back away. It shook off the forced emotion and growled, and she once again sprinted. Amid the blur of leaves and scattered bits of sunlight, she didn't care where her feet landed. Weaving around the trees, she exploited its bulk and took sudden corners it couldn't follow. It fell over twice on tight turns, crashed into a stump on another, yet still it did not relent. Starvation offered powerful motivation.

She wondered if this justified murder. If this creature caught her, it would kill and likely eat her. Was killing it first justified? Her moral quandary came to a sudden halt when a graze whiffed over her hair. She grabbed the top of her head, but found nothing.

Confusion didn't have time to set in. Before she could think two words, an explosion from behind threw her forward. A roar of fire mixed with the wounded yelp of an injured dog. She crashed to the ground on her chest, rolled head over heels into a tree, and wound up facing to the rear upside down, staring between her legs at the canid, which came to a halt a few yards behind her, lying on its mauled face and breathing in a slow, raspy gurgle.

Althea let herself fall over sideways, then forced herself to stand despite the pain of a dozen splinters in her legs and back. What remained of a small tree waved back and forth, blown in half amid a cloud of smoke some distance behind the dog. At that moment, she realized what had touched her hair—a tripwire grazing her head.

The creature caught the brunt of it; the charge blasted the skin from the left side of its head and reduced its arm to a mangled ruin. It looked up at her, menacing eyes gone pleading. She examined the blood on her legs from the wooden flechettes embedded there. Biting her lower lip, she wiggled and plucked out the largest of them before she staggered around the wounded creature. It made no attempt to keep its gaze on her.

Pity filled her heart, and she collapsed by its head. It shifted, licking her foot with a slimy tongue. Althea wondered if it had enough reason to know it was at her mercy, or merely wanted to taste her before it died. Regardless, she put her hand on its forehead and made it sleep.

This creature's body felt strange in her thoughts. Somewhat human, yet somewhat not, it contained a life force nonetheless. It had thoughts, crude and primitive like an animal on the surface, nudged along by an undercurrent of ration somewhere deep inside. She held on with two fistfuls of fur, her body convulsing from the power she forced into the thing. In the blackness of her closed eyes, she visualized its damaged shapes flowing together to become whole. The mass of its being coalesced upon the canvas of her senses as shifting amoeba of various colors merged. Black spots poisoned the overall form, straight and unnatural things with lines that didn't feel organic.

The metal had to go.

She forced her fingers under the first plate she found, between the dead material and the hot, infected skin. Bracing her knee for leverage, she wrenched it loose from the flesh as she commanded the living body to divest itself of pollution. Wires and cables stranded out from the wound as she lifted and tossed the bloody hunk to the side. One by one, she pulled and tore at the metal bits with the urgency of a child opening gifts, saving the mechanical eye for last. Althea studied the inorganic black strands threaded deep into the creature's thinking shape. She couldn't simply rip the eye out. At her urging, the canid's body repelled the device over the course of minutes. She lifted the crimson sphere and its dangling cobweb of wiring away as it exuded forth.

Placing both hands over the empty socket, she shuddered with exertion. Minutes later, a new eyeball swelled up to touch her palms. The rest of the gory cavities closed, forms pure and untainted by blackness. Sensing no more hurts within the large creature, she dropped her connection to it.

Arching her back, she reached up behind herself and wiggled splinters out one by one. Points of pain, little more than annoyances, winked in and out as her body purged smaller invisible bits of wood she couldn't find or reach. She sprawled in the mulch, half-awake and coated in sweat from the effort. The Wagon Man had forced her to work to the point of nosebleeds from the strain. The amount of harm in this creature had almost gotten there.

Althea slumped face down in dead leaves, and slipped into unconsciousness.

DREAMLESS SLEEP ENDED AN UNKNOWN TIME LATER, REPLACED WITH THE blur of her hand above the forest floor.

Althea sat up and rubbed her eyes, calm and still tired until she spotted the dog crouching about ten yards away, staring at her. Prey instinct chased all traces of sleep out of her. Her heart skipped a beat at the realization she had been helpless next to the thing that had tried to eat her. It no longer swirled in a mess of anger and pain, but gave off confusion. When Althea made eye contact, its emotion changed to gratitude. It lowered its head at her, this thing not quite man and not quite canine, and backed into a curtain of foliage, before shambling away into the woods.

Heavy thuds and snaps reverberated from the trees as it bounded off. She smiled at the wavering patch of plants, debating if she should move or fall over and nap again. After several minutes of sitting and staring at her legs, she wobbled upright amid the scattered bits of bloody cyberware. She picked up a metal strut with a length of wire hanging from the end, and held it out in front of her as she staggered forward—another of Reed's tricks to find trip lines.

The sound of running water changed her course. A tiny creek bubbled among the trees, sunken into the soil in a channel that might have been natural. She sat on the edge, letting her feet dangle in while scooping water over her face. Her grimy chest-cloth soaked dark as she drank. The effort it had taken to mend the beast taxed her entire body into aching. She wanted more sleep, despite the painful hunger.

"Hey, lookit thar." A man's voice came from behind her, too close.

"Whazzat? Girl?" replied another.

Someone cleared their throat. "Dunno. Could be. Blonde, worth a lot na matter wot 'tis."

Oh no! Althea closed her eyes. Only slavers would say that. She brought her feet up under her and stood, bracing for the next few minutes of hard running. As she started to move, the *click* of a gun came from behind.

"Don you run, ya hear? We kin sell yas even if yas gots one leg."

"It girl." The first voice again.

The throat clearer spoke again. "How you know 'dat?"

"Skirt."

The *thump* of a punch followed. She whirled around on three men, only two standing. One wore camo pants beneath a leather vest studded with all manner of trinkets and dangling objects. He laughed at the man on the ground while aiming a bolt action rifle in Althea's direction. The man who looked to be the source of the attack wore a skirt made of irregular panels of cloth knit together and covered with things Rachel called license plates.

"Go away." Althea tried to summon up her psionics—Aurora called it that, not magic—but she was too tired.

Even the attempt hurt.

"Ho my." The man with the rifle shuddered as he saw the glow. "Look." He pointed with a gasp.

Althea sighed at the irony of deciding to put aside her hesitation at using her powers to escape, but lacking the energy to call them. She would let them capture her and deal with them after she slept and got her wind back. As exhausted as she was, a day or two locked up would only serve as protection. A degree of comfort came with their knowing her as the Prophet—she wouldn't be added to a harem or harmed.

"Yes, I am the Prophet." The words came heavy with sleep, and she trudged over to them.

Bouncing with giddiness, they surrounded her and examined their find. A hand on her head pulled back on her hair enough to make her look up. They forced her eyes wider with their thumbs. Seeing the light up close, they cheered. When they shoved her to the ground and gathered her arms behind her back, she tried again to radiate fear. Fatigue reduced the emanation to a point it only made them nervous.

Rope circled her wrists and then her ankles as they bound her. She struggled to remain calm. After a full sleep, she could order them to release her. Healing the mutant had drained her to a state beyond exhaustion. She let her face fall into the soft wet mulch of the forest floor, biding her time. In an odd sort of way, the ground felt comfortable.

An eerie whistle passed overhead, followed by a muted *snap* of a gunshot. It seemed strange and unfamiliar, not as loud as it should've been. She realized the odd hissing had been the projectile passing close overhead. A wet *slap* from a second shot came from the man in the skirt as he gurgled and collapsed, clutching his side.

"She's ours!" The one in camo yelled and fired at something.

Hot brass fell on her, finding a spot of exposed back between her shirt and skirt. She squealed and rolled, absorbing an unintentional kick to the stomach from the other man scrambling to run away. He tripped over her and hit the ground, managing to crawl a few feet before the strange gun went off three times in rapid succession. His back burst in gouts of crimson, and he collapsed. Bent in half, Althea spotted the source behind long gouts of bright blue fire.

A man stood ten paces away, one hand holding a boxy handgun with little lights on it aimed at the scavs who found her. His eyes hid behind a band of silver plastic that caught the fading sunlight. A coat of dull brown leather framed him like a cape. He strode toward her, heavy boots crushing twigs and dead leaves. A few days' worth of beard ran along the ridge of a chiseled chin and an array of small boxes and objects burdened his belt. Travel-grime darkened his skin, though Althea knew he was like her, a scarce commodity slavers called 'white.'

She stared at the ground, shuddering at the tug within the ether as each man died. The icy claw at her heart hurt worse with her hands pinned behind her. She struggled to free herself, wanting nothing more than to run again and leave all of these men behind. Already tired, she wound up on her chest, heaving gasps of air into the leaves as she squirmed in protest of the ropes. The strange man walked up, stuffing his pistol into a holder on his hip next to a huge knife. The cold leather of his coat gathered in a heap on the backs of her legs as he crouched over her.

He picked at the rope around her wrists, loosening it.

"Thank you." She went limp and smiled.

He pulled at her arms, looking her over. "Damn, you're a special kind of scrawny, aren't you?"

The voice, dry and drawn out, seemed like it belonged to a much older man. Before she could pull her hands free, the ropes drew closed with a jerk that made her yelp. He tied her wrists *tighter*.

Althea wailed, squirming in an attempt to look back at him. "What are you doing? Please don't, please let me go!"

The binding on her ankles constricted as well. "Damn bandits can't tie a knot to save their asses. You could'a gotten loose pretty easy."

She writhed. "Ow! It hurts. It's too tight."

"Don't fight and it won't hurt so much. I ain't gonna harm ya. Just collectin' ya."

Althea froze in dread. "Are you Aurora's friend?"

"Don't got friends," said the man in the long coat. "Ain't no such thing. Friends are only enemies that don't have the balls to admit they'd cut your throat the minute it suits their purposes."

"That's not right."

"You sit tight a minute." He gave her a light smack on the ass and wandered away. "Don't slither off."

Her fear became anger. Grunting and wriggling, she squirmed, but succeeded only in making the ropes pinch. Her mood returned to panic when a scrap of burlap blocked her eyes and knotted tight against the back of her head. The man grabbed her by the armpits and pulled her onto her feet, and after a few seconds, up and over his shoulder like a sack of grain. A dense, musky fragrance clung to him, a mixture of spice and sweet tobacco.

She struggled, held in place by a firm arm across the back of her legs and her weight pulling her down. "Where are you taking me?"

"To your new boss."

Her wriggling ceased. "Owner?"

The man laughed, a dry evil thing that made her shiver. "Nah, kid. You got lucky. The Freddie wants to hire you. I'm here to arrange the interview."

She bounced as he walked, occasionally testing her ability to slip loose. "Hire? What does that mean?"

"You know about tradin' or money?"

"Yes," she said with a meek voice.

"Hirin's when you give a person money in return for them doin' work."

Althea tried to shake the blindfold off. "It is wrong to make people pay for my help."

He patted her twice on the back of her thigh. "You can take that up with The Freddie."

IN THE DARK

T he walk felt like it took hours. Althea went limp after a few minutes of pointless struggling, dangling over his shoulder. She came close to crying, but the eerie lack of elation the man displayed kept her too frightened. Most who captured the Prophet couldn't contain their joy. This man radiated no stronger emotion than if he had found a shiny rock to take home.

He held her legs tight to his chest, his fingers digging five numbing points into the side of her right thigh. The constant motion while hanging half upside down made her sick to her stomach. She gurgled as he took a series of hard steps descending an incline and swung around a corner. The hiss of a breeze passed by somewhere above her, but she felt no wind. The tingle of the energy field swept over her legs, and the air grew warm and dry once more. Back in the Badlands dust, his boots scuffed on sand.

Minutes later, a heavy metallic creak made her picture a door opening. The arm across the back of her legs moved. She let off an involuntary yelp when she fell backward. He caught her and guided her to soft cushions. Althea recognized a seat, but it confused her that he hadn't stooped to put her inside. She'd never seen a car or buggy this high off the ground before. A hand on her knee pushed her legs in before reaching across and securing some kind of strap over her. It pulled tight and pressed her hips into the cloth and her wrists into her back.

"Ow." She whimpered and squirmed in one last desperate attempt to get loose as the door slammed.

At least half of her life thus far been spent as a captive, but nothing had made her feel as helpless as she did in that moment. The blindfold added a scary twist she hadn't yet been unlucky enough to experience. The ability to see in the dark had left her always aware of her surroundings, always aware of which direction danger would come from. Being trapped in complete darkness frightened her almost as much as being wifed.

Still air inside the space held the scent of wood smoke and flavored tobacco. The fabric against her legs felt soft. Carpeting, another new experience, teased at the tips of her toes when she strained to feel for ground. Helplessness changed her struggling into crying, and by the time the man opened the door on the other side, the blindfold had soaked through.

The vehicle rocked as he climbed in. "What are you cryin' for?"

She turned her head, trying to gawk at him for asking such an absurd thing. "You're mean. I don't want to go with you, and I hate being tied!" She surprised herself at the demanding tone in her voice, yelling the last part.

"I'm just doing my job."

"Being mean?" Squirming didn't get her anywhere but sore.

He laughed again. His lack of emotional radiance frightened her. She knew people well enough to understand the sight of her in her current state should elicit some degree of emotion: anger, pity, sorrow, greed, or the other one she so feared. To this man, it generated nothing at all. Not even the pleasure of finding a great prize. He seemed in no hurry to run off to whatever master he served, taking his sweet time fussing with something. Minutes later, the stink of pipe smoke carried the thick scent of clove to her. The man exhaled, took another drag, and let the air seep past his teeth.

Althea coughed, trying to turn away.

"I hunt runaway slaves. Be happy you're a special request. I don't usually let the quarry ride up front." He paused, then chuckled. "'Course, ain't usually little kids I need to catch."

The seat beneath her filled with vibration as the machine came to life. "I'm not a slave."

His dry chuckle slid under her skin and made her squirm. "I suppose that's a matter of perspective. Regardless, I have a certain skill set that comes in handy tracking people down."

She tried her best to sound demure. "Please untie me. I promise I won't run."

The rasp of a chuckle came again, strengthening the reek of clove. "Oh, I've never heard that before. Nice try, kid, but I ain't gonna take the chance."

He ignored her begging and struggling for several minutes. Once it became clear she couldn't escape, she slumped forward and bawled. When that failed to elicit any form of response, verbal, emotional, or otherwise, Althea tried one last thing.

"I hate this. Will you please put me in a cage instead?"

He remained quiet for a moment. "Nawp. That's not a natural thing to ask. You're sneakin' up to somethin'. You can stay just like that. It'll only take us a day and such to get there."

She slouched. The thought of being helpless for so long made her sick. Already, her hands and feet had gone numb. "Why did you tie my face?"

"Two reasons," he said, fatigue etching his voice. He didn't seem to like talking with his prey. "One, they glow. The natives out here'll recognize who you are and create problems. That's for their benefit so I don't have to kill a dozen people on the way to Vegas."

"Vegas?"

"Town called Vegas, north o' here a ways. It's where The Freddy runs his place."

"What's the other reason?" she asked in a small voice.

"Yer one of them psionics. Don't want'cha messin' with my brain. Gotta look into my eyes for that, and I ain't havin' it."

"You know psionics?"

"Aye." He exhaled again. "You Scrags think its magic."

Althea shivered in her seat, unable to contain the fear that gripped her. "Please take it off for a little while. I'm scared. I promise I won't do anything."

A minute passed in silence before the desperation in her voice paid off. "Fine. But..." He hooked a finger under the rough cloth against the side of her head. "You keep your face pointed forward or to the side. I catch you looking at me even a little bit, I'm gonna hit you so hard you won't wake up until Vegas. If I even think you're trying some of that psio crap, you're gonna hurt like you've never known pain."

"Okay." She looked to her right, trembling.

He tugged the blindfold down, leaving it draped around her neck. Althea timidly looked around, shying away from him. The strange machine did appear to be a car of sorts, though it rode high off the ground and only had one bench seat. Instead of a rear seat and trunk, a long open wagon-like bed stretched out behind a flat window. Most surprising of all, the console near the wheel had lots of glowing stuff. This not-quite-car didn't look like it even came from Earth. Or, maybe the awful man had found a before-time driving machine that somehow hadn't been destroyed.

Terrain zoomed by outside. The bizarre, out-of-place forest had long disappeared into the distance, replaced with a field of sand-brown blur broken by the occasional flash of a piece of scrub. Careful not to look at him, she ventured a glance ahead at the road. It led off in a perfect straight line before diving into the creeping flames of the setting sun shimmering across the horizon.

After shifting to force blood into her numb hands, she put her feet up on the dashboard, trying to find some way to get comfortable. She studied the knot between her ankles, wincing as she jostled from the motion of the ride. The pressure made the veins in the tops of her feet bulge more than usual. Her attempt to wriggle some blood flow past the bindings left footprints in the dust. Althea gave up and sank against the door, watching the terrain blur past. She looked up from the ground at a mirror bolted to the door, which offered a view of three metal boxes in the truck bed. Scraps of cloth covered bars at the ends of cramped one-person cages. She stared down at her lap, feeling stupid for running away. No fight remained in her. She marveled at how sleep stayed so far away despite her exhaustion.

"You look tired, kid. You should rest. The Freddy's got a lot of work for you."

Castoff glow from her eyes sank onto her extended legs. "What does he want?"

The man leaned back in his seat, smiling. "He's got himself a nice little stable of whores."

Overcome by terror, she lapsed into a panicky fit of struggling.

He cackled. "No… Calm down, kid. You're the Prophet, right? That's not why he wants you." The man pulled her chin toward him. She almost wet the seat when she made eye contact, remembering his threat to hit her. He appraised her before shoving her head away. "'Course in a couple of years, you're gonna be a god damned looker."

Althea cowered away, hoping he didn't think she tried anything. "What does he want me for?"

"See, whores tend to pick up all sorts of nasty things, but they keep the gamblers happy. The Freddy likes happy gamblers, so he needs healthy whores. The Freddy wants you to keep his girls clean. His men get shot up now and then, too."

"He's going to keep me in a cage." Althea pouted.

"That depends, I suppose." The man leaned out the window, tapping his spent pipe on the outside of the door.

"Depends?"

"On if'n you accept his offer. Slave or employee dependin' on how you answer. If he thinks you're gonna run off, yer probably right 'bout that cage." He sucked something out of his teeth. "I suggest you say yes. No one says 'no' to The Freddy."

She relaxed. The same old routine. Raiders remained raiders even if they had fancy names and fancy huts. They were still men. Men with minds. As soon as she got where this man took her, she would force them to let her go. Her current companion gave her a dreadful feeling, but she wouldn't allow herself to be owned again. Something about this person frightened her into not wanting to influence him, but The Freddy would have a change of heart and let her go. If the whores were slaves, she would take them with her. The thought of freeing another harem made her miss her friends.

"It will be dark to you soon." She looked to the right, out the passenger window.

"Yep. T'will," he said, his voice emotionless.

"I can see at night. Want me to sit there and hold the wheel thing so you can sleep?" The silly suggestion came out faster than she could think. She didn't even know how to work this metal beast.

He laughed and patted her on the leg. "Again, nice try, kid. I almost like you."

Pushing her feet into the dashboard, she tried to slide out of the over-tightened seatbelt. "If you crash and get hurt, I will not be able to touch you to make your hurt go away." The suggestion of her being trapped in a wreck still failed to provoke any kind of emotion.

She found his silence ominous.

"If I'm dead, you won't get paid."

He frowned. "All right. I'll give you that."

Fifteen or so minutes later, he pulled off the road, stopping near a small decaying building standing alone in the expansive nothingness.

Four smashed metal objects in a neat row beneath a collapsed slab of roof told her it was something once called a gas station.

"Is the beast hungry?" She made it a point to keep looking away.

"Relax kid, I ain't like that."

"What?" She looked at him before realizing she did, then ducked away with a whimper. "I mean the metal beast."

When he reached for her, she tensed, but he only tugged the rag back into place over her eyes and tightened it.

Blind again.

He laughed, still a sinister sound that made her feel cold. "It doesn't eat gas. It's not as ancient as it looks. Besides, old fuel don't last that long. Nothin' left here but dust."

"Raiders use it," she mumbled.

"Nah. Those idiots burn ethanol or alcohol. They pour the same shit in their buggies that they drink." Finally, emotion surfaced—disgust. "Cretins. We're gonna sleep outside so I can hear if shit tries to sneak up on us."

She scrunched her eyebrows together—not that he could see them. "It doesn't sneak... it just lays there and smells bad."

The man chuckled and got out of the truck. She jumped at the slam of his door. Boots scraped over concrete slabs, around to her side. Her door opened with a rush of warmth that chased away the stagnant smoky air. Althea couldn't help but tremble as he leaned in over her, but exhaled with relief when the belt released her with a faint metallic *click*. Again, she went over his shoulder, but only for a short time while he collected something from the truck bed and carried her for a few paces.

Gravity upended itself. He set her down sitting on a raised concrete island, her back against a square metal pole she remembered holding up the roof over the pumps, the painted steel neither warm nor cold against her back. None too gently, he wound a few coils of rope about her chest and snugged it up into her armpits.

When she realized he intended for her to spend the night tied to the post, she cried. "Why are you so mean to me? Please don't do this. What if the bugs find me? What if you die in your sleep? Please put me in one of the cages. Nothing can get me in there."

He walked off, ignoring her mewling. She wriggled and tried to stand, but the cord around her chest snagged on something after an inch. Her feet slipped forward, dropping her back to the ground.

He laughed at her from a short distance away. "You Scrags sure don't give up. Maybe that's why you're still around out here."

"Please... I'm scared. I can't see if anything is coming over to eat me. I don't want to die." She couldn't stop squirming.

A gravelly sigh slid from his throat. "Calm down. I ain't gonna let nothin' touch ya. I don't usually sleep."

Crinkling plastic preceded the sound of munching.

She stayed quiet for a few minutes, listening to him reload his pipe and light up. Out here, the scent of it came in small traces. After some time, discomfort made itself known, and she lifted her head. "I have to make water."

"So make it," he said past a full mouth.

"Let me out?" She waved her head back and forth trying to face him.

"Heh. I've been trackin' runaways for longer than you been alive. Don't cha think I've heard that one before, too? If'n you gotta go, go. Yer already filthy. Little more gunk won't change a damn thing."

Not being able to walk off and go made the need to do it stronger. "I'm not lying. I really have to."

The scuff of boots on dirt came closer. She felt him inches away, his face hovering in front of hers, and wondered if he could see blue spots under the cloth.

His breath caressed her cheek with the warm rot of dead meat. "Nice try, kiddo. If I had a sack of coins for every slave that tried the 'gotta pee' routine, I could give up runnin' all over."

Her voice came a hair's breadth above a whisper. "Don't make me sit in it... Please." The pole refused to allow her to lean away from him.

"Not that I'd give up this life." A series of pats on the cheek became a harsh pinch of her jaw. He gripped her face between his thumb and forefinger, pushing her head against the hollow steel with a bell-like ring. "I love to hear them beg."

The crushing hand let go. Two seconds of tense silence passed before a harsh slap knocked her head to the side. She cried out in shock and pain, struggling at her bound wrists. Her hands couldn't cradle the stinging hurt, which made it worse. This man had an emotion now —pleasure.

"Oh... one more thing."

His leather glove tightened around her throat and squeezed. She strained but couldn't move, couldn't see, and couldn't breathe. Althea froze in terror, every muscle in her body tensed.

His breath pulsed over her ear, his lips an inch away. He spoke in a dawdling, placid tone that slid into her head like a disgusting tendril. "If'n you make one little noise and attract anything over here during the night, I'm going to teach you what happens to slaves that don't listen. Trust me, you don't want me to. I'm startin' ta like you... I'd *almost* feel bad."

Althea squirmed, desperate to suck in air, but couldn't. Her head pounded. Fear like nothing she'd ever experienced screamed in her mind. This man could kill her.

He let go with a contemptuous shove, leaving her to cough on the inrush of desperately needed air as he walked away.

She didn't have to make water any more.

KARMA AND DOGMA

Silence surrounded the old gas station save for the rusty creak of a piece of roof rattling in the intermittent wind. Althea shivered, not having even breathed loud enough to be heard for several minutes. The breeze set something above her ringing against the pole, an unmelodic sound that kept time with her heart.

Tightness gripping her wrists and ankles reminded her of the ruse from Vakkar's camp. Tied to a post for real, she wondered if fate decided to take revenge on her for lying.

Until she had met this man, the cruelest thing done to her was being stuck in a cage too small to let her stand, unable to reach a dying man. No one dared strike the Prophet, much less threaten to choke her. Everyone wanted to control her, her present circumstances made it clear that they had all been afraid of her, or at least afraid of the stories. Everyone who owned her had really been frightened of what she might do if she got angry.

Not this man.

A choice of lesser evils. She tried to swallow away the soreness from having her neck squeezed. Though, she'd much prefer a too-small cage to being blind, immobile, and completely at the mercy of such an awful man—or whatever else came wandering by and find her like this. A cage, at least, kept as much out as it kept her in. The shape of his hand still burned along her cheek. She wanted Den or Rachel to come save her, but worried what this evil man with his strange gun would do to them.

"You're evil." She tugged at her hands, voice but a whisper. "You can't let me sit in pee all night."

The scrape of boots came around in front of her, then the cool touch of his coat settled upon her legs. "Open wide."

Althea shivered, terrified of what he wanted to put in her mouth.

She attempted to ask 'why,' but the man stuffed her voice back down her throat with a crumbly thing he jammed past her teeth. It flooded her mouth with the flavor of peanuts. Food reawakened her starvation. Ever since she healed the dog, she'd been famished. She half choked on it, trying to chew far more than she should have taken in one bite. Enough remained packed in her cheeks to muffle a scream when cold water fell in her lap.

"Maybe you weren't lyin' 'bout havin' ta piss." A metal pail rattled somewhere in the terrifying blindness. "Still not riskin' it; yer worth too much. Can't be too careful with you psionic types. All it'd take is one second o' starin at me, and you'd have me offin' myself. Still hungry?"

Althea mumbled, unable to speak with a mouthful of peanut mush, so she nodded. "Mm hmmf."

"Eat up." He patted her on the cheek, lightly this time. "And don't make a damn noise."

She shrank away, waiting for the slap, but he didn't hit her again. When the second nutrient bar tapped her cheek, she bit it, holding onto it with her lips while nibbling at it. If she dropped it, she knew he would let it stay in her lap all night.

Some men just have to die, said Rachel's voice in her mind.

Althea had never been so frightened. Trembles ran down her body. Her arms and legs rocked with her subconscious need to free herself. After swallowing the last of the ration, she lifted her knees to her face and tried to lick the wet from her skin. The food had been so dry. Her shirt was soaked, and she wanted to wring it out and drink. Asking for water would require speaking, and her fear at making noise mutated into anger at being treated like this.

Wriggling like a fish on a hook had thus far served only to make the rope dig in and hurt, leaving her no closer to freedom than begging had. This man aside, enough dangerous things roamed the Badlands that being tied up and blindfolded amounted to a death sentence. She had all she could do to rein in panic. Anything at all could come by and make a meal of her, and she could do nothing about it. The cord across her chest crushed her into the metal pole, and the warm concrete upon which she sat had already started to hurt since she couldn't shift her weight. Despite her complete exhaustion, sleep would not come easy.

The agate bounced against her chest as she struggled, reminding her of Den. She gave up and let her body go slack. The rope kept her from falling over as despair came. She wanted him to save her, wanted to be with him. Panic reached a crescendo, made worse by her dread at what would happen if she released the scream so desperate to get out of her lungs. Her mind voice shrieked out into the darkness, begging anything or anyone for help. Second to being wifed, being tied had been her deepest fear, but she hadn't experienced blindfolds then.

Psionic energy welled up inside her and exploded into the world. Althea knew she did something, but had no idea of what. She held still, terrified the man might have seen something. When he didn't react, her emanation offered a degree of hope out of her intolerable state and she let it surge, writhing against the rope to empower it with every ounce of her fear. She wanted someone to save her from this man. All her terror and helplessness channeled into a great spike of mental energy.

The slave-catcher burped somewhere off to her right.

Stuck sitting in a frigid puddle, she sagged limp and exhausted. No longer having the strength to protest her bindings, she cried without sound. The emanation had no effect on anything, and her spirit came close to breaking. A steady breeze chilled her wet shirt. Fluid dripped from her nose, blood or snot, she couldn't tell. Drained to the point of delirium, and with sleep out of reach, she hung like a rag doll with no sense of time.

⚨ ❦ ▦ ◌ ♋

THE SCREAM CAME WITHOUT WARNING, A PRIMAL THING FROM THE ESSENCE of a man's soul. It snapped Althea out of the hazy non-space in which she floated. She tried to look around at skittering on concrete, but couldn't see past the cloth over her eyes. Something big ran by close. She thrashed to get away from the imagined giant roaches, but couldn't tell where they came from—or move.

Deep snarls accompanied the tearing of cloth; she forced her body still. A gunshot, that strange-sounding gunshot with the blue fire, preceded a distant ricochet and the plastic clatter of an object hitting the ground. Something heavy smashed into something metal, an impact that jarred the pain in her tailbone. Althea whimpered out her nose, fighting her desire to struggle. She hoped the monster she couldn't run away from might fail to notice her if she could only stay still enough.

Motion attracts predators.

A threatening noise, deep and feral, preceded a roar, another howl of agony, and a loud rip. The man gasped evil words and grunted. Footsteps staggered closer to her. She drew her legs to her chest, shivering, and screamed at the approaching violence she couldn't see or escape.

Growling came from right beside her. A wail of agony preceded a spray of hot liquid across her face and legs. She spat the taste of blood from her mouth. Fingers, slick and weak, closed around her ankle above the rope. A heavy voice grunted, and the hand slipped away, followed by the scrape of dragging. The deep growl became a roar muffled in bubbling liquid. A man's scream ended with a loud *crack* that made her jump. The chill of a departing life brushed past her heart.

Silence.

Involuntary shaking wracked her. Blind and tied to a post, she could only listen to the squeaking roof and the unknown thing tapping against the metal somewhere above her whenever the wind picked up. Whatever had killed the slave catcher had dragged him off somewhere to eat. The mushy sounds of it chewing filled the back of her throat with peanuts. What would it do after that? Every fiber of her soul wanted to scream for help. That she couldn't move made her want to writhe harder. The slave-catcher's death stranded her out here completely vulnerable. Trying to wriggle her right wrist out of the rope failed. The man had bound her so tight she couldn't even turn her arm. She considered the trick with her thumb, but lacked the energy to do it. She'd need to sleep first, and she couldn't possibly sleep like this.

Every small scraping sound became a flock of giant bugs in her mind, searching for her unprotected flesh. She jumped and cringed at snaps in the distance, fearing a pack of millipedes on their way to get revenge on her for stabbing one. How desperately she wanted to hear the rumble of a raider buggy. She would happily submit to a leash to get off this damn pole. The enveloping tranquility that came to dwell in the aftermath of murder frightened her more than the grisly noises of the slave-catcher's demise. Not knowing and not seeing sent her shivering out of control.

A low growl thrummed in the air, resonating from everywhere. Althea realized she whimpered and held her breath. The sense of an apex predator wafted in the air. A strong emanation of rage approached. The presence of body heat drew near, mixed with the scent of damp fur and carrion. Something huge hovered inches away from her.

"P-Please…" The weakest whisper left her lungs.

Warm slime slid over her cheek and a tendril of drool ran down her neck. The second time it happened, she recognized the feel of a huge, flat tongue. The third pass lifted the blindfold. Crouched before her, the mutant she had helped the other day tried to force a smile out of its canine face before cleaning the blood from hers. Its rage melted to affection. After bounding a few paces away, it looked back with an expectant pause. When Althea didn't follow, it took another step and glanced over its shoulder a second time. She didn't get up. It tilted its head.

She tossed the blindfold aside with a sharp nod, then whined, "I can't follow you. I'm tied."

Not expecting it to understand her words, she wriggled and squirmed, struggling to sit up away from the pole. It bobbed its head up and down and took another step back. Affection mixed with confusion. Frustrated, Althea lapsed into a futile search for freedom with brute force. Seconds later, she sagged forward, out of breath.

"You can't talk, can you? Do you know what I'm saying?" Bending her legs back, she strained to reach the knot between her ankles, but only brushed it with a fingertip before the cord across her chest hurt too much. "Help me. I can't move."

It bayed into the air, apparently clueless as to why she hadn't gotten up. Sniffing the air, the creature ambled back to her on all fours and nudged her as if to suggest she stand. She raised her legs toward its face, shifting her feet back and forth hoping it realized the man had bound her ankles.

It sniffed her feet.

"Yes. Please bite the rope." She held them higher.

It licked her soles, making her squeal and laugh. When she recoiled from the flailing tongue, the mutant leaned down and slathered drool all over her face again. She had nowhere to go, and clamped her mouth and eyes shut to avoid tasting dog spit while attempting to turn away from whatever angle the flailing drool-brush came from. She gasped as it swiped across her thighs, and then fell into uncontrollable snickers as the dog man lapped all the blood from her legs.

When it finally stopped, she spat before looking up, still giggling.

Sensing her happiness, it bounded away and waited for her to follow. Obviously, she hadn't gotten up because she needed a bath first.

"Oh…" She whined. "You're going to leave me here all night, aren't you? Silly dog."

She sighed at his lack of understanding spoken words. Of course, she had seen hermits and nomads every bit as stupid. She stared at him and projected a sense of distress, a wisp of fear tinted with urgency.

The canid tilted its head and emitted a soft whine. Then, inspired, it trotted around out of sight behind the pumps. Althea couldn't turn far enough to see where he went.

"Hey, come back. Don't leave me like this!" She let her head loll back against the post with a dull metallic *clonk,* closed her eyes, and let out a sigh of exasperation. "Silly dog."

The position left her staring straight up at a scrap of cable hanging from the roof, tipped with a metal fitting, the source of the disharmonic song tapped into the post.

Something warm and squishy poked her in the cheek. When she glanced to that side, her nose brushed a large strip of raw meat held in the creature's mouth. It poked her in the face with it again, leaving a bloody smear below her nose.

"I'm not hungry. I'm tied," she yelled.

The color drained from her as she realized where the meat had come from.

"Eww!" She recoiled and coughed, convulsing as she fought the urge to vomit. "No! Bad dog."

It shrugged and swallowed the offering before licking the smudge from her face. The essence of peanuts returned as she struggled to keep down what little she had eaten. A desperate fit of wriggling, screaming, and twisting again failed to convey the message to the dog-man. It continued licking her in an effort to get her back to happy. It evidently understood she had become upset and whined in confusion.

Althea gazed deep into its huge brown eyes. The glow mesmerized it. She saw no point in asking it to cut her loose; it couldn't understand her words. The man-dog had thoughts in its mind, images and concepts flirting with the reason of man but flashing by in bursts of primalistic urges far short of cognition. Somewhere, deep within the bestial nature of this thing, lurked the unrefined seed of human potential. Althea tried to bend forward, making the ropes across her chest dig in, and projected the feeling of being tied down into the mind of the creature.

It sniffed. The wet nose in her armpit destroyed her concentration with another fit of giggling, but this time, the dog seemed to sense something wrong. Grasping her about the shins, it tugged at her.

"Ow," she cried out as it tried to pick her up.

The beast man's head swayed back and forth, taking notice of where her body attached to the post. It lowered her to the ground and picked at the rope with a single claw.

"Yes." She grinned, bouncing. "That's it. Break it."

He drew closer, sniffing at the rope and flooding her armpit with hot, moist air. The tongue flicked at the cord. She squealed when it forced its tongue into her armpit, licking. Uncontrollable giggles lasted until he stopped trying to get a tooth around the rope. In response to her laughter, it licked at her fervently, pleased at the happy sounds she made.

Circling the post, it walked out of her field of view. The chest-rope tugged a few times. The man-dog snarled, then yanked.

"Ow," she wailed. This creature had the strength to crush her chest if it pulled with all its might. "Don't pull on it! You'll hurt me. You have to cut it."

Its face came around the pole, wide eyed with an apologetic look from her cry of pain. She focused on the image of a piece of rope sliced in two. Its little stump of a tail wagged, and it ducked back out of sight. It scratched and slashed at the back of the post, but its natural claws lacked the sharpness of the metal ones she had removed. After a series of rapid swipes, the line of pain cutting into her armpits went slack. The rope slid down into her lap and she rolled away from the pole, gasping for breath. The mutant bounded off, yipping with glee, and looked back at her once more. When she still didn't follow, it whined.

Althea shook her wrists at it, hoping it would recognize rope and repeat what it did. Ambling over, it crouched, nuzzled at the knot, then nibbled at it. Grumbling became giggling when it abandoned that knot and licked around her ankles.

"Stop it!" She gasped with nervous laughter, then made clawing motions in the air. "Use your claws."

It whimpered. She read concern—worry, even. It feared hurting her. She sighed and lay there on her stomach. Her new position offered a clear view of a scattered, gory mess on the other side of the pumps. She remembered the huge knife the slave-catcher had on his belt. Inspiration brought renewed energy. Pushing with her feet and squirming her shoulders around, she slithered like a sidewinder along the ground toward the dead man. The canid followed, confused by her bizarre motion. When she hit the blood slick, her toes slid more than they pushed, but she eventually dragged herself over the gore and up to the carcass.

The canid had hollowed out the man's chest, devouring most of the vital organs. She picked at scraps of skin and clothing with her teeth, pulling them out of the way in search of his belt. When she found it, she bit down on the knife handle and tugged. It didn't come loose. Momentary despondence passed as reason returned. This man had strange items. His knife might be strange, too. She scooted closer and studied it. A plastic button on the side stood out as odd, and no leather cord held the blade in the sheath. The button had to be responsible for the knife not coming out.

With a disgusted grimace, she stuck her tongue out and pushed the button, trying her best to ignore the taste of blood. The knife popped out a quarter inch. After spitting to the side, she nipped the handle in her teeth and rolled away onto her back to draw it free. She blinked, confused by how little it weighed. This weapon felt like a toy, like some of those flimsy plastic ones the Seekers sometimes found in the Lost Place.

Althea dropped the knife and shifted around until she got it in her hands. Stretching out on her stomach again, she folded her legs up behind her and threaded the blade with care between her calves before pulling with every ounce of strength to force her ankle-bindings into the edge. The blade sliced far easier than she had anticipated it would. The knot failed in seconds, and the strength she'd put into the effort slapped her legs into the ground.

When the stunning pain in her shins faded, she twisted over, staring at the knife behind her. The surface caught the glow from her eyes in a way only metal could, though this blade had a *far* sharper edge than any she had ever seen. Given its lack of weight, she had only one possible explanation: she had found a magic knife!

Now, of course, she had to find a way to cut her hands loose. She could sleep and use the thumb trick in the morning, but that hurt so much she decided to try to do something right away. Besides, she didn't want to sleep with her hands tied behind her back. She couldn't hold the knife and cut her wrists free at the same time, and a quick glance at the grinning canid made her think it would take too long to train him to use it.

She got to her feet and paced around, thinking about a way she could untie herself. As she neared the post, she eyed a small hatch on the opposite side of where she had been sitting, the snag that caught the rope when she tried to stand. She pulled it open with a toe, revealing a bundle of wires inside the post running up to the roof. Althea sat near the opening, working the knife handle-first into the tangle of cables with the edge facing upward. The canid watched, whining as if it thought she wanted to hurt herself.

Straining to look over her shoulder, she positioned the knot between her wrists above the edge and pushed down. The knife slid out and stuck in the concrete like a dart.

"Nooo," she whined.

The canid's hand on her shoulder pulled her over and laid her on her chest. It seized the knife in a clumsy grip with half-human hands. A wet nose in the middle of her back made her laugh and kick her legs in the air. It held her forearm with one hand, trying to maneuver the weapon against the cord without touching her skin. She watched, shaking with anticipation as this creature learned before her eyes.

When the dreadful tightness released her arms, she turned around and hugged the furry thing that saved her. The licking tongue descended upon her. Soon, its fur-covered body became a mattress more comfortable than a metal post and rope could ever be.

ALTHEA DRIFTED OUT OF SLEEP AND SNUGGLED INTO THE LEATHER WRAPPED around her.

She breathed a soft sigh of relief. When she realized she no longer clung to fur, she sat up and found herself laying upon the concrete island among the old pumps, wrapped in the slave-catcher's coat and covered with what had to be every bit of scrap cloth within a mile radius of the station. The canid perched on the roof of the building nearby, having guarded her all night.

Seeing her stir, it bowed its head once and fell out of sight. Althea radiated gratitude, despite a sense of sorrow. She knew it had to return to its own ways. People out here would not react well to a creature such as him, even if she had pushed his mind closer to humanity. Althea picked up the knife and tiptoed over the blood slick, which had partially dried into a sticky mess. She recovered the plastic scabbard and inserted the knife. The blade locked in with a *click*. Satisfied, she attached the sheath to the rim of her skirt.

After taking a seat on the pump island, she leaned forward and rubbed the rope burns until they healed. While kneading her fingers around her ankle, she gazed at a cluster of large birds pecking at the heap of gore on the ground. She hadn't asked for anything like that to happen to the slave-catcher when she cried out for help, but this time, she accepted the man's fate had come of his own choosing. He could have let her go, but he chose not to.

She stood, thinking about Rachel and feeling doubly stupid for holding it against her. It sort of made sense how it felt to kill when necessary but not take pleasure in it. That man had hurt people and enjoyed it. Though she'd rather he hadn't died, she couldn't argue that the world was better off without him. She whispered an apology to the wind for judging her friend. For a moment, she sat with her elbows on her knees, staring at the debris of the man that had abducted her, not quite sure how to feel.

Eventually, she got up and walked to the edge of the road, pausing with her arms folded across her chest. Strands of blonde and scraps of leather danced in a gentle breeze while she stared out over the black path of macadam stretching out into desolation, pockmarked and cracked from centuries of disuse. It was late in the day already, too late to travel. Waning sunlight gleamed in the windows of a small building beyond the pumps, and she decided to spend one more day here and then figure out what to do with the freedom she once more possessed.

She sighed at the desolation.

Loneliness made the cold breeze colder.

21

INDEPENDENCE

Althea awoke, her body threaded among a series of springs poking out from the cushions of an old ochre couch in the service station office. After extricating herself with care from the wobbling coils, she clambered upright. Her right foot came down on a six-inch roach, which burst, whitish goo oozing between her toes.

Cringing at the sensation, she hopped over and sat on the edge of a nearby desk, pulled her foot to her face, and sniff-tested the guts for edibility. Erring on the side of caution, she decided not to eat it, and scraped the muck off on the rotting green cushion of a squeaky, metal-framed chair.

Judging by the light, she figured the time at an hour or two past dawn, but still felt as though she needed sleep—however, she also needed food and water. Althea crept to the door and went outside, squinting into a strong, warm breeze. After finding a spot to relieve herself, she padded around the gore over to the giant grey vehicle that brought her here. Held aloft upon fat knobby tires, the truck's running boards hung at the level of her chest.

At the rear, she pulled herself up onto the bumper and peeked over the tailgate. Three metal cages sat against the back of the cab, each large enough to hold a man down on all fours. Some had bits of hair clinging to the bars or bloodstains inside them. Fortunately, they held only the misery of former use. Among the cages, the slave-catcher had packed boxes of supplies, and she soon found the cache of peanut bars and some bottled water. Not wanting to be in the presence of cages, she sat under the truck with her meal and watched the buzzards continue to pick at the man while she ate until she could force not one more bite.

The door proved a little tricky, but she managed to open it while hanging off the side of the truck. She climbed up behind a large wheel and examined the dials, buttons, and levers in front of her. She had seen raiders drive plenty of times and knew the little flappy bits on the floor made the buggies go ahead and stop, and the wheel did the turning.

The cold pedals did nothing when she stepped on them. The wheel was locked in place and wouldn't turn.

She muttered to no one in particular. "Did I break it?"

While searching for a way to make it work, she leaned into the center of the wheel and the most horrendous blaring noise she had ever heard came out of nowhere. An explosion of black feathers filled the air from scattering buzzards.

Althea jumped down out of the truck screaming, and sprinted away from the awful sound, not slowing until the truck was far out of sight. Out of breath, she collapsed to her knees and glanced up at the sky, squinting at the lack of clouds. The dirt had already become hot, and it would only get warmer as the day progressed. She spun in place, staring out at the horizon sliding across her vision. Letting her eyelids droop, she opened herself up to the world around her. The agate could let her find Den, but how could she find water—a far more immediate need.

An urge flashed for an instant. She continued to spin and it flashed again. After a few more spins, Althea realized the feeling lined up with a certain facing. It could be water, it could be Den, but it didn't feel alarming. With nothing else to do, she went in that direction.

Midday came and went. She had become parched and famished by the time she reached the crest of a small hill and gazed down at another forest of strange trees sprawled out a distance away. These appeared different from the ones she had been in before, much larger. Plants had to mean water. Giddy with anticipation, she ran herself wheezing into the woods.

Soon after the ground beneath her feet changed from warm dirt to cool mulch, she heard the sound of running water. Following her ears, she walked until she located a wide creek. She approached, leaving tracks in the wet sand framing the water like coffee-colored glass. Althea leapt into the brook and plunged into frigid water that came up to the base of her ribs.

She adored every inch of it.

Ducking beneath the surface, she gulped down mouthful after mouthful, and then rubbed her hands all over to free herself of the sticky residue of canine affection and muck from crawling in dead man.

Her thirst settled, she perched upon a submerged rock, armpit deep in the flowing brook, and pulled the magic knife out of its sheath. Poised, she squatted motionless for a time with her eyes locked on the water. A flash of silver caught her attention and she dove after it like an arrow, striking true and spearing a fish. With her prize in hand, she waded out. The waterlogged leather around her waist threatened to slip off with each step; she held on to it until she knelt by an exposed flat rock upon which she set her dinner.

The magic knife made short work of the scales as her precocious expertise let her clean and gut the fish with ease. She lacked the luxury of cooking, so she ate her fill of it raw and settled into the cool mulch.

With agate in hand, she opened her thoughts and searched for Den. Minutes of stillness rolled by until she saw him. He led a hunting team, stomping among the trees with desperation radiating from him. Knowing he searched for her brought a smile that faded when the reason for his urgency became apparent. Flashing images of Braga shouting appeared in her head, a sense he had one more chance to find her or Yala would be his wife.

Alarmed, she sat up cross-legged, clutching the pendant between her palms. Alas, the vision did not provide any sense of time. It could have been two months ago right after Vakkar's men took her. It could be right now, or it could be yet to occur. Opening her hands, she gazed down at the trinket balanced in her palm. Voices of the women drifted around her in a taunting cloud. First crush, she is only twelve, puppy love, aww how cute, she will get over him, Zhar's laughter.

Althea flung herself to the ground and sobbed. She had failed to use her powers to prevent being taken away from Den, she had failed to use them to stay with Rachel, and she wound up all alone. She curled on her side into a ball, clutching the pendant. After a moment, her sorrow become anger. Althea didn't need to worry about the chief or what he wanted. When she found her home, she would change Braga's mind for him.

Assuming Den still wanted her.

22

FOUNDLING

S oft brushed against her face, waking Althea from the fitful sleep of regret. Grey fur, wrapped around a rabbit of immense proportion, filled her view. The critter looked almost as big as her, staring with unblinking eyes and a twitching nose while it munched on something green. Sensing her awake, it stopped chewing and went still.

"Good morning," she cooed.

At the sound, its ears shot straight up. After an instant, it darted off in a panic, its huge back feet showering her with leaf mulch. Laughing, Althea fell over backward at the creature's reaction. When she could breathe again, she ate more of the fish and took a drink from the stream. Remembering what Reed taught her, she dug a cat hole with the knife, covering it afterward, then waded into the water to clean herself.

Picking a direction based on gut feeling was inexact, but she had no better option. Over the next several days, she walked, fished, and slept under the trees. Upon finding a small lake, she left her clothes on the bank and spent a few hours frolicking in the water.

When she resumed walking, she wondered what sort of magic made this place grow in the desert, but found no explanation as she followed wherever her feeling led. A new companion joined her: loneliness. Plodding along with a pout plastered to her face, she didn't notice the unusual patch of greenery in her way.

A metallic clank preceded a flash of pain and a faint *snap*. Flailing, she fell over to the side as something crushed closed around her left leg. From the look of it, her ankle had broken.

"Oh, no," she whispered.

The pain was easy to ignore, being trapped less so. She possessed almost enough strength to open the jaw trap unaided, and after a forced surge of adrenaline, she pulled the metal teeth aside and slid her foot out of it.

"Aww, dammit. Sorry, kid," a man's voice called out from a nearby ridge. "Jimmy, some little kid just wandered inta one o' yer traps. Looks hurt," he yelled back over his shoulder.

Althea shoved her ankle back into place, gritting her teeth as the bones scraped. The area filled with warmth as she mended herself. After a dull pop, she flexed her foot around to make sure she'd fixed it all the way.

"Hang on, girl. Jimmy'll make a splint and we'll get ya put to rights." The man trotted up behind her.

"I'm okay, thanks." She smiled at him.

The look of concern on his face for a wounded child shifted in an instant to greed when he noticed her glowing eyes and intact leg. Althea felt the change in his mood, and her smile ran away.

"Shee-it! Jimmy! Get down here!" He sprang at her with a cry of "Yee-haw."

She rolled, leaving him kissing leaf mulch. Scrambling to her feet, she sprinted and leapt across a narrow part of the creek.

"Hey, you ain't sa-posed ta run!" The man picked himself up, yelling for his friend as he followed.

"Wot da fuck is up your ass, Jon?" a deeper voice bellowed in the distance, followed by the tromp of a heavyset man rushing down a hill.

"Git da others. It's the damn Prophet. She here!"

Tears streamed from the corners of Althea's eyes as she ran. Finally, she found people, but it again became the same old routine. These men had even been cruel enough to tease her with the promise of being kind at first. She was not a child, nor even a person, merely the Prophet—a commodity.

More voices shouted in the distant forest, at least six or seven men. She doubted she could control them all at once, and ran harder. The terrain grew uneven and she slipped down an embankment, landing flat in soupy mud by the waning creek. Lifting her face out of it, she spotted a large opening cracked into the base of a tree up ahead, which gave her an idea.

She flung herself into the goop and rolled in it, rubbing the cold mire over her entire body. Satisfied, she scrambled into the hollow and threw leaves and twigs on top of herself, which clung to the wet mud. Huddled in a ball, she clamped her eyes closed to stop the light and listened to the men as they drew closer. The hardest part of this trick would be holding still.

Chilly glops of mud slid down her skin. She kept her breaths slow and body motionless. Shouts sprang up all around her as they fanned out in a search pattern.

No. She clenched her hands into fists. *I will not be taken.*

Her present circumstances didn't match the glorious power-flinging way she had daydreamed about securing her own destiny, but her plan might succeed despite its humble nature. One man walked right past her tree without slowing down. The muck worked: every inch of her coated in the same dark brown as the wood let her blend into the tree interior. It would be full dark soon, and they would have to give up. She could peek, but they would see the glow. The disguise only needed to last a little longer. A number of insects crawled on her, but she ignored them.

Shouting came from nearby, the first man, the one called Jon. He bellowed commands to the others before cursing and leaning against her tree. She almost gasped as the wood shifted, suppressing the need to tremble. Althea dug her toes into the saturated dirt to further mask her human shape. Jon grumbled under his breath, angry they had lost track of a little girl. She had ceased being the Prophet to him. His ego bristled at a child eluding him in his woods.

Althea focused on futility and hopelessness. Unable to see past closed eyes, she projected the emotions in an unfocused radiance. The man's yelling grew incoherent. Seconds later, the tree shifted when his weight left it. Plodding slurps accompanied his stagger into the mud. She pictured him holding his head as her induced emotions dominated his thoughts.

"Screw it. She gone," Jon yelled. "Let's get back in a'fore it dark. Mebbe she come smellin' food."

"Yer an ignant sumbitch, Jon," said an unfamiliar voice. "You'da been nice to 'er, coulda had her. But no, you gotta jump on her like some kinda squealin' inbred wolverine."

The men exchanged curses and argued into silence. She didn't move for another half hour, despite three bugs' desperate efforts to climb her face. When she ventured a look, the forest greeted her in black and white.

Dark. The light from her gaze glistened on muddy arms and legs. She shifted to face the woods, waiting a while longer before being brave enough to emerge from the hole. Althea crept along in ankle-deep mud, away from the direction the voices had gone. Running would make noise, and the men might still be close enough to hear her.

Minutes later, a canine howl echoed from everywhere, urging her up to a run. The *splat, splat, splat* of her steps in the wet dirt fell quiet once she veered away from the creek onto solid ground. Her hair clung, matted down by the drying mud. *What a sight I must be. If they see a girl made out of mud with glowing eyes, they'll shoot me.* Of course, Althea knew first-hand how legends could spread. At a distance, someone could mistake her muddy form for a girl made entirely from wood. The sight of her could spawn new tales of magical wood nymphs with leaves in their hair. The Badlands harbored strange creatures, and she had made herself into one of them.

The drying mire formed a second skin that tugged at her as she ran. Eventually, her flight sagged down to a jog, and then to a fast walk, which continued until the sun came up hours later. She zombie-staggered into the dawn, happy she had finally eluded capture, and happier still she did so without anyone getting hurt. Hunger growled from her gut as the fatigue of walking all night caught up to her. She wanted to fling off her clothes and jump in the lake again, but lacked the energy—as well as a nearby lake. Collapsing in a heap, she crawled up to a tree and went limp on the ground.

Exhaustion made the earth feel as if it fell away from her. She floated without gravity. Hunger proved too strong to allow her to sleep. She lacked the energy even to forage for food, but she kept herself *free*. An hour or two vanished in an instant; a nap snuck past her veil of discomfort. Motion drifted in the bleariness of her vision. Blue legs stepped into her vision, as did rifles. At least a dozen men gathered around her.

Why? She sobbed in her mind. Lacking the strength to do anything at all, she hung all but lifeless in the arms that picked her up.

A man's voice vibrated her body. *"Pobrecilla..."*

Althea tried to read his emotion, but lost the battle to stay awake.

SISTER KARINA

Althea remembered the woods and the running, and the men with blue-covered legs. She found herself awake, but didn't move or open her eyes. The fragrance of wood smoke hung in the air and a feeling of something soft existed between her head and the hard ground upon which she lay. She didn't want to look and see a cage. She didn't want to move and feel a collar around her neck or bindings on her arms. If she kept still, she could pretend she still had her freedom.

"Are you awake?" asked a young woman. She sounded close, within arm's reach.

Fearful of what she would see, Althea remained quiet and feigned sleep.

"You must be hungry." Fingernails teased at her stomach.

Althea jumped up at the touch and stared at a slim girl in a peach-colored dress kneeling next to her. She had brown skin like the people in Den's tribe and long black hair down to her waist. She looked young, stuck in the short time when she counted neither as a woman nor a girl. Perhaps around Yala's age of sixteen.

Althea clasped her throat and felt no collar. She sat up and scooted away; astounded she hadn't been restrained.

"Hey, easy." The girl rose on her knees, reaching toward her. "Don't be afraid. Can you understand me? *¿Entiendes Español?*"

A man's voice came up through the floor in another language. She knew it was called Spanish, but didn't understand it too well, only basic words, and nothing when spoken fast. He said something about dinner and cleaning.

The older girl patted herself on the chest. "Karina." She pointed at Althea and made an expectant face.

"I'm not stupid." Althea cowered against the wall, shaking. "Just scared."

This small room had smooth white walls and a dark hardwood floor. She had been lying on a thick rug with a pillow. A proper bed rested along the far wall. It looked slept in and had a few dolls draped over the side. A wooden box with many metal handles on drawers sat across from it by windows that peered out into the daylight sky. Stunned by the sight of intact glass, Althea didn't notice the girl's approach.

Her well-worn dress stopped at the knee. She was barefoot as well, and had a pink flower tucked behind her right ear that looked as if she picked it this morning.

Karina put a gentle hand on Althea's shoulder. "Why are you shaking? Oh you poor thing, you look terrified." She reached forward, holding both her hands, and pulled her toward the bed.

Althea followed, confused by the entirety of her situation. When the girl hugged her, she didn't know how to react.

"Please don't put me in a cage. I…" She looked down at her feet and cried. "I promise I won't run away." The words came out of her on their own. As much as she had promised herself she would stay free.

"Cage? What… *Dios mio*, what has been done to you?"

She looked up at the young woman's face, at the pity in her stare. This girl didn't look like a raider or a slave. Maybe she'd been found by one of the good villages.

"I'm Althea."

Karina smiled and fussed with her tangled mess of blonde hair. "You have such pretty sapphire eyes, but you're so dirty."

"Thank you." She ventured a hesitant smile.

The older girl stood and led her out of the room. The door turned out to be unlocked, much to Althea's surprise. They walked into a hallway with peeling wallpaper bedecked with little blue patterns on a white background. The place looked ancient, kept intact by an endless patchwork of repairs. Each section appeared in good condition, but the materials didn't match. Karina stopped in a small room with an elongated bowl big enough for a person to fit inside. A familiar strange white vase with a lid sat nearby. She had seen them before, but never one with clean water in it. When Althea stooped to drink from it, the older girl grabbed her by the chest cloth and pulled her back.

Karina made a face like she prepared to vomit. "That's a toilet! We don't drink from that. It's for doing your business."

"What's business?"

Karina explained.

"Why would you waste water by doing that to it?" Althea blinked.

"The water takes the mess out of the house, so we don't have to dig holes."

Karina twisted a metal thing on the wall by the long bowl. A pipe sticking out of the tile belched water, which began to fill the vessel.

The astounded look on Althea's face made Karina laugh.

"Wait here." She tapped Althea on the nose and walked out.

The running liquid proved too tempting. Althea leaned over the big bowl and put her face in the flow, gulping down her fill. Karina returned with two large pails of steaming water and almost dropped them laughing at the sight. After shutting off the faucet, she poured the buckets into the giant basin and smiled.

"You are filthy. Before you eat, we have to clean you up. Do you know what a bath is?"

"Yes." She answered with a polite tone. Now the big bowl made sense, despite not looking at all like the metal tubs she had seen before. "Is this for me?"

"Mm hmm." Karina nodded. "I'll give you some priv—"

Althea hooked her thumbs under her skirt and shoved it over her hips to the floor. She flung off her chest-cloth, stepped over the tub edge, and lowered herself into the warm water. Dirt stained it brown in seconds.

She glanced up at the shocked woman. "What's wrong?"

"I guess you don't want to be alone." Karina giggled.

Althea took the washcloth Karina handed her and bathed herself, ignoring the strange white block.

"Aren't you going to use the soap?" Karina knelt behind her, nudging the bar.

"Soap?" Althea blinked.

"Soap is what makes you clean." Karina took the small brick and rubbed it into the washcloth, making suds, then ran the cloth over Althea's shoulders while offering a sad smile. "Let me do your hair then. The bubbles hurt if you get them in your eyes."

"Okay."

While Althea played boat with the soap, Karina worked the lather into her hair. She rambled on about how pretty it looked and admitted a little jealousy of the bright blonde color. Althea stopped playing with the soap, overcome by the gentle caress upon her head plus the protective, caring emotion radiating from the young woman. After a minute or so, the combination grew too much and Althea burst into tears. The tenderness with which this woman treated her touched upon a nerve that had atrophied years ago, and made the past six hurt much more.

"What's wrong?" Karina leaned over.

Althea sniffled and sobbed, "You're nice."

"Why are you crying?"

"People aren't nice to me." She wiped at her face. "When I was little, a man kept me in a cage."

Karina pulled her into a hug, soapy hair and all, rocking her slightly side to side. "Why would anyone do such a horrible thing?"

Althea sniffled. "I'm the Prophet."

"You?" Karina asked, surprised. "I always pictured the Prophet as a man in a white robe with a beard." She laughed. "Esteban thinks it's a pretty woman with big boobs."

The sobbing sputtered into a giggle, but levity didn't last long. "He had a wagon, and took me all over the Badlands. He would make people give him pay things so I would help them. If they didn't, he would not let me help." Tears bored holes in the foam upon the opaque water. "Some died right in front of me."

"Aww." Karina cuddled her over the tub wall.

Althea stared at the thick layer of soap and dirt. "One day, men with guns refused to pay. They killed the Wagon Man and took me. People always take me away."

Karina resumed washing Althea's hair. "You're in Querq now. There are a lot of us here. We have an army. We will ask the council to let you stay if you like. You can be safe here."

Althea slid down into the water, resting her head against the porcelain and almost falling asleep. She looked at her toes poking up from the muck, and curled them over the far end of the tub. "I have to find Den."

"Who's that?" Karina scooped water into one of the pails. "Sit up, please, and keep your eyes shut."

Althea complied. Water fell over her, taking the soap out of her hair. "A boy. We were to be joined."

Karina worked the washcloth over her back. "Wed? How old are you, ten, maybe eleven? Oh, no. That's way too little."

Althea leaned forward and hugged her knees. "Twelve, I think."

"If that's true, you aren't eating enough. You're a stick." She smirked. "Sorry, I guess that's kind of mean if you were kidnapped."

"He is the son of Braga, the chief. The only boy who wasn't afraid of me." She closed her eyes, adoring the feeling of being cared for.

Karina stroked her hair. "I see. Well, the Badlands are a big place. We can ask the council, but I think you will be happier here with us."

Althea shivered. "Am I..."

Karina gently squeezed her shoulder. "No, Althea. You are free to leave if you wish, but you should stay. You're too little to be out there on your own."

She poured another bucket of water over Althea's head, sending the last bits of soap from her hair sliding down her back, and moved to leave.

Althea sat up, reaching. "Don't stop..."

Karina couldn't resist the desperation in her tone, and repeated the hair-washing process. "If you'd like to stay, we could be sisters. Would you like to be my sister?"

Althea picked at her fingernails under the water. "We don't have the same mother."

"That doesn't matter. You need a family, and we have room."

Althea looked up into the girl's brown eyes, sensing genuine warmth. She lifted a hand out of the muck, clasping Karina's, and leaned almost nose to nose with her. "I would like that... to have a sister."

She stood. "Come on, dry off now and let's go get something to eat."

Althea climbed out of the tub and started for the door, but a hand on her arm arrested her nymph walk.

"Hey, where are you going?"

"Outside to dry off." She blinked at Karina, confused.

Another lesson followed: how to use a towel. According to Karina, only Scrags living out in the weeds air-dried. She considered this to be civilization, and people didn't do such things here. Althea thought it silly to be embarrassed, but offered no protest.

Once she had dried herself, she dressed and followed Karina out into the hallway.

"We'll need to get you some proper clothes."

"I like it." She clung to the leather tatters. "I made it."

Karina shook her head. "You're too old for a security blanket."

Althea stopped walking and smirked at Karina as if she were dumb. "This is a skirt, not a blanket."

"You're too much!" Karina laughed and hugged her.

She led Althea to the kitchen where a man sat at a battered table with three place settings laid out. Similarity in their features told Althea they had to be related. Most likely father and daughter.

A thick black moustache spanned his wide face, and his flannel shirt resembled the sleeping bag guts she had slept in at the raider camp. She sat in the chair Karina pulled out for her, and noticed blue cloth covering his legs. His familiar scent confirmed this man had found her in the woods.

Sensing no malice in his thoughts, merely a raised eyebrow at her glowing eyes, Althea smiled at him. "Thank you for helping me."

"You look like a different person without all the dirt." He smiled.

She stared, bewildered by the presence of a man who didn't look at her as some kind of prize. The genuine kindness that lingered in the tiny wrinkles around his eyes stole the words from her mouth.

They ate eggs and some meat cut into thin strips. Karina sent odd looks her way as she picked up her food with her hands, but said nothing about it. Her hosts conversed in Spanish here and there over the meal. Althea grasped enough to understand Karina asked her father if she could stay with them. After they finished breakfast, they left the house together and walked along a white stone path. The area resembled the Lost Place, but less run down. Karina told a story of how the place had once been a massive city, and only a small fragment of it remained. Their people had found it and built it up, creating a wall around the inner parts.

On the way to the center of Querq, Father introduced her to passing people. They paused by a garage where several men covered in grease set about keeping cars working. These men made the fuel the machines ate in small quantities, so the people used them only used for emergencies. Karina's father knew one of the men, and wanted to bring Althea to see him. He had been with the group that found her, and had asked about her health.

When they left that place, they passed under a large hanging sign where two roads crossed. The greater part of it consisted of plain, shiny metal where the paint had shattered away around ancient bullet holes, and the entire left end had cracked off. A little right of center, a strip of green remained with white symbols on it. Karina explained it read as the name of the city, 'Querq,' but Althea thought the scrap of metal was far too long for such a short sound. She also didn't understand how funny markings turned into speaking.

She held her new sister's hand as they walked, stepping on dirt or grass whenever possible to evade the hot white path. Other citizens came out of homes ranging from houses like Karina's to dwellings that looked like they used to be cars or trucks no longer able to move.

Querq was an island of life in an ocean of destruction; to the north and east, the skeletal remains of ancient towers loomed, covered in nature's attempt to reclaim the Earth. A foreboding evil wafted about the crumbling mass of steel and concrete, as if the decay itself stared into her heart. The sight struck Althea with a sudden, somber quiet. She hid her face against Karina's side.

"What's wrong?" The older girl patted her on the back.

Althea pointed at the crumbling blight.

"She can feel the death upon the old buildings," said Father in English while offering a comforting glance. "Such sadness in your eyes, child."

Althea looked up at him. "Yours are sad, too."

He straightened, gazing off over the horizon.

Karina leaned forward and whispered with her cheek against Althea's head. "My mother died trying to have my brother. We lost them both. He never talks of it."

Althea's heart sank. She bowed her head. When she reached out and grasped his hand, he twitched as if startled, then looked down at her with a melancholy smile. A minute passed in silence as they stood at the corner of an old street.

"Well." Father took in a breath. "The council is waiting. We should go."

THE RAVENS PERCHED

Father and Karina brought her to a white building where she met a man they called Doctor Ruiz. He gasped at her glowing eyes, astonished, and wanted to see her right away. After following them to a room inside, Althea sat in obedient quiet while he poked and prodded her with various bits of cold metal, asked her to take deep breaths, shone lights in her ears and mouth, and bonked her in the knee with a little hammer. She didn't much care for the thing that went around her arm, hissing in puffs as it tightened, but he took it off before she could complain.

She giggled when he ran a finger over her spine and tapped her back. After asking her to touch her toes and stand up slow, he guided her to step onto a wobbly slab and played with some little weights on a sliding bar. Clucking his tongue, he indicated the exam table again and she climbed onto it once more with her legs hung over the edge.

"You are undernourished and small for your age." He glanced at his papers.

Althea smirked at him. "I know that and I'm not a doctor."

"Have they always been like this?" He shone the little light right in her eyes.

She squinted, trying to blink away the dancing firefly that lingered in her vision. "Yes."

"I've never seen anything like this. Do you have any problems seeing?"

"When it's dark, there is no color." She kicked her feet back and forth, staring at him.

He drew the blinds, making the room dim. "Can you still see color?"

"Yes. Not dark like this. Dark like dark."

"Darker than this?"

"Yes." She slid off the exam table and walked into a small closet, pulling the door closed behind her. "Dark like this."

"You can see in there?" Dr. Ruiz sounded amazed.

"Yes. No color."

He opened the door long enough to hand her a dingy piece of laminated paper with funny marks on it, and pushed it closed. "Read the first line please. I'd like a little proof."

There was a long pause. "I can't."

He smiled. "Okay, Althea. It's fine. You don't need to make up stories. We will welcome you anyway."

"I don't know how to read. I can see a picture of a baby in a circle on this bucket, with a line over it." Althea pondered the image for a few seconds. "Why would someone put a baby in a bucket?"

When no one replied, she opened the door and peeked out.

Karina, her father, and the doctor exchanged glances. The doctor almost fainted when she spoke to him telepathically.

Someone told me I'm sighmonic.

"Umm." He struggled to regain his composure. "Aside from malnutrition, she's perfectly healthy. I will not object to letting her stay. I'd love to do a blood analysis, but the machines we have here are too old."

Althea stood in silence, her head going back and forth as the adults talked. They had gone to Spanish and words came too fast for her to bother trying to listen. She paced about the room, touching the strange drawings of people with no skin and all those things called words, wondering if the bizarre pictures were how doctors saw the life-shapes.

A loud, wet cough drew her attention to a door. She wandered out into a stagnant corridor, away from the meaningless din between the grown-ups. Tracing her fingers along the wall as she walked, she passed a woman in white who smiled at her and almost dropped a tray full of small paper cups upon noticing the blue light.

The sound of the coughing pulled her along a hallway the color of sand, the floor shiny, smooth, and cold. Windows on her left flooded the area with daylight, creating large squares of warmth upon which she walked. The woman in white had abandoned whatever she had been doing to follow her, but remained back a short distance. Althea peeked around the wall, staring at a silver-haired man lying in a bed. The tiny room reeked of sick, despite the billowing curtains waving in the breeze from the open window.

"Don't go in there, child. He has TB." The woman reached for her.

Althea ducked the grasping hand and darted over to him.

"Doctor Ruiz!" the nurse yelled.

The man wheezed and lifted his sweat-covered face to smile at her. "I suppose that's it, then. Sure as hell took you long enough. Let's get it over wi—" He struggled to speak, but succumbed to a coughing fit.

Althea clasped his hairy arm with both hands, pulling it against her body with his fingers brushing her cheek. The nurse's shouts grew blurry in her consciousness as the indistinct shapes of the man's essence filled her thoughts. Something black and evil shifted in the center, orbiting his heart like a buzzard waiting for its meal to die. She focused, screaming in her mind at the blackness, ordering it to get out. It recoiled from her, flying up and away from the beating life-shape. When it tore loose from where it lurked, she sensed a hurt inside him. The darkness refused to leave easy. Blood pooled in his air-bags. She channeled more power into him, compelling his body to repair itself.

When she opened her eyes, the man rolled to his side and vomited a vile mass of glistening grey slime, tinged with venous streaks of indigo and blood. The doctor ran in and seized her by the forearms, ready to drag her out of the room. He froze at the sight of the slime on the floor and the man's color returning.

Althea looked up at Dr. Ruiz and pointed at the pulsating, gooey thing. "Put that in fire. It will make others sick. This man will need food."

The nurse made the sign of the cross and backed into the corridor, muttering. Karina's jaw hung open. Father, stoic as ever, took it all in stride. Althea stood in place, watching the doctor scramble to destroy the sick. The nurse returned with food, and the man looked markedly better in minutes. The now-healthy elder muttered something in Spanish and smiled at Althea.

Doctor Eduardo Ruiz had seen many things in his life, but this left him speechless. Althea tried to answer his questions about what she did. The look on his face said her descriptions of red and black shapes and a 'sick' living in his air-bags would have left him patting her on the head with a patronizing smile if what she did hadn't actually worked.

Karina took her hand, guiding her out of the room, leaving the stunned doctor to tend to the man.

"Karina?" Althea looked up as they went outside.

"Yes?"

"What did that man say right before we left?"

The older girl shrugged. "He apologized for thinking you were someone else."

By that time, word had spread and a crowd waited outside the clinic. More than a hundred formed a line, including numerous children. Most of the men had rifles, but none at the ready. Althea clung to Karina's side at the sight of so many faces. The older girl threaded a protective arm around her, and Althea smiled up at her new sister.

The gathering fell in around them as they took her into the center of town where more armed men walked patrols. Althea glanced at two trucks that looked as if they could still drive, parked in front of an imposing building at the center of a square. Huge guns sat upon posts in the back, the men behind them waved at her and smiled. Beyond the trucks, a stone pedestal crumbled into a heap of ivory bits. A statue had been there long ago, but aside from rubble, only one stony leg from boot to knee remained standing.

Father led her past stairs and down a hallway to a large chamber with a vault ceiling covered in flaking plaster. Small sculptured babies posed around the edge of where the ceiling met the wall, most with broken wings, and some headless. Althea walked among rows of old, red-cushioned chairs, down a narrow path to a hollow space of bare floor in front of a counter as tall as Father. She craned her head back to peer up at five people seated way up high, two women and three men.

Billowy black robes obscured their figures, and they cast shadows upon the wall behind them like gargantuan crows perched along a fence. Little blocks of dented wood in front of each one had scrawled words. Every noise made in here echoed.

They looked down at her. She shrank back against Karina, feeling small, a tiny savage among an army of civilized men. She managed a weak smile, sensing their curiosity. The crowd flowed liquid into the aisle-veins, soaked up by the waiting chairs.

"We are here in the matter of Fernando Guererro's petition to accept a foundling Scrag into the community." The man in the center appraised her. "Is this said foundling?"

Father nodded. "Yes, your honors."

"Hello, child. What is your name?" The man smiled with grandfatherly charm.

"Althea." She looked down, shying away from the blackbirds. "Some call me the Prophet, but I don't like it."

A murmur spread over the crowd behind her.

When asked where she came from and where her parents were, she recounted her tale of being stolen at the age of six from a village long forgotten, and how she had been abducted over and over again ever since. The traveling salesman who spent years dragging her around in a cage had made sure all the Badlands knew her and what she could do, and now she paid for it. She didn't really know her exact age. Twelve was her best guess.

Raiders didn't care about things like birthdays.

The council made faces at each other. She sensed pity and anger, as well as the predictable anticipatory glee. Althea felt grateful Karina had remained at her back with a hand on each shoulder, and leaned into her while staring at the globs of reflected light that swam across the shiny floor. Glittering specks fanned out in a radial pattern under the gloss, frozen in material the color of rust. Stone, she assumed, from how cold it was under her feet.

"Karina is nice. I don't want your people to get hurt because of me."

A male judge with a nose like a bird's beak smiled, thin lips curling back in an attempt to be friendly. "Raiders are not much of a threat to us, child. Our army is four hundred strong and growing with each generation." He rambled on about things like tactics, strategy, and technology, but most of it went over her head.

"What do you want to be when you grow up? What can you contribute to our town?" The woman on the far left cleared her throat before and after she spoke.

"I can help people," she said, smiling.

The judges, and some in the crowd, chuckled.

"That's very admirable." The grey-haired woman forced a smile, though her tone came off condescending. "How do you help people?"

"I make the hurts stop and the sicks go away." Her plain tone set the council abuzz.

Doctor Ruiz stood up from his seat in the crowd, and testified about what she had done moments before. Althea had never heard such big words before: 'tuberculosis' sounded funny, as did 'expunged.' She stifled a giggle.

Some voices called out, offering legend about the Prophet. A lot of it made Althea want to laugh at the exaggeration. One doubted the Prophet could be a mere child, another thought the Prophet was a man wearing a crown of thorns—he claimed to have seen a picture once.

"I can't see the future. I can't touch a cow and make it calf, and I can't make people live forever... but I can heal."

More laughter made her grin. She smiled at everyone, savoring Karina's embrace as the council pronounced their approval of her request to join the community. The ravens seemed to take strange delight in how she had no blood relation to anyone here.

The raider buggy had raced along for almost an entire day. The land here was dry and mostly barren, nothing like where Den's tribe lived. Althea's heart fell at the thought she would never see him again, but Karina's touch comforted her. She may have liked Den, but the rest of his tribe viewed her with a mixture of fear and distrust.

Althea smiled and leaned against her new family.

Querq would be an excellent home.

A NEW LIFE

F lickering candles on the table sent wobbly shadows cavorting around the walls. Father had made a thing he called an enchilada, and set it on a plate in front of her. She sniffed at the food as if studying found treasure. When Karina arrived and everyone had a plate, Althea snatched up the hot, gooey thing with both hands and bit down on the most amazing taste she had ever known.

Her eyes lifted, sensing the silence. Father and Karina stared. She looked shocked and he seemed amused. Althea pulled the soggy food log away from her face, chewing with hesitant bites while shifting her gaze back and forth between them.

When she tore another piece away from it with her teeth, Karina blurted, "What are you doing?"

"Eating," Althea muttered past a mouthful of food.

"Enchiladas aren't finger food. You're making a mess!"

Father chuckled. "She's wild, hon. She doesn't know any better."

Karina moved around behind her and shook her arm until she dropped the enchilada back on the plate. After wiping her hands clean with a cloth, she gave a quick lesson on how to use a knife and fork. Father covered his mouth to hide his laughter at the faces Althea made. Leaving her to attempt the awkward task, Karina returned to her chair and demonstrated.

Trying to eat with a fork frustrated Althea. The small portion of food kept falling back to the plate. She stabbed at it like a spear, mashing it into bits. Despite Karina's gentle encouragement, after five minutes, the fork and knife went flying over her shoulder and she had the enchilada in a two-fisted grip again, stuffing her face.

Father laughed, no longer able to contain it. Karina stood, but he waved her off. When she finished all her food, Althea licked her hands clean and then the plate.

"*Ella come como un perro, padre.*" Karina shot a flat look at her father.

"*Tomará tiempo.*"

Karina looked at Althea, shaking her head. "We need to get you some real clothes."

Althea frowned. "I like this clothes!" She clung to her skirt defensively. "It won't break when I run and swim. Your clothes would."

"Oh, you don't have to run for your life anymore." Karina ran a hand through Althea's hair. Without all the dirt, it hung straight and neat.

"She is still feral, Kari. It is going to take her time to adjust. You should not rush her along."

"What is feral?" Althea looked over at him.

He leaned back in his seat, exhaling. "The way you have lived, without parents, without schooling... like a wild thing."

"Oh." Althea shrugged.

"At least let me find you a new shirt. That thing is going to fall apart, and you are getting too old to run around without a top." She ruffled her hair.

"Den gave me this." She bunched a fistful of the tattered cloth over her heart.

"It's pre-war. It has holes in it and its barely hanging on. It's only a shirt, and it's not even a whole one... just a scrap of cloth."

Althea's gaze sank to the strip of metal around the table reflecting the glow in her eyes. Like Den, the shirt wouldn't last forever. She wondered if the harem girls had been right. Had he already forgotten her? "Okay."

"Tomorrow, I'll make chorizo so you can practice with the fork." Karina patted her on the head. "C'mon, help me with the dishes."

Father gathered his things and went out to hunt. Other men waited in a group by the porch, greeting him with smiles, nods, and shoulder patting. The girls gathered the dirty plates, forks, and cups from the table, leaving them in the sink while they went out back. Karina carried the metal tray of embers from the stove to the burning bin behind the house and added small pieces of scrap wood. One pail of warmed water would be enough for the dishes.

As they sat in the fluttering orange glow, Karina told stories of suburbs, of backyards, and of houses. She spoke of this thing called 'electricity' that could make light in the darkness and water magically hot from the sink. The elders had tried to find this mystical thing, but so far had not been able to.

The water still came out of the tubes, but only cold. When Karina was younger than Althea, she had to drag buckets of water to the house from the middle of town. Now, they only did that when the pipes stopped working. Wisps of steam circled the top of the pail and the embers threatened to die out; the water had become as warm as it could without using more wood.

Once more inside, they stood at the sink, Karina elbow-deep in foaming water and working a cloth over the plates. Althea took each one from her in turn, drying it and setting it in a neat stack on the counter. According to Karina, this ritual, 'doing the dishes,' once happened all the time.

"Why use plates if you just have to wash them?" She took a cup and worked the towel around it.

With a chuckle, Karina shook her head. "Because, that is how people eat."

"My magic knife was stolen." Althea put the dry cup on the counter next to the plates.

"Father is keeping it safe. Little girls don't need such things. You can ask him for it when you're older."

Althea glowered at the indignant frown that reflected at her from the pale green plate she dried. Being called a little girl felt insulting at first, but here, she didn't need to go fishing, or hide from people who wanted to steal her. She'd found an entirely new world.

"Well, that's the last of them." Karina stuck her arm into the water and pulled the stopper. "Want me to show you how to braid your hair?" She grinned.

"Will it hurt?" Althea blinked.

"No, silly." She drew in a breath to continue, but stopped at a heavy banging at the front of the house.

Althea jumped at the noise and crawled into the cabinet under the sink, trembling. Edging away from the doors, she crawled deeper, around old rusted cans and numerous startled insects. Thinking someone had already come to take her, she cried. Karina's muttering grew faint as she walked out to see who had come to visit.

She expected Karina's scream any second, but instead, a frantic man erupted, shouting *"Luisa se está muriendo! Luisa se está muriendo!"* He quieted to an indistinct murmur.

Footfalls on the kitchen floor thudded closer. Althea cowered against the wall. The doors flew open, revealing Karina crouched and extending a hand.

"Easy. Hey there, calm down. No one will hurt you."

Althea sniffled and relaxed, having sensed no alarm in the older girl's mood. She let Karina pull her out into the light and stood. A man, younger than Father, waited in the doorway, grinding a denim hat between his hands. He gave off great alarm and worry. She knew right away someone he loved was in danger.

"Felipe's wife, Luisa... She's having a baby and it's not going well." Karina cried, remembering her mother.

Althea ran to him eagerly, all traces of fear gone. "Take me to her."

Karina tugged her along by the hand, following the man down the streets of Querq to a boxy once-vehicle serving as a house. A small crowd gathered outside, chanting in Spanish, and some held candles. Doctor Ruiz's yelling pierced the thin walls. The crowd parted for her, and she ran ahead under a faded blue canvas awning, up the folding metal steps, and inside.

A woman lay on the kitchen table amid an array of blankets and pillows, swollen with the presence of an unborn baby. She had Karina by a few years, and dripped with sweat. People swarmed over her in a panic while Ruiz rambled on about not having this or that. The nurse she'd seen before dabbed at blood where it welled out of the pregnant woman. Felipe ran past Althea to hold his wife's hand. Luisa had taken on a pallid complexion and appeared only vaguely aware of his presence.

Ruiz looked up, holding a large knife darkened by candle fire. Seeing Althea, his emotions faltered between relief and jealousy.

"She has lost a lot of blood; I don't think..." He stopped when her husband glared at him.

Althea put her hands on the distended belly and linked her power to the woman's life essence. The shapes formed in her mind, both the woman's as well as those of the infant.

"The baby is pointed wrong." Althea opened her eyes. "He is upside down."

The man squeezed his wife's hand. "You hear that, Luisa! It's a boy!"

Ruiz grumbled and nodded, hovering over her with the knife.

"Don't hurt her," Althea blurted.

He froze. "I can get the baby out. It's called a Caesarian section."

She had never heard that before, but did remember seeing a knife used in a birthing once. Nothing about his presence radiated malice, so she relented.

"If you... I dunno, if you can do anything for Luisa, do it. I'll handle the baby." His tone implied he already considered the woman a lost cause.

Luisa cried out, arching her back and lapsing into a violent shudder before falling still with a vacant stare at the ceiling. Felipe wailed. Ignoring the chaos around her, Althea leapt forward and grabbed the woman's side, forcing power into the shapeless forms in her mind. The shouting around her muted as if her head had gone underwater. Luisa's heart-shape was still and unmoving—it had stopped. Althea felt the life wanting to slip away, anchored only where her hands touched the woman's belly.

The heart-shape hadn't been idle too long to save. She would not allow Luisa to give up. Althea pressed her fingers in, emitting a diminutive grunt while wrestling with Luisa's torn energies. The blood-presence surged in response to Althea commanding the woman's body to create more.

Telepathically, she spoke in a loud authoritative tone. *No Luisa, not yet. You are too young.*

A single heartbeat rolled like thunder over their linked consciousness.

She shuddered, focusing on the heart-shape, wanting it to resume beating. The heart thumped once more, and a second and third time, picking up speed until it beat at the rate it should. Althea focused on small rips and tears surrounding the infant that allowed the blood-presence to go places it didn't belong.

Luisa's body mended. A slice above the unborn baby opened, divided in a neat line spreading from left to right. With a hamster's growl, Althea concentrated and forced it closed. Again, it ruptured and again she mended it.

"Kid..." Ruiz's voice pierced the depths; the noise of the room flooded in. He sounded uneasy. "Hey kid..."

Althea looked up. "I'm not finished."

Luisa raised one arm. Her husband ceased sobbing and grabbed her hand.

Ruiz looked as though he'd seen a ghost. "I'm trying to cut the baby out and the skin is sealing behind the knife." He pointed at three red lines across her stomach, blood trails with no wound. "Let me get the child out first."

She offered a weak smile. "I'm sorry."

"Luisa should be bleeding from this..." He looked at the incision, speaking with grim finality. "She must have lost so—"

"I'm telling her not to bleed." Althea exhaled, concentrating on keeping Luisa's blood-shape inside her. "Hurry up."

With a skilled touch, he cut the woman open and extracted a healthy baby boy. As soon as he pulled the infant clear of his mother, Althea closed her eyes and redoubled her effort. The chaotic rush of the real world faded, her consciousness plunged into placid darkness. She sent forth a surge of psionic power, her fingers ablaze with tingles. After mending damage, causing another surge in blood production, and controlling Luisa's heart-shape back to normal speed, she swooned into the table from the exertion. Althea's senses re-entered the outside world. She propped herself up on her arms and gasped for air.

Color returned to Luisa's skin. No sign of any incision remained. Felipe scooped Althea up into a fierce hug and wept on her shoulder. She couldn't understand his rapid Spanish, but the overwhelming gratitude radiating from him made language unnecessary. He set Althea in a chair, then doted on his wife while the women cleaned Luisa up and covered her with a blanket before placing the wailing infant in her arms.

Ruiz flopped into a chair next to her, offering her a towel to clean her hands. He looked at her for a moment, still appearing to struggle with what he had seen. "Nice work."

Althea smiled at the baby. "You too."

26

QUERQ

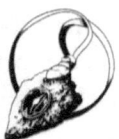

Althea examined the new garment, turning to look at herself and tugging at the clean white cloth. Karina had found this thing she called a 'tank top' for her; it fit snug to her chest and left her shoulders open. The rag Den gave her went into a drawer. She would keep it to remember him even if she no longer wore it, but she'd keep the skirt as long as she could. It suffered the rigors of the Badlands better than cloth. She knew she would eventually grow out of it, and hoped by then she could trust fate to let her keep this new life.

Father called. Time for breakfast. Today, Althea tried to use the fork thing, but grew frustrated by the food slipping off more often than it made it to her mouth. Karina drew her into her lap and helped, holding her hand and working the infernal device for her until she started to get the hang of it. They laughed, and for an ephemeral moment, Althea didn't think of herself as anything more than an ordinary girl.

After dishes, Karina had to go away for a time to something she called a 'job.' Everyone over the age of fifteen had a task assigned to them, a necessary thing to keep Querq prospering. Althea decided to wander the city. Doctor Ruiz suggested her 'job' eventually be with him, learning what he called medicine. The concept sounded alien to her, but it involved helping others, so she hadn't objected. An official job would wait until she became a little older, and a lot caught up on how to be 'civilized.'

For now, the council decreed she should enjoy the last bits of her childhood.

The morning passed in a blur of screaming children and strange games. Most of the kids here treated her nice and invited her to join them in play. The small ones were happy in a way Althea had forgotten how to be, and those her age or slightly older regarded her with reverence. She lost herself in the frolic of youth, her bliss interrupted only briefly by tending to the occasional scuffed knee.

After a time, the children dispersed, each back to their respective homes, and her wander resumed. The townspeople all doted on her, some even bowing or blessing themselves as she went by. Althea felt awkward at their adulation, offering polite smiles and asking those able to understand her to treat her like a normal person.

Querq was bigger than she thought, and roaming it for most of the day left her tired. Streets, backyards, and dried-out swimming pools all ran together into a blur of disorientation. She sat on the curb to catch her breath. Closing her eyes, she leaned back and let the sun fall on her face. The shouts of distant small children filled the air, interspersed with the occasional raised voice from one of the watchmen reporting an all clear.

A din of shouting came out of the murk of ambient noise, growing louder and louder from two men ranting, lost in some manner of dispute. Curious, she jumped up and ran across the street, ducking past a gap in a piecemeal wooden fence into a yard. Among a mess of pipes and metal scraps, a pair of men yelled and waved their fists at each other. The one on the left had white hair, the second man much younger, with black hair.

"Why are you so loud?" Her innocent question stalled them both in mid-argument.

"Juan has taken the voltage regulator from one of the water purifiers for his mechanical gate." The older man pointed at a machine that looked more like a stack of random junk.

"Bullshit, old man. I never touched it. The gate motor is still missing the regulator."

"That's because you hid it until I stopped looking for it."

"Why is that blinking?" Althea pointed at flashing orange light inside a rusting metal box. The machinery within chugged with a labored thrumming.

"It's running hot, gonna burn out without the regulator, and we're all gonna be drinkin' shitwater," the white-haired man yelled even louder.

Juan waved his arms up and down, pacing. "I did not."

Althea peered into the accused man's thoughts, finding no trace of memory indicating he had taken it. "He didn't do it."

"The hell you say?" the older man stammered, no longer yelling.

He didn't do it, said Althea telepathically. *You just don't like him because he wed your daughter.*

The man babbled and looked at Juan who had folded his arms in an 'I told you so' stance. Spanish muttering followed. Althea understood it as an apology.

"While you two fighted each other, the pump broke more. You're both being stupid and risking everyone getting a sick."

The older man pressed his fists to his hips and scowled at the dirt. After a few seconds, he nodded. They both resumed searching for the missing part. She strolled out of their yard and went down the street. A passing member of the Watch spun on his heel when he spotted her, and came jogging over.

"Althea," he yelled.

She stopped, resisting her instinct to tremble and back away from a man with a gun coming toward her. She stood her ground, but stared at her toes.

"Althea, there you are," he said, out of breath. "Karina has been searching for you."

"Oh!" Althea looked up, all traces of fear evaporated. "I…" She glanced around. "I don't know where I am."

"Come, I will take you home."

She took his hand, letting him lead her along the coarse white path.

"It is wonderful to have you here with us." He smiled at the clouds. "Do you like it here in Querq?"

Althea nodded. "Yes, but I wish people would stop bowing to me. I'm just a girl."

The watchman chuckled. "Aye."

After two blocks, Karina's distant calls for her pierced the ambient noise. Althea ran ahead, pivoted back to smile and wave at the watchman, and hooked right at the next street. She spotted her sister standing tiptoe on the front porch, her skin dark against a long yellow dress. Althea yelled and jumped; the white of a smile appeared on Karina's face. Racing down the street, she bounded up the steps and into a strong hug that lifted and spun her around once before her feet again made contact with the painted wood.

"Where have you been?"

"Querq. I got lost." Althea looked down. "I'm sorry."

Karina pulled her in the door. "Come on, we have things to do."

With the last bits of remaining daylight, Althea helped with household chores. She reveled in the normality of it, despite it being work. As a prized pet, she never did anything but sit around and heal people. Helping out around the house made her feel like part of a family.

Father waited at the table since it was Karina's turn to cook. She attempted to teach Althea the art of making a tortilla. Later, flour covered them both, and Father's mood had improved. The life she brought into their home had pulled him somewhat out of the doldrums he'd been stuck in after the loss of his wife. Though she respected his need for grief, it had been four years. Althea prodded him ever so slightly with a cheer up.

With the dishes done, Karina sat behind her on the back porch steps and brushed her hair to the glow of a lantern and many peals of laughter. After a while, Father stumbled into the doorway, a silent, pointing golem of deprived sleep. Stifling their snickers, the girls ducked under his arm and went off to their shared bed. Karina had given her a white cotton thing to sleep in that no longer fit her. On Althea, it hung down to her shins. She studied it before sitting on the edge of the bed.

"I can't run in this."

Karina laughed. "It's not for running. It's for sleeping. It's called a nightgown."

Althea brushed her hand over the material. "It's soft. Like a blanket with arm holes."

They both giggled.

"Hush before Daddy gets mad at us. He needs to sleep." Karina held the covers up so she could climb in.

ALTHEA WOKE WITH THE SUN, LYING ON HER SIDE WITH KARINA CLINGING to her as if clutching a large doll. The sun breached the line of earth, sliding into the sky and tinting the horizon outside the window orange. Althea clasped her hands over the arm encircling her chest. The 'nightgown' proved stifling in its warmth, but she kept still, at ease with the loving presence of family.

When Father knocked at the wall to wake them, Karina stirred in her sleep, squeezing her tight. Althea squirmed at the warm breath down the back of her neck and patted Karina's arm to rouse her. The girl didn't move until Father entered and gave her shoulder a gentle nudge. He hugged both girls as they clambered out of bed. Leaving them to dress, Father headed to the kitchen. Moments later, a loud clamor of pots and pans rang out.

Freedom from the nightgown came over her like a pleasant autumn breeze. Much to Karina's discomfort, Althea stood for a moment with nothing on, fanning herself before reaching for her day clothes. Once again, Karina tried to convince her to discard the pile of tatters. Althea put it on anyway, followed by her new white 'tank top.'

While tightening some of the knots in the leather, she spoke without looking up. "It fits me better."

"I have other things that would fit you."

Althea checked the skirt, turning in the mirror. "Before-time clothes fall apart if they become wet or if you get grabbed." She explained how people only wore what they found on scavenging trips, and those who didn't scavenge only had what others abandoned or gifted to them, like the chest-cloth.

Karina pulled her into a hug, patting her on the back. "It's okay, Thea. I know you miss him, but that life is behind you now. You're safe here."

It surprised her not to feel like crying thinking about him. At the village, only Den seemed to trust her. Most feared her, the *chamán* tolerated her, and Palik went back and forth between wanting to kill or cage her. Here, everyone adored her. This place, this family, felt safe as though not even being the Prophet could ruin it. She peered up at Karina and asked with an impish smile if she ever liked a boy.

"I was sweet on Dominguez, but the council disallowed it. The boy they said I could marry is an asshole." She grumbled.

Althea blinked. The face she made at the literal interpretation of the unfamiliar slang made Karina laugh herself gasping. The attempted explanation of the meaning only confused Althea more and she settled for the simpler explanation the word meant he was not a nice person.

"They tell you who to marry?" Althea tilted her head.

Karina smoothed her hands over her dress. "There are only six hundred or so people here. We have to be careful to avoid inbreeding."

"Huh?"

"If people too close to family have a baby, it will not be healthy." Karina described some of the things Dr. Ruiz had said about what happens.

Althea listened, thinking it fit her memories of malformed raiders and other sub-vocal horrors she had seen. Karina explained that to prevent problems, the Council kept records of families and relations.

"Oh. Yes. Inbeading is bad." Althea thought for a minute, furrowing her brow at Karina's giggles. "What do the words mean on those bits of wood?"

"Those are their judge-names."

Thinking about how battered the blocks appeared, Althea's eyes widened. "Wow, they must be very old."

Karina laughed. "No, the judge-names are very old. The judges are not so old. When a judge dies, a new one takes the judge-name."

"Maybe a new one will let you wed?"

"I'm high on the list for outsiders if we get a new man around here." Karina giggled.

"What if he's an asshole?" Althea asked innocently.

Karina burst into peals of laughter, which soon infected Althea.

Gunfire rippled in the distance. Althea screamed and tried to run, but Karina dove with her onto the bed, holding her by the wrists. Althea squirmed, gaze darting about in search of a hiding place, reason lost to feral panic. Karina, shocked she had such trouble containing a malnourished twig of a child, rolled on top of her to keep holding her down.

"Althea!" Karina's fifth shout pierced the veil of terror.

She stopped struggling, breathing in rapid gasps, staring at Father who appeared in the door.

He reached the bed in two strides. "What happened?"

Sensing the fight leave her, Karina relaxed her grip and sat up. "Gunfire outside... It scared her wild."

"They're coming," Althea wailed, leaping to cling to Father.

"Relax, child." His hand cradled her head to his chest. "It is just the hunters gathering food. The shots are too few to mean raiders."

She looked up at him and then blushed at the floor.

He patted her back. "Do not be ashamed, girl. You have had a hard life."

Father talked on the way to the kitchen. Althea had no idea what 'prey instinct' meant or why she had it, if she should keep it, or if she should discard it like the chest cloth. He figured she would grow out of it. She sat on a tattered old chair with a blown-out red cushion that felt like thin leather over a board and stared down.

It started with the gunshots, a haunting feeling this would not last. She received no phantom vision like when she dreamed Den would die, merely a twisting discomfort in the deepest part of her gut. She didn't want to tell them why she picked at her food. People believed the Prophet saw the future. If she spoke a word of this, they might take it for truth rather than her insecurity. Was it? Could bandits take her away from this place, away from her family?

"They can try," she muttered in a cold, stern voice that didn't sound like her.

"What's that?" Father looked up from his plate.

Karina blinked, having sensed the wave of rage. Her voice sounded hesitant, almost trembling. "Are you okay?"

The defiant mask melted to her usual smile. "Yes. Sorry. I had bad dreams."

27

FEVER DREAM

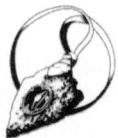

Knocking.

Father went to the door. A moment after, the worried voice of another man floated in from the living room. Althea overheard enough to understand his daughter, Corinne, had gone missing and he wanted the Prophet to find her. The two men returned to the kitchen, the guest declined an offer of food. Althea's suspicion of a trick disappeared when she read genuine worry from him. Dread clung to him like a garment.

"If she is hurt I can help, but I have not seen her." She felt ashamed at being unable to offer anything, and lowered her gaze to the table.

"Prophet, please. You must be able to find her." He slid to his knees at her side, taking her hand.

"Sam, if she cannot do anything… You know how stories grow tall," said Father, his voice somber.

Althea wanted so much to be able to help him, but couldn't think of how. The man tugged desperately at her arm, jostling her back and forth. The agate pendant tapped against her chest. The touch of it gave her an idea. She looked up at him with a hopeful smile, and jumped to her feet.

"Do you have a thing she liked?" She held up the pendant so he could see.

The man thought, urgency clouding his mind. A moment later, he nodded. "Yes, she made a bracelet for her husband."

The four of them fast-walked six blocks to a small building made of rough beige stone with large windows. Fading words on the glass surrounded a circle of red and white splotches with a brown edge, one triangular piece separated from the rest. Inside, brick-colored floor tiles traced a path alongside a counter behind which wide metal doors hung open into blackened chambers repurposed as storage spaces. A handful of chairs identical to the ones from their kitchen piled against the wall. The floor bore the scars of a dozen bolted-down tables and booth seating, removed to allow the trappings of a home. Rope hung about here and there, draped with sheets to section the large area into smaller rooms.

At the center of it all, a young man paced a circle, pausing at their approach. Althea walked over to him and looked up into his eyes. As soon as he recognized her, he collapsed to his knees, bowed, and kissed the tops of her feet. She tensed with a startled squeal.

"What are you doing?" She tried to pull him up by his shirt.

Father intervened, lifting the man away from her.

"Praise the Prophet. She has come to help." The young man, no older than twenty, held his hands to the ceiling.

She squirmed with awkwardness. Two other villages in her past had treated her like this. One even carted her around on a hand-carried chair, refusing to let her touch the ground. Raiders had walked right in and grabbed her. No one lifted a finger to protect her, thinking it was her will to be taken away. Perhaps since she hadn't used her powers to defend herself, it *had* been her will.

"Get up. Please don't do that." She folded her arms. "You don't have to bow to me."

The man bowed three more times, offering a timid apology.

Althea stepped closer, taking hold of his arm and lacing her fingers around the braided leather bracelet. "She made this for you?"

"Yes." He put a hand on hers, holding her tight to his arm.

Closing her eyes, she rubbed the material, searching for any emotion embedded in it. Her focus deepened. Wooziness came on, then burning as if boiling water spilled in her lap. After a flash of light and a vision of brown rocks, the pain moved up into her stomach and grew stronger.

The hot flash of fever spread over her, followed by disorientation and icy cold on her legs. She whined at a sensation as though a sharp stone edge, slick with algae and cold with running water, raked across the sole of her right foot. A burst of agony exploded inside her shin, a broken bone. Icy coldness covered her, and her throat closed off, making her unable to breathe. When reality returned, she found herself sprawled on the ground.

Althea gasped and pushed herself up off the floor. A feeling like water lapping at her face persisted. She fought for breath, unable to decide between cradling the phantom cut on her foot or the burning between her legs. Karina and Father each took an arm and lifted her, looking worried.

"Are you okay? You just fainted." Karina wiped the tears from Althea's cheek.

She hadn't noticed them; pain drew them forth without thought. Her mind searched for words but she couldn't speak. Father carried her to the tattered green sofa and held her until the shaking subsided. Corinne's father and husband paced and muttered, exchanging anxious glances.

The security of Father's presence calmed her. After a few minutes, Althea's body reoriented itself to the here and now, leaving the vision-senses behind. She hugged him, and waved the worrying men over.

"She is sick." Althea put a hand over her bladder. "There is fire here. She has a sick and does not know the world around her as it really is. She walks a dream."

"Is she alive?" Sam gathered Althea's hands together and clung to them.

Althea offered a pained expression. "Yes. I think so, but she is in danger. There is water, very cold water. I think she fell into it. Her leg may be broken." She tapped her right shin.

"Where?" asked Father.

"Shallow, fast water full of rocks as big as my head. Square and sharp."

"Corinne has not been missing long enough to get far." Father squeezed her hand. "I know the place of which she speaks."

The young husband started for the door. "We must go now."

"Easy, Carlos." Sam patted his son-in-law on the shoulder.

"We cannot wait." He yanked the door open. "She is alone in the river. What if bandits find her?"

Althea looked at them, shivering. She understood the reason for the feeling she had earlier. They would insist on bringing her out to the river, out of the walls and safety of this place. The raiders would come and take her away from Karina and Father—and so it continued.

"Okay. We should go help her." Althea tried to remain stoic, but her face twisted as tears came.

"She feels Corrine's pain." Carlos sighed, bowing again and muttering in whispered Spanish.

Father carried her outside. She clung to him, in no state able to walk, wanting to savor her last few minutes with this family as much as she could. Men's voices shouted in a blur around her. Losing herself in his scent, Althea kept her face hidden in Father's jacket, and wept.

She would help this woman whatever the cost.

ALTHEA LOOKED UP AT GENTLE ROCKING.

She lay in the back of a truck like that awful man had driven, sitting in an open space behind a small cabin. Ten men accompanied them, all dressed in blue jeans and blotchy green shirts. Every one of them carried a rifle, though only two of the weapons appeared to be the same type. One resembled what Rachel called an 'M4' but a bit longer. The remainder of the rifles all had wood parts like the ones the raiders had who stole her from Den. Two other trucks, each with a dozen more men, rode on either side. The second truck carried a machine gun too large for anyone to hold, mounted on a post to which a standing man clung.

She put an arm over Father's shoulder, pulling herself up and looking at the ground. If bandits tried to take her, there would be death. Perhaps that is what she sensed, a battle rather than losing her family.

Althea shivered. What if Father was to die?

"Calm yourself, child." He kissed the top of her head.

"I don't want you to get hurt," she whispered. "Please be careful."

He smiled.

The man next to him slapped the side of the truck bed. "Fernando cannot be hurt. He is too stubborn for even Hell to want him."

All the men laughed.

The water she had seen raced past them, intermittent streaks of brown-green scrub shot past in the beige blur of the dirt. Metal, hot and smooth, caressed her legs with the grit of sand. The wind whipped her hair about. Someone ahead of them shouted, and the truck slowed to a stop. The men got out, but a hand on her shoulder held her back.

"Wait here, child." An unfamiliar man smiled at her. "We found her."

Althea ran to the front of the truck bed, climbing up the roll cage to peek over the roof. Standing on her toes, she watched the men approach a fluttering ribbon of coral-colored fabric in the water. Two stayed in the truck with her, six others surrounded it. She twisted left and right, searching the endless dust, but found no sign of raiders or bandits.

A wounded moan came from the woman. Althea pulled herself up, beckoned by the pain in Corrine's voice, but a hand clasped about her ankle kept her from leaping over the roof to run to her aid. She looked back at the man with a hurt expression, trying to squirm out of his grip.

He smiled. "Calm down, child. They will bring her to you."

She clung to the roll bar and tugged at her leg. "They are hurting her."

The dry calloused hand held her until the others carried Corrine to the back of the truck and laid her in a puddle of water. One did not need to be the Prophet to detect the presence of sickness on her. Bone protruded from her right shin, and she mumbled an incoherent ramble in words neither Spanish nor English.

Sam held her husband back, knowing he would get in the way. Althea fell to her knees by Corinne's side, placing her hands with care around the splintered bone. The sense of her energy flooded Althea's mind, torn blobs of color where the leg cracked and the bright yellow glow of infection shone from the center. Her moaning lessened as Althea blocked the woman's ability to feel pain. She scooted around to grab the broken limb with both hands.

Althea's heels skidded over the sandy truck bed as she pulled. Carlos couldn't watch, and cringed away. Grunting, she hauled at the foot until the jagged white slid back beneath the soft brown skin. The *squish* caused a cringe from most of the men. Father assured everyone Corinne couldn't feel a thing. Althea dove into the woman's life energy, reducing the voices of the men to meaningless sounds. A formless mass of red shades responded to her desires. Little shreds and free-floating scraps reintegrated into a whole bone.

Althea shifted to set her hands on Corinne's abdomen. The yellow presence of sick writhed in the non-space of her thoughts. Strand by strand, the ethereal tendrils it sent into the woman's body withdrew into a central mass as Althea purged the poison of infection from her blood. With a final grunt of exertion, she forced the entirety of it apart from the rest of the shapes and directed it into the bladder.

The aroma of death assaulted the air from a slimy purulent discharge pooling below the now-unconscious woman. Some of the men staggered away to avoid the smell, but Althea merely wrinkled her nose.

"Fekshun." She looked up at the men, remembering what she once heard someone call the fragrance.

Men brought buckets of water from the stream to purge the truck after they moved Corinne.

She clung to Father on the ride back into Querq, jumping at every strange shadow or noise, waiting for the raiders. His hand on her back held her close, calloused fingers absentmindedly stroking her back. Confusion surrounded him. Althea looked up. His concern at her trembling showed plain on his face, but she could find no voice to tell him what scared her. When at long last the truck rolled through the yawning patchwork of old cars that comprised the gates of Querq, she set her cheek on his shoulder and relaxed.

Evidently, she had been wrong about raiders taking her today. That weird, unfamiliar sensation had only been insecurity... dread of being kidnapped.

She had truly found a home.

TUMBLEWEED'S

Once again, Althea roamed Querq after Karina had gone off to her 'job.' Today, people kept approaching to thank her for what she had done for Corrine. Doctor Ruiz had been telling everyone how Althea had saved her life. He rambled on about something called a UTI, and how the delirium had sent her out in the middle of the night to wash an empty basket she thought full of clothes. Father had been upset that the woman made it out of the city without the Watch stopping her.

She wondered what the Ravens would give her when the time came for her to have one of those 'job' things, too. Granted, her gifts had already done much good for the town. Perhaps then, she already had a job. With that thought, she squinted at the sun glinting among the leaning skeletons of the before-time buildings far off in the old city. Buzzard-like, they loomed over Querq as if waiting for it to die.

Most people she passed waved and smiled. Several stopped to bow or beg for a blessing. Four women the same age as Father, plus a man far older, came out of nowhere and surrounded her. Hands touched her everywhere, not grabbing, just wanting to be in contact with the Prophet.

"Please, bless my baby!" One pulled her shirt up to reveal a bulging belly.

Another had fallen to her knees, hugging her cheek against Althea's knees. "Please, watch over my husband. He's on the wall."

The third came nose to nose with her, almost in tears. "Please, I cannot bear children..."

Overwhelmed and having no escape route, Althea tried in vain to push the pawing hands away. She used her power to lift the mood of the one who sought a blessing for her husband. The woman backed away, bowing in thanks. Althea put a hand on the pregnant belly, opening her mind to the combined life essence of mother and child.

Sensing no corruption within the forms, she smiled. "Your baby is healthy."

Althea shifted her touch to the woman who couldn't conceive. She sensed a withering blackness within, hovering like evil wings over the space babies grow. Bizarre lumpy life-shapes existed without pattern or symmetry in places they didn't belong.

Having never seen such a thing before, it took her a moment to figure out how to repair this type of sick. The extra life-shapes needed to go away, and the flesh around them forced back to the way it should be. She isolated the rogue growths, and forced the woman's body to divest itself of the badness. The woman made a low groan, and sank to the ground. When Althea stopped concentrating, she opened her eyes to find a puddle of blood with a few irregular acorn-sized fleshy lumps spread out on the sidewalk. The shuddering woman collapsed onto her, squeezing the air from Althea's lungs.

She gasped, breathless. "What... did you do to me?"

Althea tried to answer, accomplishing only a whining wheeze as she squirmed. The old man intervened, grasping the woman's arms and pulling her vice-like grip open. Althea fell to her knees, searching for breath.

"There was strange growing inside you. It is gone."

"Can I have a child now?" She clutched Althea's shoulders.

Althea gathered the woman's hands and held them. "I think so, but I cannot help you with that. You will need a man to plant the baby seeds."

The woman hugged her once more before running down the street shouting the name of her husband. The old man had simply come to pay his respects, and didn't have any hurts or sicks. He ambled off after patting her atop the head. She gathered the odd nuggets of flesh in a scrap of cloth and threw them in a burn-barrel a few blocks away. After washing her hands in a puddle, she continued her exploration and eventually found herself in the shadow of the far west wall. Along the top, men with rifles watched out over the desert from a perch of concrete and steel.

The fortification looked far stronger than anything from Den's village. The Watch hadn't made it of old flattened cars stacked on top of each other. Giant metal struts held up slabs of the strange grey stone that ancient people could shape to their want. Placing her steps carefully around debris in the road, pieces knocked loose from the occasional raider attack, she approached a blue-painted metal staircase, and climbed to the walkway atop the wall.

Men and women drifted over to greet her once they noticed a little girl on their guard-walk. Some wore strange blue vests while others had pale green ones. Althea recognized it as armor, but of no type she'd ever seen, certainly not leather. She peered over the edge and frowned at the coils of razor wire tacked to the outside of the wall. The coils of metal looked like pain had taken physical form. A gentle touch encouraged her away from the edge, then an older man took her hand and walked her around on a tour of their defenses.

More of those large guns sat on pegs, as well as 'magic eyes' that let the Watch see raiders from far away. Althea adored how the people here treated her like any curious child. They didn't feel it safe for her to be on top of the wall for long, and when they encouraged her to go back down, she thanked them for protecting everyone.

A few blocks over, she found a front yard littered with children half her age. They swarmed around her, drawing her into their play. She grinned, frolicking and acting silly, reveling in the innocence of it until the adults watching them called the kids away for their midday meal.

She had much to learn in this place. Althea thought of the fork, the pipes giving water on command, and toilets. These people must be powerful if they can afford to waste clean water. She still felt guilty about ruining drinkable water each time she had to go. Father explained they tried to live in a similar manner to what things had been before a great war, lacking only something called electricity. Some small places, like the water purifier, had it, but the tiny machine could not make enough for the entire town.

A sharp *crack* followed by intermittent clicking startled her from her musings. Curiosity drew her to a rectangle of dimness in the side of a lime-painted building. A doorway without a door, it led into a dark and cool place full of older men and two women. She crept up three rough concrete steps into a dim room, but not so dark she lost sight of color.

Two men stood by a table full of strange, perfectly round rocks. They prodded them every so often with long sticks, knocking them into each other and into small nets at the corners. She watched for a few minutes, grinning when the older of the two yelled at the other for being a lucky bastard.

To her left, a row of people sat in front of a tall counter on strange seats resembling giant nails with wide, padded heads. Althea approached, intrigued by all the shiny bottles on a shelf behind it. The countertop came up to her nose, its once-shiny black surface struggling to reflect the light from her eyes. A large man, pudgy and shaved bald, smiled at her and set a glass of dull, orange liquid in front of her. A sweet, pungent scent with the tang of fermentation wafted from it.

"Yer old 'nuff ta see over the bar, kiddo. 'Ave one on the house. Name's Tumbleweed, and this is mah place."

Althea grasped the metal rail along the bar and pulled herself up to take a seat on one of the padded nail-things. Her feet couldn't reach the floor or even the ring around the bottom where the men hooked their boots. The drink smelled like fruit, citrus especially, and despite a strange sour aftertaste, wasn't wholly unpleasant even with random pulpy bits floating in it.

"S'wered ya come from?" A man to her left leaned to look at her.

Everyone in here, except Tumbleweed, looked too old for one of those 'job' things.

"I don't remember." She took a sip of the fruity substance, winced, and still couldn't make up her mind if she liked it. "Pastest thing I know is the wagon."

"Wagon?" A man to the other side glanced over.

Althea explained the small cage, the wagon that roamed the Badlands, and a man smelling of paraffin and whiskey who had taken coins and trades from people for her to mend them. A dozen sips of the orange drink left her tongue numb and made her hate the cage more now than when she had been in it. She tolerated it at the time. What else could she do? Her fate was to help people, and she hadn't much cared what they did to her in return. Another sip brought back the first week, when she still tried to escape and go home to her parents. With it came the memory of the Wagon Man laughing at her attempts to break the cage.

"Awful thing, that." The man to the right grumbled to murmurs of assent from everyone else. "Someone should'a killed 'im."

"They did." Althea blinked at the glass, fuller than she remembered it.

The bartender gestured at it. "Hooch. Make it mah-self."

She held the glass to her face, beneath her nose, sniffing at the faint fruity fizz that tickled her nostrils and made her giggle. Memories took away her smile, and she sipped more. "We went from where it was too cold to sleep to where it was too hot to move. He wanted everyone to know what I could do so people would give him pay-things. Some men came, and they stole me."

She took a long sip as she shuddered at the memory of the Wagon Man's hot blood splattering past the bars of the cage. A giant of a dark-skinned man with one eye bashed a spiked metal rod down into his head, killing him. Like when Vakkar died, she wanted to help him, but couldn't reach.

The barflies crowded around her, one old woman rubbed her back as she described the killing.

"They didn't let me out. They carried me in the cage to their camp."

Slurp.

Althea rambled on in a meandering story of how they forced her to tend to their raiding parties, men who attacked the innocent. It didn't take long before stronger raiders wiped them out and she changed hands. By then, she had grown and barely fit in the cage. The second group had taken pity on her and let her out, but they locked a metal ring about her leg instead.

Consoling hands squeezed her shoulder. She drank more of the concoction, lost in the liberty of her pain flowing freely. Aside from the leash, those bandits had been rather nice to her. They gave her anything she asked for except the ability to leave, but where would she go?

"They all died," she half muttered into the cup, teasing it back and forth across her bottom lip. "They attacked a Scrag camp a lot bigger than they thought it was. They chased small boys into a hollow, but men surprised them from behind." In her memory, a flash of machetes and spear tips flung crimson into the sky. "The Scrags cut me loose, and took me with them..."

She rambled on through many iterations of abduction by raiders or Badland gangs, looked back fondly on her time with Reed, and recounted up to when Father found her exhausted. The men seemed nervous at her mention of the machine-man stuck in the water, and two left in haste. She tried to drink more, but found her glass empty. Gravity felt weird, and the walls moved. Between the drink and her time in Querq, her indifference to captivity shattered.

"Why are people so cruel?" she wailed, falling into sniffles. "All I want is to help."

"The sands are a deadly place, little lady." The bartender took the empty glass. "Someone what kin do what you kin do... They all want it for themselves."

She tried to look at the four Tumbleweeds wavering in front of her; she couldn't tell which one of them spoke. The crowd had merged into a multi-faced entity of comforting words and reassuring hands. Such indignation radiated from them at her story, she started to wonder if Aurora had been right. The way people treated her *was* evil. Even if she helped others along the way, she didn't deserve being tethered or caged or taken against her will. Thoughts of contentment and safety filled her mind and a sudden, strong urge to be with Karina welled up.

Bracing herself against the bar and her seat, she looked past the hazy, flesh-toned blotch of her foot toward the floor. The grimy tiles seemed to move away from her as she tried to extend her toes to make first contact. The next thing she knew, the floor leapt up and smacked her in the chin. Laughter erupted around her.

"Ow." She slid her hand across the tiles and grasped her face.

Fingers closed around her arms, lifting her to her feet and steadying her. Someone had replaced the muscles in her legs with rubber, and she swayed into the bar. A man reeking of machinery walked her to a bench and eased her into the embrace of old leather cushions. The murmuring voices grew indistinct. She lay still for a while, but felt as though more time passed than she realized.

When she sat up, the world remained weird and shaky, but her legs worked a little better. She made her way back to the bar, holding onto the seat-nails to steady herself.

"Thank you for the drink."

Tumbleweed nodded. "S'okay, kid. Look'd like ya needed it."

Althea stopped at the concrete stairs out of the place, and lifted her foot toward the first step. Standing crane-like on one leg, she stared at the grey block that seemed to drift toward and away from her, making her wobble back. Her second attempt drew more laughs, and a cheer. After a glance back at the crowd, she defeated the obstacle by crawling on all fours and sprawled on the ground outside, eyes closed to enjoy the warm breeze.

After a few minutes, she wobbled upright and attempted going home. Straight lines proved elusive as she tottered past a row of buildings that, judging by the signs, had once been shops repurposed into homes. The townies glanced at her drunken gait, some laughing and others coming over to check on her.

Four buildings later, a voice called out, "Girl."

An ancient man sat on the porch steps of a run-down white building, staring at her with a look of intense curiosity. Drawn to him, she staggered closer, swaying on her feet until she nearly fell, catching herself with one hand on the wall. Continuing to hold onto the building, she crept near enough to talk. He waved at her to come closer. She blinked at a rugged face, wrinkled and brown with age and weather. Trying not to trip over her own feet as she approached, she loped a few steps closer until her hip touched his leg. He reached out to take her hand, straining to get a good look at her face.

"I think you're the one." His voice, dry and deep, covered her in the fragrance of smoke.

She tilted her head, not saying anything.

"Yes, you are." Stringy white hair shook with a series of coughs. "The last time I saw those eyes, you were just a baby."

Althea sank onto the steps, and tugged at his arm. Querq spun less after she sat down. "You knew my parents?"

He looked up and away at the sky, squinting at the clouds, leaving Althea wondering how so much hair could grow inside someone's nose. "Your mother, but I only saw her for a few hours. She was running from someone. Strange men with strange weapons."

Focusing on him, Althea looked into his thoughts. The face of a young woman with pale skin and blonde hair, wild with fear, filled his view. Dirt smudges and rips covered her sky-blue jumpsuit, but it still looked like nothing a person from the Badlands would wear. Strange tan blankets with a repeating geometric pattern too precise for human hands to produce shrouded an infant in her arms.

Her voice blurred in his memories. Men chased her. They wanted to kill her to take the child away. Within the bundled cloth, nestled a pale infant with two points of intense blue light for eyes. The sight shocked Althea out of the vision, leaving the lingering memory of her mother's voice begging this man to save her child's life.

Face frozen in astonished sorrow, quiet tears streaked her cheeks. He had been talking the whole time, though she saw the images his words attempted to describe. This man felt himself too old to take care of an infant, and had left her with a young couple in a small, peaceful village.

She stared down at the dirt between her feet. That entire settlement at the side of the turquoise lake had been wiped out because of her. The Wagon Man stole her. She had only wanted to help someone who was hurt, and he killed everyone to get her. If she hadn't helped him, those people wouldn't have suffered. Althea's gaze lifted away from the ground, toward the giggles of distant children down the street. No, a greedy man with a cart killed anyone who tried to stop him—not her.

"Never expected to ever see you again after all these years. No idea what happened to that woman, though. She ran off the same day. Reckon she wanted ta draw them men after her away from you."

A blonde woman with no weapons alone in the Badlands. Althea felt sick to think it would have been a kindness if the strange men had found her—they only would have killed her.

29

LEAD ME NOT

Black strands wavered across a square of dull blue-purple, the only color in the room. Althea lay on her side, staring at the window over the skirt she left draped on the back of a chair. The chill air had made the nightgown more appealing, velvety and warm, even if it made her feel vulnerable because she couldn't run or climb. The little sanctum she shared with Karina felt safe. She wondered if Querq would as well.

The scent of chorizo washed over her from behind, upon Karina's breath. Her sister had passed out right away, but Althea had not yet become accustomed to sleeping on something so soft. She didn't complain, rather grinned, imagining Father saying to give it time. Dirt or a scrap of blanket over a hard floor would help her drift off, but she remained in the plush bed for her sister's sake.

"What's wrong?" asked Karina in a drowsy voice. "You're not still drunk are you? You're lucky Father didn't notice."

Althea nudged her head deeper into the pillow. "I met a man who knew my mother. She's probably dead now."

Karina kissed her on the back of her head. "I can't imagine not knowing..."

"I'm sorry." Althea flicked at the covers with her toe.

The response sounded less tired. "Why?"

"For making you remember your mother's dead."

Karina kept quiet for a minute, then pulled her tight. "I got a little sister instead of a little brother... I'm happy."

Althea rolled over, nose to nose with her. Karina squinted at the bright glow an inch from her eyes, and squeezed her sister's hand. Minutes passed in a contest of who would giggle first; Althea lost.

"Hey..." Karina's voice grew sluggish again. "Sometimes I go to the garden and meditate whenever I miss her."

She felt as tired as Karina sounded. "Meditate?"

"It's when you clear everything out of your head and try to think about nothing, then the important thing comes to you. I've tried it a few times. It makes me feel better, but I still haven't seen her. Maybe it will work for you since you're the Prophet."

Althea gave her a raspberry. Prophet had become a bad word. They both giggled, but swallowed it, not wanting to wake Father.

He deserved his sleep.

🐚 🌾 🏺 💧 ♒

"IN THERE?" ALTHEA GAWKED UP AT A MASSIVE WHITE DOME-SHAPED structure.

Karina held her hand as they strode up the walkway to the door. "Yes. I'll see you in a few hours. I'm already late to the field."

After a hug, her sister hurried off.

Althea watched her run out of sight before she entered a doorway to warm, wet air hanging heavy over a concrete path slick yet rough beneath her feet. A presence here brought back her feral vigilance. She set her worry aside and crept along past old metal tables piled high with boxes and clay pots. The scent and taste of soil entered her throat while fine droplets of mist settled upon her skin. Above her, a patchwork of metal pipes leaked random streams as they carried water to clusters of immense suspended pots from which grew various vegetables.

The cupola blazed under the sun, milky triangular panels flooding the area in heat and light. At the center of this place stood a grove of trees studded with developing fruit and surrounded by a patch of grass and flowers, the spot Karina had talked about: four trees and the small wooden bench. Althea proceeded down the curving walkway stepping in many warm puddles. The path had grown slippery with algae in spots, coarse and dry in others. Soon the shade of the trees blocked the oppressive radiance from above, and she sat cross-legged on the ground by a small pond ringed with growing herbs. Resting her palms on her knees, she threw her hair over her shoulder with a nod and closed her eyes.

Thinking about nothing proved harder than it sounded. She fought the nagging distraction of the grass tickling her legs, the songs of birds above, and the gurgles of her settling breakfast.

Karina had said she should breathe. It sounded bizarre at first; everyone breathes. She meant the *way* she should breathe, slow and rhythmic. In and out, one breath at a time. Althea figured Karina had missed something in the information she had gotten from the traveler who told her about this 'meditation' thing. No wonder it hadn't worked for her. She didn't do it right.

Her prey instinct teased at her spine and sent a shiver down her back. The placidity of the place ended the moment chirping birds fell silent. She opened her eyes, breath stalled at the sight of a shadow behind an orange tree. A man stepped out of the folds of a billowing brown coat, lifting his head to peer at her from under the brim of a battered cowboy hat. Skin stretched over his skeleton so taut he resembled a walking drum; sunken eyes glimmered like rubies in their dark sockets and pinned her to the ground.

A frail hand removed his hat as he approached. Teeth the color of a decaying bog bared themselves in a sinister grin. Even the trees leaned away as if wanting to flee from him.

Althea planted her hands behind her in the grass and uncrossed her legs, pulling her feet under her as she eyed the path. He raised his hand as if to beg a moment, and she hesitated, reversing in a crawl rather than bounding into a run.

"Who are you?" She dug her fingers into the soil, clutching it, her body in the posture of a threatened jaguar.

Long grey hair danced as he laughed in a voice that resonated over the garden despite its lack of volume. "I am this place."

She furrowed her brow. "That doesn't make sense. You're a man."

Paper-thin lips parted, flashing his seaweed smile. "I am that which has drawn forth from the enmity of man."

She remembered Aurora talking about something she called a sentience.

This being had no thoughts she could read, only a radiance of dread. "Why are you here?"

He paced in a circle, gravelly voice doing its best to sound nonthreatening. "Humanity called. I answered."

Althea trembled as he passed behind her, but refused to look. When he moved into her view, she made eye contact. "What do you do?"

"I keep things as they need to be. I sustain. I feed."

"You're a ghost." She released the soil, folding her hands in her lap.

"Heh." He laughed again. "I am many ghosts."

He raised a hand and her mind flashed with images of war and death. Great machines she had never before imagined streaked across the sky, raining fire down upon the cities of the before-time. The visions lingered on people dying, especially those who couldn't defend themselves.

"Stop it." A grimace of revulsion crossed her face.

"You asked." He faced slightly away. "I am they."

She remained quiet, thinking. "All of those people, they died in the war. You're their anger?"

"I am." He glanced off. "The rage of fallen warriors called me. I came as black wolves of vengeance made strong by a feast of tender souls."

Images of angry creatures with twisted fur and glowing red eyes appeared behind him, the bonedogs that attacked Den stalking the forest. Their pale grey fur changed to ebon, their eyes lit crimson. As her vision passed a large tree, the forest changed to before-time streets filled with fire and soaked with blood. The creatures prowled amid the drifting smoke, searching. Ethereal fog rose from bodies as they passed, leaping with the form of humans into the air, but landing as wolves, joining the pack.

In a wide alley, the alpha she had killed stood in darkness, barely visible as an outline of black fur against the night. Shimmering orange eyes stared into her soul. Other wolves slinked from the shadows and merged into him. Individual shapes combined, piling on in a rising tower of darkness. The glowing spots fixed on her, rising within the building column of vapor until they came forward, becoming the eyes of a man walking out from the heart of it, the man who stood in front of her.

Althea swallowed the lump in her throat. "Is my mother in there?"

"In the sense you dread, perhaps." The weathered face crinkled with a sinister grin. "Perhaps not. There are... possibilities."

Again the visions came. A sky-blue jumpsuit fluttering from bones half buried in the sand; the same woman screaming, collared and begging while raiders wife her brutally; her mother clad in raider armor driving a blade into a man's heart and loving it.

"Stop. Please." Althea hid her face in her hands, sobbing.

"Exquisite," he rasped, drawing the word out upon a gritty voice.

Althea peered between her fingers at him, watching him savor her torment. Once she realized what he did, she scowled. "You're evil."

"You've said that before."

In an instant, Althea found herself bound to the metal post again, only without a blindfold. Instinctual panic at being tied kicked in and she struggled for some seconds before she stared at the man, who appeared as the slave-catcher. Immense roaches scuttled along, moving past him as if he didn't exist. They converged on her, antennae twitching with anticipation. She stopped squirming and frowned at the knot between her ankles. Rather than frightened, she became angry.

"This isn't real. You aren't that man."

The garden reappeared. She sat with her hands in her lap, no ropes binding her.

"I am now. You sent him to me." The entity frowned, and let off a disappointed sigh. After a moment, his mood shifted and he chuckled. "You should have let him take you. One of The Freddy's girls is dead because you aren't there."

Althea looked down. If she had gone with him, she wouldn't know Karina or Father.

"There... succulent guilt." He leaned back, inhaling as if smelling a wonderful dinner. "You prefer being here even if it means the fat man's whores die."

She snapped her head up, glaring at him. Determination made fists out of small hands. "We can go save them."

"How many people from Querq would fall fighting The Freddy's men? Two... six... perhaps a dozen? For what? Trading the lives of men with families for a bunch of meat-holes used by anyone with a few coins? Either way, someone dies."

This being disgusted her. She shivered at his words, at his meaning. "Why must there be such suffering?"

"Human nature, girl. The war burned away the false notion of 'civilization.' The primal essence of which your kind is made clawed its way forth from the crumbling ashes of humanity. The strong dominate the weak. Those with power take what they want. The natural order." He made hand gestures as he spoke with a cadence devoid of emotion.

Zhar appeared a few feet away, rifle in hand and pride on her face. She spoke in his voice. "A few are strong and take their freedom in blood. The weak get what they deserve."

Rachel appeared, dying at her feet, blood gushing from her mouth.

"Killed this bitch for warning you," said Zhar in her normal voice before laughing.

"Liar!" Althea screamed.

Zhar and Rachel disintegrated into smoke.

The man walked into view. "Querq is a quaint attempt to cling to the old ways, but we both know how *civilization* worked out in the end. Order is fleeting. The corruption of the human soul will drag even this place into the hands of savages in time. Humanity is what it is, and no matter what people try to make of themselves, they all return to the same thing. Everyone wants power."

"People do not have to be like that." She stared at him.

"Yet you wonder why you are traded like a prize? Your idealism is naïve. Humanity takes what it can get away with and kills what it cannot understand. Just like your little Den."

The garden vanished again. Cool, wet grass changed to hot sand beneath her. A band of metal locked around her right ankle bound her with a chain to a stake in the ground. Dead raiders lay scattered around the wreckage of a camp. She had scurried as far away from them as the tether would allow. Den stood over her with a spear pointed at her heart, a disdainful sneer on his face. Nalu walked up behind him offering a look of suspicion as he pulled the stake from the ground. He dragged her into his grasp by the tether and placed her, chain and all, into a wooden cage. Den shouted in anger, upset with Nalu for collecting her. The spear came in past the bars, driving her into the corner of the cage.

A trickle of blood ran from the point upon her chest as Den spoke. "Bad things follow glow-eye. We should kill it." He glared at her like an animal too dangerous to be allowed to live.

Althea shook off the projection and cradled the agate in her hands. "That is a lie. Den wasn't like the others. Palik wanted to kill me. *Palik* put his spear into the cage."

The sentience laughed. "Once the fog of their aboriginal superstition lifted, he wanted you for himself." The raspy words came from everywhere, yet he made no footsteps. "What better way to become chief than have the great Prophet as a wife." He pointed at her. "Do not think for a moment you are any better. One boy out of an entire village doesn't fear you, and you think you love him? You sought to use each other. Hah.

You hoped the others would treat you better if you became the chief's wife. There was no love. Love is a lie."

Smooth stone slid between her fingers as she rubbed the pendant. The emotional link it held to Den defied this creature's words. Her tears slowed and came to a halt. One straggler ran down her cheek as she raised her eyes and fixed him with a glare.

Authority crept into her tone. "You're lying. I won't let people do that to each other."

After a wheezing laugh, he appeared on the other side of her. "No, I suppose you'll try. You are a bit of a fly in the ointment, but you do have a purpose."

Althea looked downcast at the grass in front of her. "I'll not help you spread pain."

"Oh, but you do." A boot stepped into the corner of her vision. "Every person you keep alive only survives to feed me longer. All you accomplish is giving them more time to suffer. If you let them die, their agony ends." His last words trailed off into a corpse-whisper. "Now, now. Neither one of us wants *that*, do we? I wish them alive a little longer to feast upon their wretchedness, and you cannot bear to watch them die."

She looked away from him, searching the swaying oranges for answers. "People don't have to suffer just because they live."

"Life *is* suffering," he rasped, lunging close enough to make her fall back on her ass. His voice dropped to a whisper. "So naïve. I hope you live a long life so I can enjoy you. Mankind will suffer no matter where it dwells. It is the way they are built. They crave it." Behind him, images of raiders manhandling Aya, Ramani, and Zhar filled in out of the smoke. "All seek power at the expense of others. Out here, it is the same as beyond the great walls of flame."

She got her feet under her but stayed crouched, remembering the stories. Far enough west, they said a standing curtain of inferno cuts off the land, destroying all who approach it. It is the place where the souls of the damned go. Her mother appeared and cried out in agony, burning, her charred body standing amid a curtain of conflagration. Althea took a breath and dispelled the image, unsure if it came from her worry or this creature's influence.

She focused on memories of those she had saved. "I've been a captive for most of my life. I don't care what they do to me as long as I am helping people."

"Now who is lying?" He stood and paced off to the left. "You have been here a week and look how fast you have attached yourself to the girl, Karina, and her father. Every minute you spend with your *sister*, you cry about the life you could have had if only you were normal."

A ring of six-year-olds formed around her; no longer giggling, they teased her about her miserable childhood and sang a rhyming song about glow-eye living in a cage.

She cringed. Captivity hadn't bothered her when she knew no other life. A taste of family here in Querq made the past hurt.

The man drew in a long savoring breath as she wallowed in sadness. "Perhaps something foul should befall Karina. I'm sure your lamentation would be delicious." He grinned again.

Sorrow became wrath.

Althea leapt to her feet. "No. You will not harm them. I will not allow you to hurt my family."

A pulse of white energy welled up around her and the old man spun with dread in his eyes. His sudden fright melted into an accusatory grimace, then a pointing, shaking finger as he took a step back. His reaction confused her, even more so when he retreated from her next step. She advanced, scowling at him.

"Do not harm my family. I forbid it."

"You..." His finger quivered. "You do not belong here. Your soul is not of..." He glanced to his right, his nonchalance returning. "Their death will not be my doing. Raiders are here. They have come for you."

Her anger gave way to worry. "You influenced them. All the evil, you make it happen."

"I must sustain." He approached as if to put an arm around her shoulder. "Weak men do what weak men do. I merely hasten the inevitable."

Althea glowered. "Stay back."

He seemed afraid once more, and halted in place. "An arrangement then. I shall clear the way for you to find your little Den. What I ask of you is a gesture to acknowledge the workings of the universe. You must accept my place here. We are two sides of the same coin, and cannot exist without the other."

She looked down at the pendant, tracing the edge with her thumb. "What does that mean?"

He stepped close again. His breath, hot corpse-rot, blew over her face. "The raiders will lose. One of them will not die right away. Let this evil man who has come to take you away from your so-called *family* perish, and I shall ensure you see Den."

A frown spread across her face. She thought of Karina, of Father, and of this thing's lies. He could mean finding Den's remains.

"I don't trust you. You will let me find him dead. Leave him alone. I'd rather never see him again than have him hurt." Her voice quivered.

He flashed a grimacing smile like a snake oil salesman caught in a lie, then held his hands to the sides. "All right, you win. Let the raider die, and you shall be reunited with a living, healthy, wild boy."

"Joined to Yala and no longer wanting me." She stared down, at the blades of grass between her toes.

The entity cringed. "Yet you deny being a Prophet." He laughed. "Let the man who threatens your family perish, and I shall bend fate to give Den back to you as it was before."

Althea's thoughts ran from Den to Zhar, how she had said a twelve-year-old couldn't really fall in love. Even Karina had hinted she only liked him because he didn't fear her. It had been hard for her to say, and harder still to hear. She knew the look in his eyes right before she left. It had to be more. This creature offered her a chance to have him back. Karina and Father appeared in her mind for a fleeting instant, replaced with a cage she could barely turn around in. Her little arm reached out past the bars at a man that couldn't pay, watching and feeling him die ten feet away. The vision of Vakkar's death came next, once more stuck behind metal, unable to reach a dying man.

She crossed her hands over the memory of the icy chill in her heart.

"No. He is wounded and no longer a danger. I will not let him die." She raised her head to look at the entity, but he had vanished.

She spun around and spotted the back end of a huge black wolf vanishing among the rows of corn on the far side of the trees. Althea wanted to shiver like a frightened little girl, but she squinted at it instead—angry.

Althea muttered at the waving stalks. "Stay away from them."

Gunfire rang out in the distance. She jumped up and ran, splashing over the puddle-strewn concrete path to the exit. An ethereal whisper from nowhere made her pause.

"You do not belong here."

Clinging to the doorframe, she cast a nervous look over the empty garden before rushing outside, leaving a path of wet footprints on the dry walkway. In the street, a crowd of people scurried about. Men and women with rifles ran one way while children and the unarmed went in the other direction. Karina emerged from the sea of bodies and hurried to her. Althea flew into her arms and cried, overwhelmed with relief at seeing her sister alive and well.

After a moment, Karina pushed her head back with a gentle hand and stroked her hair. "Thea, raiders attacked. There are wounded."

She sniffled and tried to control her crying breaths, clinging with a two-handed grip on Karina's arm. After a moment of watching people scurry past, she looked up at her sister.

"One of the raiders still lives. Please have him brought in with the others."

Karina seemed frightened by the eerie calm in her voice. "W-what?"

Althea stood tall. "I will not let him die."

30

EXILE

The soft whisper of Althea's name tickled at her ear, pulling her from the depths of sleep into the reach of a gentle hand that shook her by the shoulder.

She squinted at Karina, sitting up behind her. Her sister's face was a mask of worry drawn in tones of grey. The sun had not yet started to come up. Father stood in the doorway, surrounded by a halo of color from the lantern in his hand. Deep shadows flickered about his face; something had to be wrong. Shaking off the grip of fatigue, she wiped the crumbs from her eyes and sat up.

"Thea, Felipe is here." Karina's voice carried a contagious nervousness.

"What's wrong?" Althea looked between them.

The hissing lantern drew close as Father approached and took her hand. "Althea, Doctor Ruiz is here with Felipe."

"Oh, no." She threw her legs over the edge of the bed. "Is it the baby?"

"I'm afraid it is…" He pulled her into a hug, almost forcing the air out of her. "But not the littlest one."

Sorrow surrounded him, making her anxious. "What is happening?"

"Father, what…?" Karina clung to the arm bearing the light.

His voice slipped out around the lump in his throat. "Felipe brings warning. Hector Santos is causing trouble for Althea."

Karina furrowed her eyebrows. "Hector? What could he do?"

"His brother died in the attack yesterday, the one man we lost." Father's face sank into the crook of Althea's neck. He choked up. "Felipe has said Hector has the ear of the council... They want to—" His voice choked off.

Doctor Ruiz edged into the bedroom, following Felipe, a large bag slung over his shoulder.

"Yes." Felipe shambled over. "He is trying to convince them it is too dangerous to allow you to stay here. I thought they would disregard him, but they are listening. They want to send you away."

Althea clung to Father, trembling. "No..."

Her pitiful attempt at a voice knocked the last brick from his stoic wall. The lantern slipped from his fingers to the floor with a *clank*, and he embraced her with both arms.

"Not just send you away..." Doctor Ruiz added. "They consider a plan to trade you to the chief of the Buffalo Skull."

"That's bullshit." Karina sobbed. "They're no threat to us." She looked at Father. "They can't do this. It is slavery! The council forbids it."

"I've brought some things. You can disappear into the old city before they come for you. It's the least I can do since you saved Luisa's life." Felipe smiled.

"No. No. No." Karina pulled at Althea's nightgown. "We can't let them do this."

Althea's eyes welled with tears; the urge to cry grew stronger each time Father's hand caressed her hair. The monster from the garden did this. He made the council turn on her. If he could influence the ravens, he could harm her family.

"I do not want you to get hurt because of me." Althea slid out from between them, moving to her day clothes resting on the chair. "An evil here has made their minds for them."

She tugged the nightgown over her head and threw it to the bed. As much as she tried to act stoic, she could not stall tears. Karina tried to stop her, swiping the shirt while Althea tightened the skirt about her waist.

"Father, if they cast Thea out, I am going with her." Karina gave up her tug-of-war and whirled on him. "Even if they give me to the Buffalo."

"Please stay here where it is safe." Althea put a hand on her sister's cheek. "I don't want you to become a slave."

"No. I am going with you." Karina squeezed her hand numb.

A long silence hung in the room. Father gazed at the floor with a grim frown. "It is settled then. Our family will leave."

Karina dragged Althea into Father's arms.

Overwhelmed by their feelings, Althea couldn't find the ability to say anything. They embraced for minutes, Father's hand continuously rubbing up and down her bare back.

Felipe cleared his throat. "We haven't much time."

Althea hurried with her sister down the hallway to the stairs, the men behind them. She clung to Karina in the living room while Father gathered some things in a bag. Eventually, Karina handed over the tank top, and Althea wriggled into it. No one spoke as Father led them outside, following Felipe. Absent the sun for several hours, the streets of Querq were cold and quiet. Althea trudged at a pace as if they led her to execution. Karina squeezed her arm and Father kept a hand on her shoulder. Althea saw the town in perfect clarity; every building, street, and hunk of debris brought memories from her short time here. Laughing children, smiling faces, even the annoying worship she had been trying to avoid all cascaded in her mind. Karina cried, the only sound the entire trip to the end of the southeast road until they stopped at a dead end packed with debris.

Althea stared up at the crumbling buildings of the old city beyond the wall. Chunk by chunk, they invaded Querq, littering the road with concrete acorns fallen from steel trees. Felipe's escape route yawned ahead. A corrugated metal pipe traversed the wall to the heart of the decaying city, too small for an adult to fit. Althea squatted, grabbing the top of the pipe and peering into its grey depths. Father would not be able to go down this. Even Karina might not make it.

"You cannot go this way." She sighed. "It is better if I go alone. You should stay safe here."

The sun lapped at the horizon. Karina lost her composure and her ability to speak. Althea looked away from the tunnel, glancing up at Father's face. Tears upon his cheeks caught a glint from the hesitant sunrise. That explained his silence. He didn't dare attempt to talk while he might sound emotional. She glanced again at the circle of rot waiting for her at the end of the tunnel. Den's smiling face flashed in her thoughts, followed by Rachel asleep under the table. A tear splattered on her foot as she realized history repeated itself yet again. She couldn't let her family get hurt.

She set one foot in the pipe, her toes grasping the edge, and looked over her shoulder at the people she loved. Her knuckles whitened against the metal rim when Karina, sensing a final goodbye, turned away and sobbed into Father's chest. Althea wanted to join her, bawling, but her quivering lip stalled at the sight of Father's tears increasing.

Althea had regretted abandoning Rachel. She'd even regretted surrendering to the raiders who took her from Den. All along, she had the power to protect herself, but never did.

She let go of her sadness, replacing it with determined anger. Althea removed her foot from the pipe and planted it upon the ground. After a scowl down the escape chute, she spun on her heel to face them.

A pulse of rage she didn't intend to radiate brightened the light in her eyes and gave Father back his stoic disposition.

"No. I am home. I will *not* let that thing win. I am not leaving."

She stormed off, back the way they came, leading Father and Karina by the hand away from the forgotten alley. Karina was a mess; shocked out of her sobbing by the abrupt change, but too stunned to do anything other than stumble along. Felipe stood by the pipe and blinked, speechless. Doctor Ruiz smiled.

Felipe scrambled to catch up, running alongside her, the canned provisions in his bag rattling. "Althea, please, you must leave before they see you."

"No." She didn't look at him, stomping along. "The evil makes them think this way. It's not real, and I won't leave my family. I won't be stupid anymore." She narrowed her eyes and muttered with an angry growl. "I will make it leave them alone."

Karina's grip on her hand tightened.

Althea marched into the heart of Querq, right to the council building. Not willing to let go of their hands, she reared back and kicked the door, leaving a dusty footprint upon the dark-stained wood next to the knob. The door swung into the wall, filling the huge chamber with a thunderous crash that startled the assembled into silence. The judges, perched along their bench, had ceased murmuring in whispers with a small group of men and gawked at her. She sensed a wave of elation from Felipe before he ran off, dropping his bag with a dull clatter.

Everyone at the bottom gawked at her tromping down the smooth path between the auditorium seats. The clap of her feet upon the polished stone rang out with each step on her way to the edge of the open space in front of the council. The judges traded glances, whispering. A crowd of men to the left of the bench huddled closer, as if afraid of the little girl staring at them.

Hector stood at the forefront of the group, arms folded over the rim of the wooden pedestal, barely tall enough to raise his chin past it. He pointed with a scowl at Althea. Hate permeated him; he blamed her for his brother's death.

"Is this how our noble council conducts itself?" Father had found words again. His fists trembled with fury hidden from his voice. "Secret meetings before dawn, conspiring against a child?"

"Calm yourself, Fernando." The eldest jurist raised his hand. "This is an emergency session, not a vote."

"Emergency?" Karina blurted. "You're going to sell my sister to the Buffalos."

"Emilio is dead!" Hector yelled, pointing at Althea. "Because of her."

The woman judge on the far right banged a little hammer, glaring at the out-of-turn yelling.

Father fumed. "Emilio is dead because he forgot to duck. He was grandstanding!"

Hector tried to lunge at Father, but his friends held him back. The hammer continued, ignored by all.

Karina's voice teetered at the edge of shrieking. "Raiders attack us with or without her. If not for Althea, we would have buried fifteen instead of one. Did you forget about the people she saved?"

Silence. The hammer ceased at last.

The judges looked at each other. The younger woman among them cleared her throat. "The question does remain if that particular raider attack would even have occurred if she was not here. To what degree is she responsible for an increase in their activity?"

"You're not seriously blaming her after all she has done for us?" Doctor Ruiz blinked in disbelief. "How would they have even known she's here?"

"The Many," said Althea. "He is making you all hate and fear."

The Ravens exchanged looks.

Remembering how the disgusting old man shied away from her, Althea focused on the same desire to force him away, aiming it at the judges.

"More will die if she stays." Hector waved his arm at her. "She couldn't fix Emilio."

Althea glanced down, lost somewhere between guilt and anger. "He died right away. I could not do anything for him. I'm sorry."

"They cut him in half," Father shouted, spit flying from his teeth as he traced his fingers from shoulder to hip over his heart. "Even the Prophet has limits."

Karina flung a wave at Hector. "He shouldn't have jumped down from the wall to try out his new sword."

"You bitch." Hector lunged, but his friends held him back again. "He fell."

"Stop it." Althea's shout echoed over the silence that followed. When the reverberation faded, she spoke in a soft tone. "The land here is evil. It feeds from pain and suffering. It is making everyone angry. It wants me to hurt. It wants you to hurt. It is making you all think and do things you would not do. I feel so much anger from everyone, and it is not real."

Two of the five jurists gave her a pondering look. The eldest in the middle, the grandfather, offered a sympathetic smile. The other two squinted with suspicion. One of them asked her to explain herself in more detail. Althea told them about the vision in the garden, the man who asked her to let the raider die.

"He wanted to trick me. If I had let him die, even though he was a raider, it would make me no better than they are. He wanted me to do evil."

"You save one of them, but let Emilio die?" Hector shouted. "Which side are you on? ¡Ella es un traidor!"

Doors creaked open, causing all to look. Felipe had returned with most of the town in tow. They filed into the room, few bothering to sit. Some of the Watch who had been wounded yesterday led the pack.

A voice cried out, "She stays!"

Another yelled, "Keep Althea!"

One by one, the shouts mingled together into a din. Grandfather whacked the bench with another wooden hammer, making the wooden judge-names bounce until all fell quiet. Hector grew agitated at the show of support which vastly outnumbered his small cadre of friends.

Hector looked back to the ravens. "How many more raiders will attack us trying to take her? If we give her to them, they become our allies. More protection from other groups, and they won't come after us to get the Prophet."

"They will not be your allies," said Althea in a voice quiet, yet stern. "They will take me and then they will have me. They will owe you nothing but pain. Will you continue to give them your women and your guns to keep them happy? Raiders are raiders because they do not know how to stop taking."

An unruly murmur swept across the crowd. The Ravens pounded their hammers again, trying to bring silence.

Hector hit the bench with his hand, accenting every other word. "Even if they don't stay allies, they will not attack as hard if she is not here."

Father moved up behind her and rested a hand on each shoulder, squeezing. "Then her gift helps the Buffalos, and they become stronger. That would threaten us more than her staying. Listen to yourself, Hector. You want revenge for your brother's death, but it is not Althea you should blame. She cannot heal death. Your bother was dead before she could reach him."

The murmur of the crowd sounded like agreement.

Hector stepped forward, holding his arm out at Althea. "The Prophet is in your minds, forcing you to feel sorry for her. She is enslaving us all."

"I can't believe you." Karina let go of Althea's hand, advancing toward Hector and his friends. "Althea might be the Prophet, but she's a little girl, too. Not even twelve years old! How can you consider sending her back to a life of slavery? Out there, she is just a thing to be taken and owned... a power to control. Here she has a family. *¡Es mi hermana!*" She stared, pleading, at the judges. "Please don't do this to her. She's suffered so much already. Don't take away my sister because of Emilio. How many more will die if she is gone? How—"

The *crack* of a gunshot stalled all sound until its echo faded.

Karina crumpled to the floor with a look of pure shock on her face, dark crimson spreading down the front of her dress.

Hector, eyeballs bulging with rage, lowered his arm at the gasping young woman, aiming his pistol at her head.

Althea screamed, overcome by anger. Her emotion, impossible to fit into words, flowed along a wave of psionic force. Gargantuan shadow-judges danced against the polished white marble, drawn by the radiant fury burning from her eyes. Hector's hand wrenched about with a splintering *squish*; the weapon tumbled from the upside-down wreckage of his fingers.

The miserable crunching of disintegrating bones followed a rapid twist that shot up his arm until it stopped with the *crunch* of cracking ribs in the side of his chest. The mangled limb resembled a wrung-out dishtowel. Half its normal diameter, the arm turned dark purple and leaked blood from various places where the skin had torn. Hector's cry of anguish ended with a spray of blood from his mouth. He fainted from the excruciating pain, his friends too stunned by what just happened to even attempt to catch him. The expression of pure rage on Althea's face made his supporters back away.

Felipe gawked at Hector, muttering. *"Oh Dios mío, qué poder tiene esta chica!"*

She ignored the stares, collapsing on her knees by her sister. The shot had gone close to the heart, and she had little time. Althea tore the dress to expose the wound, placing her hands on either side of a geyser of blood. Searching for enough calm to use her powers, she poured energy into the warm flesh. The blinding anger within her fell away, forgotten, as her heart swelled with desperate love. Within the formless shapes, she found the small gash in the side of Karina's heart from which the blood-presence surged, and forced it closed. The bleeding lessened. More power flowed out from her, and the rips in the life-shapes sealed.

Karina's skin shifted under her hands. The bullet nudged its way out and slid from beneath Althea's fingers, falling to the floor with a dull *clack*. Somewhere behind her, people scuffled. From the sound of it, many men fought to keep Father away from Hector. Angry Spanish overpowered the banging gavels.

The shifting forms of Karina's life-shapes became whole again. Blood, pooled in her air-bags, soaked back into her veins, guided by Althea's power.

I'm so sorry. This is my fault, she sobbed telepathically into her sister's mind.

"What… happened?" Karina coughed.

"Hector shot you," said Doctor Ruiz. He had kept pressure on the wound while Althea worked. "You're going to be fine."

The wail of a wounded man's voice rang out in the chamber.

"Hector Santos…" The grandfather's voice hazed in the distance. "For the mur"—he almost dropped the gavel when Karina sat up—"attempted murder of Karina Guererro, we hereby exile you from the settlement of Querq."

Five hammers came down in unison.

Karina wrapped her arms around Althea, unconcerned her chest lay bare and bloody. After a tight embrace, she leaned back and locked eyes. "I don't blame you… I'm glad you stayed." She squeezed her tight once more before flashing a silly grin. "You'd better mend Hector's arm. You'll feel bad if you don't."

Father removed his jacket and wrapped Karina with it.

Althea giggled with relief despite her tears, and offered a begrudging sigh. "Yeah..."

THE WATER MAN

The cart squeaked along, a rickety wooden thing held up by old mountain bike tires on either side. Althea pushed it down the winding path leading to the enclosed farm at the southeast corner of town. Every so often, her feet sank ankle deep in the crumbly dry dirt. The orange of the late morning sun flooded the area with warm light and shifting shadows between the stalks of corn and other planted goods set between rows of metal piping.

At the sight of her approach, two dozen people left their tools in place and came over to get the water and lunch she had brought out to them. The man who usually did this was old and weak, and helping him gave her a chance to spend time with Karina. When the crowd had thinned, Althea scooped some of the ground meat into tortillas and sat next to her sister on the remains of a concrete wall. The farm workers clustered in groups of conversation around the cart while they ate.

"So... Now that this is your home, are you ready for a real dress?" Karina asked in a teasing tone. "Or are you still feral?"

Althea lifted her eyes from the food, making a cute snarl as she mimed a dog tearing at its meal.

When their laughter subsided, Karina tickled her in the side. "In a year or two, you can just wear my old ones. I guess we can wait." She ruffled her hair. "Are you okay?"

"Mrf?" She tried to speak past a mouthful of ground chicken and beans.

"The other day, with Hector…"

She looked down, swinging her legs back and forth. "I have never been so angry. He hurt you. It just happened. I know it hurt. I did it to myself once, but not that much."

"Why?" Karina gasped.

"I don't like handcuffs." Althea stopped eating, gazing into her plate, and explained what she did to herself to escape.

"Oh." Karina pulled her into a hug. "You don't have to worry about that anymore. Father and I won't let anyone hurt you again."

Althea smiled and shifted sideways on the crumbling wall. She put her feet up and leaned into Karina. "I'm happy."

Karina reached an arm around her as they chatted idly about a couple of chores they would do later once she finished her 'job' for the day.

"Will you clean my hair tonight?" Althea tilted her head to look up.

"Bath night's not for two more days. Once a week, remember? It takes wood or charcoal to make enough water hot."

Althea sighed. "Brush it?"

"Okay, but you'll do mine as well." Karina gave her a light nudge. "C'mon, I gotta get back to work. The others are looking at us like I'm lazy."

"All right." She reluctantly hopped down and stretched.

"Don't forget the water man." Karina called out in a sing-song tone as she strode back among the rows of vegetables.

After running around collecting plates and stacking them on the cart, Althea meandered around the edge of the planted area to a jagged metal structure made of patchwork sheets welded together in a shape that resembled a giant clockwork mushroom. From its roof, a jumble of small copper tubes sprang out like the legs of a spider that had fallen butt-first into a hole and got stuck. She gazed down their length, out over the field where trickles and drops of water fell onto the crops.

She slapped the door a few times with an open hand after her knock proved too feeble to make noise. "Hello? Water Man?"

A throat noise, barely intelligible as speech grumbled from within.

"Are you hungry? I have food and water."

The man inside grunted again, though beckoning. She grasped the handle and shoved with all her weight against the monolithic door. It creaked a rusty groan into the darkness on the other side, leaving her winded by the time she could squeeze past. After catching her breath, she ladled some of the meat mixture onto a pair of tortillas and poured a cup of water. She entered the strange metal hut carrying the food, stepping with care along plates of metal stamped with raised diamond shapes. The wet, sometimes oily, surface threatened to take her feet out from under her as she avoided a minefield of sharp scraps, old tools, and invisible slippery spots.

Ahead, lit by a beam of sunlight from a single round window, a heavyset older man wrapped in the largest pair of leather coveralls she had ever seen sat next to a wall full of small wheels and valves. Dark grease smeared his face and arms. His massive, armor-tipped boots skidded in a futile attempt to slide a wheeled chair to the left to reach one of the knobs. The smell of fermented sweat mixed with a metallic taste in the air. When she came close to him, the odor of rotting meat drowned out any trace of the food.

"Here you are." She smiled and set the plate down.

Jowls wobbled as the large head swung around to look at her. White fringe framing his cheeks caught the light, appearing to glow. "Wot we got 'ere?"

It occurred to her she had never seen this man before; perhaps, like her cart, he couldn't fit through the door. She grinned. "I'm Althea."

"What 'appened to Aldo?" He picked at the tacos, inspecting them.

Althea imagined him counting every grain of rice. "Aldo is feeling tired and sick today, so I am helping." She tapped her big toe on the floor while gazing around at the strange machines full of knobs and valves. "He isn't sick, just tired."

Satisfied at the food, he flipped the tacos closed and lifted one to his mouth. "You should be off, 'fore Ornry smells ya. He don't much like kids. Ate the last one what came in here."

She gasped, taking a step back in shock before she realized he told a story. "That's not nice to say."

"Hmmf," he mumbled. "The bones are in that box."

Althea frowned; his emotion confirm he lied.

A large, broad-headed dog with small eyes scrambled around the corner, claws scraping for traction on the smooth metal. His coat looked like someone spilled strong coffee randomly over a white animal. The animal's legs flailed in a blur, claws striking the metal with a *skiff-skiff-skiff* of uncoordinated locomotion.

The water man shook his head and his bushy white eyebrows came together. "Best run off now 'fore he gets ya."

Ornry emitted a whining growl and clambered to a stop against Althea's legs, knocking her into the workbench. After a moment's glance and a tilted head, he licked the strip of exposed stomach where her tank top had pulled up a little. She giggled and crouched to pet him, getting a face full of tongue in the process.

The water man stopped eating and blinked at her. "Well hrmf. Ornry don't much like no one. You 'ave a dog before?"

She pulled the animal's head away from her face long enough to blurt. "Sort of."

"Well." He resumed eating. "You must be okay then. If Ornry likes ya. He'll bite ya though if'n ya bother me wit' too many questions."

The dog spun itself in a circle and flopped on the ground with a belabored wet exhale. She crouched near him. Her skirt bunched up on the floor around her feet in a cascade of leather strands. Balancing on her toes, she rubbed the dog's side with both hands. Ornry adjusted himself, exposing more belly.

Althea smiled at the fat man. "Ornry likes you 'cause you give life to the town." She skritched her fingers down the dog's back, making his day. *What is that bad smell? It's not the dog.*

"Bah." He slurped the meat sauce from his fingers.

"It's true." She gave him an earnest look. "You send water to the fields and make food grow. That is life."

"Fancy way puttin' it. I just water the damn garden." He grumbled, searching for his drink. "G'won now, git on outta here. Place is startin' ta stink of kid."

Seeing the water man grimace as he shifted to grab the cup of water, she stood and approached him. Ornry convulsed on the floor, trying to wriggle close enough to receive skritches while lying on his back.

"Are you hurt?" She weaved back and forth, fighting his effort to avoid looking at her.

"Bah. Jes' me old leg wound, acts up now and then." He scooted the chair back, rotating away.

Ornry whined.

She stooped to rub the dog's belly again. "It must hurt a lot if you never walk."

He glanced back at her with an imperious lifted eyebrow. "What makes ya think I don' walk?"

She blinked as if it was the most obvious thing in the world. "'Cause you're so big."

The innocence in her reply left him unable to be angry at the insult. He babbled for a moment before his brain assembled a line of words to push out of his mouth. "This job makes me sit all day long. It be important. All them wheels and valves don't turn themselves. Gotta send just 'nuff water here and there, not too much… not too little." He bit a taco, murmuring while he chewed. "Check filters, burn wood for carbon, change carbon, maintain pressure, oil valves… lot o' work."

Ornry whimpered as she moved away from him again. She crawled over to the man and knelt on the frigid metal, peeling the leg of his pants up. The stink of dead meat grew stronger. He pounded both fists down on the desk in front of him, making all the little needles in their round windows shake. Sweat broke out on his face.

"Don't touch it." He gasped. "Damn it all, go away! I don't need no children in here gummin' up the works. Yer gonna touch somethin' and it's gonna break." The pain in his voice only increased her determination to help. "Take me a week jes' ta figger out what you broked."

When he reached down to shoo her hands from his leg, she grabbed his oily fingers and concentrated. As she told his mind to stop accepting pain, a look of dumbfounded elation came over him and his continued grumbles about how annoying he found children to be came to a woozy halt. She had a feeling it had been a long time since he hadn't been in constant pain. After working the cloth up and away from the fester to which it adhered, Althea discovered the source of the stink—the man's leg rotted, much of it dark green.

She re-swallowed her lunch and sat back with an arm across her face, looking up at a man lost in euphoria. Ornry protested the intensified stench, rolling away and putting a paw over his nose. Once acclimated to the smell, she touched the hot, sticky shin and focused on the forming shapes of his tainted essence. For minutes, she fought with the corruption, while the Water Man shuddered and gasped. The sick had spread wide throughout his vast body, poison in his blood and rot in his leg.

Ample fuel for her work lingered in his gut. At her urging, his body consumed stored fat reserves for energy to rebuild decayed muscle and corrupted bone. Warm, putrescent jelly slid between her fingers and down his leg, expelled by her effort. When the swelling receded enough, she wrenched his boot off and tossed it to the side. The smell that unleashed caused her to dry heave twice. She gritted her teeth and commanded his body to rebuild pathways so the blood-shape could reach into his blackened toes. That didn't work, the flesh too far gone. She directed his body to detach the toes entirely before regenerating a new set. Over the next few minutes, she poured energy into him until the rot receded. The Water Man slumped in his chair, so lost in the absence of his perpetual agony he scarcely noticed what she did.

Ornry scampered away from the reeking boot; a moment later, his nose peered out from under a shelf of boxes.

A jagged shard remained within the shifting red presence. She found a bit of metal stuck in his leg a few inches below the knee, a fragment of an old spearhead lurking under the skin. It lodged in the bone too deep for her to pull out.

"Water Man?" She opened her eyes.

He had swooned into the valves and knobs, lost in the throes of relief. Her voice nudged him and he let her guide his fingers onto the strip of aluminum at the center of a glistening red crater she'd opened in his leg.

She patted his hand. "You are stronger than me. Can you pull it out?"

He picked at it, wiggled it, and tugged. Half aware of what he grasped, he managed to get it to move a little. "Pliers." He pointed at a shelf.

"What?"

"Get the pliers." He gasped, waving a swollen hand in the direction of a bucket of strange things.

She crawled to it, holding up a screwdriver. "This?"

"No. Pliers, ya little clown."

Dropping it, she grabbed a wrench.

"No, that's a wrench. Two thingees to the left. No, that's a damn hammer, ya li'l fool."

Her hand moved from item to item at random until he yelled, "That's it!"

Althea scurried to his side and handed him the tool. The water man stuck one end into his leg and clamped it around the shard. He grunted and twisted it, rocking the pliers back and forth a few times before the shard pulled free with a faint *squish*. Thick, dark blood oozed out of the hole; she put her hand over it as fast as she could react. He let the pliers clatter to the ground, looking away from the sight of her arms soaked in his blood. She purged the poison from his blood and the rot from his leg, then used the rest of his water to wipe the leg clean. After commanding the muscle and skin to regenerate, she sat back on her heels and smiled up at him.

Ornry came back, tail wagging, and rested his chin on the Water Man's knee. She gathered the charcoal-like toes as well as the remnants of the sick, taking them outside to bury. When she returned, he had his leg up, flexing his new toes, aghast at the sight.

"How d'ya do that?"

The effort left her fatigue visible, but she smiled nonetheless. "I see life inside people. I know where the sick is hiding and make it go away." She leaned against the desk. "Why didn't you go see Doctor Ruiz?"

"Bah, doctors. He'd just give me an aspirin."

Althea blinked. "The hurt was in your leg, not your ass."

The Water Man stared at her. When he realized she hadn't intentionally made a joke, he bellowed with laughter, pulling her face-first into the undulating sea of flesh that was his chest. After patting her on the back twice, he let her drop to her feet. "I haven't had a laugh like that in a long time."

She bit her lower lip and shrugged at the dog.

"I knew Ornry liked ya for a reason." He scratched behind the dog's ear. "What kinda dog did you say you had?"

"A really big one. Nice, but kinda dumb." She grinned.

"Mmm. Ornry here's smart as a... umm..." He gazed around the room as though he might find a metaphor sitting on one of the shelves. "Aw hell, he's real smart."

The dog nosed at the unworn boot, whimpering and snorting.

"Yah, should prob'ly clean tha damn thing." He picked it up, cringing away from the odor. "Worse'n I thought."

Althea rubbed his shin. "Small hurts left to rot are worse than big ones."

"Yeah..." He gazed at the innocence in her eyes. "Spose'n yer right about that."

32

AMONG FRIENDS

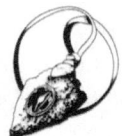

Iridescent wisps of auburn fire shimmered in gaps between buildings across the dying wreckage of old Querq. Althea leaned on the broom and squinted at the sight. Tall buildings had always made her wonder what kind of mystics could raise such things from the ground. The waning light brought with it the anticipation of Karina returning home. Smiling, she resumed her sweeping trek across the front porch, shooing the dirt out of the realm of man and back to the Earth.

She felt it in the boards first, a vibration that made the tiny particles of sand haze up into a blur above the brown-painted wood. Then came the sound, a heavy thrumming rumble not of this world. A behemoth of metal and chrome rolled around the corner at the far end of the street. A metal beast like the one the slave-catcher had, only larger. The front glowed with unnatural light, and a strip of the same ran above a window she couldn't see through.

The abandoned broom hit the porch with a sharp *clack* as she fell over herself in search of the safety of the house. Without conscious thought, she ran to the kitchen and crawled under the sink, shaking with her head tucked between her knees. The evil sound ebbed to nothing, but she remained breathless. They would be on foot now, looking for her. She wouldn't let them take her. She'd stay still and not make a sound. Not even the uncomfortable clump of skirt beneath her backside would make her move to ease it.

Perhaps an hour passed in dread silence until creaks in the floor hinted at the approach of a stealthy kidnapper. Althea closed her eyes, lest their light give her away. Breaths, warm down her leg, felt thunderous and had to stop. The worst part about having a home was how it changed her world. Being kidnapped used to be merely another day, but it had become dread incarnate. She remembered the gas station, the canid mutant, and called out with her mind for Father.

The kidnapper stopped right outside the cabinet. Althea glanced at the gap between the doors, at a shape blocking the light, and braced for the worst.

"I thought I'd find you here," said Karina. "You dropped the broom."

Shifting her weight off the tangle of leather, Althea pushed with trembling fingers at the panel of wood. Light split the darkness in which she cowered, tinged with the green glow of Karina's dress. Althea tried to force the fear out of her face as her sister pulled the door the rest of the way open.

"Guess I'm still feral." A hesitant smile slipped out from under her terror, but faded right away.

Karina sat on the floor, coaxing her from the cabinet to an embrace, staying with her and patting her on the back until the trembles ceased. "It's okay, Thea."

When calm arrived, she looked up. "I saw a monster in the road."

Karina smiled and ran a hand through Althea's hair. "It is a truck."

"A driving machine?"

"Yes. Outsiders have come to trade. They aren't looking for you. They bring supplies."

"Karina? Althea?" Father entered the front room with his rifle poised, his voice touched by worry.

"In here," Karina shouted as they stood and went to him, holding hands.

He slung the rifle over his shoulder and caught them both in an embrace. "Is everything all right? I had this feeling something was very wrong."

"We are fine." Karina smiled. "The truck spooked her."

"I'm sorry." Althea looked down. "I was so scared, I called for you."

Father muttered and glanced around, confusion obvious in his eyes. He dismissed his unease at seeing them safe. "It's only Harold and his boys come to trade. Got some new blood with him...."

Althea looked back and forth between them.

"Did they bring what the council wanted?" Karina seemed happy.

"Yeah," said Father. "I need to get back out there. You girls are welcome to come along."

Althea leaned toward the kitchen.

Karina smiled at Father. "She's still a little scared; I'll stay with her."

"Can I finish the porch after they leave?" Althea clung to her sister.

"They'll probably spend the night, maybe a day or two, but it's okay." Karina grinned. "I don't think Dad will notice."

Half an hour later, Althea was elbow deep in tortilla dough, making it herself this time with Karina hovering nearby. The pleasant normality of cooking dinner exorcised her fears. She learned faster than Karina expected; this, after all, involved hands making a mess and had nothing whatsoever to do with forks. Perhaps it made sense.

"What do we trade to them?" Althea kneaded the mush.

Karina shrugged. "Old junk, mostly. Harold wants things from the city around us, the dead parts where no one lives. It is dangerous there. Bugs, dogs, and other monsters come out at night. We know how to avoid them, so we take things for him and he brings us fresh food and medicines for Doctor Ruiz."

"Where does he get them from?" Althea looked up with a head tilt.

"He won't tell us." Karina added a pinch of salt to the mix. "They claim to go beyond the wall of fire, but that is a tall tale. He has found a before-time vault or something, and does not want us going there."

"It's not nice to lie about that. Our ancestors live there, where the good rest and the bad burn." Althea mixed the tortilla mixture with her bare hands, adding water until it reached a consistency she could pour it.

Karina made a strange gesture, touching her head, chest, and each shoulder. "It is bad to claim such things. It is why we do not ask him."

Althea took a flat pan from the high cabinet and set it on the stove before pulling the oven door open, frowning at the lack of wood. "Need burning wood."

"It's out where it always is." Karina smirked at her.

Taking a deep breath, Althea approached the door to the back porch. At some point long ago, it had been enclosed in screens, but only rickety wooden frames remained. The mournful glance she fired over her shoulder at Karina as her trembling fingers twisted the knob brought her sister out of a chair and up behind her.

"What are you so frightened of?"

Althea looked down. "I don't want to be taken again."

"Okay." Karina held her hand as they went to the pile of wood.

She selected a few pieces, stacking them on her left arm as Karina stood guard. A fat grub fell from one of the chunks, bouncing off her foot and wriggling on the ground.

"Oooh!" She stooped and snatched the thing, devouring it greedily.

Karina retched. Althea looked up, but the sight of grub-bits on her lips as she chewed made her sister convulse harder. Concerned, she dropped the wood and ran over. Much to her alarm, Karina tried to get away from her.

"How can…" She coughed and a tendril of bile fell from her lip. "Ugh. *¡Qué asco!*"

Althea followed her into the house, to the nearest bathroom, where Karina collapsed with her face over the toilet.

She paused at the door with an accusatory stare. "You told me that's not for drinking."

The thought of drinking from the toilet was the final straw. Karina's lunch came out. Althea massaged her sister's back as she searched for the problem.

"I can't find the sick."

Karina gasped between dry heaves. "You ate a *gusano*."

"Oh." Althea tucked her lower lip in to nibble bits that remained. "They're good. Lot of proteam."

"What's proteam?" Karina sat back on her heels, wiping her face.

Althea shrugged. "I dunno. It's what Reed said." She explained how he could find food from the land and knew what things she could eat and which to avoid.

"Althea?" A feminine voice called from the front porch. "Are you there? Please, we need you."

She helped Karina up and they went to see what the visitor wanted. A middle-aged woman shifted her weight from one leg to the other, trying to peek in the small windows at the top of the door.

"Something's wrong." Althea jogged ahead, feeling the worry surrounding this woman.

"*¡Gracias a dios!*" She tugged at Althea's shoulders and blasted her with Spanish too fast to understand. Seeing the look she made, the woman slowed down. "A boy has fallen. His legs, they are broken."

Althea took the woman's hand. "Bring me to him."

At the center of Querq, wailing led her to a small boy whose feet bent at wrong angles from his legs.

"He fell from there," said the old woman, pointing at a metal scaffold. "Trying to watch the outsiders."

A younger woman, no doubt his mother, hovered over him, frantic and screaming for help. Althea let go of the messenger's hand and sprinted into the crowd. People parted to allow her by. The boy saw her coming and calmed. His mother fell on her like a cloak when she knelt beside him, as if the woman needed to squeeze the mercy out of her.

"*Dale a la chica espacio para trabajar,*" said a man, pulling the mother away.

Althea took one of the boy's legs in her lap. His pained urgency faded to a curious expression once she dulled his pain. Working the foot back into place as if repairing a clay doll, she mended one and then the other. Finished, she sat and endured the exuberant adulation of the mother. She didn't expect the little guy to leap on her and kiss her on the face. Laughing, she patted him on the head before his mother scooped him up and took him back to their home. A growl from her stomach pointed out the insufficiency of a one-grub meal.

"Althea? Is that you?" A familiar female voice, laced with astonishment, shouted from the right.

She had to blink to make sure her eyes didn't lie. Rachel stood among the outsiders, sitting on the folded down tailgate of the mammoth vehicle. She no longer had the old 'M4' rifle, rather a much longer one, boxier, with blinking lights above the handle.

"Rachel!" Althea sprang to her feet and ran into a hug. "You're okay!" She cried at the visions the bad man had put into her head. "I'm sorry I ran away. I tried to go back, but I got lost."

"Hey, baby girl." She ruffled her hair. "Fancy meeting you here."

A big man with long brown hair and a beard down to his belt rounded the corner of the truck and looked at her. "You know this one?"

Althea tilted her head at him, her stare drawn to the flecks of dandruff dotting his black shirt like stars in the night sky. His clothing looked strange; his belt held many small objects also full of twinkling lights.

"Yeah, I ran into her before. This is the kid I was telling you about that helped us escape."

Two other men came over to see the child with glowing eyes. The one on the right was tall and bony, topped with a spiky explosion of black hair. Bits of metal stuck through his lip and his outfit looked like pieces of bug shell, gleaming, hard, and shiny. The second man had skin darker than Rachel's, with short black hair that clung to his scalp. His chest gleamed with a thin layer of sweat and he had the same sort of rifle across his back.

The hairy-faced man leaned toward her. "Badlands ain't no place for a little girl. You wanna come back to the city?"

Althea shook her head. "No, I'm home."

"Whoa, Harold... Check out dem eyes. She on Blue Lace?" A pulse of alarm and pity came from the dark man.

"Where the hell would she get that shit out here?" The thin guy folded his arms and smirked.

"Althea, this is Harold... but we just call him Beard. That's Darren, and the skinny one's Dean. Beard, what the hell is Blue Lace?"

He laughed. "Military drug. Experimental. It's supposed to make psionic people more psionic. It's damn illegal. The kinda stuff the cops'll shoot you on sight for selling. Military stopped using it when they found out it was deadly."

"Yeah," Darren added with a voice so deep it vibrated in Althea's chest. "Shit'll give you a mad boost for a couple of minutes, but it'll wind up making you crazy and killin' you in a few months.

"This is my sister, Karina." Althea beamed.

"Must be 'dopted," Dean mumbled, earning a slap to the back of the head from Darren. "What? Kid's white and the 'sister' is Mexican."

Darren slapped him again.

"Don't pay him any attention." Rachel smirked. "Dean still thinks I'm Dominican."

"What's that?" asked Althea.

The explanation, involving an island, largely went over her head. She got the feeling Rachel had mixed parents who had nothing to do with the place.

Althea feigned understanding. "Oh."

Rachel held her hand. "You should really come with us. The Badlands is not all there is. Society still exists." She sighed. "I slept *way* longer than I thought. Bit over 300 years. Everyone I ever knew is long dead."

Althea hugged her for a moment before she backed away with a smile. "No, I am happy here. I have Karina and Father and I can sleep in a bed and do chores and..."

"You need to go to school, to learn. This is no place to grow up. How will you get a job without education?" Rachel pulled at her arm.

"The council will give me one."

"What about hospitals? What if you get sick or hurt?"

Althea folded her arms and tapped her foot.

"Oh. Right." Rachel laughed. "Well, I'm not staying out here. I can't take the whole kill-or-be-someone's-bitch thing. I don't want to sleep with my ass to the wall all the time."

"That sounds uncomfortable." Althea's expression asked why she would do such a thing.

Rachel sighed. "I mean… aww, fuck it."

"What happened to the others? Zhar? Rama? Aya?"

"Oh them… After you took off, they blamed me for warning you Zhar intended to force you to go to her home. She wanted to—"

"I heard." Althea looked down. "I wasn't asleep. That's why I ran."

"Yeah, well, they figured it was my fault since I wasn't keen on the idea. Zhar didn't much like me anyway… guess there's only room for one alpha bitch. They're probably at Cheyenne by now." She laughed. "I tried to find my way back to base, but I ran into these guys. Beard and his guys are giving me a ride to the west. There's a real city there with flying cars and everything. I can't believe I lost so much time…"

"That's one hell of a freezer they stuck your fine ass in." Darren grinned at her as he passed with a heavy box.

She smiled at him and squeezed Althea's shoulder. "Please think about it? I'd feel bad leaving you out here in this shithole."

Althea put her hand on top of Rachel's.

"I'm happy you're okay, but this is my home now. I don't want to leave my family." Althea squeezed her hand, then returned to Karina's side. "I have to finish making dinner."

"You gonna help?" Dean shot a glance at Rachel as he hauled another box from the truck bed.

"Easy. Those two guns she had will pay for this whole trip." Beard waved at him, awe in his eyes. "Original Colt M4s that still fire. Easy million credits apiece."

"Yeah… Yeah…" The skinny guy shook his head and lurched off with a metal box toward the council building.

Karina led her home, back to the waiting pile of wood and bowl of dough.

❦

WATER SPLATTERED AROUND ALTHEA'S FEET AS SHE STRUGGLED WITH THE pump lever. The improvised machine hadn't come from the before-time.

The Water Man had made several of them before the pipe network, but the wall pipe had stopped working with the tub half-ready, the pressure too low. Karina asked Althea to retrieve water while she minded the fire.

Father had been fortunate to get a home so close to the pump. Retrieving water required only a short walk from the back porch. The sunbaked green at the bottom of a permanent puddle coated the wooden platform in a slimy growth. She pulled at the brass handle to make water come out of the earth, succeeding in lifting herself off the ground a few inches before it gave way and came down with a torrent that knocked the steel pail over and left her on her backside.

Resetting the bucket, she grabbed the lever and took a deep breath. It moved with less work once the grime had broken loose. She grinned as most of the water found its way into the container. Tonight was bath night. After a long normal day, Karina would wash her hair. Ever since her first bath here, she craved the tangible reminder of their special bond. Even after weeks, the touch of Karina washing her hair still brought tears of joy.

Her hands passed up and down through her stare at the street. She thought of the other children here. No one here feared her like the people from Den's village. In fact, they adored her. She still didn't understand the strange game with the ball where everyone would jump on whoever caught it. It beat being shunned, even if the game did cause small hurts.

The waning sunlight glinted across the water in the steel container. It would be dark soon, and her daydreaming caused her to overfill the pail. Father could carry this much, but she strained to tip it. After splashing enough out to where she could move the bucket, she heaved it into the air and staggered toward home.

The second time she needed to set it down to catch her breath, the scuff of a boot made her jump. Dean, the thin man, approached from behind. Her initial fear fell away to concern at the sight of blood dripping from the hand he clutched against his gut.

"You're hurt." She ran to him, pulling his arm away from his stomach.

Seeing a small razor cut on his palm, she offered a bewildered stare at why he had been staggering from such a tiny hurt.

"It's just a—"

A spray of pain raced up her back along with a high-pitched whine from a small pistol-like device in his left hand. Her legs failed as everything from the back of her thighs up to her shoulder burned with the torment of a thousand bee stings. She collapsed face down and tried to turn, but only her left arm would move. Dozens of green needles protruded from her skin, falling away one by one as the part of them stuck in her dissolved. The burn shifted to cold numbness and the street blurred into a mess of color.

"No." Althea stared in horror at the disintegrating chemical shards.

Poison.

Her power came slow at the urging of a mind dulled by the drug. Sped up by her psionic command, her body expelled the toxin and she made green water. Pushing herself up, she tried to scream, but only a whisper emerged. Her motion startled Dean, who pointed the pistol at her again. The evil thing covered her back in more pain. Fire engulfed her back; the weapon screamed for what felt like minutes until everything faded to black.

Dean's voice drifted out of the darkness. "Don't worry, kid. By the time you wake up..." The voice changed to that of a woman. "You'll be among friends."

33

THE GATES OF FIRE

S oft cloth brushed against Althea's skin in time with a gentle sway
that jostled her side to side. Her head felt as though it weighed
many times what it should, and the oppressive thrum of some
great mechanized presence filled the stagnant air. She stretched until her
toes touched frozen metal. Rolling onto her back, she reached over her
head and felt more chilly smoothness.

Her hand carried the cold to her cheek as she rubbed the fog out of
her senses and sat up. Her head swam with disorientation and her body
felt leaden, responding to her desire to move a few seconds late. She
looked down at her feet, stark pale against the darkness of her
surroundings. Patches of reflected light followed her gaze around a black
and white chamber that fit her like a coffin. Below her lay a pile of folded
blankets, and flat metal walls enclosed her—a cage without bars.

She remembered the whine, the swarm of angry hornets on her back,
and screamed. This time her voice came as it should, though the machine
noise outside swallowed it. She grabbed the back of her shoulder, her
fingers finding it sticky; her palm came back tinged with blood and
crystallized chemicals. She gritted her teeth and forced herself whole, a
thousand needlepoints in her skin sealing in an instant.

Althea purged the toxin from her body. Sluggishness changed to a
strong need to relieve herself. With no way out of this box, she gathered
her skirt out of the way and made water in the corner, cringing at the

burn of expelling poison. Once finished, she braced herself against the walls as the dizziness abated. The room continued rocking and swaying, proving it had not been a hallucination from the bees.

She thought of Dean pretending to be hurt, at once realizing he had put her in one of the large boxes in the bed of their truck. The motion told her they had decided to bring her with them despite her protest. The water she had been carrying home for her bath had never made it to the house, her long-awaited time with her sister stolen.

Taken again.

Althea screamed and banged at the metal on all sides, kicking and punching the unmoving barrier until her hands and feet throbbed. No one reacted to her tantrum; if anyone noticed—they didn't care. When she ran out of energy, she curled into a ball to cry, but couldn't. Anger gripped her more than sadness. Hunger as well, which came on as if she hadn't eaten in a day. Her mind called out for Father, for Karina, for the doctor, the Water Man, and even the canid.

Jostled about in the confines of the box, she rolled onto her back and braced her feet against the lid. The sense of her body filled her thoughts as her power focused upon her legs. Her thighs swelled into sinewy strands of amplified muscle. After bracing her feet against the lid, she shoved. A minute later, she relaxed, red-faced and gasping, and glared at the slab of metal that continued to defy her. She clutched the coarse blanket on either side, straining again until pain flooded over her legs. With a gasp, she gave up and rubbed her thighs. Mending the torn muscles made her hungrier. Once the hurt faded to exhaustion, she lay still for a time, drifting in and out of sleep.

Hours passed.

A bump flung her out of her near sleep into the lid. She landed on her chest and rolled upside down, crumpling against the front wall when the truck jammed to a halt. The machine sound ceased, leaving her basking in the echoing rush of her breathing. She eyed the spot where she thought the lid would open. Poised in a wildcat's perch, she waited to pounce the second it did.

"Good evening, sir," said a man outside, his voice muted by her prison.

"Howdy, officer," said Beard, also sounding distant. "How you boys doin' tonight?"

"Not too bad. What'cha got?" Officer sounded closer.

Doors opened and slammed.

Here they come.

She dug her fingers and toes into the blanket.

"The usual. Pre-war artifacts, couple of signs, couple of 'lectronic things, two old guns, and oh… yeah… got a rescue, too."

Althea scowled. She didn't need rescue; at least, not from Querq.

"Name?" asked Officer.

"Staff Sergeant Rachel E. Clarke, United States Air Force, security detachment for the 153rd Air Wing Under General Fitch. Enlistment date August 3, 2090."

Silence.

"Come again?" asked Officer.

"I know like 300 years went by. I was in a cryo unit at White Sands. We got hit with a biological weapon."

"Oh, geez." Officer sighed. "Brass is gonna have a goddamned field day with this."

"Is my enlistment still good, or is it expired?" Rachel trailed off to a whisper. "Holy shit, what is this place?"

"Welcome to West City, ma'am." Officer laughed. "Wait, what? Stowaway? Child-sized skeleton on the scanner? What are you talking about? Is it moving?"

Althea blinked. Beard said 'a' rescue. That meant one, and apparently Rachel. He didn't know she had been locked in here. Officer talking about a child-sized skeleton had to mean someone noticed her… somehow.

She cupped her hands around her mouth. "Help!" In a blur of desperation, she shrieked and kicked and slammed. "Help! Let me out!"

"Hands where I can see 'em," Officer yelled.

"Nobody move." Another voice, deeper, shouted from the other side.

Althea went quiet and listened. The truck jostled with the noises of armored bodies climbing it.

Someone knocked on a different crate. "Hello?"

"I'm here," she yelled, slapping the lid again.

"Open it." Officer said in a harsh tone, sounding close.

Beep, beep, beep, click. With a pneumatic hiss, the metal plate above her slid away to reveal a smog-filled sky bereft of stars. The acrid smell of metal, trash, and technology brought involuntary tears to her already wet eyes, and she coughed. A man-shaped creature hovered over her, covered in a shiny blue shell with the funny marks she knew as words on his chest and the sides of his helmet.

"Oh, my God, you poor thing." He leaned closer. "Take it easy, kid; no one's gonna hurt you."

Althea stared at herself reflected in the swath of gleaming silver covering the face from which Officer's voice emanated. She didn't notice the black glove until it touched her shoulder, and cringed.

"Easy, kid. I'm just going to get you out of there, okay?" He reached for her with both hands.

Despite being terrified, she had little choice but to comply. Lifting her arms, she let him grasp around her body. He lifted her out of the crate, cradling her until he climbed from the truck and set her on her feet. The metal ground chilled her bare feet. Teeth chattering, she glanced left at Rachel, Beard, Darren, and Dean with their hands against the wall; more blue men pointed guns at them. Straight ahead of her, beyond an interior gate of dull flat grey, the horizon burned with a million lights and great towers of metal and glass between which rivers of fast-moving objects flowed.

It resembled how she imagined the Lost Place might've been in the before-time, only with more light, more noise, and more stink. Things whizzed by in the air, streams of boxes clad in panels of light; larger objects resembling cars moved in neat rows much higher up. Disembodied ghostly heads, many times bigger than a person ought to be, smiled down at the earth and held up products and gadgets. The structures extended into the clouds, out of sight. This enormous city appeared to lean toward her with the overbearing lack of open land. She backed into the wheel of the truck, trying to get away from the oppressive presence, wanting to hide, wanting Father.

"These bastards kept her in there so long she wet the blanket." Another blue creature hovered over her now, perched in the truck bed by the box.

"You fuckers know it's perfectly legal to save Scrags. Why'd you lock her in there?" Officer yelled back at Beard's group.

"I don't need saved. I was taken from my family." She stomped. "I want to go home."

"Look at her eyes, Joe. Lace?"

"Get a medic down here."

"Roger."

"It was him." Althea pointed at Dean. "The others don't know. He shot me with bees."

"What?" Officer crouched, meeting her eye to faceplate. "Shot you with bees?"

"Tranq needler." The man by the box held up a tiny sliver of what looked like green glass.

Other blue men searched Dean, finding the small pistol.

"That." As soon as she saw it, Althea pointed.

Officer reached to his belt and took metal restraints out of a case. They looked somewhat different from handcuffs she had seen, but such an object was unmistakable. Althea held her hands up to him, and cried.

"Please don't tie me. I promise I won't run away," sobbed Althea, resorting to her old plea. Dread that she would never see Karina or Father again brought shivers.

He tilted his head at her and pushed her hands down. "These aren't for you, kid."

"You sick bastard." One of the blue men drilled Dean into the wall. "What'd you do to this girl?"

"Nothing. What the hell is going on? I didn't touch her!" Dean howled. "I don't even know what happened."

Rachel looked over her shoulder, past her raised arms at Althea, radiating worry.

Althea stared at the shiny ground, searching for words amid her grief. "Please… The others didn't know I was in the box. They are confused."

Beard glared death at Dean. "You shifty little bastard. If I see you again, I'm gonna beat you purple."

"Calm down, sir." Officer put the cuffs away, staying with Althea.

"That chav had nothing to do with it," said a woman, her voice coming from everywhere.

Aurora.

The blue men aimed their rifles around, searching for the source. Dean screamed and wrenched himself free of the police officer's grip, banging his face into the wall in a series of dull, metallic thuds before he slid to the floor, cheek squealing over the surface. When he sat up, his shirt split open and a flesh-apparition of a woman's upper body exuded from his chest. The displacing skin thinned his face, drawing the skull more prominent around his vacant stare and exposing the undersides of his eyeballs.

The cops leapt back, all of them shouting "whoa" in unison. Beard lifted an eyebrow, grabbing at an empty holster and grumbling about the cops taking his gun.

"What the fuck is that?" Rachel pointed.

Darren gathered Rachel behind him, and backed with her into the corner by the inner gate.

"This man is a shell. He occupied a necessary place at a necessary time." Dean staggered to his feet, shambling with a zombie's gait toward Althea. "I show myself for your benefit, little one. These police will now believe you that this man is not to blame. Don't you feel better? He will not suffer for what I have done with him."

"Take another step and you're fucking gone, whatever you are!" A red dot from Officer's pistol flitted back and forth from Dean's head to the apparition's face.

"No." Althea yelled, tugging on the hard plastic arm with both hands until she dangled from it. "Don't kill him. You can't hurt her, but you'll kill him. She's just a spirit that made him do it."

"What are you?" One of the other blue men took a step toward Dean/Aurora.

"I am a messenger, the herald of Archon. You have served your purpose. Come, little one, it is time to meet your friends."

"No." Althea shook her head. "I want my family. I want to go home."

"We kin run her back out there." Beard glanced sideways at the cops, hoping to curry favor.

"I don't think that will be possible," Aurora cooed.

Dean's body jerked. A gunshot, a scream, and the fleshy thud of body on steel followed. Althea turned, gazing up at a knife, clear as glass, stuck in Officer's side. A sluice of blood trailed the edge, dripping to the ground. The other blue man fired the instant the knife left Dean's hand; the shot hit him in the shoulder and knocked a spray of blood onto the wall that oozed down behind him. The flesh-apparition deflated, and the sense of her presence departed.

"Son of a bitch." Officer grumbled, pulling the knife out. "Fucking Nano knife? Your ass better have a BHL or I'm gonna shove this straight—"

He lurched to grab Althea as she ran for Dean, seizing her by the shoulder. "You don't need to see that, kid."

"Please. He's hurt. I have to help him." She stared at the distorted version of her face in the silver.

"Go with McMasters, he'll get you some cocoa." Officer pushed her toward another man.

"*Let me help him.*" Althea's eyes flared in time with her psionic command, and Officer's grip went lax.

He stood motionless, hand hovering as if he held her. She ran over and slid to a halt on her knees by Dean's side. McMasters glanced back and forth from her to the stunned cop.

"Dude, did that kid just psi you? You okay?"

"Huh, what?" Officer looked around. "This is a checkpoint."

"Eep!" Althea cried out at the sight of a hole in Dean's shoulder big enough to see the ground beneath him.

What kind of awful weapons did these men have? The bullet hadn't remained to be dug out—it had gone right through him. She planted her hands around the gore and opened her mind to his life essence. The five patrol officers ran up to pull her away from such a grisly sight. They stopped, awestruck, when the wound began closing. One wobbled away, sick. Her eyes brightened as she worked, soft whimpers and grunts of exertion escaping her lips. After repairing the wound, she crossed her arms over her gut and moaned from a painful hunger pang.

A hand took hers, guiding her to stand before picking her up and cradling her against cool plastic armor.

"C'mon, kid," said Officer.

She reached up, pushing the silver visor away from tired green eyes. Her fingers touched his cheek, and the sense of his life flooded her consciousness. In a moment, the knife-bite in his side sealed.

"Aww man, kid, you didn't need to see that." Officer pointed at Dean. "Get *him* to a medic, send the others to interview rooms, and someone get a fuckin' Zero down here, stat. We don't get paid enough to deal with this weird shit."

34

HOT COCOA

The tiny silver room held two metal chairs facing each other from opposite ends of a silver table. Officer set her down in one of them and folded her limp arms in her lap. Althea stared at the loop bolted to the table and imagined the leash would be attached there. She leaned forward and put her wrists on either side of it, waiting for the chain.

"Stop that." Officer put her hands in her lap again. "I don't know what they did to you, but you're safe now. No one here is going to hurt you. Would you like some food?"

"Yes, please." She swung her feet back and forth, gazing down.

Shivering from the temperature, she curled up on the chair and stared at her blurry reflection in the rough finish of the table. Officer had closed the door behind him; her heart sank, she felt certain it had locked. Cold and bare, with places for chains to go, this room had to be meant for slaves. Despite that, it was cleaner even than Ruiz's hospital.

A hole in the ceiling covered in little bars carried murmuring voices from elsewhere inside this place. A woman arrived in the same blue shell as the other men, only she had nothing covering her face. She carried food over, smiling. Two pieces of chicken, a beige glop, and a mound of little green spheres rested on a tray, flanked by a plastic knife and fork.

Althea looked at the fork and cried. It made her think of Karina. Her sister would be upset with her for not using it, but she was too hungry and too upset to dwell on it. Packing handfuls of peas and mashed potatoes into her mouth, she devoured the strange food without tasting it, down to gnawing on the bones.

A red-haired woman in a white jumpsuit had snuck in while she ate, watching her go feral on the fried chicken. Althea looked up from the fifth pass of her tongue over the plate, realizing she had an audience.

"Wow… you must've been hungry." The woman smiled. "I'm Heather. What's your name?"

"Althea." She shrank into the chair.

"Hello, Althea. I'm a medical tech, and I need to check you out to make sure you're not sick or bringing anything into the city we don't want."

"I don't want to go into the city. I want to go home," she mewled.

"We don't just let kids wander off into the Badlands. When you're eighteen, you can go back if you want. For now, you'll get a foster family and go to school, and—"

"I have a family." Althea jumped up, yelling. "Aurora took me away from them."

Heather smiled. "Well, if your parents are out there, they should come to the city where it's safe. We can talk about finding them once we make sure you're healthy."

She glared as the woman waved a strange little device over her, watching a strip of blue laser light crawl down her arms and legs. Heather turned Althea's head to the side. Warmth flooded one ear then the other.

"Open wide." Heather lifted a small wand, which shone a bright light down her throat.

This felt familiar.

The woman took a small red tube out and pushed it against Althea's shoulder. She jumped when it hissed and created a cool presence beneath her skin. She didn't react to the tiny bit of pain. When Heather did it a second time, she scowled.

"What are you doing to me?"

The woman offered a reassuring pat on the shoulder. "It's medicine that will keep you from getting sick. They're called vaccines."

"I don't get sick." Althea sighed.

"Sure." Heather flashed a patronizing smile. "Let me see those eyes."

"No, I don't know why they light up. Yes. They've always done it." With a put-upon exhale of frustration, she leaned forward and opened them as wide as she could and rolled them around to the four corners. "See? Blue light. Can I go now?"

Heather ignored her ramble, poring over her face with the same strange device.

"Interesting."

"What?" Althea grumbled.

"Your sclera are bioluminescent, like a firefly, but stronger. The rest of the eye looks normal."

"Bio loom..." She tried. This woman spoke the same word the strange little robot had used.

"Bioluminescent."

"What does that mean?"

"It means they glow." Officer chimed in from where he leaned on the doorframe.

"Then just say they glow. I knew that already." Althea called the woman dumb with a glare.

"So what's the verdict?" He looked at the redhead.

"I'm malnurmished, but you can't find anything else wrong with me. I'm small for my age, you think I'm only ten but I'm twelve, and umm..." Her insolent rant stalled as she ran out of things to say. "Well, maybe I'm not really twelve."

Heather frowned. "Her metabolic rate is sky high. Muscle density is what one would expect from a professional athlete... Somewhat *malnourished*"—Heather glanced at the untouched fork—"and probably a little feral. She's conversational, though, so she's had some human contact."

"I even walk on two legs and I'm toilet trained." Petulance dripped from her voice. "Or do you want me to make water in the corner and bark at the moon?"

Officer tried not to laugh. "Any diseases, parasites, or infections?"

"I checked her twice, nothing. Never saw that before with a Scrag; they always have half a dozen things."

She stomped, her bare foot making a sharp *clap* on the metal floor. "You're not listening. I told you I don't get sick."

A wave of discomfited concern came from Officer. "Any evidence of..."

"No. That's one damn lucky kid."

A wave of strong relief radiated from Officer.

Heather disregarded her with the same patronizing smile. "So where's the suspect that took one to the shoulder? Isn't his wound worse? Why did you send me in here for this first?"

Officer pointed at Althea. "She fixed him already."

"What? Stop fucking with me, Joe."

"Go check the surveillance vid. Dude took an eleven-millimeter to the shoulder. The kid put her hand on him and the wound just closed on its own. That's why we got Zeroes on the way."

Althea's sadness turned to sullen frustration. "Can I go now? Are you done?"

Officer glanced down the hall. "Not my decision, sweetie."

Rage boiled inside her and the glow flared. Hair whipped by an unseen wind, she yelled with a voice louder than physically possible. "I am *tired* of being kidnapped! I want to go home."

Radiant fear worked on giant roaches, and apparently just as well on arrogant medical techs. Heather screamed and ran past Officer into the hallway while he merely lifted an eyebrow and took a step back. The medic was too scared to speak; Althea sensed her fear of psionics, a terror that peaked when a man and woman in black walked into view outside the large window.

Their clothes didn't shine like the blue shells, and they both had silver pistols on their belt instead of the black ones like Officer. Heather ran, refusing to make eye contact with them. Officer moved out of their way, less obvious in his distrust, but she sensed it. He didn't fear them the same way the woman did, more like how raiders reacted to the poor idiot who had to carry explosives.

Althea relaxed, backing against the table.

"Hello there." The woman entered. "I'm Jamie. I hear you're a very special little girl."

Mike, look at her eyes.

The man in the hall reacted to the thought.

I'm sayomic, too. Althea shot her voice into the woman's head.

Jamie chuckled. "It's psionic." She pronounced it a few times until Althea repeated it properly. "We are special police officers who help people like you. They told me you just arrived from the Badlands?"

"Yes, but I don't want to be here. I have a family. I've been kidnapped and I want to go back to them now." She folded her arms, and pouted at her toes. "I missed bath time."

"Your family is out there?"

Althea took a step toward her, urgency brimming in her eyes. "Yes, and they are worried about me."

Jamie sat in the other chair, tugging on Althea's hand until she moved closer. "Are they able to take care of a girl with your special circumstances?"

"What do you mean?"

"Well..." Jamie looked her up and down. "It doesn't look like you're being given enough food, you're wearing a boy's undershirt and a skirt made from leather bits. No shoes... Are your parents taking proper care of you, is all I'm asking."

"You just described *every* kid." Althea's tone came off flat. "I get extra hungry when I make the sicks and the hurts go away."

The two exchanged a glance. Althea read their thoughts. Before they walked in, they'd watched her mend Dean on some kind of magic square of floating light. These people in black wanted her too, though it felt like curiosity more than greed.

"You know what I can do. You saw the man outside get better. That's why I don't get sick."

"Althea, is it?" asked the woman.

"Yes."

"We know of some others who have talents like yours. We call it accelerated healing. What has us confused is we have never seen someone able to do it to other people."

The man walked closer. "In all documented cases, those who have been gifted with that ability could only restore their own bodies."

Althea shrugged.

"Maybe she got some radiation or something from the Badlands?" The man lifted an eyebrow.

"You've read too many vid comics, Mike. Radiation doesn't turn you into a superhero; it melts your skin off."

"Yeah in large fast doses sure, but who knows what very low level exposure over generations can do." He smiled. "We know what we saw. Can you explain it?"

Jamie squeezed her shoulder. "Althea, there is a place we can take you where you can learn how to get the most from your abilities. It's a safe place where we can protect you and teach you."

"Home!" She stomped. "I want to go home." She stomped again.

"What if we brought your family here?" Mike patted her on the back. "Just for a little while so you can be with them while you see the school. If you don't like it, you can go back."

Althea stared at the floor. This place might be tolerable with Karina and Father, but the people of Querq depended on her, too. "My home needs me. There are so many people there I miss."

"Why would anyone want to be out there? All the creatures, the mutants, the gangs, the violence..." Jamie shook her head.

Officer made a noise, stifling a thought. Althea peeked. He wanted to say "we have gangs here, too." Some of the images in his mind looked terrifying. Flying cars, screaming people, gunfights in the streets, junkies, homeless, crime scenes, all of it swam together and made her wrench her telepathic link away from him with a whimper.

"What's wrong?" Jamie tried to be consoling, but she didn't compare to Karina.

"I don't like this place. There's evil here. I'm sick of being kidnapped so much. I was finally happy, and they took me away again." Her voice twisted with tears, but she defied the urge to sob. "I want to go home, and I want to go home right now."

"You haven't been kidnapped, honey." Jamie patted her lightly on the cheek. "You've been rescued."

"It feels the same." She pouted. "'Cept I'm not tied up or in a cage."

"That's so sad." Mike passed over a cup of hot chocolate from one of the blue men. "Here, hon. Take this. It's good."

She sniffed at it, allowing Jamie to pull her into her lap. A big swallow went down her throat like fire. Shocked by the heat, she cried out. Gasping, she fanned at her mouth. It tasted wonderful, but hurt.

"Sip it, slow." The woman giggled. "See, there's a lot you need to learn. That's why we would like to take you to the school. It's not safe out there."

"People don't hurt me. They just lock me up and fight over who owns me. They call me the Prophet. I don't want to be owned anymore, and I know I can make them stop now."

"You're in the city, Althea. Nobody out there knows who you are. It's a dangerous place for a little girl. Hell, it's a dangerous place for me." Mike laughed.

Althea sipped the sweet, warm liquid, staring over the rising edge of the cup at his blue eyes. He wanted something from her, but not the same way the raiders did. She intrigued him the way inventing things intrigued the Water Man. They wanted to help her. Neither gave off any malice, but they also didn't let her go back to her family.

"Look. We have to follow procedure." Jamie sighed. "Let's pretend for a bit the law would allow us to send you back into the Badlands; before we could do it, we'd have to at least work with you for a little while to understand what you can do."

"Why?"

Slurp.

"It's the law. We need to catalog psionics, especially when we find someone that can do things no one has ever seen before."

Slurp.

She stared at him. They feared she would be a danger to people, a thought she found ludicrous. "I can't kill people. All I want to do is help."

An unintentional pulse of radiant sadness at being thought of as a potential threat knocked them both loopy for a moment.

"Oh my." Mike grabbed his head.

Out in the hallway, four men burst into tears. Hearing them cry reminded her of Father's tears the night she almost had to leave Querq. Althea buried her face in her hands, overcome with sorrow. A distant man wailed.

"Telempath." Jamie gasped, sniffling into full on sobs. "Sadness... Please stop. Holy shit, she's strong. I can't resist her."

Althea realized she 'leaked,' and got herself under control. "I'm sorry. It made me sad when he thought I could kill someone."

"Hey." Mike tipped her chin up with his finger, still fighting the urge to cry. "I believe you, but our boss will be mad at us if we don't. Will you help us, just for a few hours and then we'll talk to her about getting you home. We have cars that can fly out there if everything works out okay."

If she's this powerful, she might be better off out there away from the corporations, said Mike's voice in Jamie's mind.

She tilted her head in curiosity. "What's a corporation?"

Jamie mumbled. "You know it's rude to..."

"What is rude?"

Slurp. The cocoa no longer burned.

Mike cracked up laughing. He thought for a moment, and smiled. "A corporation is like a gang, only they use money instead of guns."

She stared. "That's stupid. Who's afraid of money?"

"You'd be surprised." Jamie chuckled.

Slurp.

Althea glanced down at her empty cup, shrugged, and set it on the table.

MALICE IN WONDERLAND

ecause they promised to take her home as soon as they could, she
agreed to go with them. Beard's truck was missing from the space
between the gates when they walked outside. In its place sat a
shiny black car with a strip of clear glass across the roof that snapped side
to side with brief flares of blinding blue light. Mike led her by the hand to
the door; the steel ground had become colder since the sun hid behind the
jagged claws of metal and light that scratched at the sky.

Althea trembled at the city looming over her. It felt as though it would
come crashing down at any time, smothering her with a strange
foreboding darkness she sensed lurking behind the gleaming edifice of
civilization. She stood on the far side of the great wall of flame the elders
had spoken of, only it was made of metal instead of flames, with guns
bigger than cars that threw fire instead of bullets. When she had asked
about it, Mike told her it protected the city from mutants and gangs. This
place did not hold anyone's ancestor spirits. The land beyond the 'great
barrier' did not belong to the dead.

She frowned at the blue spots her eyes made on the armored door
panel until it swung up and open. Soft grey seats waited for her.
Reluctantly, she gathered her skirt up and sat. Mike reached across her
for the seat belt, and she stiffened like a dutiful slave as he pulled the strap
across her lap.

"You said you wouldn't tie me." A tear rolled down her cheek.

"This is a safety belt. It's to protect you in case we hit something."

Seeing Jamie put one on as well calmed her. She sat still as Mike closed her door. The console flooded with light in response to Jamie playing with buttons. Mike slid into the passenger seat and belted himself in.

When they floated straight up, Althea lost her mind. Screaming, she scratched at the glass and kicked at the seat. The belt held her down and she tugged at it, trying to escape. Jamie set the hovercar back on its wheels hard, struggling to overcome the radiant terror emanating from their passenger. As soon as they hit solid ground, Althea's panic receded to bawling tears. Mike leaned through the gap between the seats and held her hand.

"Hey, calm down, sweetie. There's nothing to be scared of. You're in a hovercar. It's supposed to fly." He smiled.

Althea clutched the lap belt and strained, grimacing as she tried to get out. Mike reached over and clicked the buckle off. Freedom eased her panic. He laboriously explained the workings of the seat belt, telling her to look at his thoughts if she needed to. She did, and after a few sniveling breaths, put it back on. When the vehicle again glided up into the air, she clawed at the seat, but contained herself.

The inner wall of the checkpoint fell out of view as they floated higher. She looked out over an endless sea of great buildings glimmering to the horizon. With terrified curiosity, Althea gazed around at the scenery while the car climbed to join a stream of similar vehicles. What her eyes told her defied imagination. Not a scrap of bare earth or vegetation existed anywhere. So many people lived in this place, yet this mountain of human achievement flooded with such sorrow.

Waves of bad emotions zoomed by from other cars. Anger the most popular, jealousy, greed, and depression followed. One car made her raise an eyebrow, as the mood wafting from it seemed as though someone was getting wifed.

She had gone with them only to go home as fast as possible. Whatever they wanted to do would take a few hours, and then they promised they would send her home if she still wanted to go. The city slid by outside, blurred by the haze of liquid sadness that fell from her eyes. After a while, she noticed the windows of buildings outside slid upward, and realized the car descended.

Althea peered to the front.

"There you are."

The voice, with a British accent, came from a ghostly man's head protruding from the console. He had thick brown hair, a prominent brow, and an arrogant smile. A thin mustache joined a tiny beard on his chin.

"Who the hell are you?" Mike glared at him.

Althea drew a breath. "Ghost?"

"No, it's a hologram," Jamie muttered. "Someone hacked our comm channel."

"Do holler grams have feelings?" Althea's voice trembled.

"No, they're just li—what the hell?" Jamie blinked at the head. "Mike... That fucking hologram has surface thoughts... Ow." Jamie gasped and grabbed her head.

"How amusing." The head frowned at her. "Indeed I do, but they are *not* for the perusal of my lessers."

"You realize you are intruding upon Divis—" Mike grabbed his head and screamed.

"That is quite enough prattle from drones." The head sneered at Mike. "You... time for a nap."

Mike faceplanted the dashboard, unconscious.

"You..." The head looked at Jamie and the free will melted out of her face. "Please give my guest a ride to our rendezvous point."

The eyes within the holographic head flashed to static. Jamie pulled at the control sticks and the car banked off to the left in a slow glide toward the ground. Althea hyperventilated, seeing her promised trip home evaporate. In her panic, she forgot how to work the seatbelt and thrashed at it.

The hologram chuckled. "You have much to learn, Althea. You needn't be afraid of me. I am like you."

She froze, staring, disliking the way he pronounced her name, "all-thaya."

Rage and terror collided in equal amounts in her mind, leaving her feeling neither. "What?"

"These pathetic individuals are merely psionic. What we are is something much greater."

"Don't hurt them." She writhed; her heels slid off the seat as she struggled to pull her hips free from the belt.

His laugh made her feel small. "I will not hurt them if you behave yourself. I am just borrowing them for a moment. I am saving you from the tyranny of a society that cannot possibly understand you. They only want to control you, like everyone else. If you think they would have actually ferried you back into primate land, you are sorely mistaken."

"I want to go home." Her downcast gaze fell among tangled strands of leather. A glint of chromatic light danced across the silver button, and she remembered how to work the belt.

"You *are* going home, child... to a home that can properly nurture you."

She crawled past the gap between the seats, grabbing Jamie's arm in both hands and shaking her. Android-like, the woman gazed with lifeless eyes at the passing buildings.

Althea shoved and pulled. "Wake up."

The head laughed. "You cannot reach her, child. Do not feel sorry for them. They only led you into slavery once again. Only I can offer you true freedom." Shimmering light from the ghostly head flashed patterns on her skin.

She stared at him. "Who are you?"

"I am the man who will usher in the dawn of the Awakened. You may know me as *Archon*." He gazed up and to the right, infinitely proud of his own destiny.

She blinked. "Awakened at dawn? Most people wake up at dawn."

He frowned. "Droll child. Are you truly simple, or do you mock me?"

"Sorry." She looked back and forth at the lights all over the console. This flying car had so many complicated things. She couldn't even work out how to use a steering wheel and pedals, and this car didn't have a wheel—just two sticks. "What is awakened?"

"These Division 0 fools are psionic in the way a baby crawls. You and I, we are walking—no... flying. We are a higher order. Your eyes mark you as one of us."

Althea cringed from the pride and desire radiating from the face floating over the console. Leaping forward, she swatted randomly at buttons and switches, trying to make the bad man go away.

"What are you doing, child? *Sit down!*" His voice flooded her thoughts.

She fell onto the hard plastic between the two front seats, grabbing her head. A second later, she wanted more than anything to hop back into her seat to please her daddy. She did so and grinned vapidly at him like a little girl waiting for a pat on the head. It felt like such a wonderful idea to just sit there and behave.

The smiling faces of Karina and Father flashed in her mind. A tiny scream started in the back of her mind, growing and coming forward until it erupted from her mouth; she shoved him out of her head.

"No." Anger brightened her eyes, flooding the car with blue light. She leapt into the front again, pounding her fists into the console, left and right, at anything that glowed.

A bad sound throbbed in her ears. Everything inside the car flashed red. The hologram head vanished as the center part of the dashboard went dark. The car fell like a stone. Althea floated straight up, her back against the cloth liner at the top of the cabin. Seeing the ground approaching fast, she screamed. Her arms were too short to reach Jamie while pinned to the roof. Growling, she swung a leg down and pressed her foot to the side of the woman's head.

Strange scrambled energy occupied the space where the brain should be. Nothing seemed physically wrong, but the brain felt like a machine not 'turned on.' She tried every way of pushing at it she could think of, searching for a way to purge the harmful presence before they reached the ground.

Jamie's eyes shot open. She screamed, bashing her fist into a red button. Light spread over the console. She hauled back on the left stick. Althea crashed onto the floor, then bounced up into the rear seat, barking like a kicked goose when she thumped against the seatback. She reached for the belt, but became weightless again an instant before a tremendous smash hit the car from below. Sky, road, and city flashed by the window as the vehicle tumbled end over end. It stopped for several seconds when Jamie regained control. Althea found herself lying on her back in the front seat again and couldn't explain how she'd gotten there. Her head pounded, the warmth of blood ran down her face.

Althea closed her eyes, focusing inward. Her bone-shapes had cracked: ribs, an arm, and her thigh. She cringed at the *snap* of her right femur coming back together, after which the pain of her reintegrating arm barely registered. Angular shards broke into the red cloud. She forced them away from her body one by one, wincing at the sensation of small fragments sliding out of her skin and dropping to the carpet beneath her. After sealing a minor cut on her forehead, she pushed herself up off the floor and looked around.

Her stomach growled.

The windshield had become a dented slab of metal covered in broken glass, no longer transparent. Mike remained unconscious; Jamie moaned, bleeding.

"You okay?" The woman coughed up blood.

"Don't talk." Althea took her hand.

She didn't have much energy left, but focused what little she had into the wounded cop. Althea budgeted it enough to stabilize her and prevent death. When she opened her eyes, Jamie tried to speak.

"Stim...," whispered Jamie in a weak voice, distorted by Althea's fatigue.

She did not ask for clarification, instead looking into the woman's mind. Small red devices on her belt held medicine. They would make her less tired. Althea rummaged the little black cases, avoiding the strange silver gun. In one of the pouches, she found five red tubes and took one out.

"How do I work it?" asked Althea. The answer formed in the woman's mind faster than words.

Althea pushed the end into her thigh, but nothing happened.

"Safety cap..."

After turning it over, she bit a yellow plastic cap off the end, exposing a tiny hole at the center of a metal spot. When next she pressed it into her leg, it hissed and flooded her thigh with a cool presence. Within seconds, a surge of energy replaced her fatigue. Jamie gave off confusion. She had meant for the girl to give *her* the stimpak.

"Oops," muttered Althea. "Sorry."

Revitalized, she mended the last of the hurt from the woman and turned her attention to Mike. His limp body weathered the crash a little better, and was in no danger of dying. A second after he awoke, gunshots erupted around her.

Althea tried to look, but saw only Jamie's hand as it covered her face and shoved her into the back seat. "Get down!"

The woman drew her silver pistol, firing bolts of blue light out the open driver side window. The *clink* of bullets striking the car came from everywhere. Phantom voices filled the car asking what happened. A desperate, young sounding girl really seemed to want something called 'status.' Both Jamie and Mike yelled they needed backup immediately. Althea knew a car made for an awful place to be in the middle of a gunfight. They tended to explode. At least, raider buggies did. This strange flying car would probably explode *way* worse since it was so much bigger.

She leapt headfirst out the open passenger window, slithering straight to the ground and crawling on her belly to get away. A dozen people in a mix of long coats and wild clothing that reminded her of raiders, only less dusty, continued firing at the car. The bullets bounced off without even denting it. Althea gawked in surprise, wondering if perhaps she should have stayed inside. One man tossed a sphere of flames around in his hand. The sight of the hovering fireball made her heart skip a beat.

A demon!

Althea ran, feet squeaking over the metal ground as she sprinted down a cluttered path between two buildings. One of the raiders saw her and yelled at his friends to circle around. Taking a right at the first opportunity, she dashed into a narrow alley strewn with garbage and large, wheeled metal boxes packed with yet more trash. A few paces later, she leapt over several sleeping people.

A huge man leaned out from behind a dumpster so close Althea couldn't stop and ran right into him. She bounced away and staggered back, peering up at a toothless grin and frayed beard.

"Sorry."

Bypassing the wobbling giant, she darted around the corner before he could turn to see where she went. She didn't look over her shoulder since the raiders trying to take her from the people in black could be right behind her. Turning corner after corner, she continued until a strange rhythmic throbbing noise pounded at her from an open doorway. A line of people stacked up along the edge of a building with a lime green door, dressed in clothing made of bizarre shiny materials, some with their hair aglow or twisted into weird shapes. Above the opening, funny symbols danced in the air, shifting and moving, made out of pure light like the head in the car.

A tall, bald man in a black leather vest and dark pants peered at the couple closest to the door despite wearing opaque glasses. Althea stared to the rear, terrified the man with flames in his hand would round the corner any second. In all directions, the same thing repeated itself: trash, small clouds of fog rolling along, buildings, and metal ground. The doorway into loudness looked like the best place to hide. She sprinted for the door, sliding under the bald man's reaching arm. Inside, multicolored lights flashed in the dark, pulsing in time with beating music that vibrated the air and swallowed the bald man's shout. She ran forward across a short area full of tables, and down three stairs into a dense crowd. The noise in the air grew loud and heavy, pushing and pulling the air in her lungs.

Stumbling amid a sea of undulating figures, she tried to disappear. This room held so much chaos no one could find her. The mass of people reacted like a body to a foreign object, pushing her along in a current of gyrating hips and roaming hands until it spat her out, chest-first into a rounded platform of shiny black glass upon which a naked woman gyrated in time with the music. Straps circled her thighs and waist, with small bits of bright red plastic tucked in them.

The woman stuck her rear end out at a man nearby and waved it around. He grinned and reached up to stick another little red tab into a band around her thigh.

This must be the raider's camp. Althea gulped. The harem slaves would occasionally dance like that, though she found it strange the woman wore no leash and even radiated pleasure. Althea figured her as broken as Aya.

"Totally love the blue light," a female voice yelled into her left ear. "Where did you get them done?"

A girl who looked to be about Karina's age had tucked up next to her. Red light striped across her face, a raccoon band over her eyes, and she wore a little vest that didn't cover much of anything. At first, Althea thought the girl had painted her legs black, but a belt revealed the coloration to be thin pants.

"Oh damn, girl." She reached for Althea's chest. "You need to have someone look at them boobs. Wow. Talk about *flat*. They're so small they're not even there. Mine used to be little like that, too."

This girl had strange emotions. Looking at Althea, she radiated the same feeling that she'd picked up from an older boy in Querq while he did that lip-touching thing with a girl he liked. Althea wasn't quite sure why another girl would feel that way about her.

"Umm. I'm too young," said Althea.

"What?" shouted the girl.

I'm a kid. Like maybe twelve.

The girl blinked at the telepathic shout. "Oh, shit. Sorry!" She laughed. "No wonder you're so skinny. What are you doing in here?"

Althea backed away into the throng, hiding once more among the moving bodies. The dense crowd prevented her from falling over, but swept her across the room and down a second short set of stairs onto a floor coated in a slimy stickiness where people stood in place and had seizures.

She froze, grimacing at the disgusting sensation under her feet. *Eww.* She peered down at the black surface and peeled a foot away, wondering what she walked on. No one else seemed to notice the awful miasma. Althea realized the swaying bodies and the noise followed the same rhythm. Zombie thrashing moved in time with the horrible sound, as if everyone in here fell under the charm of an evil mystic. She gasped in terror it might overwhelm her too. This cursed, sticky floor had to be why no one ran away.

A hand touched her backside. She yelped and jumped forward. Another hand ran over her head and down her back. Althea stumbled away, right into a hand that squeezed her ass again.

"Hey, cutie," said a man from behind.

She whipped around but he was gone. Spinning to the left, she found another man shaking himself at her like the rest of the afflicted while waving glowing orbs over his head. The music crashed into her mind, making the place feel as if it wanted to devour her. The emotional radiance around him reminded her of the way Vakkar looked at Rachel. He wanted to wife her. Her initial wave of panic faded at the sense he didn't want to force it. Althea blinked at him in confusion, wondering what kind of raider only wifed a girl who wanted him to. Could women here be so broken that they *wanted* to be wifed?

He shrugged as she backed away, and focused his efforts on another woman with luminous green hair. Hands grabbed her from behind, sliding around and up her front, pulling her back against an undulating body. Althea twisted out of the man's grip and darted three steps over the sticky floor, flailing her arms to recover from a slippery spot where someone had spilled a drink.

Finding an island of open ground in the sea of swaying bodies, she caught her breath and clung to her wits before claustrophobic panic could set in. Behind her, more women danced on small stages amid a sea of light, which made their skin glow in the darkness. One had catlike ears and a long waving tail, the other a colored stripe over her eyes that constantly shifted among various shades of aqua and blue. Althea stared at the tail, wondering what sort of creature she looked at.

To the left, a man covered in glowing clothing worked buttons at a counter and shook his head in time with the awful sound. Ahead, two women with pink hair stood behind another tall bench, like the judges from Querq, pouring liquid into cups and handing them out. Dawning realization came over her; the undulant bodies around her *danced* to the strange cacophony of buzzing, thumping, and high-pitched warbles no creature in this world could be responsible for.

The people she'd assumed under some sort of control appeared to be having *fun*; no one here felt like a slave or under the thrall of a mystic.

Rapid motion broke her bewilderment as a man in an iridescent purple shirt grabbed her by the hands and swung her about in the strange ballet.

"Great outfit. Neo-tribal, I love it," he shouted. "You're fuckin' brave to go barefoot in here, but it's sexy as hell. Wanna find some place quieter? They got sofas in the back."

"Dude!" another voice yelled from behind her. "That's a little kid."

He stopped dancing and stared at her chest, finally noticing the height disparity. "Oh, shit. How'd you get in here? Sorry, squirt." He dove into the crowd, overwhelmed with disgust at himself and afraid of being seen with her.

The crowd parted, giving birth to the bald man from the door who shoved his way past them. She looked up at him, cowering away from his anger. He seized her by the forearm, dragging her with a wrist-crushing grip through the dancing throng. The man elbowed men and pushed women out of the way, the stream of begging and pleading from her lost to the throbbing noise these people called music. Past the ocean of bodies, he dragged her down a dim hallway where a small group laughed in a distant room. A black door swung open at the urging of his boot and he shoved her out into a light rain. Her foot found a deep water-filled hole that tripped her to all fours. Althea crawled forward, glancing back at him.

"No kids. Go the hell home." He slammed the knob-less door.

She stared at the vibrating panel, the hard music louder in her memory than the air. With an incredulous glance, Althea peered at the shin-deep puddle, the falling rain, and the lonely, trash-filled alley. How odd. He hadn't tried to lock her up or take her.

He simply threw her out.

WHISKED AWAY

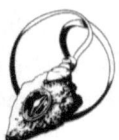

Althea trudged away from the place with the awful sounds and strange people. The rain clad her in cold, and she moved as best she could around the micro-lakes collected in the alley. Her skirt grew heavy from the falling water, and she kept a hand on it to prevent it from slipping over her shapeless hips. The wet strands did little good against the gusty winds that tore down between the great metal towers. A doorway with a tiny awning gave a semblance of shelter against the rain, so she curled up in the hollow against the wall.

Longing for the presence of Karina behind her in their warm dry bed back home, she sobbed. She had so been looking forward to her bath and the touch of her sister washing her hair. Her tears vanished into the rain that dripped from her hair and ran down her legs. The water fell from toes curled over the edge of the step into yet another puddle. She wanted to know why the world was so mean to her.

Why couldn't it allow her to be happy?

A dog barked somewhere in the night and a boot splashed in a puddle nearby. She lifted her head at three men barely past being called boys, squinting to see her. They appeared in black and white due to the darkness, dressed in leather coats and heavy boots. One had an entirely metal arm. Another had a wire sticking out of the side of his neck that went into his coat pocket. All had guns and devious smiles.

"Hey, kid. You got any left?" The one with the metal arm nodded at her and made a strange gesture.

"You look cold. We can warm you up." The wire-boy grinned at her.

"Any left?" She lowered her feet back into the water, ready to stand.

"Whatever you're on." He tapped his finger below his right eye.

"I don't have any medicines." Bracing her hands against the wall, she stood in a slow, nonthreatening way.

"We got some stuff left if you're lookin' ta forget whatever ya ran from." The third one held out a handful of small colored squares, pills, and things that resembled the stimpak.

"You ever get it on with a tween before?" The metal arm guy patted his friend on the bicep.

Wire-boy gave him an uneasy look. "Dude... wrong. That kid's like ten."

Althea's eyes locked on the oldest and widened. Sensing his desire toward her, she bolted off over the puddles without a sound.

Screaming only drew more predators.

Alleys, trash, and buildings blurred past. She didn't look back to see if they bothered to chase. While trying to take a hard right over the wet plastisteel ground, her feet slid out from under her and dumped her on her tailbone, sending her into a spinning slide that ended face-first against a huge trash compactor with a resounding, hollow *boom*. She lay stunned as the noise reverberated. A mountain of trash fell on her, and she froze like a fawn in the light. Her cheek and backside throbbed in matching pulses. Althea closed her eyes and forced the pain out of her mind.

No movement, no breath, no crying—only listening.

Distant cars hissed over the rain-soaked ground, the flying ones hummed overhead. Other musical noises floated in the air, but no pursuing boys with metal arms and nasty thoughts found her. Tucking her knees to her chin, she let herself cry, wondering how she would escape this place and get home. People, she could bend to her will, but she had no power over the metal beast of a city.

Sleep came without warning.

AN UNKNOWN TIME LATER, A HAND AROUND HER ANKLE SHOOK HER AWAKE.

Calloused fingers tightened about her leg, pulling her out of the trash pile into the street. She stayed limp, playing dead.

"Aww hell." A man's voice sighed into a wet cough. "This damn city gets worse every day. You can't be oler'n 'leven or so. What kinda sad 'scuse for a person could do this?"

A stench burned into her throat: vomit, urine, general filth. Coarse hands rolled her onto her back and folded her arms across her chest. Dry fingers brushed a gentle caress over her forehead.

"Dumped in the trash like…" He seemed to be crying.

Althea opened her eyes and looked up at a man wearing several torn coats. The stench of months-old alcohol, vomit, and a *long* time without a bath scorched her throat. He had pulled a woolen cap from his head and held it over his heart, muttering with closed eyes about some guy named Art in a place called Heaven. His face darkened with grime upon skin the color of burnished leather.

She sat up and tugged at his pant leg. The man yelped, throwing his hat in the air and stumbling backward, scooting away with the fright of ages on his face.

"Gaaah!" He clutched his fingers to his chest. "Y'aint dead." The gurgling cough returned. "Praise Jeebus!"

"Are you sick?" She stood and approached him, returning his hat. "I have heard that cough before."

"Yeah well, livin' out here." A fit of phlegm interrupted him. "Least you's not dead. Thought someone dumped ya."

She stood next to him, holding his hand to her chest. Sure enough, a shifting blackness dwelled within his life essence. Althea wanted it gone from him. Her power energized his body and sent him to his knees, convulsing. Once, then twice, then a third great shudder wracked him. He heaved over sideways and retched a glistening glob of whitish-purple slime into the alley. When his muscles again obeyed his desires, he wiped his mouth on the back of his sleeve and stared at the sinister mass, gliding off to a gutter in the tide of rain.

He blinked. With each unlabored breath, his gaze grew wider. He hugged her and she cringed from the stink. Not wanting him to feel bad, she held her breath and waited for him to let go.

"How'd ya do that one, then?"

She faked slipping into a puddle, sneaking a microbath. "I make the hurts and sicks go away."

"Kin ya do that again?"

"Yes." She stood.

"There's someone ya need ta see then." He took her hand and scrambled to his feet.

He strode with urgency in his step, almost dragging her along.

"Where are we going?" She gasped, struggling to keep up on the slippery ground.

He giggled with glee. "Ta my home. Someone needs yer help."

At the thought of a hurt person, she forgave his rush. "What's your name?"

"Marvin Jones, but people just call me Whisk."

She blinked at him. "'Cause of your whiskers?"

"Whiskey." He cackled.

"What's that?"

"Y'aint from 'round here, eh? Mars?"

"No. Querq."

"Never heard o' that planet."

Several streets later, she understood whiskey and he knew Querq wasn't a planet. Althea stopped speaking when she noticed he headed toward a round metal cage at the edge of the street. The sight of it made her legs lock, and she slid on her heels the last several inches until he let go of her arm.

"Down here." Whisk ducked into the cage and vanished over a short wall at the end of the path.

She leaned forward, relaxing at the realization the metal formed a safety shroud on a ladder, not a cage. The climb led about fifteen feet down to a sunken area. He bid her to follow. No longer worried, Althea climbed over the short wall and descended after him. Whisk took her hand once more at the bottom. The enormous trench reminded her of a deep river without water, with walls of metal instead of sand. It led off in both directions, packed with tiny homes made from old shipping boxes, some connected by plastic tarp awnings. Tattered bits of cloth drifted in the breeze, hung about like doors and partitions.

Fire licked at the air from a tall cylinder in the middle of the impromptu town, around which a few grimy people huddled for warmth. Traces of rotten food, smoke, liquor, and urine washed past her, punctuated by the ever so rare patch of air devoid of smell. One man stood a distance away, peeing onto a round grating.

"Ol' Flatline's been in a bad way for a while. Used ta be some important upsec type 'til he showed up here."

She looked up at Whisk. "I will help him if I can."

"Oi, Whisk!" a gargling voice called out. "Wheredya git the drowned rat?"

"Trash pile, tween 818 and Providence."

"Prov Street? Damn." A pile of dark shredded cloth and hair shambled over, reaching for her. "Looks brand new. Who'd throw out a doll like that?"

"She's a real kid, numbnuts." Whisk slapped his hand away from her.

"No shit." He squinted.

Althea tugged at Whisk's arm. "You got a toilet?"

"Umm." Whisk emitted an embarrassed chuckle. "Not really." He glanced at the grating. "W'aint used ta havin ladies 'round. There's uhh, one down that way in the tube wit no grating fer the number twos."

While Whisk and the shaggy man spoke in hushed tones, she crept a few steps away and looked down through a corroded lattice of metal into a pipe she could almost fit in. The air here smelled like the buckets from the raider pens. She planted a foot on either side of it and hiked her skirt up. Whisk and the other man yelped and whirled away.

Grey Tatters rocked from heel to toe, staring off at the smog. "Guess'n you're right then. 'Bout her bein' real and whatnot."

Whisk gave an uncomfortable cough. "Little warnin' next time, kid."

When she reappeared at his side, he shook his head at her. She didn't understand why they both radiated embarrassment. Whisk hadn't reacted that way when Tatter used the grate.

She tugged at his arm. "Where is the sick man?"

FLATLINE

"Y a gotsta see this." Whisk patted Grey Tatters on the shoulder, pulling him along.

At the far end of the row of crates, he stopped at a battered red shipping container with a dirty cloth curtain serving as a door. He pulled it aside, revealing a sunken man wrapped in dark cloth laying upon an old cot, covered in blankets. His lips moved in an endless series of inaudible whispers, as if he recited a silent chant. Every few seconds, his head ticked to the right. Someone had taken the time to decorate the space like a cheap motel room, adding a simple desk and chair as well as a tangle of torn curtains over a 'window' consisting of a hole.

"Can ya help Flatline?" Whisk pointed at the man.

Den's tribe had called Althea pale as a ghost, but his tribe hadn't seen many 'white' people. Compared to this person, she felt dark. Flatline even made Zhar look like she had color.

His skin resembled undisturbed snow, tinged with purplish smudges around the eyes. Eyelids painted over with bruise flicked with random spasms that continued down past violet lips over his cheeks. A shaved spot in his short, black hair exposed a metal plate behind his ear with several sockets. One still had a length of carbon-caked melted wire hanging from it.

Althea grimaced at the sight. The surface thoughts rattling around in his mind went in and out, the ramble of a consciousness trapped in a body no longer connected to it. Strange symbols flashed in his mind, as many numbers as letters, plus other glyphs she didn't recognize at all.

"Ol' Flatline here's got coreburn. Happens to them net-heads what get black iced too much." Grey Tatters scratched flakes out of his beard. "He used to poke around places he didn't belong 'til somethin' bit him in the ass."

"He bin like dat fer weeks," Whisk muttered.

"Hey, Whisk. You ain't wheezin."

"Yeah." He pointed at Althea. "Told ya you gotta see this."

She stepped over the low wall separating his chamber from the drainage trench, parting the shambles passing as curtains with her hands. Flatline's entire body shook with an attempt to move, resulting in one eye shifting to focus on her.

An incoherent moan came from him. "Whuyu."

"I'm Althea."

His thoughts gained clarity, but remained a mess.

"Wawamnt."

"I want to help you, if you like."

"Nob felp me. Whakidgondu?"

"I can try."

"Kay."

Flatline's ashen arm slid out from the blanket, fingers flapped in the erratic dance of uncontrolled nerves. She took his hand in her left, placing her right upon a forehead as cold as the ground. Whisk and Tatter leaned into each other to watch, keeping the gathering group of vagrants behind them out of her way.

"You have metal things in you," she muttered, and sensed he wanted to keep them. "Umm... Okay. They aren't making you sick?"

"Nmf." A surge of drool dangled from his lip, a raindrop of translucent slime with a cloud of blood swirling within.

Eyes closing, she searched out his essence. The amorphous forms came to her, withered and small. His thinking shape looked like a sack of tiny stones rather than a single blob. A great, wretched crack fanned out from the shadow of invading metal parts. Of all the hurts she had mended, never had she seen anything close to this level of damage in the thinking shape. One raider had a knife get stuck in there, and mending it had taken a lot out of her.

This one would sting.

She glanced at Whisk. "I may sleep after this. Don't be scared."

Drawing a deep breath, she knelt so she didn't fall, expecting to be unconscious by the time she finished. After placing her hands on his chest, she projected her influence into his body. One by one, she forced the little shards back together, gasping from the exertion. The 'cracks' turned out to be rootlike paths where the thinking shape had died. She commanded his body to reabsorb and regenerate the bad parts. His arm moved, rising to her hip and holding on. His other hand clasped her arm, then let go.

Minutes passed.

"Imfworking," he moaned. "Thoughts… clearing. I see angels. So beautiful."

A hand brushed her cheek. The caress slid down to her chest, over her heart.

A whispery voice rasped in her ear. "Silver ribbons, wings of light."

"Dang. He been in the net too long." The alcohol breath of Whisk's chuckle floated by.

Minutes stretched to an hour or more.

Her body slackened; his hand at her chest held her upright. More pieces drew together. The cracks sealed. Shuddering with effort, she fed power into him until it hurt. A dribble slipped from her nose, warmth on her lips; she tasted blood.

His other hand left her hip and wiped her face. She blinked, lifting out of the red-on-black world of their link, and smiled at pale eyelids no longer bruised. The Wagon Man had forced her to work until she bled. This time, she did it because she wanted to. She tried to say something to Whisk, but had no voice.

She remembered falling backward onto something soft.

ALTHEA'S CONSCIOUSNESS RETURNED IN THE BLACK-AND-WHITE CONFINES of a cargo box. Fleeting threads of hurt raced across her body, centering on a stabbing pain in her stomach. She sat up and wailed, curling into a ball to chase away the soreness. It had been years since she had overextended that far and hunger had advanced to the point of pain. Her cry drew Whisk, who opened the side like an awning and smiled until he saw her agonized expression.

"You hurt?"

She dragged herself to the opening, wincing. "So… hungry."

"Oh. No probo. Bennie just got a pity sack." He scurried off, returning with a plastic bag soon after.

His attempt to chuckle sent a dry, alcohol-tainted wheeze over her face. "Here, tek two. Lookin like ya could use it."

A pair of clear clamshell cases landed on the derelict cloth between her ankles, each containing a round, beige object. She picked one up, looking it over, drooling at the scent of meat. Althea bit it, gnawing on something hard.

Plastic.

"Hah!" The creases around Whisk's eyes deepened. "Open 'em first. You sure Querq ain't a different planet? How the hell you ain't never seen a cheeseburger afore?"

"What is it?" She fiddled with the offering, stymied by the container.

He took it from her and pinched the edge, popping it open. "Almost fresh."

The burger didn't have a chance. The second one went faster than the first.

"Guess'n ya like 'em." Whisk handed her another. "Night man at Cyberburger gives us a pity sack sometimes, round midnight. Whenever the vat's too low ta keep for the mornin'. They'd chuck it otherwise."

"It's good." She licked the taste from her fingers.

Her voice drew a dozen bums to her little house. Word of Flatline had gotten around, and they had come as they always did. One by one, she tended to them despite that it hurt to call on her gift so soon. Finding herself in her usual role felt comfortable in a depressing way. Even the great City-Beyond-the-Fire followed the laws of nature. These men prayed to her once she had cured them of everything from broken fingers to sores to odd things that made them cough squiggly sicks onto the ground. Their adulation brought with it a familiar sense of foreboding.

"I shouldn't stay here." She sighed. "I don't want you to get hurt."

Whisk scratched his head in confusion. Once the line of injured homeless had dissipated, Flatline sauntered over with a cheeseburger in each hand and one in his mouth.

He sucked the mouth burger down in one gulp. "Holy shit, I thought I was fucked. I don't know what the hell you did, kiddo, but I owe you big time. Coreburn's usually a one-way ride. What do you mean, you don't want us to get hurt?" He jammed another burger in his mouth. "Fuck, I'm hungry as hell."

Althea swiped another burger from the bag, chomping at it as if she had to eat it before someone stole it. "Bad people always come to take me away. They will hurt you to get me."

Flatline looked her over. "You're a Scrag, aren't ya?"

She nodded.

"Badlands rules aren't city rules. Yeah, we got our gangs here, but they don't do the whole takin' slaves thing. Cops get their panties in a knot about that."

"What's panties?" She chomped a piece of burger off.

"That..." Flatline pointed at her, chuckling while chewing on his last burger. "Is a conversation I am *not* having with a ten-year-old. The cops don't much like that, either."

"I'm twelve," she grumbled, wondering why she bothered.

"Oh, yeah, that's *so* much better. Hey, I guess you don't need my services seein as you're from the shitsmear, but if you ever do, just ask."

"What can you do?" She rubbed her belly, finally full.

Flatline rubbed his chin. "You have no idea what the GlobeNet is, do you?"

She shook her head, cluelessness written on her face.

"Okay, umm. I sneak around a digital world, grabbing information people are willing to pay me for... information other people don't want found."

"Can you find my mother?"

"Doubt it if you're from the Badlands. They don't have much in the way of computers out there. Not sure I could help."

She thought about the memory in the old man's mind. Her mother's blue clothing looked more like what the people in this strange city wore than anything from the tribes. Althea stared at Flatline, sending the image of the pale-faced woman into his thoughts.

"Whoa..." He stumbled away, holding a hand to his forehead. "That's fucked up. Is that your mom?"

She looked down. "Yes."

"Well, okay. I can try. You know what her name is or anything else I can use?"

"No."

"Well..." He laughed. "I've had less to go on for other jobs, and you did bring me back from the dead. The least I can do is try. She doesn't look like a tribal. There's records of companies going out there to do unethical crap. Might take me a couple days to procure a deck and get back into the swing of things. As soon as I got somethin', I'll come find ya."

"You're not going to hurt yourself, are you?"

Flatline shook his head. "No. Fuck that. I ain't goin' anywhere near a grade six net again. Not 'til I get my hands on some Icevest softs." He turned to Whisk. "Hey man, if you see a pizza delivery bot come out of nowhere in a few hours, you're welcome."

Cackling with glee, the strange man in black danced to the end of the drainage channel and climbed the ladder, singing.

THE STREET PREACHER

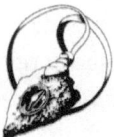

Wiping tears from her face, Althea climbed out of her metal box and squinted at the setting sun. Three days had passed since she had crossed the gates of fire, and no amount of bawling would bring her back to Karina and Father. She had to do something more than sit around feeling sad. The stiff breeze channeling along the drainage path blew icily through her clothing and tossed her hair about her face. She wandered among the fragments of a dozen shattered lives stacked around the repurposed boxes and shipping containers that formed this enclave of the unwanted.

At the center of it all, she plucked the pity sack from the ground to find it empty save for a cup of beige slime with no appreciable fragrance or flavor. The sky held no answers. Even the stars hated this place. Only the receding sun had the strength to penetrate the indigo gloam. That, at least, told her which way to go in order to reach Querq. 'Generally east' sounded good enough to try.

Narrow metal rungs hurt her bare soles, colder than the air. With the vagrants off on a search for charity, the Bumwallow—as the denizens called it—had fallen silent save for the scurrying bits of trash frolicking in the gusts and a distant gurgle from the corroded grating.

Althea put her back to the fading day and walked. The phantoms of this place followed her, inhabiting the howling gale and appearing in darting movements in the shadows at the edges beyond her sight. Being alone had never been something Althea liked. Being alone in this place frightened and saddened her more. The lack of rain amounted to the only thing in her favor. She marched past cross street after cross street, dodging the curious stares of vagrants and hoodlums. The people who lived in the bowels of this dreadful city had thoughts and feelings quite similar to the raiders.

In no mood to be kidnapped again, she didn't hesitate with the *go away* command, sending several threatening men running off in random directions when they tried to grab her.

A great glare rode in from the side along with a blaring horn. Althea crossed her arms over her face and screamed at the metal beast charging toward her. The light nearly blinded her as the monster shot by, inches away, with the screech of a demon's wail. Blinking, she faced toward angry yelling, but the trembling visage she presented drew the vitriol out of the charging man's voice. Her eyes recovered from the brilliant light, and she squinted at a long, black car twisted sideways on the strange metal road, door open, its driver looming over her.

"The goddamned light was green, stupid kid." A man, clad in dark shimmery fabric with a strange grey strip of cloth hanging from his neck, stared at her with incredulity. "Are you fucking blind or something?" He scratched at his hair in frustration. "Dammit. If I hit you, that woulda jacked my insurance rate. What the hell is wrong with you? Do you speak? Hello?"

Althea shrank in on herself and stared down at her toes. The man radiated anger at her, so she must have done something wrong. "I'm sorry. I don't know what you mean."

"Damn street kids. Don't you know what a traffic light is?" The man stepped closer.

"I don't. Please don't hit me." She took a step back, afraid of the rage billowing off him.

"Oh for fuck's sake. I ain't gonna whack a little girl. You serious you don't know what a damn light is?"

"I'm from the Badlands." She lowered her arms from her face and ventured eye contact.

His hard expression softened. "Look, kid. See that." He pointed at a glowing red circle floating in the air over the road. "They put them by roads where people are supposed to walk. If you see red, you wait for green. If you see green, you can cross. You walk out on a red light, you're gonna get creamed."

"Creamed is bad?"

"Guess it's true what they say about blondes, eh?" He laughed. "Yeah, creamed is bad. You were almost a hood ornament."

She knew he mocked her, and didn't like it. His mental imagery of the meaning of 'hood ornament' proved gruesome enough to destroy her indignation. "I'm sorry. I won't do it again. Thank you for telling me the lights."

"Strange kid. Hey, ain't it a bit late for you to be out alone? And what the hell's a little kid doing with cybereyes."

She shrugged. "Cyber eyes? I don't know what that means."

"Your eyes are lit up." He shook his head, perhaps considering it not worth the discussion. "Where you goin?"

"Querq."

The man chuckled. "Yeah, we all got 'em."

"What? No, the city, Querq."

"City? There's only two cities, East and West. Oh, shit, you mean out there in aborigine land." He laughed. "Good luck with that, kid."

She stood there in silence as he went back to his car, pulled the door closed with a dull *thunk,* and drove off. Althea hurried back to the slightly elevated walkway alongside the road and waited. The orb had returned to being red, so she didn't move. No cars came, but she didn't take a step until it turned green, then dashed across the road as fast as she could. Most of a block later, fanciful music drew her gaze to the clouds, at a strange box as big as a car sailing by overhead.

Two great panels of light shimmered below it, angled to face the ground on either side. Moving images spread across them: a field of black glinting with stars, at the center of which gleamed a long, white machine. The view zoomed in, revealing an uncountable number of glowing dots covering the long object. Shaped a bit like a loaf of bread, one end had a wider part from which plumes of energy streaked off into the black.

The music cut out and a man's voice echoed off the canyon-like walls of nearby buildings. "The senate confirms earlier reports that the CSS Angel, the largest military starship produced by the UCF to date, is slated for active duty within months. One hundred patriotic citizens are eligible to win tickets to attend the launch event and accompany the vessel on its maiden tour around the moon."

After a few seconds of empty black, the panels changed to show a man's upper body. Little bits of metal in various shapes dotted his green shirt. He reminded her of a raider chief trying to look important. Funny symbols appeared, scrolling below him.

"The admiralty is pleased with the progress the build crews are making. We are proud to see this great symbol of freedom and patriotism take to the far skies of space. The level of support a ship of this type is capable of bringing to colony worlds is an order of magnitude above what we have today."

Boring.

The fancy lights and pretty coat with all the shiny bits on it wouldn't get her home any faster. She walked another two blocks in relative quiet. She stopped again at one of those red orbs, curling and uncurling her toes over the metal curb, waiting for it to change.

"Hello." A strange little voice, not quite male, came from her right.

"Hi," she said before looking. Upon seeing no one nearby, she spun around twice. "Ghost?"

"Do you need a ride?"

She jumped. The voice again came from where no person stood. Again, Althea spun in a slow turn, searching. From a box atop a pedestal at the corner, a drawing of a small man waved at her. The sides of the pedestal had pictures of little cars around the smiling figure in blue.

"Who are you?" She walked over to the pedestal.

A human figure with a rectangle for a body, noodles for arms and legs, and a circle for a head saluted her. "I am a PubTran taxi terminal. I can dispatch a PubTran taxi if you are in need of transportation."

"Transportatoes?" She stared at the glowing panel at face level.

It emitted an insincere laugh. "Do you need a ride? Do you need to go somewhere far away?"

She jumped and clapped. "Yes! Please."

Bouncing, she waited. Minutes later, a tiny car skidded to a halt by the pedestal. Its silvery roof and doors and powder blue fenders looked quite battered. A door that took up almost the entire side swung up into the air to reveal two facing bench seats. She stooped under it and climbed into a warm space that smelled like an old shoe. The seat was much harder than the ones in Jamie's car, but still softer than a steel box. She sat, gawking at the front end, and lack of anyone driving it.

"Please state your destination." The same voice from the pedestal emanated from a small flashing panel on the wall to her left, opposite the door.

"Querq, please."

Several seconds of silence later, the voice returned. "Destination not found. Please provide additional detail."

"It's far to the east in the Badlands. An old city named Querq."

After a long pause, the voice spoke in a lifeless cadence that attempted to sound pleasant. Whenever it recited numbers, the tone dipped out of the rhythm of the sentence. "Closest match: Albuquerque, New Mexico. Population: <unknown>. Distance: estimating <Eight-hundred thirty two miles>. Estimated Trip fee: <Four thousand one hundred fifty four> credits. Warning. Badlands considered dangerous. PubTran Corporation is not responsible for injury or death resulting from this trip. Loss of PubTran equipment due to this route will result in a fee of <seventy thousand> credits to your account."

"Umm. Okay." She bounced in her seat, ready to cry from happiness.

"Please wave your NetMini past the terminal for account identification or insert credit stick with balance sufficient."

She stared at the panel for a moment, shrugged, and waved her hand past it.

"Read failure. Please try again."

Wave.

"Read Failure. We are sorry. We are unable to process your NetMini. Please reboot your device and try again. If you are a PubTran employee, please provide verbal override code."

"Please, I want to go home," she whined at it.

"Please, I want to go home," echoed back at her from the wall in her voice. "Is not a recognized override code. Voice analysis indicates occupant is a juvenile. Please locate your parents."

"I'm trying to. Father is in Querq. Please take me home." She banged on the emotionless thing.

"We are sorry. PubTran Corporation cannot accept liability for stray children. Please exit the vehicle."

Althea sighed, sick to her stomach. How cruel of this thing to make her think it would take her home.

"Please exit the vehicle."

She crawled into the cold night. The door sank closed and the driverless thing zoomed off. Plodding along, she walked for an hour, seeing no change to the endless city. No matter how many streets went by, she felt no closer to home than before. The cold ground numbed her feet. *Stupid little empty car.* Her hopelessness shifted with an idea at the thought of Beard. He could drive her home. He even knew how to get there; in fact, he offered to take her. The next time she saw Flatline, she would ask him to find Beard and bring her to him.

At least having a plan, she decided against aimless wandering and went back the way she came. The little crate Whisk gave her had some nice mildew-laced blankets she could keep warm with, far better than being out in the wind. Another block down, the sound of a man shouting drifted from an alley. His words teetered at the edge of his voice before thundering down with intense gravitas. She pictured the spittle flying. Curious, she went toward the ruckus, approaching the flickering shadows cast by fire blazing from a trio of metal cylinders as tall as she was. A dingy mural dominated the wall opposite the stage: a giant dove drawn in reflective white paint with spread wings and a flower in its beak. Trash brushed across her legs as she waded through it, one hand tracing the wall as she went.

A crowd of vagrants ringed a collection of boxes and tables set up as a stage, upon which a somewhat heavyset man in multicolored rags of gradient filth gesticulated and waved. The carpet of old green and black coats followed him like a cape, swirling about the ground as he walked back and forth. He held a metal rod five feet long with two curled bits of white glass screwed into sockets at one end and a length of wire dangling from the other that looped into his pocket.

Around his neck on heavy industrial chain, a great metal cross hung swaying and gleaming as he shambled. An explosion of white-brown, belt-length hair surrounded a face red to the point she half expected it to pop at any second. With every tiny movement he made, a grunt escaped his lips as if the act came with great exertion.

An array of shimmering holographic panels painted the abandoned building behind him in otherworldly light. The projectors dangled on wires from a network of metal rods that rose up behind his platform like crone-fingers. Some screens showed war and death, others static, two near the top had the faces of old men ranting, and a few held a still image of a peculiar brown-haired man in a robe holding up a hand with a hole through it.

She drifted among the crowd, approaching the stage from which he preached. His boots traveled back and forth at her eye level as he ranted about the 'end-times' and the 'sins of man.' His impassioned oration kept time with shifting images of fiery explosions, red desert, war machines, and wounded children flashing behind him. He screamed about something called god as well as evil, and the sins of Mars. A man put a hand on her shoulder. She looked up at a face hidden behind long strands of dark silver hair, and sensed no ill will; he gave off friendliness, welcoming her to the group. She returned his smile, and looked back at the tech-evangelist.

"How long will this continue without the voice of the *people* being heard? Death surrounds us all. In the streets here on Earth, in the skies on Mars, the greed of the money-changers goes unchecked by the blood of the innocent." He leaned back and the corkscrews of glass at the end of his stick lit up with a painfully bright glow. "The technology devours our souls. Where will *you* stand when cometh the Day of Judgment?"

She hid her eyes when his pointing finger swept past her.

Grunting, he shambled to the edge of the rostrum in front of her.

"Such sin." He extended his arm. "We live in a society where the *innocent* are cast into the streets and forgotten. Look at this child and see what evil dwells within the hearts of man. How could a society claiming to be just hurl an innocent into the streets?"

The crowd's gaze focused on her. She studied her toes, hoping no one noticed the blue light.

Air puffed from under the stage as he tromped away. "Only if you embrace the Lord can you find redemption. He shall guide us beyond the stain of this existence to the light."

Pointing at random people in the crowd, the big man asked if they had been saved. Some shouted yes. Others stared at him.

"Are you saved, my son?" The fat man pointed at an emaciated bum in dark clothes with his finger three knuckles deep in his right nostril.

The man looked up startled, and farted. The finger remained where it was.

Althea's giggle drew every eye in the crowd. She clamped a hand over her grin, embarrassed at her reaction. All the adults gave off a sense of grimness like a funeral, so perhaps she should be serious. Some of the street people gasped, others peered with curiosity. The fat man gawked, at last noticing the glow.

"On your knees," he roared. "The harbinger of the end walks among you!"

A few of them fell in place.

Althea shrank in on herself. "What?"

The preacher waddled down from his perch, grunting with each step, and laid his old lamp at her feet. Her shadow grew immense upon the wall behind the crowd. He knelt before her. When he looked up, such fear showed upon his face Althea couldn't resist peeking into his mind to understand what scared him. Through his eyes, she saw herself, standing in line with the mural; the luminous painted dove wings spread out from her little figure as if part of her.

"Please, O angel of wrath, tell us we are to be spared." He bowed close enough for his hair to tickle her toes.

She crept back a step. "I'm Althea. I'm not a angel of wrath. I don't even know what that means. Please get up, you're giving me the blush."

He lifted his face from the ground, gaping at her. "You are... I can feel the purity in you." He knee-walked after her and traced a thumb over her cheek. "Your innocence glimmers in this place like a white candle in the darkness of an infinite abyss. If not wrath, then mercy?"

"Umm. I got kidnapped. I'm trying to go home. Do you know Beard?"

"The Angel seeks the one known as Beard." The fat man grunted to his feet, rattling the lamp-turned-staff at his flock as he spun with a cascade of cloth shreds. Shadows danced and swayed. "Knowest any of ye a Beard?"

A few of them laughed.

"Bring you the end times?" He turned at her with scary eyes, bushy eyebrow twitching.

"No. Are you sick? Why do you talk strange?" His thoughts sounded in a ramble about half as bad as Flatline's baked brain. He thought her some kind of winged creature from a place called Heaven, come to destroy the world and take a select few back there with her while leaving everyone else to suffer and burn. Althea recoiled in horror. "I help people. I don't kill them."

He shambled up a short stairwell to the dais, grunting again. "She is a messenger. He hath provided us another chance to redeem ourselves." The preacher scurried to the other end of the platform. "Bear life unto others. Tend to the sick. Be ready for the end times."

Althea backed into the murmuring crowd and slinked off into the dim quiet of the next block. Every alley looked the same. Picking one on a feeling, she waded into another swath of chest-deep trash, forcing her way to the street beyond. One left turn had taken her to the strange gathering, so another left should point her back to Whisk and the others. Several steps later, she looked up at the towering structures and the glowing streaks between them. The little flying machines with their light-pictures were not so thick here. This place gave her the feeling nobody cared about it anymore.

A shadow ballet upon a windowless wall caught her eye, its accompaniment a series of muffled screams and fleshy thuds. Two of the silhouettes held the arms of a third, as a fourth struck him from behind and the dusk-form melded with the ground. Blood spattered the black phantoms on the wall.

Althea crept to the alley's edge, but stopped before looking. The police said no one in this place knew her as the Prophet. Her reputation would not protect her here. She bit her lip with anxiety, wanting to help the man, but afraid of what his attackers might do to her.

Wet plastisteel embraced her as she leaned against the building and listened.

A whispery voice, blurred by alcohol wailed, "Please, no."

The ring of a blade in the air, a sinister chuckle, then a tremendous scream. Something splattered.

She peeked around the edge. A man crouched over a body on the ground, raising a gleaming blade for the fatal stroke. Gasping, Althea leapt out, thrust her arms forward, and projected a blast of telempathic fear, hitting three men with such profound terror they sprinted away screaming, without looking back. Crinkling plastic and echoing footsteps chased them into the distance. Althea hurried over to the shuddering body lying face down in the alley. Life gurgled out of his mouth and a cavernous hole yawned in his back. She skidded to a halt, almost falling when her toes found tepid, slippery blood. Several pieces of inner-bits littered the area. She collected the blobs as fast as she could move, and like a three-dimensional puzzle, stuck each one inside the man where she thought it looked proper. Some big pieces were missing, but the heart remained intact, though it appeared mere seconds away from stopping. She looked around but couldn't find his air bags.

Elbow-deep in the man's chest, Althea established a link to his life-shapes. The pain stopped, the inner bits she'd thrown in randomly no longer appeared anywhere near the right places. They all looked so much different inside the link. She manipulated shifting outlines of color as her hands molded his flesh like clay. New organs formed as her psionic energy empowered his body to regrow. The salvaged fragments moved into their proper place while street grit emerged from the closing tissue.

Eventually, she drew her hands out of the mending flesh until her palms rested flat against new skin.

The man took a great moaning breath, as if the touch of air hurt his new lungs. He shuddered, curling into a ball, whimpering. Althea held his hand, muting his pain.

Just as well, she'd exhausted herself too much to stand anyway.

39

SCRAPS FOR THE TAKING

Aware of little more than her hand upon warm flesh and the chill of slick metal under her knees, Althea's mind drifted in a fog of indistinct time. She wanted to crumple to the ground and pass out, but the darkened alley filtering past her half-closed eyes looked anything but comforting. Vigilance kept sleep away.

A hand touched her back. "Am I dead?"

Althea shook her head, almost falling over from the momentum. "No."

"You... You're an angel." The man she had saved trembled as if he gazed upon a creature not of this world.

"I'm Althea." Her whisper held only a hint of a voice. "Did I miss a hurt?"

He patted himself along his chest and gut. "There is no pain. I..." With a sudden look of guilt, he rummaged his shredded, bloodstained clothing.

Her hand on his arm stalled his search. "You don't have to give me pay-things. Do you know a man named Beard?"

"No."

His stomach growled. Hers answered.

"Can you take me to Querq?" Her weary glance met his, and then fell after his look of confusion.

The man picked at the shredded strips of shirt draped over his chest. "I don't know where that is."

"You should eat something."

He tugged at her hand until she managed to stand. "You shouldn't be in this part of town alone; it's dangerous here."

"I'll be okay." She glanced at the trail of blood leaving the alley.

"No girl your age ought to be calm in a place like this." He looked up to the smog, and gave her a smile with a wink. "I know you're not just some kid; you heard my prayer." He bowed. "Thank you!"

The man darted off, and she touched her belly as if to acknowledge the hunger. A series of sanguine smears and footprints led from this place, deeper into the alley. *Nibblers.* But how did the cannibal tribe get past the wall of fire, and why did they leave so much meat behind? Nothing in this place made any sense.

Stark black against the grey ground, the bloody trail led her through the dark. Bodies, pressed against the walls, drew sharp breaths as they noticed two spots of glowing azure floating along in the middle of the night. Althea glanced at them, her eyes cast weak patches of light on the walls. Some hid their faces, others stared in awe, and a handful tried to follow until they tripped over things they couldn't see.

At the end of the third alley, the street undulated with a soft pink glow. She edged up to the wall and peeked around. Two blocks away, a life-sized naked woman made out of light gyrated above a black-painted door. Her slave-dance bathed the entire area with unnatural iridescence. Althea looked down. In the light, the black smear became crimson.

The trail of streaks and drips went to a stairway sunken into the metal earth, past large pipes and the smell of rust. She paused at the top and crouched, gripping the edge of the first stair on either side of her feet. Voices echoed, sinister sounding men celebrating something they called a 'score.'

Curiosity pulled her forward, and she crept down a few steps, holding on to thin vertical pipes that felt like the bars of a one-walled cage. A thin ray of light shimmered in the dust an inch above one of the stairs. Althea didn't know what to make of it, but suspected normal people probably couldn't see it. Strange things were best left undisturbed, so she gathered her skirt and stepped over it. She looked deep within the patchwork of girders, wires, and yet more pipes, into the bowels of this underground place. A small area of color dwelled within the sea of greyscale lines. Men crowded around a figure in white who held bloody air-bags to the light and examined them. Grinning, he lowered them into a glass cylinder of peach-colored liquid barely large enough for them. More inner bits filled shelves behind them, in jars of various sizes.

When the man in white moved away to place the stolen air-bags on a shelf, a sinister-looking thing somewhere between a chair and a bed came into view. A mess of buckles and straps hung from it, filling her with the thought anyone on it wouldn't want to be there. A finger of ice tickled her heart at the sight.

These men stole pieces of people, and from the anticipatory greed shrouding them, she knew they thought of the inner bits as pay-things. She glowered, stunned anyone could do something so wicked. How was this place, this fortress of metal cut off from the earth, any better than the Badlands? Her knuckles whitened and she growled under her breath. What could drive men to do something so evil just for pay-things?

Some men just gotta die, said Rachel's voice in her mind, followed by a wave of guilt. Witnessing this made the words sound closer to truth, but the thought still made her sick.

"Oi, Doc. Whazzat blue light o'er there?" A man in a black vest covered with knives and decorative chains pointed at her. Spiked fuchsia hair wobbled with his sudden motion. "You install some new whoosy-fuckit at the stairs?"

"Sounds like one o' them little rat-dogs snarlin'." Another chuckled. "Prob-lee just its eyes catchin' the light."

"Be certain." The man in white spoke in a voice like a scalpel scraping over steel.

A sharp wave of his hand sent the other three men moving toward her.

Althea scrambled up the stairs, careful to avoid the strange line of glowing dust. This evil demanded action, but what could she possibly do to them? She could order them to stop, but that would only last a few minutes. The clap of her feet on the smooth metal echoed in the endless canyon of plastisteel and glass, alarming in its volume. She slowed to a nervous, silent jog, keeping her weight on her toes, fighting the building urge to look over her shoulder.

After a series of random turns and no sign of pursuit, she stopped and sat on an overturned trashcan to rest. Heavy breaths drew in a whiff of food, and her stomach cried out in protest. Her nose led her to a curtain of light leaking into an alley from the street beyond. Edging up to the oasis of color, she flattened herself against the wall and peered around it. Along the ground floor of a building across the road, large windows offered a view of a room full of tables where a number of people sat and ate. Most hunched over their plates, ignoring everyone around them; many looked tired.

Seeing no cars or people moving on the road, she darted up to a set of plain metal doors with tall oval windows. They lacked a handle. When she reached out to push on them, they slid open with a sharp hiss. Althea jumped away, clasping her hands to her chest in shock. They glided closed without a noise. Two breaths later, she took a step toward them and they opened again. Despite being ready for it this time, she still flinched. Afraid of being crushed, she jumped past the doors and whirled about to stare at them while backing away.

Tantalizing aromas cavorted in the air, many of which she didn't recognize beyond smelling like some kind of food. To her left, a counter with those padded nail-things like Tumbleweed's bar stretched off, but the two men seated on them had food instead of orange happy juice. Booth seats ran along the wall opposite the counter. On the right side of the building, a room of freestanding tables held the bulk of the people.

Althea went into the table room, gaze wandering. A recently used spot had three abandoned plates, with scraps of bread and green strips of some manner of plant next to chicken bones. She ran to it, grabbing anything edible and stuffing it into her mouth with alternating hands. People nearby glanced over at her one at a time; some gasped with revulsion while some *aww*-ed at her, but she ignored the noises they made. A few of the chicken bones even had bits of meat left on them.

What little remained teased her, and she looked around for more, still chewing. A man and a woman a table away talked over plates they seemed done with, pushed to the side. She crept up to the edge of their booth, looking back and forth between them until they noticed her.

"Are you finished with that?" She pointed.

Not fully looking at her, the man waved a hand at the voice. "Yeah, you can take them away."

She scarfed down the woman's untouched fries and the slices of tomato and lettuce the man did not use on his burger, but stopped with a horrified face after one bite of a pickle.

When the woman got a good look at her, she scooted away along the bench seat against the wall. "Sergei, that's not a waitress. That's a blood-soaked urchin devouring our leftovers."

The man raised an eyebrow at her.

Althea stopped scarfing and offered an apologetic pout. "I'm sorry. I was so hungry, I forgot about the fork."

Everyone looked at her. She ventured a sheepish glance around, feeling the rising tide of alarm in everyone's mood. Her confusion at how anyone would be scared of her ended when her downcast gaze settled on the blood smeared all over her. She relaxed, understanding they didn't fear her, but reacted in horror to what they thought someone did to her.

"Oh, my god." A thick-bodied woman in a black uniform called out, shattering the tense silence. "Honey, are you all right?" The floor bounced as she stomped over.

"I'm hungry." She looked up at the large woman. "They said they didn't want it."

"What in the..." The woman's thick brown curls dangled around her face. She came to an abrupt halt at the sight of the blue glow. "Are you on drugs, child?"

"No. It's 'cause I'm sigh-onic." She smiled inside for saying the word right.

The level of fear around her surged. Almost everyone went from sympathetic to terrified in an instant. The overwhelming emotion caused her to shrink in on herself. She made eye contact with a few who wondered what *she* did to someone to end up bloody.

The big woman measured her with a careful glance. "Where are your parents, and why are you covered in blood?"

A few people toward the back of the room scurried out the door. Althea ventured another bite of the pickle and grimaced. "What did they do to this? Why does it taste bad?"

"That's a pickle, honey. It's pickled. Where's your momma?"

Althea chucked the ill-flavored thing back on the plate. "I don't know."

"What about your daddy?" The woman reached for her hand.

"At home."

"Did you see somethin' bad happen? Something the police might want to know about? Oh, my, that isn't your daddy's blood, is it?"

"No." She shook her head. "I found a man in an alley. Someone stole his air-bags."

"Is he okay?"

"Yes. He ran home."

"Who the hell would steal air bags?" muttered a man two tables away.

"Come on then." The woman led her by the hand through a flapping door into a giant kitchen.

Althea waved her free arm for balance while step-sliding over a layer of permanent grease on the floor.

"Dammit, Betty, what the hell are you doin' bringin' a filthy street scrap in here? You know we prepare food in here."

"Since when the hell have you given a flying fuck about sanitary codes, Hank?" barked the woman.

Betty ignored the continued ramblings of a short anemic man in a stained white apron and dragged Althea to the back of the room. She didn't protest. Trying to lock her legs and resist would only have caused her to glide. After running warm water into a giant utility sink, the rotund woman lifted her to sit on the counter with her legs hanging into the basin. She washed the blood and grime from one arm then the other before taking her time washing Althea's feet.

She endured it, staring at the wall with a forlorn expression. This felt a bit like a bath, but more to the point, it made her miss Karina, and home, even more. She didn't give in to the urge to cry.

"What's your name, girl?"

"Althea."

Betty lifted her chin, dabbing at her cheek. "Got a last name?"

"How can I know which one will be the last if doesn't ever change?"

The woman blinked. "What's that supposed to mean?" Her brown eyes glittered with concern.

"Umm... I don't have any other names..." She thought for a moment. "Well, some people call me Prophet."

"Althea Prophet." Betty rubbed her chins. "It's pretty."

One at a time, the woman dried Althea's feet with a soft, white towel and swung each leg away from the sink. "When was the last time you had a shower?"

"What's a shower?" She slid off the counter once Betty had dried her arms.

"That's a long time. Come on then, I'll get you something to eat."

"Who's paying for it?" asked Hank from behind a shelf full of battered pots and pans.

The woman made a strange hand gesture at him, just her middle finger sticking up.

Betty put her at a small table past the end of the row of nail-seats, by two doors with stick figures on them. She left her there for a few minutes, and returned with glass of white liquid and a sandwich. The scraps from the abandoned plates had taken the edge off, and she munched on this food slow enough to taste it, tapping her heels idly against the fake wooden panel below the cushion.

She savored the rare treat of fresh food. Betty said something about this being grown in a vat rather than made from slime. Althea had no idea what that meant, and couldn't imagine how anything solid could be slime. Two men walked in the strange self-opening door. Althea looked up, peering over her plate at them while licking up every last crumb.

Long black coats covered baggy pants somewhere between olive and brown. Heavy boots loaded with an excessive number of metal fasteners thudded over the floor as they approached a young woman whop stepped up to smile at them.

"Welcome to Maude's. Two? Booth or table?"

"We're not here for food. Police." He held up a candy bar. "Got a call about a street kid."

"Oh, hi detective." The woman gawked at the bar, tweaking her hair and smiling.

Althea had a sense something wasn't right. She felt him do something to the woman, something like she had done to Vakkar. Their thoughts dwelled on her and whispered the name Archon—the ghost head. She dove flat upon the bench seat. They wanted to kidnap her. Escape would require either running right at them or trying her luck with the stick figures. Plastic doors clattered when Betty emerged from the room behind the long counter, holding a plate in each hand for the men sitting there.

Althea slipped to the ground and crawled out from under the table, heading for the area behind the counter.

Betty looked down as she passed. Without a free hand to snag her, she could only yell. "Hey, kid, wait."

Althea cringed at the ruination of her stealth. She sprang to her feet and ran for the kitchen doors before Betty could drop the plates and grab her. The two 'detectives' rushed the counter; one went for the end while the thinner man jumped it, nearly knocking Betty over. Althea palmed the swinging flaps, darting into the kitchen. She circled a steel island of shelves and went toward a door at the other end, propped open with a mop, dashing out onto a raised platform where metal boxes sat in stacks behind a giant truck backed up against it. Without hesitation, she leapt off the end, landing in a somersault on the ground below. The 'detectives' tripped over the mop on their way out, one knocking a pile of boxes over. Althea rolled over to sit, facing them with a frightened gasp. Anger started to well up, but she instead focused on her sorrow at being separated from her family.

Her targeted burst of telempathy left both men on their knees, sobbing.

Althea bounded upright and sprinted hard toward the nearest alley, the agate arrowhead trailing over her shoulder, longing for the protection of her little house in the Bumwallow.

Never had the thought of being in a small metal box been so appealing.

40

APATHY

After hours of roaming, Althea stopped trying to think about where she went and let her instinct lead. She wandered for a while more, going wherever whim pulled. Eventually, she emerged from a side street and spotted the ladder, a welcome sight that brought life back to her weary legs.

She jogged to it and climbed down. Most of the bums had returned, crowding around the burn box, save Whisk in the middle of watering the grating.

"Whisk? What are police?" She walked up behind him.

"Hey," he shouted. "I'm busy. Give me a little space." He glanced over his shoulder and shifted his back toward her as if he wanted to keep her from seeing whatever he had in his hands.

She tried to peek around him. "What are you hiding?"

He swerved away. "Jesus H, kid. Give me some damn privacy."

Althea backed up, raising her hands. "Sorry."

After wandering back to her sleeping box, she crawled inside and waited. Whisk showed up a few minutes later, red-faced and rambling about personal space, and that thing he called privacy. He stooped to peer in at her.

"What are police?" She sat up, cross-legged, and held on to her shins.

"Pains in the asses is what they are," Whisk grumbled. "Never leave ya well enough alone, they don't."

"They hurt your ass?" She blinked.

"Naw, not for lit'ral. They're always chasin' us away from the beggin' spots or out the dumpsters."

"Do they take slaves?"

Whisk made a face like she had slapped him. "Slaves? Are you crazy?"

"Well…" She picked at the decaying blanket around her foot. "Someone told me they wanted to make me a slave again. And they carry umm…" Althea clasped her fingers around her wrist.

"Handcuffs?" Whisk chuckled. "Them's for criminals. They don't take slaves. They arrest bad people."

"Arrest?"

Whisk explained as best he could.

"Sounds like slaves with bigger cages."

"Naw's different. They don't sell 'em, an' they don't make 'em work or force 'em to umm, yeah I won't go there. Ya's too young."

Althea folded her arms and glared. "I know what wifeing is."

"Yeah, well." Whisk's face turned redder. "Police don't do that. They punish people that do. It's bad… and yer too little ta think things like that." He glanced away, fidgeting. "Well, you ain't little-little so's mebbe its good you know wot it is so you don't let anyone trick yas into doin' it."

A glimmer danced over her eyes. "I won't let anyone do that to me."

"Good." He flashed a sea of yellow teeth at her. A long enough conversation with him at close range would make her tipsy. "Why you askin' 'bout police anyway?"

"This man told me they were bad. He said they would make me a slave, but he would protect me." She squinted into the wind. "I didn't trust him. He felt wrong."

Whisk's belch flooded her little room with the scent, and flavor, of cheap booze. "Yeah welp, some fool says the cops take slaves, sounds like he's lyin'."

She fanned the air, grimacing. "So they're not bad?"

"Naw, they help people mostly. Specially kids. You really oughtn't be here wit us. You got one of them futures waitin' for yas. Cops'll put ya wit some fosters and give you a shot at a real life. Don't fuck it up, or you'll wind up right back here; and if'n you land up here and you ain't little and cute no more, you're screwed."

"Fosters?"

He coughed. "Aye. A family willin' ta take ya in and treat ya like their own, tho' usually temporary kinda way."

Althea slid to the side, curling into a ball upon padding that smelled of wet dog. "I don't want temp rary parents. I want Father and Karina."

Whisk shrugged. "Get some sleep."

He wandered off after easing the lid of her container closed without a sound. She stared at the puddles of reflected eye-light on the smooth plastisteel panel. This crate was bigger than some of the cages she had been kept in, and it struck her how safe it felt. Especially with solid walls instead of bars. Bad people couldn't see her.

The men who stole body parts haunted her thoughts, making her shiver into the blankets. If police were as Whisk said, they seemed like the best option for doing something about them. She trusted his opinion far more than the word of the floating head. In the morning, she would try to find some police.

ALTHEA AWOKE ON HER BACK, ARMS ABOVE HER HEAD AND FEET PRESSED into the wall of the crate. The space wasn't long enough for her to extend her legs all the way, unless she lifted her toes near the roof, which she did, stretching for a wonderful few seconds. She rolled over and stared out from half-closed eyes at the shadow of her bent knee on the wall, outlined in azure glow. A veil of unkempt blonde hung over her face.

All the running from the previous day left her legs sore, but a few more stretches worked the aches down to a point she could ignore them. A shove at the panel failed to move it, so she pushed harder with both hands. It didn't even rattle. Her heart raced, but she held on to calm long enough to check the other wall in case she rolled in her sleep and pushed at the side against the wall of their waterless river. It, too, refused to move.

Trapped.

Had Archon's men found her in the night and locked her in? Had her little house become a cage for real? She kicked at the panels, banging on all four sides and screaming.

"Help! Let me out."

Althea braced her back against one side and shoved with both legs at the other, whining when it went nowhere. She grunted and strained, channeling her power into her leg muscles to make herself stronger. The panel flew open without warning. A man howled in pain as the swinging plate smacked his shins. One of the vagrants jumped away from the box, dancing, cursing, and rubbing his legs. Althea scampered over to him, stalling the pain with a touch.

The guilt she felt would've been fitting had she killed him. She whined at him while rubbing the small cuts on his legs away to healed skin "I'm sorry."

"Fuckin' latch caught 'cause Whisk gave ya the new box. We not broked it yet."

She stared ashamedly at the ground, until he ruffled her hair. After a quick visit to the grate, she foraged the prior night's pity sack. Someone had left a couple of fried nuggets behind. She choked down the cold, flavorless things, wishing she could find a grub or two instead. It didn't seem as though any wood existed in this place. An unclaimed clamshell case that should have contained one of those 'cheeseburger' things held a glop of beige slime like what Vakkar's men had fed her.

Scooping it into her mouth, she glanced to her side at the sound of a homeless man retching.

"How can you eat that?" he asked.

She blinked. "What do you mean?"

Shuddering, he looked away. "Yer eatin' plain OmniSoy. The cheeseburger melted."

Althea blinked at it. "It's new tree-ant paste. It's not a cheeseburger."

"They got machines what turn it into cheeseburgers... but they cheap ones, so it ain't perm-nent, and they fall apart if ya don't eat it in a couple hours." He walked off, twitching and trying to keep down what little he had eaten.

She didn't understand how this slimy substance could have ever been a cheeseburger, but still licked the plastic box clean of it. It didn't taste bad; it didn't taste like anything. After tossing the empty, she wandered the Bumwallow for a few minutes before approaching a random occupant.

"Umm." She waved. "Hey."

He grinned at her, lifting her off the ground in a tight, smelly hug. She had rid the glaucoma from his eyes a day ago. "Heya, sweetie. Why you still here?"

"How can I find police?"

"Datz easy." He grinned. "Go do somethin' you don't want 'em seein ya do."

"Really?" She blinked.

He pointed at the ladder. "Naw. Up there. Gotta walk north on 804 a bit, get out of the grey zone. Cops don't come around here much. Heh, the way you look, they'll find you."

She glanced at the ladder, and back to him, tilting her head in confusion.

"Parts of the city got real bad. Real, real, bad. Kind o' things what live there even the cops won't touch, so they blacked them offa the map. Ya get a bit farther 'way from dem places, you get what they call grey zones. Not quite as bad, but still bad. Civ-lized sorts don' go there. Keep walkin' 'til ya see lights and people don't look like us." He put a hand on her shoulder, a somber, grateful expression on his face as if this would be the last time he'd see her. "Thank ya fer what ya did fer me. I'll never f'get ya. G'won, kid. You don' deserve ta be stuck here."

Althea wouldn't let police put her with those foster things. She would lead them to the man in white and then make them let her leave. If she could find them, they could fix the problem.

The rickety ladder rattled as she climbed, even under her slight weight. She had no idea what 804 meant, and the smog-filled sky offered little clue as to which path led north. After wandering for a bit, she decided on a direction with more light in the horizon than the rest. As the blocks passed, the number of people out and about increased. Some shook their heads with bewilderment at the barefoot waif walking along in a tattered leather skirt and dirty tank top. She looked wholly out of place in this fortress of glittering metal and flying machines, filled with people in their fancy blinking clothes and gadgets.

She kept going in a straight line with her gaze just high enough not to collide with anything or anyone. Between the angle of her head and the sun filtering straight down among the buildings, the eerie glow in her eyes had to be near unnoticeable.

Red and green orbs reminded her of the lesson from the other day. Not wanting to become a 'hood ornament,' she waited when her travels took her far enough away from the Bumwallow for them to stop being dark. A car passed, the color changed, and she continued until a man in a shiny indigo coat stepped right in front of her.

The tall, thin head at the top hid under a dense mop of erratic black hair that hung down to his belt. Althea glanced at a pistol under the coat, and at boots which looked as if they had once been a grey snake.

"Well now." His voice sounded deeper than his delicate frame would imply. "You're not what I was expecting. 'Cute blonde' usually means something else." He sank into a squat, far enough down to meet her eye to eye.

His neutral mood let her remain calm. "Who are you?"

"I'm Terry." He held out a hand. When she didn't react, he clasped her fingers and rendered a handshake to a limp arm. "I'm glad I found you before you got hurt."

Althea made a face at the strange gesture. "Are you police?"

"Naah. We don't need police. They don't trust us, so I don't trust them."

"Us?" She tugged her hand out of his grip.

Psionics, kiddo, said his voice in her head.

"Archon's your chief?" Color drained from her face.

"You got the wrong idea, kid. He comes off all creepy and weird, but he is really trying to protect us. He wants to meet you. We all do. We've heard so much about how wonderful a person you are."

Deception.

"I can't."

"Come on, just for a bit." He held his hand out again.

She stepped to the side to go around him. "No, I need to go now. I have something to do and then I am going home. Please leave me alone."

He grabbed her arm to hold her back, his fingers tracing somewhat cleaner smears in the dirt.

"Grr. Get off me." She glared at him.

"I'm afraid you don't quite understand. We're concerned about a child running around the city alone with no one to look out for them." He flashed a disingenuous smile. "This isn't a request."

Althea struggled. His hand slid from her shoulder, down her arm and seized about her wrist.

"Help!" she wailed at the sidewalk full of people. "Help me! I'm being kidnapped!"

No one so much as glanced over.

"Quiet, you." He yanked her off her feet and spun her chest-first into a dark maroon car, dormant at the side of the road.

He lifted her on her toes, forcing her arm up behind her back. While pinning her against the car with most of his weight, he fumbled with something she couldn't see in his jacket pocket. Expecting him to grab something to tie her with, she squirmed and shrieked. No one even looked.

"Time for a little nap, kiddo. Just relax, we don't want to hurt you."

He was too strong, too heavy. Her left hand clawed at the cold glass pressed against her cheek. She couldn't move; fire spread down her right arm. Another screamed plea brought no appreciable reaction, even after she involuntarily added sobs. Something cold and small touched her on the neck behind her left ear and pressed in hard enough to hurt—but nothing happened. Her heel found his shin several times, but he only muttered bad words and pressed her harder against the car.

"Blast. Damn safety caps. Be just a second, hon," he muttered past an object in his teeth.

She shouted her lungs empty, but no one even looked her way, their attention all absorbed in small handheld devices.

"Someone please help!" A telempathic detonation of distress stalled every sentient mind within a hundred yards; pedestrians froze in their tracks as if time had ground to a standstill and a handful of cars swerved, some going up on the sidewalk. As one, the crowd turned to look at her, pinned helpless against the side of the car with her hand behind her neck.

"Please help me," she whined again, a whisper in a hundred minds.

This time they heard.

"That guy is trying to abduct some girl!"

"Hey you, get offa that kid!"

"You son of a bitch perv, what the fuck do you think you're doing?"

"Oh, shit," Terry muttered. "Why'd you go and do that. Not very nice."

He vanished, dragged into an angry crowd by a sea of hands. Althea whirled around, back pressed into the unforgiving car, nursing her throbbing arm. She winced at Terry drowning in a sea of pummeling fists, shoes, and random objects. They called him all kinds of bad things. Althea edged around the car, slipping away from the wall of bodies into the street.

Screeching tires shot by.

She slammed her back against the street-facing side of the car. A moving one brushed close enough for her to feel its presence; a spray of water wet her legs. Althea didn't want to become a hood ornament. Motionless against cold metal for the span of a few breaths and a half dozen more cars passing, she finally opened her eyes and breathed again. When a chance presented itself, she slid to the right and climbed over the hood away from the road. Somewhere under a mass of bodies, Terry groaned.

"I got it. I'm callin' it in." A man poked at a small slab of black glass with his finger.

Althea spun, glancing at the crowd with a weak smile. The entire mass of people leaned back in one coordinated motion when they saw the blue glow.

Silence.

Not wanting to be here when Terry's friends showed up, she waved at them with a pleasant smile and ran, ducking between two bystanders who tried to grab her.

"Hey wait, kid..."

She sprinted off down the street in search of a police.

When she could run no more, she stumbled at a drunken lope until she fell onto a metal bench facing the road. As long as she had been going, her surroundings remained more or less the same. Tall buildings, some with glowing words on them, surrounded her. The city continued without end in both directions. The crowd density increased here. People dressed in strange garments and walked as if late for some important meeting. Most failed to notice her, and the few who made eye contact kept going. As curious as they might have been about a solitary ragamuffin on a bench, she wasn't their problem.

Tucking her legs up, she leaned over and snatched a half-finished bottle of juice from a trashcan bolted to the side of the seat. Sipping at it, she frowned at the street. Except for Betty, the people in this place had no hearts. Even most raiders would stop to check on a kid. She wondered if all this anger and impatience came from the 'corporations' that used money instead of guns. She threw the empty bottle back in the can, unable to comprehend how that could compel respect, fear, or power.

She'd wound up in an alien world made from nightmares painted on a canvas she couldn't have imagined possible. Althea wanted so much to be home, but before she could go, she had to do something about the man in white. It would gnaw at her soul if she ignored something so evil. Althea sat watching the cars pass while she rested. The people in them radiated anger. Some screamed at the car in front of them for being slow. Others yelled at no one at all, carrying on as if having a conversation with a person that didn't exist.

Sickened, she stood and rubbed the cold of the metal bench out of her legs before wandering several more city blocks, weary and confused with no hint at where she might find one of these police. Her chest-level view of the crowd offered an unending stream of people disinterested in her existence. Most avoided her while some shoved her out of their way when she tried to approach. This was so unlike Querq. So many people packed the sidewalk she couldn't even see the ground, and not one of them friendly—or even in a good mood.

Sad and annoyed at the way everyone here behaved, she trudged on. After passing two more cross streets, opportunity presented itself in the form of a wide open door to a room full of people seemingly free of the perpetual hurry. Perhaps someone in there knew where to find a police. Up a few steps, she looked around at the bodies mingling in the dim space. They sat at tables, most paired off in couples, and others perched upon the nail-things in front of a bar on the left. A small magic tray with baskets on it floated on its own about the room, offering its contents to whoever was close. When it passed her, she took a small bowl of peanuts and crammed them by the handful into her mouth.

A man scurried back and forth on the other side of a counter like at Tumbleweed's place. She approached, and satisfied her eyes could see over the top of it, climbed up onto one of the giant padded nails. Leaning her elbows on the bar, she swung her feet back and forth, waiting for the man to walk over.

"What's yer poi—" He blinked at her.

"I'm looking for a po—"

"Get outta here, kid," he bellowed, shocking her. "You're too young."

"I can see over the bar," she said, indignantly.

"What do you think this is, brat, Europe? Get lost. For at least ten years."

She jumped down and ran outside before he could hit her, stopping on the street and staring back at the doorway.

"Christ Jimmy, what the fuck do I pay you for?" The bartender's yelling continued at someone inside.

A thin guy with short dark hair and a tight green shirt stomped to the door, slipping in the scattered peanuts she dropped. Recovering his balance, he held his middle finger up in the air behind him. He leaned on the wall outside and crossed his arms.

"Sorry, kid, gotta be twenty-one."

She smirked.

He pointed with his thumb down the street. "Beat it."

Althea hung her head and kept walking. Two more strangers ran away from her when she tried to talk to them. No one wanted to get involved with a grungy orphan. Desperate, she lunged and grasped a man's hand. The next thing she knew, she found herself upside down, headfirst in a trashcan. Her side hurt from where he'd grabbed her.

"Hands to yourself, fuckin' little pickpocket." The can rocked from the impact of his foot.

Althea squirmed around, pulling her legs down and shifting upright in the mass of garbage. The stuff in here had been sitting too long to smell worth eating. The man took a few steps, checking his clothes. She climbed out onto the street and sighed. A little box no larger than her head zoomed over and got in her face. Awe washed over at the floating thing. She jumped when it spoke.

"You there. There is a fine for littering." The crackling digital voice sounded upset. "Error, ImDent not found."

"He put me in this can," she whined, pointing.

"You removed refuse from the receptacle and dumped it on the sidewalk. Please replace the trash where it belongs. Noncompliance will result in a citation."

A 'citation' sounded like something she didn't want. After gathering the junk she displaced during her exit back into the can, she smirked at the little flying thing.

"One more piece," said the tiny object.

"There is no more," she whined, gesturing at the ground.

"You were placed in the refuse containment device and are now litter on the street. Please return yourself to the proper receptacle."

"I'm not trash. I'm a person." Stunned that even floating metal boxes thought so little of her, she sobbed into her hands.

The miniscule annoyance drifted closer, sweeping a red line of light up and down her body. "Scan confirmed. Suspected litter is not an artificial life form." The pestering thing zoomed off after the man, nagging him about misuse of city trash receptacles, as they were not intended for disposal of unwanted children.

Althea wiped her face dry and sighed. The next person she tried to talk to shoved her hard to the ground. She landed on her ass before she could get one word out; he scurried off, wiping the hand that touched her on the leg of his pants.

Sorrow and frustration mounted. She drew in a breath to scream for help when a moving picture of a policeman smiling and waving from the side of a building half a block away caught her eye.

Grinning, she got up and ran for it. Althea slipped around a tall man lip locked with a half-naked redhead in glittering heels, and dashed into a room dim enough to turn black and white. At the far end, a policeman on a raised platform danced around in the only spot of color in the place. His uniform seemed a little tight, and a lot small. At a confused gait, she padded down the carpeted walkway between tables populated by mostly women while the police man gyrated and unbuttoned his shirt.

A group of five men seated at the closest table to the stage hollered and cheered at him. The cop let his shirt fall backward off his shoulders; huge rolling chest muscles reminded her of a raider juggernaut. She skirted up to the edge of the light and waved, bringing an end to his strange dance and changing his smile to a look of bewilderment. For a moment, he stared in silence, blinked, and pulled his shirt closed. He tugged at a small black wand hanging from his left ear that curled in front of his mouth, and pointed at her.

"Umm. George, what's up with this?" His voice thundered over the entire room. "You guys still checking ID? I think you missed one by about ten years."

"Are you a police?" The music cut out a second before Althea yelled, leaving her shouting over silence.

The crowd laughed, and a few people made *aww* sounds.

Sensing a man approach from behind, she looked up and back. Before she could say a word, he grabbed her around her left bicep, nearly lifting her in the air.

"Sorry folks." The dancer cringed. "Hey George… easy huh, she's just a kid."

"Ow. You're hurting me." She wriggled, rising up on tiptoe in an effort to lessen the pain. "Put me down."

He did, once he had carried her back outside. "Get outta here. You're gonna get us shut down. If I see you again, I'm gonna call the cops to pick you up."

"Are cops police?"

"Yeah…" He stared in disbelief. "Geez… freakin' kids today."

He slammed the door in her face, and the music resumed.

She followed him right back in.

He whirled on her. "You are some special kind o' stupid."

"I want the police." She smiled. "Please get them."

The bouncer eyed the room warily, emanating a twinge of dread. In his thoughts, he worried about a thing he called 'drugs' and a place he knew as 'the fun room,' which he didn't want the cops to know about. He grabbed her, squeezing her wrist numb while dragging her once more onto the sidewalk. The swat on the ass he gave her as a parting gift sent her up on her toes gasping for air. No one had ever hit her like that; no one had ever dared strike the Prophet.

She had no idea how to react. Althea had seen Scrags do that to misbehaving little children. The stinging pain, total frustration, and the shame of being treated like a *little* child set her off wailing like someone young enough to be disciplined that way. People walked around her on either side as she stood bawling. The bouncer stared at her with 'asshole' practically written across his forehead.

His chest appeared in the corner of her vision. She sniffled up at him. Unable to speak, she peered into his mind. Guilt, mostly, and confusion at why a girl her age burst into tears from one 'light' spank.

"Look, umm… Sorry I hit you. I ain't good wit kids." His face came as close to a smile as it could get. "Here, take this. It'll get you a free combo at Cyberburger. Go eat something."

Plastic clattered to the ground at her feet, and he vanished behind the slam of the door.

Sniveling, she stared down at a glowing hamburger the size of a thumbprint printed on a clear card with funny markings around it. Althea figured someone at a place called Cyberburger would barter this card for something to eat, so she kept it.

Rubbing the last bits of pain out of her rear end, she plodded down the street. People still ignored her, save for the occasional rough collision that knocked her sideways when someone walked into her as if she wasn't there.

The ball at the next cross street was red, so she stopped. To her right, an open door beckoned into a room full of shelves. The Lost Place had buildings like this. Den called them Sev-Levs. Sometimes they found food there, oblong yellow soft things with sweet white stuff inside them. Despite being from the before-time, they were still edible. He told her about how they used to sell conveniences. She had no clue what a convenience was, but the smiling man behind the counter might be able to help her find a police.

Clutching the card, she entered, squinting at a blast of air even colder than the outside. A strange fragrance filled the room, overpowering the small meat-sticks slow roasting under heat lamps. Smoky, yet laden with spice, the aroma clung to everything. As soon as the man saw her, he started shouting and waving an arm at her. Althea had never heard that language.

He emanated worry as well as anger, yet she had done nothing but walk in.

"You go. No steal here." He rushed around the counter, waving his hands in her face and reaching for something against the wall. "I no charity."

"Please, I need a po—"

She ducked the swing of a broom, and backpedaled out onto the street. "Please, will you—"

The door slammed with the clattering of out-of-tune electronic bells, and he locked it.

Continuing backward, she looked around at the people, the buildings, the furious face in the store window, and the starless sky. Someone shoved her to the side, on purpose. She fell, barely getting her hands in the way before her face hit the ground.

"Stupid kid, watch where you're going."

The man in the fancy black suit with raspberry cuffs and collar didn't look back. He gave off a spike of amusement. He enjoyed flinging her to the ground.

Althea couldn't take the cruelty anymore. The tears flowed before she finished crawling to the curb. The frigid surface would have been soothing to sit on if she noticed it, but her stoicism had been exhausted by the endless litany of uncaring, mean, and selfish people who lived in this awful place.

Huddled on the edge of the sidewalk, she wrapped her arms around her legs and sobbed. She missed Karina and Father so much her chest hurt.

This was Archon's fault.

For the first time she could remember, Althea decided she hated someone.

41

ENEMY OF MY ENEMY

Althea sat on the curb, chin on her knees, her feet ankle-deep in water running down the gutter, every bit as frigid as the people in this place.

Ripples spread outward from her falling tears. Once she had no tears left to shed, she looked up at the crowd flowing behind her. No one saw a lost child sobbing, merely another piece of trash they needed to step around.

The pattern in the smog had shifted, revealing the weakening daylight of an early evening sky. She lost track of how long she sat there, consumed by sorrow, but her legs had gone numb and her breaths came in the short, spasmodic bursts that followed a hard cry. Almost a week had passed since she last saw her family, and defeat took a seat beside her. The thought her home might be lost forever stole away the energy it would take to stand. She felt her sorrow leaking out and reined it in. Despite their heartlessness, these people did not deserve that.

Faces slid across her memories, some smiling and some bloody. All the people she could remember helping appeared and faded. She shivered. It didn't matter how the world treated her. She was the Prophet, and she still had a job to do. Somewhere, someone could be hurt, and she couldn't turn a blind eye to them. She smiled as one more tear came forth. What did it matter if the world was cruel? The fleeting moments of intense love and gratitude whenever she helped someone made it worth all the misery.

A tenor voice fell over her from behind. "You all right, girl?"

She lifted her red-ringed eyes, peering up at a black man in his later fifties. He appeared as skinny as she, and dressed in a dark blue jumpsuit. Grey highlights streaked his hair and beard. A word upon a patch at his breast had been drawn to resemble a speeding boxy vehicle.

"Don't look like you're doin' too well there. You need any help?"

Someone *did* exist in this place who had a heart. She jumped into him and cried from joy. He didn't even cringe away from her touch.

The sound of his voice made her feel better. "Hey now. What's your story?"

She wiped her face with both hands, but couldn't talk right away. After a few tries, she swallowed the lump. "I was kidnapped and I'm trying to go home."

"Oh my." He took her hand. "Did they make you take some kinda drug?"

"No." She thought for a moment. "Are you asking because of my eyes?"

He nodded.

"Please don't be afraid of me… I'm sigh-onic."

"Oh, I see." He patted the back of her hand. "Well, even psionics need to be wit' their folks. Come on now… let's get you to the police then. They'll be able to help you."

She bounced. Holding hands, she walked with him for a little more than a block before he stumbled to a halt. She looked up. His face had frozen in a mask of shock and he clutched his chest.

"Sit," she whispered, searching his life-shapes for the source of his pain.

He complied; she felt his pulse racing faster and faster out of control. Something reached into him from outside making his brain overwork the heart.

Setting it right proved simple, but the man had already passed out. Althea gave him a mental poke to wake him. When she stood, six young men appeared out of the crowd walking toward her, one of whom stared with intense concentration on the older man.

"Okay, *Prophet*, this is getting tiresome." A young man with a vest full of guns tossed a fluff of cobalt hair to the side off his face, and frowned at her.

Unable to risk these people harming the nice man because of her, she bolted into the nearest alley without hesitation. The clamor of their pursuit echoed off the walls. She paid no attention to their orders to stop, and didn't believe their promises not to harm her.

She ran a little more than halfway to the next cross street before her right foot came down and *didn't* touch the ground. Althea yelped in shock, gawking at the metal tiles falling away from her. Realizing she rose into the air, she flailed her arms and kicked her legs, screaming. No single point of contact touched her. An overall sense of pressure enveloped her, carrying her sideways toward a building.

"Nice catch, Donnie. Can you hold her still? I don't wanna take that bony little foot in the nuts."

Althea craned her neck enough to look behind her. A man in a light grey suit held his arms out at her. Ripples in the strange force holding her still matched subtle changes in his facial expression. Others rushed over as the force pressed her into the wall. The sensation changed from lifting to pressing and it held her arms and legs still. She couldn't even move her finger, and shrieked for help, begging them to let her go. A telempathic emanation of pity caused the force to weaken. The metal wall slid against her cheek as she slipped an inch toward the ground. A hand went over her mouth and a familiar, high-pitched whine started up.

She tensed a split second before the rain of bees swam across her back. Hundreds of tiny needles pierced her skin. This time, she felt them dissolving. This time, she knew what it would do and refused to let it work on her. None of the men noticed the luminous chemical running down her leg, forced out of her body. Or, if they did, mistook it for a sign of terror.

She closed her eyes and went limp, pretending to be asleep.

That's better. I'm being taken. Things are back to normal.

The strange force lowered her to the ground. She let her body go where gravity took it. Hands rolled her onto her stomach and gathered her arms behind her back.

No. No. Please... Without meaning to, she radiated her dread of being bound.

"You sure you wanna do that?" A voice from the left.

Someone standing by her head answered. "Ark will get pissed, wants us to be super nice to this one. She's some kind of key to his master plan."

"You wanna explain to him why we lost her?" asked a man from right above her.

"Dude... I shot a half-stick of sleepy time into her. What is she, seventy pounds? She'll be out for two days."

"Yeah, man, come on. It feels wrong tyin' a kid. 'Sides, you know how Ark gets when us peons disrespect the Awakened."

"Okay, fine, but if we lose her, I'm going to set your ball hairs on fire." The man holding her arms let go.

Another man spat. "Just get her in the damn van."

"Damn, this little bitch is rank. Where the fuck has she been sleeping?"

"From the smell, I'd say your sister's pants."

A hollow bell-like noise followed; she imagined someone's face bouncing off a metal post.

"Fuck you."

A kissing noise, lips smacked on empty air several times, followed. "Your sister would."

Someone growled. Boots scuffed around.

"Knock it the fuck off," said a girl who didn't sound much older than Karina. "I hate being out here. Let's do this fast."

"Yeah man, stinks." The deep voice quieted them. "Put her in the back of the van. The *very* back."

An arm slid around her and another scooped under her knees. She hung limp as someone picked her up. Her face slid against an armored vest, and she continued faking sleep as they carried her. The heavy sound of a sliding metal door preceded the scratchy touch of automotive carpet at her skin. When the man who put her down moved away, she risked a peek at the inside of a van. Two voices outside on the left continued to argue about how to contain her in a way that wouldn't make Archon upset with them.

The man who made her float sat in the driver's seat, tapping at the controls. Taking a silent breath, she thought about how much she missed Karina and Father. She fixated on the incredible sorrow and hopelessness that had gripped her while sitting on the street corner. Her face contorted with emotion; she sat up and opened the floodgates, letting every ounce of her emotion slam into him.

He collapsed over the wheel and sobbed as if his entire family had died in front of him.

She sat up on her knees and slapped at the glowing buttons by the door. Slapping became pounding; she shot brief glances over her shoulder at the men outside. Pounding became kicking. A chance swipe of her hand hit the right thing somewhere, and the side door slid open. A radiant telepathic burst of confusion left the others holding their heads and staring into space.

She took off. By the time they chased her again, she had a two-block lead. Althea turned at random until the sight of a shimmering pink light beckoned her toward a way to solve two problems at once.

Pausing long enough to be seen, she zipped around a corner and boosted her adrenaline as well as the muscles in her legs. Superhuman speed, no shoes, and steel sidewalk made her feet ache after four strides. She zoomed past the hologram to the top of a sunken stairway. Althea clung to the railing, half kneeling while she stole a few breaths and shuddered at the pain of overstressed muscles. As soon as the people who tried to kidnap her came into view, she waited for them to spot her and ducked into the dark, careful to avoid the strange line of light on her way down.

A passage led from the stairs into a black and white maze of tubes and girders. She ran down an open corridor for a short distance before squeezing under a low-hanging tangle of pipes. Pulling herself along the ground, she belly-crawled under the mass of plumbing to the far end of the room into a space only a child could fit. She kept going until she found a hiding place against the wall with enough room to sit up.

Motionless, she stared at the foreboding chair with the evil straps.

And shivered at the awful feeling it stirred within her.

42

THE RIPPER

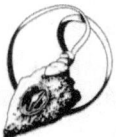

Huddled in the dark, Althea gathered her knees under her chin and glanced up at an evil silver sphere that swelled from the ceiling above the demonic chair. A dozen metal arms studded with an assortment of horrible-looking sharp things sat poised to inflict death. The bloodstained implements seemed to look right back at her like a hungry animal appraising its meal. Cold concrete touched her back. She shivered, wondering how many died there.

The raiders who had left handcuffs on her ankles for months, fearing she would run, had a 'doctor' with a similar machine. More than half the time he used it, it tore the patient to bits. While the senile old fool hadn't intended to hurt anyone, watching him laugh at explosions of blood and gore was too much to bear. By her memory, she would have been about eight or nine then. Her voice echoed in her mind, yelling *'go away.'* He had gotten up from his desk and walked out. She never saw him again. This metal-armed horror seemed to be in better repair than the one at the raider camp. It had no visible rust and at least four more arms. Still, such a device had no business being used on people. It looked *sinister*.

Archon's lackeys stumbled down the stairs. The area flooded with blinking lights and a loud blaring noise. They shouted, but she couldn't make out what they said over the clamor. Men came from deeper within and ran past her hiding spot, oblivious to the little figure covered by pipe-shadows drawn in flashing red.

Gunfire erupted, interspersed with angry yelling. She trembled with each bang, hating the violence. Two evils collided; distasteful as it was, she tried to tell herself only good could come from this. When the sound of fighting reached full swing, she crawled out from under the pipes and slipped around a plastisteel wall in search of a rear exit.

The inner hallway had rough metal gridding for a floor, too painful to run on barefoot. Holding her arms up in an effort to lessen her weight, she gingerly stepped to the first available turn. A splash of color on the wall offered the promise of daylight.

When she rounded the corner, she froze at the sight of a massive shirtless man. His arms, proportionate to his great size, gleamed, the image of a bodybuilder sculpted in charcoal-colored plastisteel. Black leather pants with armored plates on the thighs strained to contain his muscles. Tall boots covered in armor panels looked heavy enough to crush a car. Metal covered the entire right half of his face, the eye on that side, an extending lens, glowed scarlet with mechanical light.

Wide-eyed, she backed into the wall, flattening herself against it in hopes he hadn't seen someone as small as her. The giant's face tilted down, the eye-lens whirred, and long blades slid out of his hands, one per finger, each about nine inches in length. A mind whispered within the metal, thoughts simple—focused.

Little pretty thing. Should not be here. Boss want make scream. Smash. Kill.

The strength failed her legs and she collapsed to the ground in the corner, raising her hands over her face as if they would do something to stop such a monster from hitting her. Undeterred, the man raised an arm, blades poised to rip her in half. Imminent death pushed her brain to a place it had never been before. Terror welled up from the deepest recesses of her soul. Her mind lashed out with the only thought she had, a psionic emanation so powerful it stabbed her brain like an icicle.

Someone help me!

Her mental scream staggered the oaf. His arms fell slack to his sides. He stared, unmoving, into space. A tendril of drool slid from his lip. Althea trembled on the floor, gazing up at him for a minute, too frightened to move. The gunfight continued in the distance. Several rapid shots in a row dispelled her hesitation. She slid along the wall to stand up. Tiptoeing to the side, she kept her eyes pinned to the unmoving beast of flesh and metal, edging around him to the hallway from whence he had come.

She took two steps backward before a blinding flash of pain struck her on the bare skin above her skirt along her spine. Althea fell with such speed it seemed as if the air in front of her became the floor in an instant. Her arms and legs twitched out of control as an electrical buzzing crackled between her ears. Anguish overwhelming, her muscles refused to obey.

"Well, well, well." A high-pitched male voice rang out. "What have we here?" Someone clapped; a rapid staccato thing barely audible over her pounding heart.

A hand hooked the back of her shirt and dragged her along the floor past the oaf, over the scratching metal ground, toward the evil chair. The dire feeling she got from it made sense. He meant to put her on it. The sight of restraints made her twitch with renewed determination, and he dropped her. Another wave of burning agony swam over her body. Her scream squeezed past a rigid jaw refusing to open, a primal sound of agony that foamed snot out of her nose.

He brought her ever closer to the horrible contraption. She emitted a series of subhuman noises as she fought the paralyzing touch of whatever dreadful device the man in white had against her skin. It bit her again when her leg moved. Hot tears streamed down the sides of her head when the crackle sent wave after wave of disorienting misery through her for a third time.

Soft leather embraced her. He dumped her on her back atop the chair. Bands of thick material cinched tight around her wrists and ankles. Another strap pressed down on her shoulders and then her hips. Sinister cackling came from the man in white each time he secured a fastener. A wrinkled bald head with one silver eye hovered over her face. His sweat ran off in drops, landing on her cheek. Althea glared at him, searching for her power, she ordered him to release her, but her voice wouldn't come.

"Such a pretty little throwaway. Almost a shame, really." He drew a startled breath. "Magnificent eyes. Glowing. Oh, this is truly a fortuitous find. I don't know whether I should sell them or study them. I suppose I'll have to wait and see if they keep glowing once they're in jars." He pushed his thumbs into her face so hard it hurt. "From the structure of your cheekbones, I can tell you'd have been quite beautiful. You'll have to settle for being pieces inside someone rich and magnificent." Before she could invade his mind, he ambled out of view over to some kind of machine.

Images and feelings flooded into her from her contact with the chair.

Pain, horror, screaming. Many people had indeed died on it, alive long enough to see their insides removed. Feeling came back to her limbs. She writhed, twisting in an effort to find him. Blue and red light shone down from the silver ball above her, sweeping back and forth over her immobilized body as the steel arachnid came to life. Its motion gave her voice back in the form of a scream while laser lines crawled up and down her skin. She couldn't get away from the horrible seat.

Bullets whizzed overhead, clanging off the pipes above.

The man in white leaned to his side and pushed something on a distant wall. After a *beep*, his voice echoed like a thing out of nightmare over the entire building. "Will you three simpletons watch where you're shooting!"

Althea quivered at the sound. "Please, don't hurt me. I'm twelve. I'm just a little kid." She radiated pity.

"Twelve? Perfect! Just under the minimum age. Ooh, very nice. Looks like you're in excellent health. Your kidneys will be worth about two hundred grand each, and that liver... Oh yes... Intact, disease-free ovaries!" He squealed with delight. "Millions!"

Hot tears ran down the sides of her head. "Wait! I could be eleven, maybe ten," she wailed and jerked her arms against the straps. "Everyone keeps thinking I'm ten. I don't really *know* I'm twelve. Maybe I just guessed wrong."

"Even better, child parts are much harder to find." He fiddled with something on the console she could not see. "That'll be worth double or more."

"No." Her voice fell to mewling. "Please, I have a family."

"Do they know where you are?"

"No, I'm trying to get home."

He giggled and clapped. "Excellent. Then they won't find your bones."

"Please no... Why? Why are you doing this?"

He paused, tapping a finger to his lip as he considered the question. "Well, you see... The perils of modern society often take quite a toll on the bodies of those who live to their fullest. Fortunately for me, these same people tend to have gobs and gobs of money. Now, when they go and turn their lungs into crystalline dust from too much Icewhisper or their indulgence in synthetic alcohol turns their liver into pudding, I find someone like you. Some poor scrap that no one will miss, and take what they need. Don't worry, child. It will only hurt for the first, oh, ten minutes. I'll start with the non-vital parts first so you have more time."

"Karina and Father will miss me." She couldn't peel her eyes away from the orb of death.

"That is almost touching. Well, they should have thought of that before they let you run around the grey zones." Something else beeped. "Now I just need to program in your measurements so Frankie here can convert that grubby little body of yours into money."

Althea twisted and pulled at her arms and legs. Barely able to move, she rolled her head to face the stairs, and shouted, "Help!"

The rolling gunfight picked up intensity; a male voice screamed.

Robotic arms whirred to life, spinning, twisting, and clicking as calibration routines ran. Various small tools at their tips whirred or snapped. The man in white bounced up to the side of the table, sliding his fingers under the neckline of her shirt. He held up an enormous pair of scissors and smiled at the terror in her eyes.

"Now, I do need to get these shabby clothes out of the way and we can begin the beautiful harvest." He pressed on her abdomen, squeezed her leg, and forced her eyelids wider with his thumb. "Yes, yes. You are perfect."

The icy metal slid along her chest, its jaws opening around the white cloth.

"No, I'm not. I'm malnurmished. I'm from the Badlands. I have all sorts of sick inside me that you've never seen before." Althea stared into his eyes, tweaking at his emotion as he lifted her tank top. She found nothing in there to touch. This creature was broken. His emotions didn't work. He had none at all. Her best defense was useless. The scissor started to close. The man in white gazed at her, eyes bulging from his head with fascination.

"Such pretty blue light."

She whimpered. "No."

He ignored her. Fright became anger.

She commanded. "*Stop!*"

The man in white stalled as if frozen in time. A moment passed, she dare not struggle with the tip of the sharp scissor so close to her throat. More bullets clanked above. She drew several breaths while glaring at this animal dressed up like a human being.

"Pretty... blue..." A line of drool slid out of his lip, pooling on her stomach. "Glow. Blue." The right corner of his mouth twitched, teasing at a spasmodic smile.

Tugging at her fists and twisting her feet, she used her terror of being tied down to intensify the psionic assault. *"Let. Me. Go. Now!"*

His face twitched once, and again as the white of his left eye flashed red from hemorrhage. A trickle of blood fell out of his left nostril, his body shuddered, the bald head beaded with droplets of sweat. Drool rolled over his teeth. Her overpowering command had pulverized his mental faculties into a simple machine.

The ponderous scissor fell from his grip and slid off her chest to the side, bouncing on the cushion with a thump before clattering to the floor. The man in white reached forward without looking, undoing the strap pinning her shoulders. She raised her head to watch as he reached for the band around her left wrist.

Metal hands appeared without warning, crushing the man in white's arms into his sides; muted pops came as bones shattered under muscle. The gloss grey fingers squeezed the white coat crimson.

The pain broke her control, and the man in white screeched. "What are you doing? How dare you touch me! Do as you're told. Put me down this instant."

With a bestial roar, the oaf lifted the squirming little man into the air and threw him to the side over a railing. Somewhere below in the dark, a cacophony of ringing pipes and debris rose up as he landed. She sat up as much as she could, wringing her body into a strange shape in an effort to get her teeth on the band around her wrist. Realizing she couldn't bend that way, she fell limp and out of breath.

"Why did you do that? He was letting me out."

The huge heap of man looked at her, wriggling and helpless, and stepped closer. A stray bullet glanced off his shoulder with a dull *click*. She leaned as far away from him as the straps would allow, not knowing what to make of the bizarre tangle of emotions in his head. The mechanical iris enlarged and he traced his fingers over her head as if petting a kitten. Althea struggled, but still couldn't move at all. At feeling so trapped and defenseless, she trembled.

Much to her surprise, the man no longer radiated the desire to destroy her.

"Hi..." she said in a timid half-voice while lifting her right hand to wave at him. "Umm, nice metal man."

A placid female voice flooded the room. "Calibration complete. Organ harvest sequence initiated. Warning, anesthetic reserves at zero percent. Override code L-O-L accepted. Initiating procedure."

The autosurgeon came to life. A dozen octopusine little arms whirred and spun, clicking and poking the air while sharp things gleamed in the light and stabbed at nothing. Others buzzed, one glowed, and some fired test spritzes of liquid out of tiny needles. Chattering, the insidious thing rotated about and lowered with a hydraulic whine until one metal arm extended from the mass of gyrating limbs, reaching for the center of her chest with a three-inch rotary saw.

The big man watched, motionless as a statue.

She screamed, wrenching at the belts. Blood surged as adrenaline both natural and psionic bolstered her strength. In an instant, her arms and legs swelled from limp noodles to hard, defined muscles. Althea strained at the straps. A few threads started to give way, but she stopped fighting as the spinning horror nipped at her shirt. Forcing all the air from her lungs to make herself flatter, she strained to escape the rotating blade. Tiny flecks of white fabric jumped onto her face a second before it bit into skin, spraying her cheeks with blood.

Althea screamed, "Father!"

The oaf loosed a sudden roar and grabbed the saw-arm. He bent it back from her as though it were made of flimsy plastic, and snapped it off, hurling it into the distance. A grunt of anger escaped him before he slammed his fist into the killing sphere, crushing it into the ceiling. He continued snarling and huffing while twisting and tearing the machine out of its mount. Plastisteel stressed, screeching over loud electric buzzes and snaps.

Althea cringed as far as the restraints permitted, turning her face away from a shower of sparks that rained down from the wreckage. Hot flecks fell on her like a swarm of biting flies. She jerked about in an effort to shake off the ones landing on her and evade the embers that somehow got under her, lingering and burning out of reach. The large man mashed the ruined machine into the ground three times before he spun around and hurled it; a heavy metallic *crash* came from the dark.

As if called by her pained whimpering, a presence drew closer. Body heat warmed her arm from inches away. She looked toward the warmth at the metal-armed giant standing right beside the chair. The straps arrested her startled jump.

He glared at her writhing body with a sneer and tide of anger that grew stronger each time she squirmed. Every pitiful gasp as her leg or back found a burning spark enraged him. He touched her chest with gentle fingers, emitting a baleful sub-human moan at the sight of blood spreading over the white cloth. Loosing a terrible bellow, he raised his arms and the claws snapped out with a ring loud enough to mask the distant gun battle for an instant.

"No... please." She cringed away, begging for her life with telempathic radiance.

The whisper of blades caressed her with a rush of air, yet she felt no pain. The chair shuddered with a series of *clanks*. When the flurry ceased, she quivered, too afraid to look until metal arms slid under and lifted her out of the shredded straps.

Cradled into a chest so hairy it reminded her of the canid, and so warm it stalled her shivers, she opened her eyes and stared at a visage carved in the strong lines of a soldier. His one living eye met her gaze, the lens of glass and metal staring off into the dark. She reached up to touch the half of his face not metal; his unshaven cheek rough under her hand and wet with tears for what he witnessed done to her. The titan, who once wanted to smash and destroy, now wanted nothing more than to protect.

His anger had fled; in its place, regret. She felt like a four-year-old cuddled by a normal-sized man, but his foreboding presence denied her any sense of calm. Althea slipped a hand under her shirt, examining the one-inch slice down to her breastbone. A little concentration mended her skin, and quenched the strip of pain. One huge hand brushed her hair from her face, then returned the timid wave she offered moments before, tiny whirrs emanating from his metal fingers. His thoughts apologized for what the man in white almost did to her, though he lacked the ability to speak. Another stray bullet bounced off his shoulder, not that he noticed.

Metal clattered and rolled. A distant moan came from the man in white. The giant's head whipped around as if he had been slapped. Fury returned. He gingerly set Althea seated on the edge of the awful table and jumped over the railing, falling out of sight with a deathly snarl.

A cry of primal rage preceded the *squish* of crushed flesh; the man in white screamed.

Althea lowered herself to the floor, disgusted by contact with such an evil object. From beyond the railing, a repetitive spray of blood spattered the pipes along the ceiling. The man in white's cries of pain weakened to gurgles amid the repeating dull *clank* of cybernetic blades driven through flesh to the ground. The icy brush of a departing life touched her heart, but the raging and pounding didn't stop. In fact, the oaf's vengeful howls gained intensity. Not wanting to see what had happened below, she ran for the hallway.

Lost in feral panic, Althea darted over the painful grated floor, down a short corridor, and jumped onto a ladder that led out from this horrible place. She climbed like molten lava rose beneath her, flying up toward the circle of daylight beckoning from above.

43

CAN I KEEP HIM?

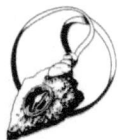

I n the comforting dark, Althea sat in the small metal room that shielded her from the horrible world outside its thin walls. Trembling, she massaged the soreness and metal fragments from the soles of her feet as her frenetic dash replayed itself in her memory. Once terror relaxed its grip on her mind, she squeezed herself into the corner of her sleeping-box and trembled until exhaustion overtook her fear.

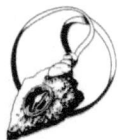

A METAL CREAK AND BLAST OF LIGHT TORE HER OUT OF SLEEP. SHE FLIPPED over with her arms crossed in front of her face. The shriek she let off made Whisk jump backward and drop the lid. It slammed, shaking the entire container. Her mind took several seconds to compensate for abrupt consciousness, and she realized where she was, and whom she had seen. Althea pushed the hatch open until it caught on the locking nub and stayed up like a canopy.

Whisk chuckled. "Rough night? Here, 'ave a snort."

He handed her a small metal bottle. She took a sip of liquid fire. Her face turned red. She gasped, and gave him an accusing stare. Coughing followed a fit of gagging and watery eyes.

"Takes bit o' gettin' used to. 'Ave another hit if yas want."

She shook her head, handing the flask back to him while trying to regain the ability to breathe.

"More fer me, then." He took a good swig, reacting no different than if he'd had a pull of water. "There's food."

Althea patted herself down and rummaged the moldy blankets. She had lost the burger card. Resigning herself never to know what this stuff tasted like fresh, she followed Whisk to the pile of scavenged food poured out at the center of their community. Along the way, she idly picked at the inch-long slice in the center of her tank top. Rather than at the pain it caused, Althea grew angry with the man in white for damaging Karina's gift. By the time they reached the center of the Bumwallow, thoughts of her sister had brought tears.

The residents sifted among the mound. They selected items of interest before wandering off to their 'houses' when they had taken their fill. Althea crawled around the pile, scarfing down the errant strip of fried potato or half-eaten nugget of synthesized chicken. One of the bums poked her in the back with something pointy. She spun around, and he poked her in the tummy with a clear plastic box. It contained a half-length turkey sub, evidently discarded by someone who noticed it's sell date had passed a whole two days ago.

"Uppity fuckers." He wheezed a chuckle out a gap in his teeth. "Actual vat-meat, and they didn't even open it. Here, kid, you take it."

"Thank you." She clung to it, hugged him, and scampered off to her container for the feast.

Althea indulged in the surprising bounty and thought about the dog man from the gas station and the way Father had shown up at the house when she called for him. She pondered Jamie and Mike, and wondered if she could bring them here the same way. To them, she had only a vague connection, not like the emotional link to Father or Karina. Then again, she didn't have much of a bond with the dog man, and he had heard her.

Screaming bums made her look up. Dozens of rag-clad men ran to the left, away from the ladder and down the drainage run. Heavy clanking stomps approached her space. She poked her head out, spotting the metal-armed oaf following the trail of dirty footprints she had left behind.

The surge of happiness he threw off when he saw her prevented her from running. She kept a tight grip on the rim of the container as he shambled over, unable to stop trembling at the sight of him. His finger blades slid back into their housings with a rapid flurry of loud snaps, and he stooped to pat her atop the head with tenderness she never expected.

Swallowing hard, she forced a tenuous smile. "Hi."

When he grinned, blood ran out of his mouth. The fright of his presence receded, allowing her to notice a number of bullet holes. He fell on his butt right outside her door, grinning like a lost puppy after finding its way home. She crawled out of the container and walked around him. Even with him sitting on the ground, she had to look up a little to make eye contact. He had been shot in the back, in the side, and several dents gave away where he had taken a few to the arm.

She stared into his mechanical eye, bewildered at how a beast that once wanted nothing more than to smash the little pretty thing sat here overjoyed to see her. She crouched, balancing on the balls of her feet, and put a hand into the bushy hair spread over his chest. Althea peered into his mind, finding his thoughts focused on her face. Her scream of deathly fear still rattled around at the back of his consciousness; all he wanted was for her never to make such a sound again. The more she looked into the images and feelings that glimmered within him, the more she came to understand what had happened.

Her abject terror at coming close to death stamped a permanent emotional imprint on his brain. His entire existence now revolved around protecting her. She bit her lip, uncertain if she should feel bad about doing that to him. After all, he had been a monster seconds away from murdering her, but did this differ at all from being a slave?

Yes. I saved him. He would have hurt people if he didn't die. This is better.

She sat cross-legged at his side and set to the task of healing him. The man had such thick muscles even the magic city bullets which had passed right through Dean had lodged in him. The presence of thin fibrous metal between skin and flesh likely had something to do with that as well. One by one, she coaxed metal slugs out of him, heavier, longer, and pointier than any bullets she had seen before. Althea normally removed lumps of metal that resembled stomped-on mushrooms. When she could find no more bullets inside him, she pondered getting rid of the foreign things in his body, but this man had far more than the dog, and none of them appeared to cause continuous pain. The electronics blended with his flesh much more seamlessly. Besides, both his arms only existed in metal. She couldn't leave him helpless.

Althea settled for mending the gunshot damage and slumped to the side to rest. The big man's adoration had grown stronger. Perhaps her telempathic imprint had been a starting point, and these feelings were genuine? She stared at him with more questions than she could answer, debating the justification of altering a man's entire personality, even if he had once been evil.

The bums returned, carrying crude weapons made of old furniture and lamps. At seeing Althea sitting in his lap, they exchanged glances and relaxed. Most resumed eating. Whisk and Grey Tatters approached, but kept a safe distance.

"Wot's that then?" Whisk pointed.

"He followed me here. Is it okay if he stays?"

A peal of thunder rippled over the smog. Whisk looked up. "Aye, but we'z bout ta get peed on. Best git inside."

She crawled into her container and gazed out over the Bumwallow as the rain came. Pooling water carried off the lighter bits of trash and ushered grime into the piss-grate. The oaf would never fit inside her container. He sat dutifully outside, ignoring the deluge with one great metal arm reached inside, to which she clung.

"Do you have a name?"

He looked at her. In his thoughts, the man in white screamed, calling him "stupid cretin," or other things that sounded worse.

"I'm Althea. Thank you for saving me."

He grinned.

She traced a fingertip over the grooves of his arm between interlocking plates, down to his fist resting on the ground between her feet. Althea frowned at her legs. Once again, she'd become a filthy thing, far removed from the taste of 'civilization' she had enjoyed for a short while in Querq. Her eyes welled up thinking of the fork and the face Karina had made when she had grabbed the enchilada with her hands. The memory of her sister's fingers washing her hair brought full-on sobs.

The big man moaned, leaning in to pat her on the head. She looked up at him, sniffling; his expression asked what made her cry.

"I miss my family. All I can remember my whole life is being taken. I've been too scared to make people leave me alone. I don't want to be taken anymore." She held back her tears, growing angry. "I'm sick of being kidnapped. I just want to go home."

He tapped himself on the chest and pointed out into the world. He wanted to help her find them.

She smiled, hugging the rigid metal arm. "I know what to do."

After crawling to the edge of the container, she peered out into the downpour, searching for Whisk. When she spotted him, she sent her voice into his mind.

Whisk? Can you please find Flatline?

He yelped and collapsed amid the heap of trash he carried. Sitting up, he whirled around looking for the source of the voice.

Althea giggled. *I'm over here.*

Whisk shot her an alarmed stare and blinked. She waved. He scratched his head until the disorientation faded, and set about re-gathering his dropped treasure with shaking hands.

Flatline could find Beard. Beard could get her back home, and her new friend would protect her on the way. Maybe the ravens would even let him stay in Querq.

44

SHEPHERD

Althea lay draped in the oaf's lap, her cheek against his chest, a trickle of drool running down over his stomach. Thick metal fingers stroked her hair, and in an awkward sort of way, she felt protected. Whisk ambled over, still keeping a nervous distance from the giant. Stiffness told her she had slept like that, likely the reason for the drool.

"Hey now. Imma go see 'bout findin' Flatline. Wot wit you fixin' him up and all, he dun wen' back to his ol' life. Hope he don't get the coreburn again." He shook his head, tossing little dark things out of his hair. "Nevermindin' that. May take me a little bit to find 'im."

Althea got up and hugged him, stink and all. "Thank you."

After a nod, he trundled off and up the ladder. Two of the other homeless men approached, one with a cut on his hand. His friend looked her up and down while she mended it.

"Hey, kid. You wana help us get some food?"

She looked up at him. "How?"

"You got the big three for begging."

"What?" She squinted from the sun while trying to look up at them.

"Well. One, yer a little kid. That gets a lot 'o sympathy. Two, yer covered in dirt. Three, yer a girl. People can't resist dem big blues. Oh yeah, and four, you look starved... like a actual street kid."

"Billy, she *is* a street kid." The other man whacked him on the back of the head.

"This sounds like something bad." She folded her arms.

"Here's the plan. There's a bunch o' food joints round here. Some let us have their throw-aways, but not 'til they close. We go to a place wit you, I tell 'em you're my kid and we need food. They take one look at you and feel guilty and all. We get food. We go outside, stash it with Charlie here, and go to another place." He clapped once. "Bingo, we swim in food!"

She turned. "That's dishonest."

"Oh, we ain't gonna keep t'all. It's fer everyone." He waved his arm at the wallow.

"All right." She sighed. "But what about my eyes? Those people are looking for me."

"You iz genius." Billy leaned back and howled at the sky.

He ran off and dove headfirst into his pile of junk. A minute later, he returned and stuck a pair of too-large sunglasses on her head, then handed her a white curtain rod.

"There. I'll tell 'em you'z blind. Keep 'em closed and tap that stick on the ground like yer usin' it to find your way along. Blind, starvin' little street kid." His eyes watered with emotion. "Oh, Charles, we're gonna eat!"

For a few hours, they walked from restaurant to restaurant. More often than not, they'd receive a little food, which went into a sack that Charlie, waiting outside, carried. She didn't do much but stand there looking sad, not difficult—she *was* sad. Althea found the wait for Whisk to come back with news of Beard painful, but at least she could do something to help these men before she left.

They returned heroes. Given first pick of the loot, she took the most familiar thing, a burrito, and some cheeseburgers for the big guy. After returning to her 'house,' she sat down to eat and stalled on the first bite, bewildered at who would put scrambled eggs inside a burrito. When the initial shock wore off, she ate it anyway. Fresh food couldn't be ignored.

Later, the oaf followed her close around the wallow while she went from container to container, healing little hurts and chasing away a sick or two. One of the bums commented he acted like a big German shepherd walking on two legs. From then on, Althea decided to call him Shepherd. He didn't seem to mind.

A woman's terrified scream came from the distance, followed by the angry bellow of a man. Her next shriek carried pain. Althea ran to the ladder and went up to the street, toward the sound of the shouting. Shepherd emitted a frustrated moan, too big for the shrouded ladder.

From the corner of an alley, she peered at a man in a fancy glowing suit that changed in a gradual sway from green to blue, then orange to red and back to green. Luminous neon pink teeth sneered from a dark-skinned face set off by a glimmering purple visor.

A pale young woman with powder-blue hair cowered away from his repeated slaps. Two black discs adhered to her breasts only big enough to cover the dark spots. Her skirt barely qualified as a skirt instead of a wide belt. Iridescent pink shoes with long struts for heels looked like something the woman had been forced to wear so she couldn't run away from her owner.

He swatted at her hand, tossing a small thing to the side that fluttered to the ground and vanished amid the trash. The woman snatched at it desperately on its way down, begging him to let her have it, but he dragged her off by the arm. A trickle of blood ran from her nose.

Althea followed, intent on freeing the woman from slavery. If she could stall a monster like the man in white in his tracks, she could deal with this glowing fool. She stepped on something that stuck to her sole, and hopped to a halt, lifting and twisting her foot over to look. A rubbery one-inch square of beige material with rounded corners and a raised bit in the center clung to her skin.

She wiped at it, but it didn't move. An annoying thing stuck to her foot could wait. She had to help that woman. When she took another step, she stared down at a bizarre tingle spreading up into her leg. The light changed. The painted words and faces on the walls moved. Giant yellow spheres with smiling mouths sang at her, things she remembered from her early childhood, songs meant to put little children to bed.

Shadows grew, colors changed, and the alley in both directions twisted into a haze. The sky turned yellow. She blinked and it went green. The buildings swayed like giant blades of grass. Painted rainbows slid along the walls and flowers burst from the vacant black squares of broken windows.

The tiniest voice she had ever heard came from her right. "We're coming to save you."

A six-inch tall woman with an orb of white hair and dragonfly wings flew up to her face and poked her in the nose with a tiny electrical spark.

The pixie giggled and waved. "Don't worry, little moggie, we're coming." She zoomed away, leaving a trail of white glowing dust.

"Hey, how ya doin?" asked a gruff man from below. The source, a fat grey tabby cat, yawned at her and trundled off.

She grinned and reached to pet it, but gawked when her hand fell to the street with a *splat*, at the end of the noodle that used to be her arm. Her fingers flowed off like rivulets of flesh from the point of impact. The hilarity of it caught her off guard, and she laughed.

The metal road surface rose up to her chest. She swam in it, paddling at the cool, silvery liquid that carried away all her sadness while the little painted stick men from the walls told her she would be with her family again soon. An army of white cartoon doves surrounded her with bright bird-song and a flash of flapping wings.

Something hit her leg. The blue-haired teen fell to the ground and vanished with a splash into the silver. Laughter came without thought, and Althea cooed and giggled at the young woman swimming around in circles.

"Where is it? Where is it?" The woman raced in circles, scratching at the trash.

The man with the glowing pink teeth stomped over. He started reaching for the teen, but stalled at the sight of Althea and bent closer, peering at her. His face detached and drooped to his belt. The dead bird on the side of his hat flapped its one remaining wing. She grabbed her big toes, one in each hand, and pulled, rocking back and laughing at him. When they stretched out, she stopped laughing and stared at her feet as if they were the deepest mystery of the universe. One by one, she stretched the rest of her toes to the same length.

"Yo, I think this little skank here pinched your Zoomer."

Althea raised her foot to her face, sniffing at the wavering noodles her toes had become.

"You little whore," said the woman, poised to tackle her.

"Whoa." The man put a hand up to the side of his head. "You feel that?"

"Yeah... It's... It's..." The woman, now a female canid with sky-blue fur, fell on top of her and licked the side of her head. The tongue slid over her scalp twice more before the creature fell onto her back, giggling like a little girl. "She tastes like Zooooom."

Althea grinned and pet the dog-woman on the belly, making her laugh.

"Yo. I ain't never touched this fuckin' shit. Why am I high?" Pink Teeth stumbled to the side, his flapping arms sprouted bright purple feathers.

Althea grinned at the man as he failed to fly, wondering where the blue dog woman went and why she pet a fish. "You're not a bird." She pointed, yelling with the accusatory tone of a triumphant seven-year-old.

"No, Ah ain't. And who the hell you is?" He grasped a fistful of her shirt and pulled her up to eye level. "You got a lot o' nerve freelancin' in my yard."

Althea stared down at the noodles waving out from under her skirt that had been legs. The sight made her laugh again.

"Neebo, she's just a little kid." The blue-haired fish did a backflip out of the glimmering silver and fell back out of sight. "She ain't workin."

The pink teeth parted, and kept expanding into a huge tunnel. She imagined flying past them into a swirl of bright colors.

"I know some dudes that would pay for this," said Neebo.

"That's sick," said the fish. "She's too small."

Althea tilted her head at the flashing lights in front of her and struggled to make sense of the fluttering mass of face. With a sudden burst of inspiration, she jammed her finger into one of the whistling openings. He let go of her and howled. The fall happened in slow motion, her jelly legs did nothing to support her, and she splashed into the metal water. She rolled onto her chest and tried to swim toward the blue-haired fish, who floated upside down making bubble-pop sounds.

"She just tried to pick mah damn nose." Neebo sneezed and snorted. "Damn she's fucked up. Gotta be a first trip."

The water lost its fluidity; stinging seeped into her hands from slapping the hard ground. Amid the chorus of singing graffiti, one sharp nibble of hurt crawled up her arm and into her brain. She suspected something had gone wrong, but not what. An army of battered rag dolls crawled out from under an old dumpster and swarmed over her, giggling, chattering, and tickling her. Althea squealed with laughter and rolled onto her back, staring up at giant bees dancing in the blue-violet smog far above. The Wagon Man had smoked something once and the cage had kept her basking in it. He had given her a doll he'd found that looked exactly like the forty crawling over her. The smoke had made her feel listless and funny.

At that moment, she knew she had been poisoned.

She covered her eyes, tuning out the silly things that played and sang, ignored the fish, and peered inward at her life essence. Wispy strands of something orange drifted within her like kelp snagged on a branch. Anchored to the sole of her foot, they reached up her leg toward her brain. Althea wanted it out. The strands receded as she forced the poison to her bladder. Her head throbbed, her eyeballs ached, and every muscle felt like mush.

After a minute or three of lying motionless in pain, she sat up and pulled her foot into her lap. Althea splayed her toes apart and picked at the little square until it peeled away, revealing a tiny pad covered with a pattern of tiny hexagons in metal thread, soaked with a foul-scented liquid.

She tossed it aside and used a piece of trash cloth to wipe the wet spot away. The woman lay on the ground nearby, blowing spit bubbles like the fish had been. Althea dragged herself closer. The older girl had a blackened right eye. Blood dribbled from her nose, and a number of bruises decorated her forearms. The absence of a hallucinatory high shared upon the wings of Althea's telempathy caused the woman to groan. Althea took her hand and concentrated, mending numerous small hurts.

"Come on, kid, your fine ass works for me now," said Pink Teeth. "Get you cleaned up, some food, place to live, you'll be doin' good for yourself."

Althea glanced up at him from where she knelt. "No."

"Damn, girl, you're some kind of pretty. Bet you won't even need much work done."

He reached for her. Althea cringed and raised her arms to protect her face. Rather than hit her, he grabbed her wrist.

"No. Go away." His emotion made no secret of what he wanted her to do for him. Her blasé tone became angry, and her eyes flared bright. "*Now.*"

Pink Teeth blinked, bewildered, and shook his head. "Yo, Haggis, Little E, need yo' asses pronto…"

"Yo." yelled a deep voice from a nearby alley. "On the—what the fuck is thaaaa?"

A loud *squish* preceded splattering. Someone's internal bits bounced into view.

"Shit!" screamed a high-pitched male voice.

Two gunshots rang out; flashes of azure lit the alley, projecting nanosecond shadows of a massive claw-handed silhouette looming over a smaller man. A horrible scream of terror changed to one of agony before it cut to silence.

"No!" screamed Althea, struggling to run toward the death she felt in the air.

Pink Teeth held onto her arm, staring dumbstruck at the maw of the alley. She whined and pulled, but couldn't get away.

Shepherd emerged from where Pink Teeth expected his friends to be, claws out and dripping blood. All his attention locked onto the hand clamped around Althea's arm, sparing none for the bullet hole in his left pectoral. A mangled bellow of rage exploded from his throat as he held his arms to the sides. The pimp turned two shades paler.

"You don't have to hurt him." Althea glanced from Shepherd to the bad man. "He's going *away*. Right?"

Pink Teeth sprinted out from under his one-winged hat, which spun to the ground, and took off down an alley, his footfalls echoing to silence.

Shepherd relaxed and retracted his blades. He trotted over to Althea and emitted a grunt of concern. Althea gave him a sad look and darted around the corner. One man, or what was left of him, leaned against a dead car. From about where his stomach upward, he ceased to be. A cone of bloody mess painted the wall behind him. Thicker chunks still slid down toward the alley. Not far away, a severed arm clutched a large pistol. Another body, somewhat smaller than the other, lay twitching on the ground. His abdomen had ruptured, and much of what belonged inside him dangled out onto the road.

"Why!" wailed Althea, wasting a second to gaze up at Shepherd with a wounded stare that made him moan and slouch.

She rushed to the still-living man's side and grabbed handfuls of his guts, stuffing everything back into him in a haphazard scramble. At the point when adding anything more forced something to squeeze back out, she concentrated on her power. After she shut off his pain, she forced his body to make its blood-shape larger, and then nudged the rest of the blobs back to where they belonged. In the periphery of her awareness, Shepherd kicked at the ground.

When she finished, she wiped her bloody hands off on the man's purple dress shirt, stood, and folded her arms at Shepherd. "They hadn't done anything yet. You can't just kill everyone you think is bad."

The massive man hung his head. Confused, and a little guilty for making him sad, Althea approached and reached up to touch his cheek. His half-metal face attempted a smile. She looked into his thoughts. Shepherd had expected these men to hurt her and the mere thought of it had enraged him.

"Thank you for helping me." She hugged him.

He perked up.

"Killing people hurts me too." She whined. "Even if they're bad."

The man groaned and sat up. Shepherd growled, sending the man limping off as fast as he could move.

"You're shot," she whispered, tracing a finger around a small hole in his left pectoral.

Shepherd shrugged.

AT ALTHEA'S URGING, SHEPHERD HAD CARRIED THE WOMAN TO HER LITTLE room within the Bumwallow. Something remained wrong with her, a hurt nestled deep in her brain that would take time to fix. She knelt at the young woman's side, feeding her water and bits of food scavenged earlier by Whisk and his friends. It reminded her of how she had taken care of Rachel. She sagged, fighting the urge to cry. That felt like a lifetime ago. She missed her friend, and still felt bad over running away, but knowing Rachel made it to the city where she wanted to be helped ease her guilt.

The older girl batted at Althea's hand. "Go away, kid."

"Shh. Be still. You're hurt. You need to drink this." She tipped an old synthbeer can full of water at the woman's mouth.

"Blech, what is this?" She choked it down, making faces at it.

"Water."

"Ugh. From what planet?" The woman blinked, rubbed her nose, and forced herself to sit up. When she made eye contact, she froze. "Whoa, you some kinda Lace-head brat?"

"Everyone keeps asking me that, but I don't know what it means." She crawled into the girl's lap and pushed her against the wall with a hand on each shoulder. "Please sit and let me help you."

One of the black domes popped off the teen's breast. Althea tried to put it back where it came from. The young woman blushed and swiped it from her grip.

"Lace. It's nasty shit. When you're on it, you feel like a god. Makes your eyes glow green... Gets into your soul. People'd kill their own mothers to score, but that shit's a death sentence. Yuji was on that crap. It killed him after two years." She squeezed the small dome and it beeped, adhering back into place. "Only way you can help me is if you got a Zoomer around here to make up for the one you stole."

"I'm sorry. I stepped on it as accident. I didn't want to." She showed off the red mark on her sole. "It's bad. You shouldn't touch them."

"I…" The woman recoiled from the foot hovering close to her face and shuddered, breaking out in a sweat. "I need it. I need it bad."

She placed a hand on either side of the woman's head and concentrated. The darkness within the girl's thinking shape shifted, twisting with flaring black threads that pulsated down her spine.

Althea gathered a surge of power and closed her eyes.

"No… You don't."

ARCHON

People on the street knew the young blue-haired woman as Andromeda. The mother who had abandoned her four years ago called her Violet. At the time her mother left, the girl had been Althea's age. Delirium and fatigue made for a short, but emotional conversation before they fell asleep in a pile.

Violet's shivering had jostled Althea awake in the middle of the night, so she covered her with all the bedding and made do with cold metal. Althea's eyes popped open. A thick mass of dense, cold air crawled over her, startling her awake for the second time. Her sleep-deprived brain, further stymied by the temperature, seized. The eerie chill faded by the time she had the presence of mind to sit up. She wrapped her arms around herself, teeth chattering.

In the black and white space, as dark as could be, Andromeda smiled at her. Althea blinked and wiped her eyes. When next she looked, the older teen's head had lolled against the wall, eyes shut with sleep. Althea pushed the side wall open with her foot, letting in the night air, warmer than the interior of their cargo box. The Bumwallow hung in silence, all the residents asleep in their cubbies. Nothing moved.

After a powerful yawn, Althea curled on her side, letting her guest keep all the blankets.

"YOU MUST BE FREEZING," ASKED VIOLET, LOUD ENOUGH TO WAKE ALTHEA.

She pushed herself up to sit before squinting at a face ringed with a sphere of blue hair. "Huh?"

"You were shivering. The cage doesn't bother me." She patted the bare metal.

"Cage?" Violet gave off fear until she pushed at the flap and the door swung open with ease. "Why did you call this a cage?"

"It's a metal box." Althea shrugged. "Cages aren't always locked."

Shepherd peered in. Violet screamed, startling a flock of bums as well as a few birds. The big man tilted his head with curiosity and looked at Althea, as if to ask what was wrong with this woman.

"Don't worry." Althea crawled outside and stood beside him. "He will protect us."

"What if Neebo's boys come looking for me?"

"Who?"

"The guy who wanted to grab you. That's Neebo."

"Pink Teeth?" She grinned.

"Yeah. And his boys are gonna come after me."

Althea shot an accusatory look at Shepherd. "No, they won't."

He shrugged with an apologetic grin.

A long black car came to a halt on the street by the ladder, giving Althea a bad feeling. The urge to run grew strong, but she didn't want Pink Teeth to take Violet. She reached up and pulled the container closed, pressed her back against it, and folded her arms, acting casual. Whoever came to cause trouble, she would send them away.

The rear door opened, revealing a short woman with stark white hair in a pixie cut. Her grey-blue coat fluttered around her shins in the breeze, exposing shiny black pants and knee-high boots with thin, raised heels. Althea couldn't quite tell her age. By size, she appeared a teen, but had the poise of an adult woman.

She pulled her sunglasses down her nose. Ice-blue eyes peered over them, locking stares with Althea. A hint of a smile formed. She stepped to the side as a man emerged from the grand car. His thick mane of chestnut hair was groomed to perfection, including a thin mustache and goatee. He held his gaze high and surveyed the homeless below him with a displeased glower, then stuffed his hands in the pockets of his long, tweed coat.

As soon as she saw the nose, she recognized him. The floating head —Archon.

She'd come so close to going home... Whisk would be back any minute now with Flatline or at least with the knowledge of where to bring her to meet him. She clenched her hands into fists, refusing to be taken.

"Go away," Althea yelled. "I'm not yours. I don't wanna go with you."

"What's going on?" Violet's voice sounded muted from inside the closed container.

Althea patted it. "Stay in there. Please."

"Foolish child." Archon stepped off the edge and floated to a graceful landing in the sunken trench some twenty feet below.

"Ladders are so gauche," muttered the white-haired woman.

"There is much you lack the refinement to understand." He held his arms out in a disarming gesture. "You have such potential. Stop frittering it away in this grotty hovel."

The woman climbed down the ladder.

All the bums gawked in silence. Watching this man fly had stolen the breath from their lungs.

"I don't want to understand your fine mints. I know you're bad." Althea slipped one foot behind the other, creeping backward. "I want to go home to my family. You are not my family. Please *leave me alone.*" Her eyes flickered.

He smirked into a smile, then a full grin. "It seems you are learning a little, but you have a lot of work to do."

She gulped at the dismissal of her attempt to influence him, her voice carried a desperate whine. *"Please leave."*

He closed his eyes, facing away while weathering her mental assault. His odd accent grew more pronounced. "You are getting closer, dear, but still falling short. Come now, child. Stop with the games and let us be off. You are superior to these wretches." Archon held out a hand bedecked with two gold rings.

Althea glared, clinging to Shepherd's metal arm. "You want to take me like everyone else. I'm not owned anymore."

He sighed, pinching the bridge of his nose with exasperation. "Fine then, if you insist on doing things the hard way, we shall." With that, he produced a pistol and held it to the white-haired woman's head. "Come now, or you can watch her die."

The bored tone to his threat confused her. He didn't seem likely to do it.

"What the hell are you doing?" the woman whispered.

At her not seeming frightened, Althea peered into her thoughts.

She cannot stand to see people hurt. Just play along, dear, replied Archon with telepathy.

Althea's frown deepened. "You're lying. I see your feelings. You like her."

The woman cracked a little grin.

"Since you insist on being cheeky." He whipped his arm forward and shot a hole in the wall over Grey Tatter's shoulder. "The next one won't miss."

The man hurriedly produced a small gun from his pocket.

Archon raised one eyebrow. He waved dismissively, and the bum flew across the drainage channel, striking the wall face first with a loud fleshy *thump*. Grey Tatter screamed and twisted against the metal. An invisible force rolled him onto his back, feet off the ground.

"Stop it," Althea yelled.

"Come on then, luv. We'll pause on the way an' get you some proper brekky." The woman in the coat smiled.

"Certainly. I think we can spare a moment to feed the urchin." Archon again sounded bored. "Come with us, and he lives. Dawdle and he dies. There are quite a number of tramps here to play this game with. How many shall it take?"

Shepherd roared and grabbed an empty plastisteel shipping box. Archon raised both eyebrows. The giant hurled it hard enough to knock himself over onto all fours. It sailed to an abrupt halt a few feet away from Archon, motionless in space for seconds, before rocketing back at the metal-armed guardian. Shepherd leapt into a punch that launched the deformed box into the wall with a tremendous hollow *thump*. He leaned forward, preparing to charge at them.

"That yobbo may be an issue. Would you mind, dear?" Archon mumbled.

The woman leaned back, raising her arms to the sides. An upwelling of energy surrounded her, invisible to the eye. The air tingled with an ozone scent seconds before a cobweb of crawling electrical arcs threaded up from the plastisteel ground and jumped to various points on the big man's body.

With a bestial wail of agony, he fell, shuddering and twitching out of control. Althea stared in horror at him, then at Grey Tatter, who gasped for breath.

"Stop. Stop. Stop." Althea stomped her foot in time with each word. "Please don't hurt anyone else!"

The woman relaxed and the lightning receded. Shepherd's skin had become hot to the touch. Spasmodic trembles rocked him.

"He's merely stunned, luv. Best come with before he gets up and I give him worse." The woman beckoned her with a wave.

Althea knelt by Shepherd's head, wiping the sweat from his brow. "Please watch after Violet. I don't know if I'll see you again."

He moaned in protest.

"They'll kill you if I don't go." She closed her eyes, forcing the tears back. "They'll kill Whisk and everyone here." She considered trying to terrify them into fleeing, but she'd never seen anyone make lightning before. Something bad would probably happen if she scared that woman, especially near too many innocent people who could be hurt.

Head down, she stood and plodded over to the first two people she considered hating.

The woman broke a twenty-second staring contest first, looking off to the side. "James, I got a dodgy feelin' about this nipper. Maybe Aurora was right... maybe we—"

Archon leaned to the woman with a rushed whisper. "Bollocks. Get her in the car. Oh, dear." He took a step back from Althea, covering his nose. "You eh... tend to the ragamuffin. She rather needs a bath."

The woman took her by the hand and walked her to the ladder.

"Spare us the sniveling plea." He peered between his fingers at her. "I know how you feel about being on a tether. You do not believe me now, but I am trying to elevate you from this life. If only you knew your potential. A magnificent person like you deserves so much more than what life has given you. Are you not displeased with how the world treats you?"

She stared at her dirty feet.

"Fine then," he snapped. "Up you go."

Althea dragged herself up the ladder, glaring doom at the stained metal inches behind it. The white-haired woman guided her to the door of the overlong car and put her in a rear-facing seat before sitting opposite her. Archon entered from the other side, taking a spot next to the woman. He tucked himself as far away from her as he could get and still be inside, one hand over his nose.

"I'm Anna, but you can call me Pixie if you like." She smiled in an attempt to be disarming.

Ignoring her, Althea looked out the window at the bums. Grey Tatter staggered out of sight into his box while the others collected to watch the car roll away. A sad bellow from Shepherd made her cry. Cool breezes came from all around her, thick with the sweet scent of clean.

"We found ourselves a cute little moggie, didn't we?" She winked at Archon before wiping at Althea's face with a moistened cloth. "You 'ave such pretty eyes."

She sat stone-faced, disregarding this awful woman's attempts at motherly care. The street fell away from the window as the car went into the air. Angry and frightened, she clutched her fingers into the soft black seat and gripped the carpet with her toes. Flying terrified her. She stared at her lap not to have to see the buildings flashing by.

Trembling came. Fear of what awaited her mixed with the despair of being so close to going home and getting taken away yet again. She wallowed in sadness until blurry shouting pierced her veil of misery and the fragrance of burned electronics picked at her senses. After a few finger snaps in front of her face, she opened her eyes to Archon's hand inches away. Pixie curled to the side, bawling.

"Stop that straight away." He seemed to want to give her a light slap, but hesitated at the thought of touching her. "You're going to make us crash."

A flash of sparks and smoke burst from behind her. The sobbing man behind the wheel halfheartedly swatted at the console where fire had erupted. Everything swayed and rocked as the car dropped out of the sky.

"I'm not doing that sparks," she whined.

A force seized Althea's head, making her look at Pixie.

"No, Annabelle is. That telempathic sobby drivel you're radiating has sent her all sixes and sevens. When she becomes upset, electronics tend to go a bit wonky... usually in rather disastrous ways. It would be best for all of us if you put a lid on it."

"Huh?" Althea looked back and forth between them.

He sighed at the roof of the car. "Look, child, cut the telempathy, or I'll stop it for you."

Folding her arms, she realized her longing for Karina and Father had been leaking. Archon showed little reaction, but Pixie wept inconsolably. Althea sighed and stared at the floor, trying as best she could not to allow her emotions out. The car leveled off and the ride continued in quiet broken only by the driver's occasional sniffle.

"Hey..." The woman reached out and held her hand. "I was pretty messed up when Archon found me, too."

Althea glowered. "I'm not messed up. You're kidnapping me."

"You're living with tramps," she said, raising her voice. "You're a child. A special, pretty little child. The street is no place for you. All we want is to give you the home you deserve. You've got nothing to fear. We won't hurt you."

"I have a home. Why won't you let me go there?" She squeezed the woman's hand.

"That wretched place is no home for someone like us." Archon glanced at her. "I've been searching for you for a long time. That wasteland you people call the *Badlands* is dreadful, worse than the street detritus we found you with."

"Querq is nice. I miss my family." She pulled away from Pixie's attempts at consolation, huddling against the door.

Will you hurry this along, please? Her stink is seeping into the fabric. We will smell it for months.

Althea frowned at overhearing his telepathic request of the driver. "Sorry I stink. I don't want to ruin your car. You can just let me out anywhere."

Archon chuckled. "Clever girl."

Pixie reached to comfort her again, but she cringed away, drawing a sigh. "Didn't Aurora say she was all sugar and spice? She seems a wee bit petulant."

Glaring, Althea shouted, "I am not your pet!"

The woman covered her mouth to stifle a laugh. "No, sweetie. Petulant doesn't mean that."

"Yes, Lauren did say that... always the obedient little captive." Archon shook his head. "She went and got herself attached to some Badlands drek that created the illusion of safety. You see, child, your feelings for the man and his daughter are not real. Given the conditions in which you have grown to this point, you have attached yourself to the first people to be nice to you. In a few months, you won't think of them again."

"You're lying," said Althea, furious.

The driver roared and pounded a fist on something.

"Sodding hell," growled Anna, sparks lapping out of her into the seat, lofting the stink of ozone and molten plastic. "She's doing it again."

Althea swallowed her rage, half-whispering, "You are a bad person."

Her abilities didn't affect Archon at all, leaving her feeling like a normal kid trapped in a situation she couldn't escape. She ignored Pixie's continued attempts to be soothing. The city slid on outside, each passing building the same as the one before it. After a while, the buildings changed, ruined and dead like the Old City surrounding Querq—only larger, and metal instead of concrete.

She scooted to the window and pressed her hands against the glass, staring down at a large swath where the towers became much shorter and crumbled. Up ahead, an industrial complex spread out along the ground amid a network of pipes and conduits running between a foreboding edifice of dark metal and four large, hyperbolic towers, dingy white against the sky.

The driver steered for the structure at the center. Eerie lime fluorescence in the windows stared up at her like the eyes of the thing from the garden. It had wanted her out of the Badlands; she had sensed the desire quite strong within it. Something about her had scared a creature made of hatred and suffering, and she wondered if Archon took his orders from it. The idea that creature might be presently feeding from Karina's sorrow made her angry all over again.

A flurry of sparks leaked from Pixie, creeping over the seat.

Althea reined in her mood. "Sorry."

They landed on the roof. Pixie took hold of Althea's left wrist and guided her out of the car. A wash of sour air laced with the scent of metal and oil blew by. The stiff breeze had a pleasant warmth despite the bad smell. Althea stifled a gasp at the discomfort of stepping barefoot on sun-warmed metal, refusing to let these people take delight in her misery.

Pixie led her down the steps of an elevated landing pad and along a greasy walkway to a door. A man and a woman with tiny rifles stood astride it like guards, both in battered, mismatched clothing. They radiated jealousy as soon as they looked at her. Althea gave them a confused glance.

The four towers, their white-painted sides streaked green to brown with rust and grime, reached far into the air above this roof, ringed with flickering lights and spiral catwalks. The most awful, low-pitched howl rumbled inside them from the wind. Althea shied away from the scary, monolithic things, and swallowed hard, at a loss to understand this place.

"It's bad here," whispered Althea.

"Just an old power station," said Pixie.

"Indeed." Archon gestured at the grounds with a sweeping motion. "I thought it an appropriate metaphor."

Althea crept to the roof edge, peering down at the vast rusting network of pipes and abandoned vehicles. "There is only ruin here."

Archon frowned.

46

AS WOLVES LIKE DOGS

Pixie pulled Althea along a series of staircases and corridors, past dozens of rooms. Some looked untouched for many years. Fallen pieces of ceiling tiles littered ancient desks and broken chairs. A handful of offices had been repurposed into small bedrooms. One held a twenty-something man playing with strange gadgets full of blinking lights. A pair of teenage girls sat on a bed together chatting while cleaning guns. The last occupied room they passed held two blond boys younger than her, each concentrating on a scrap of fabric. Althea leaned to watch, catching sight of a wisp of smoke and a sputter of fire before Anna pulled her away. One of the boys mumbled something in another language she'd never heard before.

At the far end of a long hallway, a right turn opened into a huge white-tiled room full of toilets separated by flimsy partitions. A bright orange plastic curtain blocked off the rear corner, near a metal bench and a row of small metal cubby holes with doors.

Pixie stopped at the bench and let go of Althea's arm, then pulled back the crinkling tarp to reveal a three-foot-wide clear cylinder connecting from the ceiling to a thick metal disc on the floor bedecked with blinking lights, small panels, and vent slats. One side of the tube had a narrow, curved hatch.

"I don't like it here," whined Althea.

"Oh, rubbish. Come on then, peel yourself out of those 'orrible rags and let's get you cleaned up. I bet you're pretty under all that dirt."

In a place devoid of stink, Althea realized she reeked. The lack of a bathtub made her suspicious, so she stood her ground. "No. I want to go home."

The white-haired woman radiated a twinge of guilt, but kept it off her face. "Come on, mite. Don't make this unpleasant. It's for your own good. Those filthy things are not healthy."

"I don't get sick," said Althea, with more petulance than intended.

Overhead lights faltered, as if a decrepit bathroom in an abandoned power station didn't frighten her enough while the lights worked.

"Althea…" Pixie reached for her.

"Okay!" She yelped and jumped back.

After a momentary staredown, Althea peeled her shirt off, then let her skirt drop to the ground. Anna took the battered tank top and skirt, pinching them with two fingers at arm's length, and dropped them on the bench before prodding Althea toward the cylinder with cold fingertips to the back. She stepped up inside, whimpering.

The woman closed the hatch behind her. To her left, a metal panel at chin level flashed with blinking lights. She glared at her naked reflection in the tube. This was new; since she'd made her skirt, no one who had kidnapped her had ever taken it before putting her in a cage. She didn't have clothes when the Wagon Man kept her locked up, but she'd been little then. Few Scrags that age wore anything. But now, having her clothing forcibly taken away felt a little too much like being put in a harem.

She liked these people even less.

Pixie hovered at the gap in the curtain, tapping her foot expectantly. After five minutes of silence, Althea spun around wearing an expression midway between pleading and cross. "How long do I have to stay in this cage?"

The woman gazed at the ceiling. "Oh, for fu—fudge's sake. Haven't you ever used an autoshower?"

Althea crossed her arms. "No."

"Shall I assume you've not a clue what a bath is then?"

"I know what a bath is." She pushed at the hatch, which didn't budge. "This is a cage, not a bath."

"Righto. Well, think of this as a bath while standing up. The machine does all the work; all you have to do is stand there. I'll walk you through how to work the controls."

"I don't like this!" Althea banged on the door. "Karina washes my hair. Let me out! I don't want this bath."

Anna showed no reaction to her tantrum aside from pointing at the control panel inside the tube behind her. After another minute of glaring, Althea pouted at the flashing symbols that turned her chest green with reflected light. Words blinked below each one, and an animated wheel in the corner formed a sliding scale from red to blue.

"Right then, hit the one labeled full wash, set the temp to preference and—"

Althea glanced back over her shoulder. "Which one is 'fool wash?'."

"The one labeled 'full wash.'"

Althea blinked at her.

"Bother... you can't read, can you?"

"Read?" Althea tilted her head.

Pixie sighed.

"Can't you do it for me?"

"How am I supposed to do that?"

"We can both fit in here."

"I'd recommend against that." Archon's voice echoed from out of sight by the door. "Having a shower with that one can be... uncomfortable."

Pixie blushed. "I umm, sometimes have a bad reaction to water." With a weak smile, she made a little spark dance between her fingers.

"You've *no* idea," said Archon with a hint of remembered pain.

"Oh." Althea sulked at the panel.

"Touch your finger to the third square in the second row. The temp looks fine. All you have to do is stand there and try to stay calm."

"What will it do to me?"

Pixie grumbled. "Warm water, soap, hot air... Nothing bad."

Althea didn't sense any deceit, and poked the screen as instructed. She jumped when the disc under her feet rattled and whirred. A pronounced *click* came from the hatch, sounding much like a locking bolt. In a panic, she threw herself into the cylinder, slapping at it and screaming, "Let me out! You tricked me. It's a cage."

She continued wailing until warm water sprayed on her from above. Pixie leaned against a column in an attempt not to fall over laughing. Althea bristled at being mocked.

It's not fair!

A metal ring slid down out of the ceiling inside the tube, spinning and spraying her from all directions with cascading waves of hot water. Squealing, she moved away from the edge as the rotating jets doused her from head to toe and then back up. Gagging and sputtering, she tried to find a way to turn where she didn't feel as though she would drown, but couldn't avoid being blasted in the face. Spray raked like tiny claws all over her body.

Once the ring stopped, Althea looked at the floor. Dirt-streaked water swirled, devoured by a small grating in front of her toes. She accepted that Pixie hadn't lied. This cage-like thing really was only a strange kind of bath. Drops of water fell from her nose, offering the juvenile distraction of trying to adjust how she stood so they would fall right into the little square holes without touching the drain.

The machine came to life again, the ring spinning in the opposite direction and covering her with white foam. Remembering Karina's warning about soap, she closed her eyes and clung to the hand railing, waiting for it to end. After the suds, more warm water left her dripping. She clutched the railing tight, hating every ounce of this thing that made her feel like an object being cleaned rather than a person. Her longing for the loving caress of Karina washing her hair leaked down her face in the form of tears. She hated the clinical automation of this tube. This machine matched everything else about this giant city—no love. No wonder everyone who lived here became heartless.

The shower vanished and she found herself in the farm fields of Querq, chest-high wheat tickling her bare stomach. A short distance away, Karina toiled, her gaze downcast and her face joyless. Althea raised a hand and called to her, but got no reaction.

"Karina." Althea screamed. She tried to run to her, but found an invisible wall in her way. "I'm alive."

Karina stopped working and looked up, craning her head with a joyous glint in her eye as though she had heard something on the wind. Seeing nothing, she bowed her head and wept. The sight of her made Althea cry as well. Every ounce of emotion in her heart projected the desire to tell Karina she was okay and doing her best to get home. Her sister looked up at the clouds again, smiling despite her sorrow. Karina dropped the farm tool and ran off. The field faded back to white-painted walls, and Althea found herself curled up on the floor of the tube, staring at droplets of water on the clear barrier.

The sprayer ring emerged from the base and slid upward, back to the roof. Fury welled within her, a nascent emotion she had not often called upon. Regardless of what they did to her, that these people had made Karina so sad brought rage. Archon must have some trick to shield himself from her power. Sneaking away would be her only chance.

"Okay, it's done. Let me out." She stood, kicking the door, but Pixie had gone.

Althea scratched and pushed at the hatch, but it refused to open. Before she could escalate to screaming and banging, the entire tube shuddered and whirred. She cringed as the cylinder filled with hot fast-moving air, a tornado in a bottle.

The torrent subsided after a few minutes, leaving her dry. Seconds later, a *click* came from the door and it popped open. She leapt out before it could change its mind and close again, and ran to where she had left her things. Her clothes were gone, replaced by a plain white dress, an impractically tiny scrap of fabric with two holes in it, and a pair of floppy pink cloth strips set atop simple, flat white shoes. Only the agate pendant remained of her old things.

At the loss of her beloved skirt, she buried her face in her hands and cried. Why did these people have to be as cruel as possible? Defiantly, she put on only the agate amulet and stormed out.

Pixie caught her at the door. "What are you doing?"

"Going home." Althea tried to duck past her.

The woman grabbed her by the shoulders and twisted her about, directing her back into the room. "Go get dressed. You can't run about starkers. You're not out in the tribes now. First lesson of civilization: people wear clothes."

She struggled to get past the woman for a moment, but couldn't. "I want *my* clothes!"

"They're right there for you." Pixie half-carried her back over to the bench.

With a sigh, Althea picked up the strange little scrap, wondering who would bother with it. It was so small it offered neither warmth nor protection. She couldn't even figure out where it belonged, or why these people would give her such a ridiculous choice. She tossed it aside and chose the dress.

Pixie chuckled. "Never saw smalls before?"

"What?" asked Althea.

"Underpants?"

"They're so small. Why would anyone want them?"

Althea pulled the dress on over her head, having seen Karina wear them. The hem stopped at her knees, the material as soft as the nightgown. Running, climbing, and swimming would be harder, but possible. Wearing a modern garment brought weight to the worry she would never see home again.

Head down, she trudged over to Pixie. The woman sighed and shook her head, seized her by the wrist, and dragged her off at a brisk walk.

Althea kept up, alternating her gaze from the floor ahead of her to the woman at her right. "Why are you jealous?"

Pixie stopped. "What? Jealous? Of you?"

She nodded. "Yes. I can feel it."

The woman glanced away and resumed walking. "You're still small enough to have a decent life."

Althea winced at Pixie's grip on her wrist growing tighter. She stared at the woman, reading her emotions. "Someone made you really sad when you were small like me. You want to be a kid again, don't you? You're not all bad. Not like him. You don't like being mean to me."

"You've no idea what my life's been like, I—" A flat stare from Althea stopped her voice in her throat. "Oh, well. I suppose being kept as a slave in the Badlands is just as miserable. How could you even want to go back there?"

"Querq is big and safe. I'm not a slave there. I have a real family. I have to do chores and help and everything. They miss me." Althea wiped a lone tear off her cheek. "Love is not where you are, but who you are with."

Pixie stood for a moment in silence radiating guilt, shame, anger, and despair. Momentary hope faded when the woman discarded all emotions other than annoyance and dragged her along faster. Althea didn't protest, sensing the woman had become angry at herself, not her.

HER HAIR BRUSHED BACK STRAIGHT, ALTHEA PADDED WITHOUT A SOUND into a cavernous room, shockingly posh compared to the crumbling decay outside. A long, silver table surrounded by white chairs dominated the right side. Pixie's fingers in her back nudged her forward, closer to Archon who sat at the far end. Althea gasped at an aura of pink-purple energy surrounding him, until she realized the light came from an alcove of holographic screens at the far end of the room behind him where a handful of young people sat at consoles, making little dots move around the floating slabs of light. In the dark, their faces took on the color of whatever showed on their terminals.

"Well, well." Archon looked her up and down, smiling. "That is quite a bit of an improvement. You're quite adorable, actually."

Pixie tugged at the dress, adjusting its fit. "She wouldn't let me brush her hair, and she's apparently petrified of socks." She suppressed a giggle. "Didn't even realize what smalls were."

Althea winced at the pressing spots in her back as Pixie urged her over to a chair.

Archon chuckled at her lack of shoes. "Our stone-age darling will acclimate to the modern world soon enough. What she wears—or does not—is of little concern. Much more important she begins her training and education. Her primitivism is amusing in a quaint sort of way."

"Well then, p'raps we should buy 'er some animal furs and a spear?" Pixie continued to giggle, and sat in the next chair. "It was hard enough getting her to use the shower. She can't read. She even asked me how to free the little man from my NetMini." Having lost the ability to speak due to her laughter, she held up the device, pointing at the head reading a news broadcast.

Althea glared at being mocked. "Can I have my skirt back?" She looked at the woman, figuring her more sympathetic.

"Sorry, luv. I tried to wash it, but it fell to bits."

"No… I made it…" Althea's lip quivered, but she refused to cry in front of them.

Archon rolled his eyes. "Truly a magnificent job you did. Eat."

Another woman with skin the color of fresh snow and lemon-blonde hair past her knees walked around and set a plastic plate in front of her. Althea gasped. The whole of the woman's eyes were jet black and gleamed like gems. Clad in a tight leather skirt and sweater, both white, she carried the hint of familiarity, a presence exploding into recognition at the sound of a voice that came without moving lips.

"Hello, little one." The placid voice of Aurora, the flesh-creature, swept over her mind.

Althea leaned away, casting a wary look at the food. Three wooden sticks impaled chunks of meat coated in a brownish-red seasoning, next to a pile of rice.

"We tried to get something as familiar as possible to what you were used to." Archon gestured at the plate. "Teriyaki chicken. It's better than desert lizard, rat, or whatever the devil else you eat out there."

Althea sniffed the offering. In her current mood, hunger had been a distant thought, but the smell of food that hadn't been in the trash for days coaxed it out. She took a handful of rice and stuffed it into her mouth, losing a fair amount in the process.

Archon looked amused, but gave off disdain. Pixie thought it cute. Aurora circled the table and sat, putting her feet up. Apparently, she disliked shoes, too.

He watched her eat with her hands, shaking his head. "The cretins have done some damage. You have a lot of work ahead of you. Althea, you are very special. It is an honor to have you here."

"I've already told you what I think of this." Aurora frowned at him.

"Oh, I'm sure we can bring the little wild thing back to society." Pixie reached to pat her on the head.

Althea looked at her and growled.

"Reminds me of Binkley. He was food aggressive as a kitten," said Aurora.

Pixie's gaze softened. "Aww."

"She's manipulating you." Archon pinched the bridge of his nose again.

Althea jammed another handful of rice into her mouth. Pixie reached for the spoon.

"Please refrain." Archon waved her off. "She will become all mopey about that mongrel *sister* of hers, and it will set us back a month."

Althea grabbed the spoon defiantly, and shoveled at the rice.

He smiled. "Now then, Althea." He lowered his hands to the table.

"Altheeeea," she said in a petulant tone. "You're saying it bad. Not all-thay-a."

He again pinched the bridge of his nose, shivering, trying to hide his indignant anger. After a moment, calm.

"You must have a great many questions for us. First, let me begin by welcoming you to our little group. You have met Annabelle. She has a talent with electricity. This is Lauren. Her talent allows her to find people for us, and she is quite the clairvoyant."

"Am I then?" The ivory-skinned woman made a sarcastic face, scratching in the air with a clawing gesture. "Then why don't you believe me?"

Althea glanced at the women before staring at Archon. "What is your talent? Being an asshole?"

Two men at the distant terminals gasped in shock, while a teenage girl among them burst into giggles. Aurora smiled. Pixie laughed.

He forced a saccharin smile, but couldn't hide his displeasure from her. "I am a telepath, mostly. Your abilities over the body are almost as impressive as what I can do to the mind."

One of the empty wooden sticks leapt from her plate, spun over, and lanced down into Pixie's hand, sending a spritz of blood across the silver beneath it.

"I dabble with Telekinesis as well." He brushed a finger at his lip.

Pixie screamed, removing the lance from her palm. "Bloody 'ell! What was that for?"

"Because you laughed at him." Althea gave him a dire look before taking Pixie's hand and mending the tiny hole. "He wanted you to see me help someone."

"As I stated before, you are one of us. You are of the Awakened." Archon held his arms out to the sides to accentuate the magnitude of the statement.

"Thank you for the food and the dress, but I don't want to live here. *Please take me home to Querq.*" Her eyes flickered.

He smiled. Brushing off her suggestion, he produced one of those stimpak things from his pocket. "In the Badlands, you are like a goddess. While it comes in handy, and you are quite powerful, it also makes everyone want to take you away. Here, you can be free of that. Your abilities are impressive, but they are not the only way to stave off death. Here, with me, you can have a normal life." Elbow upon the table, he twirled the red cylinder in his fingers, staring past it at her, his voice half a whisper. "Technology is… wonderful."

The skewer again leapt up and impaled Pixie's hand. Telekinetic force held Althea tight to her chair. The stimpak floated up from his hand and glided across the table.

Pixie stuck herself in the arm with it, and the small wound closed. She scowled, wiping the blood from her hand. "You can be a right bastard sometimes, James."

The force pinning Althea to the seat stopped.

Archon shook his head. "As great and powerful as you are, child, you have much to learn. What you tried to do there, most call Suggestion. An idea, sent into the mind that echoes louder and louder until it sounds and feels like something you want to do anyway. Unfortunately, I know that little trick as well, and I have had a bit more practice at it than you. Would you care to be upon the table on all fours, scampering about and barking like the animal you were raised to be?"

"Careful, James." Aurora winked. Her voice filled the room, though her mouth remained closed. "She'll honk in your loafers."

"No, please." Althea looked down.

"Then you will not try it again. Not that it will work. You see, when you try to use an ability on someone who also knows the trick, you had best be better than them, or it will accomplish bugger all."

"You don't need to humiliate her." Pixie shot him a dark look, still rubbing her hand.

He stood and paced around the table. "She humiliates herself, refusing to rise above her primitivism, wanting to return to that wretched husk of civilization running about in leather scraps whilst carrying spears. No, she is destined for far more. This girl is quite powerful, young, and... pretty. If not a bit peevish."

Althea looked at Aurora, sensing a touch of annoyance. "He keeps telling me I'm pretty and saying nice things, but it won't make me like him."

"Child, when you have come to accept the life you knew is little more than a pale remnant dwelling in the shadow of the real world, we will teach you to grow your power. The place you think of as home has been forgotten by mankind. There is nothing for you there but obscurity and death."

"I don't care if I have an obscurity. I want my family," said Althea, her voice undercut with a subtle note of sorrow.

Archon froze with his mouth open, making a face as if he had been slapped with a raw salmon. "Good grief, you little dust flea... obscurity isn't a thing you can hold. It's a state of existing where—" He fumed.

"You want to own me like everyone else. You want to own me and use me to do bad things for you."

"She has changed, Archon." Aurora smiled. "Not the docile little pet you hoped for?"

He swiveled to stare at her with a pained expression of frustration. Aurora didn't look at him, but smiled.

"There are things at play here you do not see, child," said Archon. "This city in which we hide holds people who think they run the world, think they order this society. They are terrified of us. They want to control us, cage us, or eliminate us." Condescension wrapped his voice like syrup. "The so-called police are no better than your Badlands raiders. In fact, they are worse. They will stick in you a tank and poke you with needles to see why you are what you are. Governments are all the same.

They do not see a little girl. They see something they could use as a weapon or a threat they need to destroy."

Althea folded her hands in her lap. Anger, fear, desperation, and a need for power swarmed around him as he ranted. She couldn't separate the lies out of what he said; regardless of any potential truth, he believed himself.

He calmed, lowering his voice to something almost approaching comforting. "If you don't accept your destiny with us, they will find you, and they will keep you away from everyone you could ever love."

She glowered at the floor. "Why do you want me so much? What can I do? I know your feelings. You don't want to protect me. You want me to do something."

Archon chuckled, an exasperated titter, while forcing a smile. He gestured toward Pixie as if to say, 'this is what I have to put up with?' "Well, you see, Althea…" He circled back to his chair. "I have spent many years gathering psionic individuals who share my particular distrust of the government, trying to help them build a better life. I have been searching for a way to help them know *true* power."

"Awakened?" Distrust scrunched her face.

"Exactly." He thrust an arm at Aurora. "See, she does understand. Because of your special gift, the way you can *help* people"—his excitement dropped to normal conversational volume—"you are in the unique position to help all of us. It's a bit like what you did for that Flatline chap."

"How do you—?"

"Know about him? Oh, merely a trifling thing I like to call *being the most powerful telepath in the world*."

Aurora rolled her eyes; at least, she gave off an emotion to go along with that sort of gesture. The solid jet orbs couldn't really roll in a way anyone would notice.

"If you are able to stitch back together a brain in such condition, you have the power necessary to facilitate the awakening of all of our brothers and sisters. You can *fix* their damaged minds and unlock their true potential from the handicap of banal normality." Archon whirled about, seeming a bit like the street preacher as his voice gained volume. "We can be free of the tyranny of those who do not understand, live in a place they cannot touch us." His fists balled, held with triumph before eyes wild with anticipation.

He let off an emotion nothing short of terrifying.

"You really think she can just zap people awakened?" Pixie blinked at him.

His victorious smile broke into a disdainful frown, bathing the room in derision. "No, of course not. It may take months or years, but between my study of the brain and her ability to manipulate living tissue, I will find the answer."

Aurora made cat-scratching gestures at him, which sent him into a storm of internal rage.

Althea nudged herself forward, transferring weight onto her feet. Pixie gawked at Archon, emanating a mood as if about to start an argument. Aurora winked at her with an amused half smile. Archon turned his back, lost in a ramble about DNA sequencing, throwing around words as big as Shepherd. He vented to the wall, ruminating about both the brain and how the government would destroy them all.

Sensing opportunity, she bolted from the chair and sprinted out the door. She made it one foot into the hallway before she floated off the ground and hung there, pedaling her legs at nothing.

"Well, you are certainly a determined little scamp," said Archon behind her. "I'll give you that much."

Sharp footsteps from his fancy shoes came closer. She glided forward, kicking and screaming as he floated her to a small room with a glowing orange bed, a plain metal desk, and a chair. She landed gently on her toes. Before she could even turn around, the door closed and locked. Althea let out a pulse of rage at being kidnapped again, which ignited a screaming match in the hallway between Pixie and Archon. Sparks danced over the wall. The shouting fizzled out in seconds. Althea ran to the door, pounding on it, but couldn't escape. She gave up after a few minutes, her fists numb, and dove headfirst into the pillow on the strange, glowing bed.

With thoughts of her family flooding her mind, her anger faded and she bawled herself to sleep.

47

A IS FOR ASSHOLE

For a fleeting dream moment, Althea curled up in her own bed, arms wrapped around Karina. The glow of sunrise in the bedroom window changed to an even orange, flooding her senses with light and heat. She opened her eyes, but everything remained blinding orange. Comforting warmth embraced the entire front of her body. When she propped herself up, her hands sank into a gelatinous mass encased in thick, clear plastic. The luminous slab spread out below her in the approximate shape of a mattress.

Althea rolled on her side and wiped her eyes clear of crumbs, then found herself staring at a trio of bizarre, plump creatures a few inches away from her toes. They hadn't been there when she had drifted off to sleep. Screaming, she fell backward off the squishy pad onto the floor.

After hiding in a ball for a moment—and nothing coming to eat her—she risked a tentative grip at the mattress edge and pulled herself up to her knees, peering over the glowing orange slab at the little green and blue monsters. Six black eyes stared at her impassively. Not one of them moved.

Sensing no life within them, she crawled onto the bed and poked at one, knocking it over. Feeling foolish, she took a deep breath and sat cross-legged on the pad. She'd never seen stuffed animals before, but they came close enough to rag dolls for her to understand. One of the strange people must have left them there trying to make her feel better.

She found herself in a small room upon a small bed. A rusty-wheeled chair lay askew by a green painted metal desk with two flat objects upon it. Shiny black glass backed with silver plastic, the objects had the general shape of books but only a finger-width thick.

One door led out of the room. The lump in her throat grew large before she touched the knob. As expected, she found it locked. Rattling, twisting, and tugging did little other than make noise. She considered banging and screaming again, but these people wouldn't listen. Althea pouted at her new dress while pacing a circle over the dingy blue throw rug. Perhaps an hour later, someone knocking distracted her.

"Hey, kid. I'm Kim. I'm gonna open the door and give you some food. If you run away, I'm gonna get in a lot of trouble, so please don't."

Althea sat on the bed, letting her feet dangle as her anger simmered. A wisp of a girl with long, dark hair entered bearing a plastic tray. The smell of something sweet followed. She set the offering on the desk and rushed backward to block the doorway. She might have been fourteen. Althea could probably overpower her, even without her abilities.

Nothing stood out as obvious or unusual about the girl: no glowing eyes, random sparks, or strange skin color. Her black shirt had a picture of an evil man with wings and fangs, and she wore a ludicrous amount of bracelets, which jangled as she folded her arms over her chest. Baggy pants and thick boots made her look like a kid trying to dress up as a raider.

Althea scooted off the bed and moved to the squeaky chair, sniffing at the plate, which contained three strange, puffy brown disks stacked on top of each other.

Althea picked one up and studied it, making the girl laugh. "These tortillas are wrong."

"Pancakes," said Kim. "They told me you wouldn't use a fork."

Althea gave her the side eye.

"What? You never saw pancakes before?"

"No." The food smelled sweet and safe, so she bit off a piece and chewed. "You seem nice. Are you captive, too?"

"Nope. I'm not 'wakened like you are, just psionic. Ooh, I love your eyes." Kim grinned, edging closer. "Archon says he's looking for a way to make us all 'wakened. He wasn't born that way... he found it later. He said you're the one who can make us powerful."

Althea glanced at her for a moment, then grabbed a cup of brown liquid at the edge of a tray. What she expected to be a drink turned out to be a sweet, viscous syrup with an unusual flavor she'd never tasted. She coughed and sputtered. Once the initial shock at the thickness wore off, she scoured the wonderful substance clean from the plastic cup with her tongue.

"You're a messed-up kid." Kim shook her head. "Who eats pancakes dry and then drinks syrup straight? Gotta pour the syrup over the pancakes."

She shrugged. "I don't like him."

"Oh, he acts all big and mean, but he just likes to sound important. Once you get used to it here, you'll see he's right."

Althea licked the sticky from her fingers. "Did he take you away from your family, too?"

A spike of rage from the girl made Althea lean back.

"No, the pieces of shit kicked me out. They couldn't handle having a psionic kid."

Sadness.

Althea jumped to her feet and hugged Kim. "I'm sorry for making you sad."

Kim squirmed. "Stop. Stay back. He said you'd try to trick me. If you run away, you could get hurt. The government will kill anyone they find that's 'wakened. An' I'll get in trouble for lettin' you get hurt."

Althea let go and moped to the bed, sitting on the edge. "I don't believe him, and I won't trick you. I'm sad your parents made you go away. I have a family and Archon took me away from them. I wanna go home."

"My parents are idiots. Dad's a politician and he said it would hurt his career if it got out he had a psionic daughter. If I see him again, I'm gonna kick him straight in his constituents."

Althea's memories swam with the street full of people shoving her around. "I hate this place. Everyone is so mean."

"I'm not mean." Kim ventured closer. "None of us are."

"Are you locked in your room, too?"

Kim laughed. "No. I'm happy here. I want to be with Archon and help him. He won't lock your door anymore once you uhh, stop being wild."

Althea fidgeted. "Can I have a pail?"

"A pail? Why?"

"I have to make water."

"Eww." Kim grabbed her by the wrist. "Come on. I'm gonna get my ass handed to me if you run away, but piss in a bucket? Eww. That's just *so* primitive! Are you serious? If you gotta go, just hit this button." Kim pointed at something on the wall. "Someone will come check on you."

Kim led her to the room where she'd showered earlier and let her use one of the toilets before she dragged her back to the same room. The older girl took one of the black things from the desk, fiddling around with it until a cartoon rabbit appeared in midair. She explained about holograms, and that the device was called a datapad. This one taught small children how to read. Other datapads contained various lessons, and Archon wanted her to get started right away so she could 'catch up.'

"The better you do with these, the faster you won't be wild anymore. I used to hate school, but now I kinda almost miss it. Archon can be an ass sometimes, but he really does love us all. Think of him like a replacement daddy." Kim smiled, and left her there with the rabbit.

Althea wanted to yell, "I have a father," but didn't blame Kim for what Archon did.

"A is for apple..." The diminutive cartoon bunny waved and bounced around, speaking in an irritating, chirpy voice. "Aaaa-pelll. Can you say 'apple?'"

"Sorry, Althea... I gotta," murmured Kim from outside.

Even expecting it, the *click* of the lock shot down her spine like the crack of a whip. She couldn't help herself, and dropped the annoying datapad on the bed before hurling herself at the door. After a few minutes of struggling against the unmoving handle, she spun around, staring at the four walls.

"C is for cat. Can you say cat? Trace your finger over the letter C now." The holographic rabbit changed into a cat.

Ignoring it, she glanced up at a slat-covered hole in the ceiling that offered freedom. Althea dragged the desk away from the wall, positioning it below the vent. After catching her breath, she climbed up and grasped the vent cover. The thin metal grate refused to budge. Her effort to pull it open lifted her feet off the desk. She hung on it with all her weight, bouncing up and down. It gave way with a sharp *squeak*, dropping her back to the desk on her feet. Once she recovered her balance, she tossed the cover onto the bed and clapped dust from her hands.

"I'm sure you'll get it next time. D is for dog. Can you say D?" The rabbit made a barking noise.

She eyed the hole, squatted a little, and vaulted up to grab the edge, then pulled herself up into a metal-walled tunnel filled with a strong, cold breeze.

When she oriented herself on all fours to crawl, her dress bloomed in a frigid blast of air conditioning from behind. She shrieked at the cold and whirled the other way, squinting into the wind with chattering teeth.

"F is for frog. Can you say F?" asked the electronic rabbit, followed by strange croaking noises.

"F is for freedom," she grumbled, clambering forward.

The metal tunnel creaked, banged, and buckled from her passage. She climbed over a number of grilles that peeked into other tiny rooms, but found little of interest and nothing in the way of an escape route.

Frigid aluminum numbed her hands and knees, but she kept going down what felt like an endless shaft. After a right turn, the powerful wind died down. A moment's more crawling brought her to a flat metal square blocking the passage. It appeared to be attached on a pivot along a central strut. Banging on it with her hands proved ineffective, but after she shifted around and kicked it a few times, it gave way and spun horizontal in the middle of the tunnel. Flat on her stomach, she pulled herself under the flap. Beyond it, stagnant air offered wonderful warmth even if it did smell of mildew.

Althea crawled onward, past several broken vent covers offering opportunities to leave the shaft, but all led to the same immense room filled with a row of crumbling machines lined up like gargantuan pigs at a trough. Not only did it remind her of Vakkar's factory, the fall looked terrifying, so she continued.

She went left at the next crossing, scampering down another tunnel into a colony of rats. She gave off a mild telempathic radiance of trust and calm. The furry creatures swarmed her with affectionate licks and rubs while she crawled through their home.

After two dead ends, and avoiding an offshoot from whence the repetitive moaning of wifeing came, she found her way into a larger square chamber with a massive dead fan and a vertical tunnel. Althea climbed up onto of the blades, big enough for her to sleep on. Holding the central strut for balance, she stood on the wobbly perch and pulled hand over hand, spinning the fan into place below a vertical passage. Metal ridges every two feet served as a ladder. Her fingers and toes ached, but she forced herself to climb. After twelve feet of ascent, the shaft turned ninety degrees at the top. While crawling over the rim, a metal burr opened a six inch cut down her left shin. She fell on her side, curling up to cradle the injury while biting her lip to keep from crying out. Once the momentary paralysis from sudden pain faded, she clutched her leg to her chest long enough to mend it.

The tightness of her surroundings made her wonder if she would ever see the outside world again. A foul odor crept into the air, stagnant and organic, worsening the farther she went. Her need to get out of this tiny space urged her forward as fast as she could crawl. Up ahead, a four-way junction offered the hope of moonlight coming from the left-hand path.

She made it to within six feet of the light before the vent collapsed out from under her.

Althea screamed, plummeting straight down past fraying sheet metal. Thirty feet below, a rectangle of eerie green water raced toward her. She closed her eyes, grabbing at thin air, desperate to stop falling before she went *splat*. An odd sensation rippled over her mind as though something psionic happened. A disorienting shift came as her plummet somehow slowed, but before she could open her eyes to look, she plunged into the water.

Loud whirring machine noise cut off the world as she sank below the surface in a pool as hot as a proper bath. She kept her eyes and mouth clamped shut. A few seconds later, her toes slipped in slimy muck on a hint of tile. Waving her arms to keep her body oriented up, she let herself sink until she could plant her feet firm in the ooze, then kicked upward.

She broke the surface, gasping for air and opening her eyes. After a few initial panicky strokes, she paddled in silence. Huge walls, small white tiles traced in smears of rust and grime, surrounded her on all sides with at least fifteen feet between the rippling surface and the way out. She floated in the horrible smelling bath, treading water while rotating in search of something to climb. Far above, a tiny black gash in a strip of metal crossing the ceiling made her gulp. The drop didn't look like one she should have walked (or swam) away from alive. She shivered at rows of broken lights and a strange intricate lattice of rails over the pool with some manner of robotic arm twisting out of it. Everything basked in decay. Far on the other side of the pool, a rickety ladder clung to the wall.

Maybe I'm dead. She swallowed, fending off the horrible sadness at the thought of how Karina would react.

"Did you see that?" asked a woman, her voice echoing in the massive chamber.

Althea clamped a hand over her mouth, holding back the urge to gasp.

"Nein, habe ich nicht," said a sleepy sounding male. *"Halluzinieren sie wieder?"*

"What?" asked the woman, exasperated.

"No, I haven't," replied the man with a heavy accent. "Are you hallucinating again?"

"I haven't touched the shit all day." Tapping light footsteps came closer. "I saw a bright fucking light. Like a military flare or some shit."

People approached the top of the pool. Althea took a deep breath, shut her eyes, and went under the opaque green, paddling downward. She floated in a hot black void until her lungs screamed for mercy. Not trusting the people to have wandered off already, she commanded her body to wait. The thumping of her heart in her ears slowed so much it frightened her, but being caught scared her more.

When she could tolerate the lack of air no more, she lurched upward and gulped a breath, seeing stars. Pain as though she'd been stabbed in the chest paralyzed her for a moment. She held her hands over the ache, whining in silence until it passed. Fortunately, the people had already left.

She swam across the ancient pool to the ladder. It had wider, flat steps that didn't hurt her feet like the round rungs at the Bumwallow. After a cautious peek over the top, she pulled herself up onto a narrow concrete walkpath surrounding the pool and wrung her dress out as best she could without taking it off. Streamers of water spattered around her feet. Her dip in such a warm pool made the world feel colder.

The room had three doors, two on the longer wall and one only a few steps away from her. Unfortunately, the close one was locked. She scurried to a pair of steel double-doors, terrified of making the smallest sound. One gave way, allowing her into a dusty staircase. She made it a few steps down before the sound of bored teens and clonking shoes approached from the next switchback. Tears flowed from sheer frustration. She doubled back and ran upward, rounding the corner and taking another flight before anyone saw her.

A metal door capped the stairway off at the end of the next set of ten steps. With the voices still approaching from behind, she threw herself into the door and shoved. It opened with much less resistance than she expected, leaving her stumbling out onto the roof.

The metal surface warmed her feet, blotched here and there with sticky or oily patches. She glanced over her shoulder at the door when it closed with a soft *clunk*. Conversation in the stairwell drew louder. Althea rushed around the edge of an enormous boxy machine and into a strong breeze that lifted her hair off to the left like a flag and made her soaked dress icy. She frowned at herself, her new dress smudged and clinging, and lamented the loss of her beloved skirt. It had been the first piece of clothing she'd ever worn, and took weeks to put together from scraps of raider armor. She once thought Jake foolish for showing off his pants to everyone because he believed they meant he'd become a man, but now she understood—and felt silly that losing a pitiful tangle of leather could make her so sad.

The creak of the door startled her back to reality. She dropped to all fours and crawled into a low, dark space beneath the vibrating machinery. One pair of sneakers, one pair of combat boots, and a young woman's bare feet in some kind of neon-blue rubber sandal went right past her without hesitating.

"Tati's telling everyone she saw some kinda bright light in the old coolant tank," said the owner of the sneakers.

"Bullshit." The woman replied. "Tatianna's a fuckin' junkie. She's seeing Flowerbasket is what she's seeing. Radioactive water doesn't glow that bright."

"It does not glow at all," said a deeper voice from over the boots. "Cherenkov radiation is blue, not white, and there are no materials in there strong enough to produce the effect. That room is an outer loop coolant reserve. The water it holds never went into the core. Also, all the rods have been gone for at least a century. The water isn't that radioactive anymore."

"Cherenkov?" Sneakers laughed. "Why is it always something Russian, Ivan?"

"*Bliad!* My name is *Gamed*, not Ivan."

All three chuckled after the sound of a light slap.

"Guard duty sucks," said the girl in the foam shoes. "Wanna hide out in the generator room?"

"Sounds good. Generators need guardin' too." Sneakers trotted away.

"*Da*," said the deep voice, exaggerating his accent.

Althea huddled in the dark, motionless, until the stairway door slammed. After another ten minutes, she crawled out and inched to the edge of the roof, squinting at the massive white towers still thrumming with the vibration of the wind. She leaned forward, only enough to peek over the side. The ground was at least four stories below, and she could find no way down aside from jumping.

"Impressive, aren't they?" asked Archon, behind her.

She gasped, clutching her chest. She let her knees buckle so she didn't pitch over the side and fall. Once she could breathe again, she glared at his shoes. "Yes."

"Cooling towers. Many years ago, this place was a nuclear power station until they gave up on the technology." He sidled up to her. "It was too hard to control, too dangerous when things got out of hand... Just like us."

Althea half cowered, trying to hug herself warmer.

"I must say I find your tenacity quite amusing. It would be nice if the others showed the same degree of motivation. You know that one fellow is still crying because of what you did to him in the van? We have to feed him because he refuses to eat on his own."

She looked down, feeling a smidge of guilt. "He shouldn't have tried to kidnap me."

"Heaven's sake, girl. You are not kidnapped. We are your real family."

"I won't help you take over the world." She curled into a ball against the short wall at the roof edge.

Archon moved to her side, pulling her up to her feet and putting an arm around her back. "I don't want to take over this world, child. I want to create a *new* place for people like us. I want you to be safe."

"You want to make people obey you. You're just a raider chief in a silly coat." She grabbed her hair so it stopped whipping into her eyes.

"I understand you have the wants and desires of a child. You want this so-called family you have attached yourself to. You want things to be as they were, and you want everyone to be happy and love each other." He managed a pained smile as if choking those words up had wounded him.

She shot him a sidelong glance.

"You are very special, my child. There are so few of us, and the government would like to keep it that way." He patted her shoulder. "If they thought they could not control you, they would have no problem at all putting a bullet right here." He tapped her on the chest, over the heart.

"Is this because of the garden?"

"Garden?" he asked, giving off genuine confusion.

Althea shook her head. "I thought you were someone else."

"Oh, that sentient Badlands twaddle? You know, Thea..."

"Don't call me that," she snapped. "Only Karina's allowed to call me Thea." She scowled. "An' Father."

He sighed, gaze rolling to the clouds. "Cheeky little thing. Fine then. I do know more about you than you think. Such as, your real mother."

She tried to hold back the eagerness on her face. "You knew my mother?"

"Not personally. I have information. Perhaps I would share it with a loyal companion. If you say you will not try to run away, I will tell you." He patted her on the back. "All you have to do is promise, and I'll not rest until I can tell you exactly where she is, or bring her to you. I know you keep your promises."

Her heart sank. For years, she had promised not to run away to avoid being tied, and look where it had gotten her. She pictured the vision of Karina crying in the field. "I'm sorry. I will not promise you that. I have to go home."

Archon lifted an eyebrow. "Well, that is certainly out of character for you. I do not know whether to be impressed by your honesty, or pity your foolishness. A smart girl would have lied."

"It's bad to lie."

"I suppose pity then."

"You could pity my family instead and take me home." She glared.

"Your mother"—he tapped a finger on his chin in thought—"worked for a western subsidiary of Matsushita Electronics, if I recall." He paused, giving her an expectant look.

Red formed around her eyes, but she shook her head. "I won't promise."

"Some codswallop about advanced hyperspace drive research. They attempted to open gateways to other dimensions or realities. A fool's errand. From what I hear, the project was a contemptible failure. The prototype exploded and killed most of the poor sots working there when they tried to turn it on. That is one of the reasons they put those things out in the Badlands... So no one valuable dies if they fail."

Althea shuddered at the evil words. "Every life is valuable."

He smiled. "Whatever energy that thing threw off when it imploded affected you in the womb"—he took on a dour tone of sarcasm—"and filled you with insufferable optimism and sweetness. Perhaps they opened a portal to candy land?"

She scowled.

"You are a bad person. I don't trust you." She lifted her head to look at him. "You only care about what you want. You don't care you had to take me away from people who love me, and you don't care Pixie is sad inside."

His face flashed red. "Your mother tottered off pregnant as a foaling cow, injured and bleeding, lost in the Badlands. She threw you away before she ran off to die in a hole, alone and unloved."

It felt like a lie said only to hurt, but it worked. Althea bowed her head and wept. The gentle hand on her left shoulder became a harsh grip on her arm.

"If you so desperately crave your wild tribesmen, perhaps I can make you feel more at home until you come around." He took a pair of handcuffs from his coat pocket and dangled them in her face. Neon blue fur covered the loopy bits. "Try skulking off like this again, and I'll fix you with these for a month." He rattled them at her.

She stared through the rings at him, facing her second worst fear, helplessness. Her heart yearned to be home. Rachel's words rang true in her mind.

Althea turned her back and held her hands behind her. "Put them on me now then. I don't care what you do... you'll be waiting a long time." She let her head sag forward. "I will not stop trying to go home."

She tensed, waiting for the awful feeling of metal around her wrists, but nothing happened. Sensing a twinge of distaste and a tiny bit of pity from him, she glanced back.

He'd put the awful things out of sight, back into his pocket. Bluffing.

"Althea, I'm trying to offer you a *different* life from what you are used to." He slid an arm behind her, coaxing her into a walk at his side. "As long as you've lived, people lock you up and keep you on tethers, take you away from anyone you love."

"Just like you." She trudged, staring down.

"Bollocks." He scowled over the wall. "You're supposed to be nice and cheery and full of sugar and smiles and... ugh."

"I will not make your friends stronger so they can kill people who don't join you."

Althea evaded a pat on the head with a scowl.

"You are entirely missing the point." Archon sighed. "No one is forced to be here."

She stopped and glared at him. "So I can go home? Or am I forced to be here?"

He let out a long-suffering sigh. "You are still a child who is incapable of understanding what is best for her. You will come around soon enough."

The march back to the dormitory passed in silence. He didn't speak again until they arrived at her room where Pixie waited, leaning in the doorway.

"Deal with this…" He shoved her toward the door and walked off.

Pixie hooked a finger in the collar of her dress and pulled her in. "He really isn't always like that."

A strange metallic smell hung in the air, mixed with smoke. The haze surrounding the vent in the ceiling gave away the source. All the edges of the cover looked molten. She wouldn't be taking that way out a second time.

"He's bad." She sulked to the bed and sat down hard.

"Aww." Pixie sat nearby, patting her on the back. "You're looking at it the wrong way, dearie. There are people out there who want to kill us because of what we are. He's just trying to do what's best. You are so pure and innocent you cannot see it. Sometimes, people have to do not-nice things to survive. He wants you to help him teach the little ones how to stand up and walk. When someone disobeys, he gets angry because it endangers all of us."

The short woman continued trying to be friendly. She sounded like an attempt to impersonate an older sister—without any sincerity. Her words carried a whiff of pity for a little girl in her situation, but she mostly wanted Archon to be happy. For some reason, whenever Althea made eye contact with her, she gave off sorrow, and a little guilt.

Althea pouted in silence, not responding to anything Pixie said until she gave up and went to leave.

"Wait."

Pixie paused in the doorway, glancing back. "Yes, dear?"

"I know you're not all bad. You don't have to be like him. Something hurt you, didn't it?" Althea gave her a wide, innocent stare. "I can help."

"I had it a bit rough comin' up in London." Pixie sighed. "Bad memories is all. I'm not hurt."

"He doesn't treat you very nice. He hurt you in the hand."

"That wasn't like him." Pixie rubbed her hand, a far-off look in her eyes. "He's not mean. He just… thinks clinically all the time."

Althea frowned at the pile of datapads on the bed. "He said he'd chain me for a month if I try to run away again."

Pixie walked back in and ruffled her hair. "Oh, he's just bluffing. He's a big softy. He wouldn't do that to you. He really does adore children, even the petulant ones."

"Is that why the handcuffs had fur? So they don't hurt?"

The woman's face went bright red. "He showed you those..." Embarrassment billowed out of her, and she couldn't bear to make eye contact.

Althea reached up and put a hand on her arm. "Pixie? Is he keeping you captive, too? Does he make you wear them so you don't run away?"

"Sometimes... No..." she stammered. "It's not what you—"

"Help me!" Althea grabbed her arm and shook it. "We can both get away."

Pixie teetered at the verge of tears. Tiny sparks crawled up onto Althea's fingers. "Stop. Don't. It's... I can't talk about it. It's not so I don't run away. It's... bugger. You're too little."

She rushed out and slammed the door locked behind her.

Althea fell back onto the bed, confused. Her impact disturbed the electronics piled at the other end.

The smiling rabbit appeared. "A is for apple. Can you say apple?"

She thought of Archon, narrowed her eyes, and muttered, "Asshole."

48

LOYALTIES

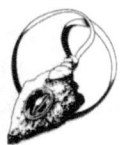

Althea slid from the bed and crept to the door. Rattling the handle reminded her for the hundredth time she was locked inside the little room. The vent wouldn't budge, even if she made herself stronger. Kim dropped off eggs and toast not long ago, but didn't stay to chat. Archon had ordered minimal contact until she changed her mind. He knew she hated being alone and worried she would influence someone un-Awakened.

She considered *making* Kim help, but didn't out of fear she'd be punished. Freedom wouldn't be worth another person suffering. She sulked to the desk, propped her head up on her arm, and picked at the eggs. She glared at the fork, refusing to touch it. Not until she returned to her family.

"If I ever find my way home, I'll always use it." Althea cried. "I don't care if I drop food. I don't care if they laugh at me."

She ate about half of her meal before she couldn't stand the taste. After crawling onto the bed, she curled into a ball and closed her eyes. Her life had been an endless cycle of abduction as far back as she could remember. Her first set of parents lingered at the distant edge of her memory. She'd only been five or six when the Wagon Man took her from them, and didn't even know if they survived his attack. The cage in the wagon, countless raiders, other villages, Den, Vakkar, and now even Archon. Even in this supposed *civilization*, she remained a captive because of what she could do.

She curled up on the bed and cried out with her mind for help, at the edge of desperation. If only she had used her powers at any of a dozen different moments to save herself, she wouldn't be here. Archon worried her. Her magic didn't work on him.

A hand brushed the hair out of her face. She looked up at onyx pools set into a porcelain face, and gazed into their endless darkness. The woman had appeared out of thin air with no clothing on. The door remained closed and locked.

Althea drew a gasp, but held still. "Aurora?"

The woman smiled and sat at the edge of the bed. As always, her lips didn't move. "I heard you beaconing."

Pushing herself up to sit, Althea stared past her feet at the rug. "I don't like it here. This city has so many bad people, and everything is dead."

"Because of what you are, someone will always want your power. Your only true freedom is choosing who benefits from it."

"I want to help everyone. I'm tired of being locked up. Why can't people just come get help when they need it? Why do they always want to keep me away from other people?"

Aurora leaned closer, brushing a hand over Althea's head. "Your fear of mistreatment lets people own you, so they do. You haven't accepted this yet, but some people don't deserve your help."

Althea broke eye contact, looking down, thinking of Archon.

She continued stroking Althea's hair. "The time will come when you will not save his life. You will watch him die."

Something about Aurora had changed. She didn't seem as scary in person. "Why is your skin so white? Why are your eyes black?"

"Why do yours glow?" Aurora tapped the tip of her nose. "Many Awakened have little quirks about them, sometimes not so little." She chuckled. "For me, it's obvious. I can't talk with my mouth. I make telepathic voices in people's heads. Most telepaths have to send their words into one brain. Mine go everywhere all at once. Not to mention, I'm white as a ghost and my eyes are black." She examined her fingernails. "It's caused some issues."

"I have a Querq, too." Althea pouted.

Aurora threw her head back. Disembodied laughter reverberated in Althea's brain. She swiped a finger across the girl's cheek below her eye. "I mean these."

"When people see the light, they know who I am and either take me or worship me." The tone in her voice gave away both as unappealing. "What about Pixie or Archon?"

Aurora smiled. "When Annabelle becomes emotional, her control of electricity goes a bit wonky. I don't know what Archon's peculiarity is; perhaps he doesn't have one because he was not born Awakened."

Althea blinked. "He wasn't?"

"No. He used to be a big important professor at a fancy school across the sea. He spent many years searching for a way to increase his power and found it. He became Awakened long after he was born."

"Why are you here?"

"Curiosity." Aurora smiled. "As well, it seemed proper to facilitate others like us meeting."

"But he's bad." She stood and stomped. "How can you help him?"

"There will always be bad. People could not know good without bad to compare it against. Things will happen, though good or bad depends on what people do. I'm lucky enough to peek a few pages ahead at the script every now and then. I told him bringing you here wasn't a good idea, but he has chosen to pursue you nonetheless. I knew he would, and I also know what will happen, so I didn't put up much of an argument." She traced a finger along Althea's jawline. "I am sorry for taking you away from your family."

"You didn't seem sorry when you made that man get shot." Althea gawked at her in disbelief. "Why?"

"I needed to ensure those mercenaries didn't stay around long enough to drive you back out there. Please believe me when I say I knew your stay here would be temporary, and I needed to prove a point." Aurora resumed playing with Althea's hair. "I wanted Archon to understand the nature of what I see, and know the folly of rash decisions. At times he can be like a small boy, demanding what he wants no matter how foolish. When dominoes fall, they have to land on someone. There is more to you than he can imagine. He senses great power yet to be unlocked, but he is mistaken in its nature."

Althea sniffled. "A strange man thought I came from some place called Heaven to end the world."

Aurora laughed. "Then, like Archon, he was only half right."

"What do you mean?" asked Althea, a bit of pleading whine in her voice.

"No ordinary person could suffer your life and emerge with such untarnished innocence. Archon did not entirely lie to you. Your mother was present when a portal opened to another place, and it did collapse and destroy the entire facility."

"What other place? What happened? Where is my mother?"

"There isn't time." Aurora smiled. "When we meet again, I will explain more."

"Wait. Don't go." Althea grabbed her by the shoulders. "I know you can send yourself places. That's why you have no clothes, isn't it? You're part ghost. Can you please tell Karina I'm okay?"

Aurora stood and glanced at the closed door. "You can tell her yourself soon enough. Damn. He's early."

"Who—?"

The door wrenched away from the hinges, drawn into the hallway where it clattered to the ground out of sight. Althea scrambled to the back of the room, her scream becoming a cheer when Shepherd squeezed himself past the doorway. With an angry growl, he leapt for Aurora and grabbed her about the throat.

"Don't hurt her." Althea yelled.

He hurled the ivory figure at the wall, but she disappeared into it like a dissipating spirit.

Althea stared in awe at a trace of glowing fog.

Shepherd scooped her up and emitted a groan of urgency. After squeezing her in adoration, he sidestepped out of the room. She cuddled to his chest, her eyes closed, rocking back and forth with his run. Shouts and gunfire chased them. He skidded around a corner a second before bullets hit the wall behind him. Althea pressed her hand against his skin, concentrating on boosting his adrenaline and endurance.

He ran faster. Hallway after hallway blurred past them. He stopped short several times, avoiding shouts and the chirps of arming weapons. Aurora said she could tell Karina herself. The woman had known Shepherd would be there. That had to mean she was going home.

Althea kept her head down and her eyes shut, concentrating on bolstering Shepherd, huddled tight against him. He navigated the decaying building at a frenetic dash. Different chemical smells drifted by. She sensed his worry. He didn't want to confront anyone with guns while carrying her. Each time he found a corridor with so much as a single armed teenager, he went in a different direction. His heavy tromping steps became metallic clanks when the ground changed from concrete to catwalk.

Althea opened her eyes. Shepherd loped across an elongated metal walkway from the uppermost floor of the primary building to the side of the cooling tower complex. As they neared, the great monoliths stretched so far above her she could no longer see the top.

"That is quite far enough," Pixie yelled from in front of them.

Shepherd slid to a halt, before setting Althea down on her feet and shoving her behind him. Nine-inch blades slid out of his fingers and locked. His lens-eye whirred as a growl rumbled in his throat.

"You know how this ended for you last time, cretin." Pixie held up a hand, a tiny lightning spark dancing from finger to finger. "Now, get out of the way."

Althea clung to his side, staring around his hip at her. "Pixie, please don't hurt him. Please don't do this. Let me go home."

"I can't do that, mite." Pixie tossed a lightning bolt between her hands. "If anything happens to this lunk, it's because you are running away. If you don't want him hurt, turn around and go back to your room."

He growled, stomping toward her with murder in his eyes.

"No! Don't hurt her, either," Althea wailed.

Pixie shook her head with a sigh, then flung her arms forward. A scintillating streamer of blue lightning arced from her fingertips into the metal railing, dancing along until it engulfed the huge man. Barefoot on the metal, Althea had nowhere to hide and convulsed with burning tingles that crept up her legs.

She fell to the ground, twitching out of control and shrieking. The big man lurched to one knee. He moaned in sorrow, exuding guilt that Althea's scream of pain had been his doing.

The light and crackling ceased.

"Had enough, then? Or do you want more? On second thought, you're going to be a needling little problem as long as you're around."

Another smaller crackle; Shepherd gurgled.

Stop it, both of you! Althea tried to yell, but her jaw remained closed.

Shepherd grabbed the railing, the whirring of his metal arms ground down to a belabored drone until a section of the balustrade gave way with a deafening *crack*. He staggered backward as it broke, recovered, and swung the length of pipe at Pixie. She ducked the bar whooshing over her head, and tossed another arc of lightning into the improvised weapon.

Rigid and shuddering, the big man fell to the side, draped over an intact section of railing. Foam sprayed from his mouth with an anguished gurgle.

"You had your chance." Pixie poured more energy into the arc. "I'm doing you a favor, you poor sod. Bloody 'ell, you're not even human anymore."

Althea reached out, clawing at the air toward the woman. She felt the lightning killing this man who had come to save her, this man who only tried to help her because of what she had done to him. Her magic made him want to protect her like a daughter. Now, he would die because of it.

"*Stop!*" The child's scream flooded the woman's mind, louder than the sizzling electricity.

Althea's desperate need to protect her protector mixed with her newfound rage, and she commanded the woman's throat to close. Pixie grabbed her neck with both hands, eyes widening. A constricting wheeze leaked from her nostrils. She reached one hand toward Althea, horror and astonishment in her expression. She murmured and fell to her knees.

Eyes rolling back into her skull, Pixie loosed a weak gasp before flopping face down on the grate, unconscious. Althea stopped forcing the woman's throat shut, then slumped, out of breath, against a strut below the handrail. Shepherd moaned and pushed himself up. Althea dragged herself to the unconscious woman's side. Shepherd raised his claws, but Althea held her hand up.

"Please don't."

She put a hand on Pixie's cheek and her hair fluffed up with static electricity. After making sure the woman remained alive, she sent a flood of sleep into her brain that would keep her out for at least an hour. Doing that made her think of the *chaman*, how she'd snuck out to warn Den. That day felt like a lifetime ago.

An immense metal hand drifted into her peripheral vision. Althea stood, clasped two thick, artificial fingers, and glanced up at her guardian. "No one has to die."

The door at the building end of the walkway flew open; more of Archon's loyalists clambered out with guns at the ready. The teen girl with the strange blue sandals led the way, her tiny machine gun faltered once she got a good look at Shepherd.

"*Go away!*" screamed Althea.

The wall behind them became a shadow play in the radiance from her glare.

No longer afraid, she gathered her anger and added a blast of radiant fear atop her psionic command. If she could make Badlands roaches flee, she could deal with Archon's people. Althea took a step toward them, arms out to her sides, eyes burning like tiny stars.

She snarled.

The punks stopped, some trembled, the girl in flip-flops fainted, and several sets of pants became wet. The instant the still-conscious ones ran away, Shepherd scooped her into his arms once more and ran in the only direction he could go from here—to the other end of the walkway.

His great strides carried them up the spiraling catwalk rimming the outside of the tower.

49

WHEN GREAT MEN FALL

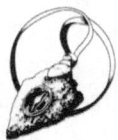

S hepherd ran higher into the air upon the bouncing walkway, around and around the spiral. Soon, they reached the apex, a narrow viaduct leading straight across the first tower's maw into a dense cloud of dark smoke rising from within. The swaying metal bridge spanned a chasm of air filled with the taste of metal, broken by puffs of mist and fog. The walkway continued across open space to the adjacent tower, from which they could reach the ground away from their pursuers.

Althea pointed at the connection, patting Shepherd on the shoulder to get his attention. He nodded and stepped out onto the suspended path, which swayed with his mass.

"Well, that is most unexpected," said Archon. He emerged from the billow of dark fog in front of them, one hand along each railing. "Once again, you impress me."

"Stop. Aurora warned you taking me was a bad idea. Don't you understand?"

He smiled. "I understand she is overcautious. Precognition is not an exact science. Her visions of the future present the most likely outcome, but knowing the outcome allows me to change it."

Althea stared around at the howling wind. "What if she sees what will happen because you know she was going to see the future? Wouldn't she see what would happen because you reacted to what she told you would happen? I had a dream Den would be hurt, so I tried to warn him. I got taken away because I left the village. Now I know the 'hurt' was losing me. If I stayed where I should have stayed, maybe he wouldn't have been hurt. Maybe I saw myself causing him pain."

Archon pinched the bridge of his nose. "You are wounding my head, girl. I always hated theoretical philosophy... and time paradoxes are a torture from the tenth plane of Hades. I think you *did* save that little tribal scrap from some terrible unseemly event, but by doing so you, put yourself at risk. You do not honestly think those raiders found you on their own do you? Aurora borrowed your little boyfriend's new wife and led them right to you. We are trying to elevate you from the tribals."

Flushed, she didn't know whether to cry or scream with rage.

Sensing her mood, Shepherd roared and charged. The grating bounced under his weight, making Archon grab the railing with a panic-laden moan. He gave off a spike of fear when he looked over the edge. Althea fell on her ass, hooking her arm around the banister.

The giant bore down on Archon, who barely managed to let go of the swaying ground long enough to focus his telekinesis. Shepherd floated up, but rammed his claws into the catwalk to anchor himself, fluttering like a meat flag from Archon's attempt to fling him away. Metal crumpled between cybernetic fingers. Shepherd glared at Archon as if daring him to keep pushing and join him in death when the entire trellis failed.

Archon slammed the oaf down. Shepherd smashed into the bridge, bouncing Althea up to her feet. An uneasy groan leaked past Archon's teeth. Her tormentor appeared ready to faint from vertigo. The instant the metal fingers pulled loose from the grating, Archon grinned and thrust his arm out again, no doubt intending to fling him off the walkway. Shepherd reacted faster than expected, grabbing a fistful of tweed coat. The pair flew up, spun over, and came down; Archon's fear of heights killed the telekinetic effort.

Archon landed on his back, pinned under the growling Shepherd, who clamped a metal hand around his neck and hauled him into the air. Archon clutched a plastisteel wrist too large for him to close his fingers around. He gasped for air, on the verge of fainting as Shepherd dangled him out over the deadfall.

Althea opened her mouth to protest, but the giant hesitated, twisting to look at her as if knowing she wouldn't want him to kill.

She shivered, not so sure this time.

In a blink, Shepherd vanished, caught in a telekinetic spin that left Archon on the walkway and the big man sailing into darkness, his silent fall interrupted by a loud metallic *crash* and scraping a distance below. Althea leaned out over the edge, screaming.

Archon got to his feet, then dusted his coat back into place. "Well then... now that he is out of the way."

She sobbed at the blurry man coming toward her, her eyes awash with tears. "Why did you kill him?" As he drew nearer, she backed up, hand over hand clasping the railing.

"Well, he was trying to kill me, and I often have a somewhat dim reaction to attempts on my life." He paused to ponder the situation. "You know, I do find it curious every time you develop an emotional bond with someone, it gets broken. So sad, really. You ought to love someone you cannot be taken from." He tried his best fatherly smile.

She backed up, clinging to a secondary railing below the main one.

He peered over the side, smirking. "Very well then, since I broke your toy, I'll see about getting you a new doll to play with. Perhaps one a bit smaller and easier for you to dress. Wouldn't you rather have a nice princess or something?"

"I hate you." She cringed in guilt, despite meaning it. She'd never said that to anyone... even the Wagon Man.

He smiled with a dismissive chuckle. "If fathers had one sterling credit every time a daughter said that to them, they could pay for proper schooling. Come now, it is quite unsafe up here."

Archon reached for her hand.

She leapt away, scooting backward across the grate. "Everyone I love gets hurt because of me. Aurora said the only freedom I'll ever have is choosing who I let use my power." She grasped the railing and gazed into the dark below. "What if I choose nobody?"

"Oh, come now, girl. You are not about to fling yourself into oblivion. I know you better than that. Think about all the good you can do for the new mankind."

Althea retreated, careful to place her steps around holes. His smile grew, his best false 'trust me' face slithered into her mind. He started to feel like her father, her protector. She winced, knees buckling, and put a hand to her forehead, but kept edging away. The platform widened behind her; she had reached the edge of the tower where they had started. He pushed into her consciousness and flooded her mind with a hundred rapid-flash images of his smiling face. Only her grip on the bannister kept her from swooning to her knees.

He wanted to *force* her to love him like a father. Never before did she imagine anything worse than being wifed, but this…. She wouldn't allow it. The blurriness in her head drained away the instant she clung to the truth that he lied in her mind. An odd warmth spread along her back.

Archon froze like a statue, gawking at her, all the color drained from his face.

She shook off a lingering headache, and an inexplicable flood of courage swelled in her chest. Althea drew in a breath, feeling taller.

Archon staggered. "H-How is it possible... I cannot..."

Distant metal banging grew louder than the howling gale.

"You're bored of talking and just tried to *make* me love you." Althea scowled. "I can't love evil."

Archon scoffed. "I'm not *evil*... I am merely doing that which must be done. You would have them kill us all." Again, he tried to batter into her mind.

A new power welled up inside her. Pure white light radiated from behind her, reflecting as bright wavering threads in his terrified eyes. A trickle of blood fell from his nose.

He screamed; the shock of it brought her out of the trancelike state, and the glimmering light vanished as fast as it had manifested. Althea gasped at the sight of metal blades erupting from Archon's body, soaking his stomach and thighs with blood. Shepherd had come over the side of the catwalk, a bloody mess as well, and driven one whole hand of nine-inch blades into Archon from behind. Althea grabbed the railings on both sides to keep her balance upon the bouncing catwalk. She tensed every muscle, but didn't shout or look away. Archon glanced down at the gleaming blades protruding from his body with a smirk of drunken disbelief on his face.

"Bollocks," muttered Archon. "So that is what she meant by claws."

Shepherd rose to his feet, lifting the wheezing man into the air. Blood burst from Archon's mouth. He looked down, lips curling into a grimace of disdain and anger. Shepherd's body rocked from unseen telekinetic force; Archon slid from the blades and collapsed on all fours. His blood dripped over the grating, falling into the abyss below.

The big man staggered backward, driving his claws into the floor to keep from falling again. Archon dragged himself a few feet closer to her before sitting. He glanced at Althea and tried to speak, but only produced a wet gurgle.

She took a step back.

A glint of defiance shone in his face. Archon snapped his gaze to

Shepherd and raked his fingers at the air, sneering. His eyelids flared open and the giant howled with torment. Sparks flew from the cybernetic limbs. Shepherd's entire body shuddered and twisted, back arched. He screamed in agony.

With an explosion of blood, Shepherd vanished, except for two metal arms embedded in the catwalk by their claws. Frayed wires sparked from the shoulder of each artificial limb.

Althea jumped to her feet and ran to the railing, staring down at Shepherd's armless body painting a crimson stripe along the white thermacrete tower. He locked eyes with her for a fleeting second before sliding over the inward curve and falling out of sight. She reached after him as if she thought she could catch him.

A tiny whisper left her throat. "No…"

After seconds of silence, a resounding metallic *crash* came back up from below. He had fallen much farther that time.

Lowering her weight off her toes, she leveled a glare down at Archon. Heavy bleeding had laid him out on his back, gazing wearily at the sky above. An incredulous chuckle launched a crimson glob from his mouth, as if his imminent death was so far removed from his expectations of how the day would go, he found it humorous.

"It has been a few weeks since I've stepped in warm blood." Althea glanced down at her stained feet, her voice cold and creepy. "Is this what you meant by reminding me of home?"

A second bubble of red saliva burst from his mouth. "Not entirely." He winced.

"I suppose you're expecting me to save you now." She squatted, touching her fingertips to the blood on the floor and drawing lines on his face. "Even after you took me away from my family and killed my friend."

He forced a smile, his voice labored. "That was kind of the hope here, yes. We Awakened have to help each other; no one else will. We are one."

"You really ought to have listened to Aurora. You don't understand what you've done." Althea put a red dot at the tip of his nose. "She told me I would watch you die."

Archon's detached joviality fell away to dread. She stared at him with an emotionless face. The moment she sensed fear, she managed a sad smile and slipped her hand past the shreds of cloth to touch his stomach. "But not today."

Althea shut off his sense of pain.

"Oh, that is wonderful." He moaned. "Yes, child. Good girl. We are of the same order."

She waited for a lull in the gale and spoke in a somber tone. "I'm nothing at all like you."

Archon wheezed into unconsciousness. She closed his wounds only enough to halt the onrush of death. He would not die this day, but he also would not hinder her escape. Once certain she had done enough to let him survive, she cleaned the blood from her hands on his jacket and stood.

Her hair and dress whipped in the howling gale. She shot him a dire stare, imagining Rachel yelling at her to kill him.

Guilt washed over her. Head bowed, she walked away, heading toward an enclosed ladder that led to the wailing depths.

She needed to say goodbye to a friend.

50

ELYSIUM

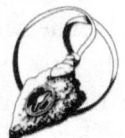

F og and mist whirled around Althea. She descended a narrow
ladder into the heart of the thrumming machinery. The cyclone
trapped by the tower tugged at her climb, threatening to pull her
slight frame from the rungs at one careless step. She ignored everything
except for the metal bars moving past her face and the sameness of the
dingy white wall, broken only by the intermittent flash of her hands in
her vision.

Neither sadness nor anger followed her down. She felt nothing except
the cold metal on her feet and the tenebrous presence of the structure
engulfing her. The walls grew narrower and then wider as she sank
deeper into a place filled with the mournful wails of the captive wind. She
knew Shepherd was dead despite being too far away to feel his life depart,
yet she needed to see him one last time to apologize for what she had
done.

A lattice of metal vent ports spanned the tower near the bottom, warm
enough to feel from several meters away. The ladder continued past it
toward a network of pipes only inches above the ground a short distance
deeper. Her fallen protector lay out upon the grid, at the center of a crater
of smashed metal slats and leaking water. She stretched one leg out,
hooking her toes on the platform before pushing herself off the ladder.
Althea caught her balance with a wave of her arms before walking a pipe,

maneuvering like an acrobat to where Shepherd's impact had flowered the steel tubing.

Blood no longer gushed from his mangled shoulders, and his vacant stare didn't turn toward her. The red glow from within the lens had faded to an almost imperceptible electronic ember. Althea stepped over a bent pipe and climbed up to sit against his side.

"I'm sorry." Grief fell on her, and she bawled. "You didn't have to do that." She sniffled, collapsing over his chest. "It's my fault."

Sob after sob fell out of her; she lost the ability to see as well as breathe. She witnessed people die many times, but for him, she felt responsible—as if she had killed him herself.

A glimmer of light flooded the base of the tower behind her. Althea looked up. A mass of writhing ribbons of pure white stretched out to either side of her like wings. They rose into the air, ethereal trails banishing the darkness with light so pure it tinged blue at the edges. Her sniveling breaths calmed, and a pass of her hand rid her cheek of tears. Scintillating energy wreathed her arms, wafting like vapor into the air. Too sad to care what happened to her, she leaned forward, and embraced the giant's neck. After kissing him on the forehead, she fell onto his chest.

"Thank you."

She hated that he had died. Blaming herself, she wished with all her might to fix the worst hurt of all. Regret and contrition surged. The radiance grew blinding, and all the strength seeped from her body.

Althea hugged her fallen guardian tight and closed her eyes, calling Shepherd's name and wailing apologies in her mind.

A CREAK OF METAL.

"I think she's in here... What the hell is that?" asked a man, intruding upon Althea's perfect calm.

A different voice said, "Fuuuuuuck this, I'm outta here."

Time hung in a cloud of non-space; Shepherd's chest hair tickled her cheek.

Pain twisted her insides, a sensation as though she had run herself to the point of vomiting. Time held no meaning.

"Deal with that. I'll go after those idiots," said a familiar female voice.

Althea lifted her head to look, but floated alone in an ocean of blue-white light. "Jamie...?"

Energy surged out of her.

A warm breath burst over the top of her head.

The blinding white light around her became all-consuming.

WHIRLING WINDS AND THE TOUCH OF A HAND ON HER BACK FADED TO SOFT warmth that enveloped her. A strange smell came to her senses, the scent of clean. Struggling to breathe, she inhaled the sweet air. She clutched her fingers into a squishy bed.

Resignation sapped the will to move from her heart. They caught her with Shepherd's body. Archon's people had found her and taken her back to her room. For a time, she lay without moving or opening her eyes, too afraid she would try to get up and find herself tethered. Footsteps shuffled somewhere nearby, followed by indistinct and unfamiliar voices: a woman talking, and far in the distance, a small child laughing. Doubt crept into her mind. She hadn't seen any little kids at the power plant.

When her eyelids parted, pure white surrounded her on all sides. She leaned up, holding an arm over her eyes until they adjusted to an unreal place that seemed nothing like the evil city or her home. The light came from a window out to blue sky, tinged by smog. The floor, white and immaculate, gleamed with a perfect reflection of everything above it. This didn't look like the place Archon had taken her.

A dull green blanket covered up to her chest. She spent minutes staring at the tents her feet made. Archon had threatened to handcuff her for a month if she tried to run again. Since her arms lay above the blanket, obviously free, she feared what she would feel if she moved her legs. A small silver cylinder clung to her right forearm by virtue of a sticky strip. From its end ran a thin rubber tube to a pad on the back of her hand. The presence of a tiny needle under the pad, inserted into her skin, intruded on her senses.

To the right, a small alcove held a toilet behind a little door next to one of those bath machines. A grinning stuffed rabbit stared at her from the silver table next to the bed. The scent of food teased her and then vanished. After a tentative pause, she pulled at her right leg, shocked that nothing held her down. She sat bolt upright, rubbing her legs and arms while reveling in the lack of restraints. Instead of a dress, she wore a snug, stretchy white garment like shorts and a shirt in one piece, but it had no apparent means of opening.

Althea pulled the plush rabbit into her lap. She squeezed it, crying before she realized why. It smelled like Karina. Her brain struggled to explain how it could.

The rubber pad behind her knuckles reminded her of the drug Violet had so craved, but she didn't feel loopy. She peeled it and licked a droplet of blood from the back of her hand where a short, plastic needle came out. Fixing such a tiny hurt happened as a reflex rather than conscious thought. Althea cringed, peeling the cylinder from her arm. The small strip that held it in place took some peach fuzz with it as it came free.

After rubbing the spot, she leapt from the bed and dashed to the window, gawking at the ground so far below it made her dizzy. The height scared the air from her chest. She recoiled from the glass, spinning around as her surroundings overwhelmed her. With nothing else to do, she clutched the plush rabbit and cast a fearful glance at the world outside.

She abandoned the window as an escape route and went for the door, but hesitated with her fingers over the handle, expecting it to be locked. When it opened with ease, she almost cried from joy. She stuck her head out the gap and peered into a busy hallway. To the right, it led past a series of other doors to a wide area with a large desk where strange false people sat. They wore white uniforms and hats bearing little red crosses. Gaps in their skin revealed metal underneath, the way they moved appeared unnatural, and they had neither thoughts nor emotions within them.

The other side had yet more doorways and ended in a small room with empty seats, fake plants, and many windows. An old man sat in a chair floating above the ground on a pad of light.

She slid a leg past the barely-open door, extending her toes to the floor outside as if an ounce too much pressure would set off alarms. Transferring her weight to the outstretched leg, she slid out of the room and stood there. When no shouting started, she crept in the direction of the desk, the rabbit tucked under one arm. Beyond the other doors lay rooms with beds like the one in which she had found herself, some empty, others with people in them. She drew near the counter, squeezing the plush toy and slowing her steps, her gaze locked upon the machine-people behind the desk. If they didn't look up, she could walk right past and escape.

At a sudden loud chime from the left, she jumped to her right, landing in a crouch atop a cushioned bench.

She flattened herself into the wall away from two silver panels that slid apart to reveal a cube-shaped room with no windows. Four men and two women walked out of it and went in different directions. She wondered how long they had been trapped in there, and didn't move until the strange cage closed again. Still breathing fast from the scare, she eased herself back to her feet but managed to take only one tentative step before a voice startled her from behind.

"Hey there, kid. Glad to see you're awake. You've been out for three days."

Althea jumped, falling once again atop the bench. Mike, one of the 'Zeroes' from the flying car, had come up behind her. His black uniform made him look like a hole in space against the stark whiteness everywhere. The shock of being snuck up on shifted to annoyance and then to worry as she thought about what Archon told her police would do to people like her. Whisk said the police were nice to kids, and she trusted him far more than Archon. She sat up and pulled her legs under her, placing the stuffed animal in her lap.

"Where am I?"

He smiled. "This place is called a hospital. It's where sick people go to get better."

"I'm not sick. Does the government want to kill me?"

He gave off shock, then confusion. "No, of course not. Our abilities are no different than guns. Having them isn't a problem—it's what you do with them that matters." Mike smiled and spoke inside her head. *Look as much as you like, sweetie. I trust you. We have a lot to talk about.*

Althea found no deception, so she relaxed. With a tentative smile, she climbed off the bench and reached for his outstretched hand.

"There are some people downstairs who want to see you..."

51

VISITORS

Althea followed Mike, stepping tentatively along strange, smooth hallways full of strange things, staring around at the commotion. The mixture of fear and wonder in her eyes attracted several nurses and staff happy to see her up and about. Few understood the nature of why she felt so frightened; none could know how a child of the Badlands felt here.

Mike came to a stop at one of those large desks where three false women with glowing eyes and odd lines on their faces worked. All had plastic faces with permanent smiles.

She shied away, positioning herself behind him.

"Nothing to be afraid of, Althea. They won't hurt you."

"The dead should not move." She shivered.

He patted her on the shoulder. "Dolls were never alive. They're machines."

Althea thought back to the one stuck in the river. "Do they want to purge taminants?"

Mike blinked, then looked into her thoughts. "Oh... oh, my. No, Althea, not at all like those things. These are administrative workers. They answer questions and help people. Think of them like a computer you can talk to."

Her eyebrows scrunched together. Her mouth opened. He laughed at the look.

"I'll explain what computers are later. Right now, we have to get you checked."

"I don't want to be checked." She stepped back, clinging to the stuffed rabbit. A ripple of silence ran over the area as every person within a hundred meters inherited a wave of angry distrust.

"Easy." Mike leaned on the counter to steady himself. "I promise you, we will not hurt you. You need to see a doctor before they will let you leave. Then, we can see your visitors."

She sagged, staring at her toes. At least she'd found a spot of warm sunlight to stand in, a momentary escape from the smooth, white and frigid alien surface everywhere else. After a few brief words with the machine-woman, Mike again took her by the hand and walked her down a different corridor to a small room. Inside, a large cylindrical tube dominated the space, while two small beds sat closer to the door. Althea stared at the tube with a tilted head.

"Is that shower meant for two people?"

Laughing, Mike guided her over to one of the beds and lifted her to sit on the edge. "No, it's a medical tank. You don't need that now, since you're not hurt, but you were asleep for several days, and no one could explain why you wouldn't wake up. We only want to make sure you're healthy."

"I feel fine." She folded her arms over the plush rabbit. "Well..." Althea let them fall onto the bed at her sides. "Maybe a little tired."

"Yeah... I imagine you might feel a bit drained after—"

"Good morning," said a dark-skinned man in a white coat, entering at a brisk stride. "Welcome to Ancora Medical. I'm Dr. Bailey."

Althea stared at metal strips along the sides of his head, studded with winking blue lights. She trembled at the white coat and looked at the ceiling above her—no metal octopus, and no straps on the bed. Even better, the man gave off concern and curiosity, no malice.

She relaxed, and remained quiet as the man waved a small device over her, connected to his head by a wire. Green laser lines slid down her limbs as it passed; she stared at the flashing emerald stripe until it vanished over her toes. He lifted her arm, flipped her wrist up and tapped it before setting it back in her lap. A small device the doctor pressed to her shoulder pinched and left a droplet of blood behind. Althea frowned at him, willing the minuscule wound closed in an instant. He plugged the machine into a console and watched funny symbols spread out next to various colored blobs. Whatever it meant, it made him smile.

As expected, he spent a great deal of time checking out her glowing eyes before he handed a small silver disc to Mike.

"She is a little undernourished, but I see no evidence of any permanent injury. Brain chemistry is consistent with a post-comatose state, though from these results, I would have said she'd been awake for a week, not hours. They tell me you have a theory about what put her in a coma for three days?"

Mike tapped his head. "Psionic stuff. She overextended herself. Extreme fatigue. She isn't undernourished. Her abilities drive her metabolism way above normal."

The doctor tapped on a datapad. "I've updated her file. Am I signing off on her discharge to the department, or does she have a parent?"

"I'll get back to you on that," said Mike.

"Can we go now?" Althea slipped off the bed.

Mike took her hand. "Do you want some slippers or sandals or something?"

"No. I don't like how they feel and they make me walk funny." She smirked at the floor. "I'll lose them when I get kidnapped again anyway."

"That life is behind you, sweetie, but we can worry about that a little later. Come on."

She padded along, holding his hand and feeling lost. He led her around a corner and up to a doorway. Despite the apparent safety of this bizarre place, it felt *wrong*. No wind tossed her hair, no earth under her feet, and no…

Mike pushed open a door.

"Karina!" She shrieked at the sight of who waited on the other side.

Before her legs gave out, she sprinted into her sister's waiting arms. Karina collapsed to her knees, burying her face in the crook of Althea's neck and sobbing as she tried to crush her with a hug. The poor plush rabbit turned into a pancake between them. Althea squeezed as hard as she could, unwittingly detonating a pulse of telempathic joy that shared her mood with everyone inside of a quarter mile. Neither girl was in any condition to speak for the better part of five minutes. When at last she regained her composure, at least most of it, Karina ran a hand over Althea's head.

"You missed your bath."

Althea flashed an impish smile. "I'm sorry. I know you told me not to get kidnapped after dark. I won't do it again."

"Is it true Beard did it?" asked Father.

Althea hadn't noticed him in the chair off to the left. She dragged Karina over and climbed onto his lap. He palmed the back of her head, pulling her cheek gently against his chest. She closed her eyes, adoring the feeling of having a dad. Karina held on to her right hand. After Father ceased stroking his hand over her hair, she leaned up and shook her head.

"Beard did not know. Dean had a bad spirit in him. It made him do it."

Father stared into her eyes for a long moment, his elation well hidden from anyone other than a telempath. "They said the man who took you is no longer a threat?"

Althea cuddled against him, basking in his joy at being reunited with her. "He won't bother me again." Remembering Archon also made her think of Shepherd. She sniffled, and then bawled into Father's denim-covered shoulder.

Karina rubbed her back. "I missed you so much."

"He was a bad man." Althea sniffled. "He hurt people. He killed my friend."

Father patted her on the cheek, then slid his hand to her shoulder. He pushed her away enough to look her in the eye. "Did he do anything to you?"

She cringed at the awful thought on his mind. "No, he did not wife me. He wanted me to do magic to people's thinking shapes. He killed Shepherd." Althea sputtered into sobs. "It's my fault he died."

Father relaxed, letting her cuddle once more. She tucked her legs up, curled entirely on his lap. He held her in stoic quiet, the polar opposite to Karina's display of emotion. He didn't have to act it out. Althea picked up on his emotion directly and found solace in his quiet strength. Karina sat on the nearest chair, keeping hold of Althea's hand.

"We found Querq," said Mike, leaning on the doorway. "Jamie and I ran out there without permission. We thought you'd like to see your family again."

"Thank you," said Althea. "Can we go home now?"

Mike held up his hand. "Not just yet…"

Althea pouted.

"There are some other people that want to meet you; it's really up to them."

"You can't keep her if she does not want to stay." The reserved hostility in Father's voice vibrated her chest. "If you are this city's Watch, she has done nothing against the law of your elders."

"Oh, no." Mike chuckled. "It's not that. She has special talents we have never seen before. All they want to do is meet her. We can help each other, and there's something"—he peeked out into the hall and waved —"else."

Althea's eyebrows drew together. She stared at the wall, listening to Father's breathing. Thoughts of Querq drifted across her mind, the kids she played with, the Water Man, Ornry, everyone there that needed her so much more than this fancy place with their fancy little red things that could do what she could do. She scowled, remembering Archon demonstrating the stimpak. This strange police man had brought her family back to her; she could tolerate the bad city a little longer.

"Thank you for bringing my family to me. I will talk to your elders, but I will not let them keep me."

Mike moved into the room, pointing at her. A shadow fell over him. Althea twisted around to look. Shepherd ducked in past the doorjamb. His tight grey sleeveless shirt did little to obscure his bulging chest muscles and... living arms. Black baggy pants and boots, clothing from this future world, covered the rest of him.

Althea crumbled her fingers into her mouth, pale as a sheet and trembling at the sight of him. Silent tears rolled down her cheeks; she forgot how to breathe. All strength left her body. The rabbit rolled out of her lap to the floor. Shepherd approached her, a warm smile on a face no longer half-metal. His eyes held full sentience. He took a knee beside her and put the stuffed animal back in her grasp.

"Hey, kid. You okay?"

If not for Father holding her, Althea would have fallen to the floor. She reached out, clasping three of Shepherd's fingers. His new arms didn't look much smaller than the ones Archon had ripped out of him.

"Y... You're alive." She sniffled, gasping as her smile let in the taste of salty tears. "I'm... I... How?"

"I remember going over the edge, falling, and a loud crash. When I got up, everyone was gone. It was so damn quiet, I couldn't even hear myself breathing. I saw this mangled body lying in the wreckage and figured I'd bought the farm. Guess that ghost stuff is for real. I got up, but this black shadow came at me. I don't know what it wanted, but it seemed pretty interested in my hide. I ran for a while, but it cornered me in one of the dead end hallways. It got real close, but then backed off. Then I heard you crying... You were calling my name, so I went to you."

Father squeezed her shoulder.

"When I got back to where I landed, you were there. Streams of silver light came out of your back like wings. You were floating there, over my body like an angel... a sad little crying angel. It wasn't your fault I died, but you kept apologizing for it. I heard your voice in my mind asking me to come back."

Althea wiped at her face with both hands, still dumbstruck mute.

Mike exhaled. "We have been trying to keep a lid on this. I'm not sure if she actually did bring the dead back, but—"

"She did." Shepherd glanced over his shoulder at him. "That freak tore a pair of Class 4 assault cyberarms off me, the ones that require torso bone replacement. Then I fell ten stories. I was dead."

Althea sniffled, reaching out to touch Shepherd's all-human face. "How... Daddy..."

Father comforted her. "Easy, girl. Some things should not be questioned. Be happy with what is. Do not worry about the why of it."

"Is"—she looked at Father, then Shepherd, then Mike—"this why I was asleep so long?"

"We think so." Mike nudged the door closed. "Your large friend here is the main reason the brass is interested in you. We had a telepath come in while you were out." He bowed his head, emitting a sad sigh. "Whatever happened to you out there made her cry. She was able to ascertain the nature of your gifts: Accelerated Healing, Telempathy, Suggestion, and a little Telepathy. However, we have no idea how it is that you can do some of the things you can do. Mostly use Accelerated Healing on other people. We've only ever seen it work on the person with the ability."

"She is the Prophet," said Father, matter-of-factly.

Althea hissed. "I hate that word. Please, Father, can I just be Althea? Prophets get put in cages and kept on leashes. I have a family."

Karina leaned into a three-way hug. "I like that."

"So, what's your story?" Father glanced at Shepherd.

"I was once in the military, UCF Colonial Expeditionary Force. I remember distant planets, dropships plunging down into the atmosphere of new worlds. A lot of it is fuzzy, something about there being more money in mercenary work, but I got my ass shot up more than I can count. Pretty sure I took a few rounds to the head, brain damage or something. This one job for a nutcase is the last thing I remember. It's all a damn blur now, nightmares of red and killing and this little twerp in a lab coat." Shepherd gestured as if crushing a man's head.

"Some men deserve to die," Althea whispered, so soft no one noticed.

"What's that?" Father tilted his head.

"Shepherd saved me from a bad man." She gazed at him with adoration in her eyes.

Father finally smiled. "Well then, I owe him my thanks."

A DESTINY HER OWN

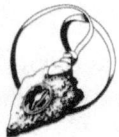

At Althea's insistence, Karina had hovered nearby while she used the autoshower. The sight of the tube brought back the last strong memory associated with it—the vision of her sister in the field. This, in turn, had left her wanting nothing to do with the impersonal bathing device. With Karina in sight, she tolerated it, but it couldn't replace her bath.

Jamie, Mike's partner, had dropped off some modern clothing for her. The plain white dress had a one-inch silver disc at each shoulder that held it closed across her chest. The hem ended halfway down her thighs. She balked at socks and kid's sneakers, but begrudgingly accepted them when Jamie pointed out they would keep her from touching the 'bad city.' As soon as she climbed into the rear seat of the Division 0 hovercar, they came off.

Her left hand held Father's; her right held Karina's. All three shared several minutes of nerves as the vehicle slid off the roof of the hospital tower. Althea stared at her knees, picking at the carpeted floor with her toes. She didn't really want to go with these police to visit their bosses, but Jamie had talked her into it as a gesture of thanks for reuniting her with her family. These people treated her like a person, like a little woman that had her own wants and needs, not like some prize for the taking. For that, she found it possible to respect them.

The ride ended far too soon when Jamie set the car down on the roof of another building. Althea slipped her feet back in the uncomfortable socks and shoes before rushing with everyone amid high winds to the shelter of a door flanked by two armored men. Father seemed most interested in their weapons, but didn't dawdle long enough to ask them any questions.

Jamie led the way into the building. More people in black, some armored, came out of doors to look at her. Many gasped at her glowing eyes. Father and Karina continued holding her hands. She squeezed a little tighter each time a new face popped up. Following a belabored explanation of the difference between elevators and cages, Althea gulped and allowed them to bring her inside one.

Her knuckles whitened as the doors closed, and she tried to burn holes in the steel with her stare until they parted to reveal a different outside than the one they had left. He led her past rows of plants both real and false in a plush lobby. A man jumped up from behind a large onyx desk and ran over, excited to see them.

"This way," he said, before jogging off down a corridor. "Wow, they really do glow."

She looked down.

Transparent security doors parted for them, and the entourage made its way down a white-painted corridor with blue-grey carpet. Althea stared at all the modern things, clean and unthreatening. This building was a world apart from the Bumwallow. She shot a forlorn look at the floor, thinking it cleaner than many plates from which she had eaten before. When they arrived at a small waiting area and took a seat in a row of violet chairs, she looked over at Mike.

"Mike? Why do people like Whisk live outside if there are nice places like this?"

"Whisk?" He raised an eyebrow.

Althea explained.

"Oh, homeless people." Mike rubbed his chin. "That's a hard one. Some actually prefer it. They call it 'rejecting society.' Other people have horrible luck, or mental issues, while others have addictions that control their life. I can't give you one clear reason for them being there."

"Fringers lack motivation," said Jamie. "They're only out there because they're lazy."

"That's an unfair generalization," said Mike, whirling on his partner. "You can't just lump them all together like that. There's a difference between fringers and homeless. Technically, off-grinders are different as well."

"Semantics," muttered Jamie.

Althea tuned out their resulting debate, leaving her chair to sit in Father's lap once more. She smiled, closing her eyes and basking in the gentle motion of his breathing. He kissed her lightly atop the head.

"I won't let them take me away again." Althea let her feet sway idly. "I won't let anyone do it anymore."

"If you can bring back the dead, I imagine you can do whatever you want," Father whispered into her hair.

She giggled for a moment, but fell somber. "I don't know if I can do that again. I don't know how I did it."

"Althea?" A young blonde woman with green eyes appeared at a doorway. "They're ready for you."

Her uniform seemed fancier than the others did, more little shiny bits. Althea stood, squinting at the new arrival.

"I'm not going alone."

"That's fine, dear."

Althea followed with her family close behind along another corridor, past two men with rifles. The escort waved her hand at a silver square on the wall. A happy chirp emanated as a door opened, leading into a large meeting room. Seated at a wide black desk, two men, one pale and older, one brown, flanked a grey-haired woman.

Althea looked up and to her left at Father. *They have judges, too?*

He squeezed her hand, then shrugged, whispering, "I imagine so."

This city is so big. Why do they only have three judges?

Father shrugged.

All three elders appeared entranced by her glowing eyes. The woman leaned on her elbows, overhead light shifted along the whorl of grey hair pinned up behind her head.

"You must be Althea. I've heard so much about you. I am Division 0 Chief Jane Carter. I am in charge of the special police that have been helping you. On my right"—she gestured at a hard-faced older man, mostly bald—"is Deputy Director Johannes Burckhardt, my immediate subordinate." Carter indicated the somewhat younger looking man on her left with dark hair and caramel-colored skin. "This is Mikhail Kovalev, Regional Commander for West City."

Althea stepped on her impatience to go home, and remained polite. "Yes. You wanted to see me?"

Mikhail leaned back, sliding a finger across an amused smirk. Althea came close to smiling at him; he seemed to like her. Burckhardt on the other hand struck her as the kind of man who hated everything, even the air he breathed. Althea squinted at him. He felt just like the raiders. He wanted to use her power.

"This one's at least ten, Johannes. Ready to strap an E-90 on her hip and send her out?" asked Mikhail, already snickering at his own joke.

The comment earned a hard stare, but no reply. Althea bit her lip, sensing Carter wanting to laugh, but hiding it.

"We have been reviewing your case files and find them very intriguing. Someone with your abilities is rather vulnerable to exploitation if not protected."

Althea tilted her head. "What's exploitation?"

"I mean, people will want to take advantage of you, make you do things you don't want to do." Carter chuckled softly. "I'm sorry, dear, it slipped my mind you have not had proper schooling."

"Oh. Like him?" She let go of Father's hand long enough to point at Burckhardt. "He wants my power. I feel greed."

Burckhardt shifted, coughing into his fist. Carter shot him an accusatory look.

Mikhail appeared about to burst with laughter. "Don't mind him. He's like that with everyone."

"We would like you to stay with us here," said Burckhardt. "We have a special school for gifted children. You will be able to learn how to be part of the modern world and at the same time be protected and safe from anyone who would hurt you."

"You want to learn me. You are just like Archon; you want to make me do things." Althea released her handholds and took a step forward, making fists. "This place is no better than out there. You want to cage me with fear instead of bars. I want to go home. I do not like this place, or that man."

Burckhardt drew a breath as if to speak.

Mikhail held a hand up, silencing him and earning a glare. "I would caution you, Johannes, don't antagonize her. Read the report on her Telempathy before you wind up a basket case."

"Bah, Telempaths." Burckhardt waved dismissively.

Carter lifted an eyebrow. "You find us weak, Johannes?"

Color drained from his face. "No, ma'am. They are just not..."

"I see." Carter cocked her head at him. "Psionics are all about weaponization to you. Pyrokinesis, Telekinesis, Mind Blast... Everything else is a mere toy, am I right?"

Burckhardt's face reddened.

Althea frowned at the imprints her toes made in the tips of her shoes as she lifted and dropped them. "I don't like to hurt people. I am not a threat to you."

"If not a threat, you are certainly careless," scoffed Burckhardt. "You let that Archon fellow live. Who knows what sort of trouble he—?"

"That is not her concern." Carter's voice started loud and dropped back to normal. "If this girl would spare the life of a man who killed her close friend, I very much doubt she could present a threat to anyone."

"Just don't shoot her sister," mumbled Mikhail.

Karina gawked, then clung to Father.

Althea gasped. "How do you know...? Oh, the lady who watched my dreams."

Mikhail grinned, tapping the tip of his nose before leaning toward Carter. "She lashed out at someone who shot her sister. In a moment of great emotion, she has the potential... But, I am confident such a thing is only possible in the most dire of circumstances."

"Yes," said Carter, her ice blue eyes softening to a grandmotherly stare. "Even now, she feels sad for the man she injured."

"Corporations would want her genetic material," added Burckhardt. "We already know someone acquired a DNA sample from the Myshkin woman."

"Yes, but she was not as this one is," said Mikhail.

"Awakened?" asked Althea. "That's what Archon called it."

Burckhardt rolled his eyes. "Puffed-up, arrogant bastard."

"What do you plan to do with your gifts, girl?" Carter sat up straight, raising one eyebrow.

"I want to go home to Querq. There are people who need me there. We don't have the little red sticks that make hurts go away. I don't like it here, everyone is so mean." Althea gazed into the warped reflections on the shiny desk, memories of her day spent wandering the city nearly brought her to tears. "I want to go home. I was happy there. All I want is to be with my family."

Karina walked up behind her and set a hand on each shoulder. Althea smiled.

"That's the Badlands. We cannot guarantee your safety there."

Burckhardt poked his finger into the desk repeatedly in a stabbing motion. "We need to keep her here and protected."

"You want to understand how I can do the things I can do. I do not like this place." Althea looked to Father. He didn't seem interested in this place either.

"I don't care where we live, as long as we are a family," whispered Karina.

Althea took another step at the table, glaring at Burckhardt. "I will not let you keep me. I am going home." She lit off a pulse of mild dread.

Carter leaned back, eyes fluttering. "Very well. Perhaps it would be best to keep you out of arm's reach of biomedical companies. If you are willing to help us as well, should the need arise, I am sure we can come to an arrangement."

Althea relaxed.

Mikhail pulled his hand away from his mouth. "As strange as it sounds, she may actually be safer out there. I doubt there is much roaming the desolation she couldn't handle, now that she is of a mind to do it." He winked at her.

"This is highly irregular," said Burckhardt, slapping the table.

"You will have ample opportunity to review the results of her training. We can work with her just as easily out there away from prying eyes as we can within the city. And she may yet consent to brief visits should the need arise." Carter offered her best grandmother's smile. "I'd offer to take you on a tour of our facility, but I think you'd rather be home."

"Yes, please." Althea leaned back into Karina, pulling her sister's arms over her chest.

A SPIRIT TOLD ME

Althea sat sideways on the porch steps, resting her head on Karina's shoulder with her legs crossed at the ankle. Clothes hung on a line running from an eyebolt by the door to the far corner, casting dancing shadows on the road. The scent of floral soap hung thick to her sister's hair. The long awaited bath/shampoo now over, she basked in the quiet warmth of being home.

She had taken an extra-long time in the tub, staying until the water became cold. As it had her first day here, the gentle touch of Karina's fingers washing her hair brought tears of joy, only this time, Althea hadn't been the only one crying. A faint breeze flapped at the hem of her dress.

An iridescent blue dragonfly circled about the porch before coming to a lazy landing upon her big toe. Its wings twisted and fluttered to the side for a few seconds before it shifted to face the wind. Karina continued raking her fingers in gentle strokes at Althea's damp hair. Happy to be home, the past several weeks grew ever distant in her memory. Soon, she would let all thoughts of the bad city fade away. She had been much happier believing in made up stories about a wall of fire at the edge of the world beyond which only the dead lived.

Karina looked up at the struggling light bulb at the center of the porch. "It is so strange to see the lights on. Do you think those electricity cubes are dangerous?"

Althea shrugged. "I dunno. Since they told us not to touch them, I think so." She tilted her foot, grinning at the insect as it moved to compensate. "They are in the power works now, no little ones are allowed inside. Not even me."

"Your new friend seems nice."

"Shepherd?" Althea squeezed Karina's arm. "He was scary when I first found him. A bad person made him do bad things. He's happy here."

"He is strong enough to use the plow alone." Karina fell quiet, as if lost in a daydream. "I'm surprised he didn't want to stay in the city with his modern life."

"He doesn't like it there. There are bad people who would hurt him, org-nized crimes."

"What's that?"

She flexed her toes, wondering how much she could move before the insect decided to fly off. It remained. "I dunno. He said they would hurt him. Besides, he wants to protect me."

"Well, you did save his life." Karina tickled a giggle out of her.

"Are you gonna marry him? You said you had first choice if a new man came to Querq."

Karina loosed an embarrassed laugh. "He's almost as old as Father, Thea. I'm only sixteen. It wouldn't be right. Besides, the city people are making us strong. Soon, others will learn of it and new men will settle here. Querq will grow. I will have a baby of my own someday. For now, I'll settle for taking care of you."

Althea nestled tighter, leaning her head against Karina's. She giggled as the dragonfly tickled its way across her foot. A moment later, the sound of men shouting to each other drew her attention. Two members of the Watch atop the wall in the distance cheered, enjoying some kind of games with their new rifles. Gouts of blue fire belched from the front as they whooped and hollered while unloading bullets on some poor, unsuspecting pile of scrap metal.

She frowned. "Why did they have to give us city guns? Why does there have to be death?"

"Be happy they let you come home. They must want very much to protect you, because they have given Querq so much. We were strong before, but now our city is a fortress. If we have such weapons, the day will come when no one dies because they will be too frightened to attack us."

The dragonfly flicked out its wings, curved its body upward, and took off. Althea sighed, watching it glide away down the street. She thought of the apparition in the garden. "Some bads don't care about guns, but I will stop them."

"I gotta pee. Will you be okay until I get back?"

Althea sat up and swung her legs off the step. "Yes." She grinned. "I'm not scared anymore."

Karina stood. Althea closed her eyes, leaning back on her elbows and enjoying the breeze in her hair. Soft footsteps thudded in the porch as her sister stumbled into the house. She took in a deep breath of clean air, held it, and let it out. Querq had none of the sour smell of that awful city. She swished her foot back and forth over a dirt path that many years ago had been a paved road. One Division 0 hovercar glided overhead, a black rectangle against the sky with a cyan glow at each corner. A throng of children chased it, cheering. Medical supplies, clothes, gardening technology, toys, and stuff for schooling had gone over well with the locals.

The gleaming vehicle circled, descending out of view past a row of houses on its way to the town square. Althea had gotten more than her fill of the high-tech city and felt no urge to pursue it, content to wait for Karina's return. Ion engines whined off into silence.

An eerie feeling settled over the area. She sat up straight and looked around at a quiet street. Nothing appeared to explain the foreboding sensation on her mind. Althea eased forward to her feet and backed up the stairs onto the porch, clenching her fists in annoyance.

"Who's there? What do you want?" she asked, refusing to be afraid.

"Relax, girl." A cloud of fog coalesced, from which a rather naked Aurora stepped out.

Althea regarded the paper-white woman for a few seconds before offering an unimpressed smirk. "What do you want? I thought you were too *civilized* to run around with no clothes?"

Aurora smiled, sauntering over to the hanging laundry. "No, that's Anna. I thought you'd disapprove of me wearing one of your friends. You didn't seem to much fancy that last time. I can't take objects with me when I cross into the astral world."

"You can't wear people." Althea held her ground. "I... I mean you *shouldn't*. I told you to leave me alone."

The woman held her hands up. "Calm yourself, girl. I am not here to take you away again, and I am not here on behalf of Archon." She offered a genuine smile. "I wanted to see what you looked like when you were happy."

A silent staring contest ensued. Aurora's all-black eyes held as much warmth as possible given her outlandish appearance.

"Fine." Althea folded her arms, tapping her right big toe into the porch like an impatient woodpecker. "What do you want?"

"I assume you are aware that he lived."

"Yes. I know."

"You could have let him die."

A petulant sigh escaped her. "No, I couldn't. You don't understand."

"Well, you know he's only going to hurt others." Aurora pulled her hair out of her eyes and held it down. "By the time this is over, more will die. I suspect a great many will if things go wrong. You could have prevented it if you left him there."

Althea gazed at her feet. "It's bad not to help. If he harms others after I mend him, it is his choice. That is not my fault. If I had let him die, that would be my fault."

"You will see him again, child."

She snapped her head up and glared.

"Not against your will. When the time comes, you will choose to be involved."

Althea bit her lip. "I don't want to see him again."

"Do not worry yourself about it now. Enjoy your home."

"Will they be hurt?" Althea took a step closer.

"If you do not follow your instincts, the possibility exists." Aurora closed her eyes for a few seconds. "However, you are not one to ignore your instincts. You will encounter a burning phoenix with sharp talons, but she has a soft heart."

"What does that mean?"

Soft *thuds* from Karina walking across the house grew louder. Aurora glanced at the wall for a few seconds, and back to Althea.

"You will understand when the time is right. Before I go, one more thing. Ask your father to send a patrol to the east into the foothills. Along the path they know as Four Zero."

Aurora's body collapsed into a glittery silver mist barely a second before Karina stepped onto the porch. She skidded to a halt in the spot where the visitor had been, and shivered. At the look on Althea's face, she ran over and took her hand.

"Is everything all right?"

"I think so... Is Father still home?"

"Yes. He is in the kitchen. It is his night for dishes."

Althea strode into the house, dragging Karina along by virtue of refusing to release her hand. Father stood at the sink with his sleeves rolled up, taking his sweet time cleaning up after dinner. Murder had several definitions, and what Father did to the Spanish song crashing over his teeth was one of them.

"Father?" She stopped right behind him.

"Yes, child?" His smile flattened at the urgent look in her eyes. "Is something the matter?"

"Can you ask a patrol to go to path Four Zero? East?"

"I can... Did you have a vision?"

Althea's face went blank. Saying 'yes' would be a lie. Inspiration struck, and she grinned. "A spirit told me to look there."

LOST WOLF

T he brush snagged less and less with each successive pass through Althea's hair. She sat on a small bench, back to Karina, fingers digging into the cushion as she grimaced. Soon, the tugging smoothed out and the brushing became pleasant. Althea relaxed, letting the motion of it pull her head about. The new nightgown they had gotten from the bad city stopped a few inches above her knees. The gossamer material didn't feel as confining as the nightgown her sister gave her, which made it better for warm nights. She scooted her feet back and forth over the rug as Karina tended to her hair, and overacted her disappointment when it became her turn to do the brushing.

After switching places, Althea spent a few minutes pulling at Karina's much thicker mane with her fingers before subjecting her to the brush. She cheated, telling the older girl's body not to notice any pain until the snagging lessened. All the while, they chattered about nothing of any importance. Karina thought one of the city police was cute, and he was only twenty-one. Five years difference wouldn't upset Father too much. Althea shrugged, having no idea how he would react.

Once Karina had enough of her hair being pulled, they settled into bed. Althea stared at the ceiling, holding Karina's arm to her chest like a doll. Father had been gone for hours, though she didn't feel any unusual worry. The mixture of concern for him and happiness at being in her bed once again made her want to stay awake and enjoy it. More and more, the bed felt comfortable. The appeal of sleeping on a hard floor or dirt grew distant. The room hung in silence for some time, the only movement the creep of a square of moonlight across the ceiling.

Karina fell asleep within a few minutes. Althea closed her eyes, not particularly trying to sleep or stay awake. The rhythmic, quiet breathing behind her made her feel tired, but still, she remained aware. A while later, the tromping of heavy boots echoed over the whole house. She sighed, expecting someone needing her help. She slipped out of bed, not disturbing Karina, and had finished changing into her day dress before Father's bellow came up the stairs.

"Althea?"

"Yes, Father, I am up."

"We found a boy. He needs your help."

Althea's yawn stalled at the concept of a wounded child. She darted out into the hall and flew down the stairs, halfway between falling and running. Father caught her at the bottom, hugging her before taking her hand and walking with her outside. Blue saturated Querq at this hour, the city lit by a pale, full moon. Most of the townies slept, save for the defenders on the wall and a man from the city sent to teach them how to operate the strange electricity boxes. Guardsmen waved at her as they passed.

"There is no need to run, Thea. You have time." He rubbed his thumb over the back of her hand. "If he spent another day out there, he might be beyond your help. You are truly a gift."

Althea thought to correct him, thinking of Shepherd, but even she doubted her ability to ever do something like that again. She wondered if she had been able to bring him back because Shepherd's death had been her fault. Perhaps such strong guilt and love had been the key. For a split second, she wondered if she could do the same for her family if something happened, but she did *not* want to picture them dead. The mere thought made her shiver.

"Oh, Althea... you don't need to be frightened." Father pulled her against him with a hand on her shoulder.

"I'm not." She fought off the dark ideas in her head and smiled. "I am happy you were not hurt."

He chuckled. "It'll take something a little tougher than a couple of Bonedogs to take this piece of saddle hide down."

"Bonedogs?" She gawked up at him.

"Yeah, five or six of the little furry bastards. We got one, but the rest took off."

She scowled at the decaying shadows of Old Querq in the distance. *You have the whole Badlands. Leave my home alone.*

When they arrived at Dr. Ruiz's clinic, she ran ahead of Father and followed the pointing finger of the nurse to a room.

Inside, a boy of about fifteen lay on a bed, sienna skin stark against the white linen. A dense mass of black hair upon his head had clumped with dirt, sweat, and blood. He faced away, rasping for air. She ran to him, noting dozens of small wounds. Crude bandages of plant leaves had been removed from animal bites on his legs; thorn marks, a healed arrow wound in his shoulder, and bruises covered the rest of him. The scent of alcohol wafted up from a steel bowl full of dirty gauze pads, no doubt the work of the nurse.

"Please bring him water. Food too, he will be hungry." Althea grabbed his arm, closing her eyes and opening her mind to the essence of his life.

She found no major sicks, much to her surprise, and proceeded to force his body to mend an uncountable number of cuts and bumps. By far, the worst was the arrow strike, as it possessed the taint of a nascent infection wrapped around a fragment of metal still stuck in bone. His skin split open at her command; tissue undulated and moved around the sliver, forcing it out. One by one, the smaller marred lines in his life-shapes sealed. He stirred, and his breathing lost the raspy wheeze.

A thin cord tugged at the back of her neck. She opened her eyes, gazing down at his hand, turning her agate arrowhead pendant between his fingers. A glint flashed over it. She reached up to guard it, grasping his fingers. She started to pull it away from him, glaring into his eyes.

But recognized him.

"D... Den?" Tears slid down her cheeks in warm trails.

He sat up, gathering her hands and holding them together. "I said I would find you. I am no longer of the tribe." He flashed his crafty-fox grin. "You are still pretty, even if you are too pale."

She gulped, wide-eyed with shock. Her breath fell into erratic flutters as she traced her hand over where the raider shot him in the leg. "Y... You almost died."

"Almost." He winked.

Before he could say anything else, she leaned up on tiptoe and did that lip-touching thing.

fin

ACKNOWLEDGMENTS

Thank you for reading Prophet of the Badlands!

Additional thanks to Jackson Tjota for the cover illustration, Ricky Gunawan for the interior art, and Alexandria Thompson for the cover layout.

I'd also like to express my thanks to "the group" for the inspiration to create these characters. Martin Capdevielle, Pam Harris, Arcelio Serrano, and Ed Soroka. The Awakened series is loosely based on a game I ran, though as they say, some names have been changed to protect the not-so innocent.

This series is somewhat unconventional in that the first five books each focus on a different character, with their stories combining in book six. (However, Althea remains my favorite and she creeps up in the other books.)

I'd also like to thank Althea for making a drastic change to the story. I'm an outliner, and I arrange everything ahead of time before writing. My original outline called for her to be exiled from Querq and wind up in West City as a ward of Division 0. However, while writing the scene where Karina washes Althea's hair, the two formed a much stronger emotional bond than I had anticipated. It felt as though Althea appeared in the room beside me, shaking her head when I got to the exile part. She refused to give up on her new family and demanded I change how the story went.

And so, I did.

ABOUT THE AUTHOR

Originally from South Amboy NJ, Matthew has been creating science fiction and fantasy worlds for most of his reasoning life. Since 1996, he has developed the "Divergent Fates" world, in which *Division Zero, Virtual Immortality, The Awakened Series, The Harmony Paradox, and the Daughter of Mars series* take place. Along with being an editor at Curiosity Quills press, he has worked in IT and technical support.

Matthew is an avid gamer, a recovered WoW addict, Gamemaster for two custom RPG systems, and a fan of anime, British humour, and intellectual science fiction that questions the nature of reality, life, and what happens after it.

He is also fond of cats.

Visit me online at:
   Facebook: https://www.facebook.com/MatthewSCoxAuthor
   Amazon: https://www.amazon.com/author/mscox
   Pinterest: https://www.pinterest.com/matthewcox10420/
   Goodreads: https://www.goodreads.com/author/show/
7712730.Matthew_S_Cox
   Email: mcox2112@gmail.com

OTHER BOOKS BY MATTHEW S. COX

Divergent Fates Universe Novels
Division Zero series

- Division Zero
- Lex De Mortuis
- Thrall
- Guardian
- Harbinger

The Awakened series

- Prophet of the Badlands
- Archon's Queen
- Grey Ronin
- Daughter of Ash
- Zero Rogue
- Angel Descended

Daughter of Mars series

- The Hand of Raziel
- Araphel
- Ghost Black

Virtual Immortality series

- Virtual Immortality
- The Harmony Paradox

Prophet of the Badlands Series

- Prophet's Journey

Divergent Fates Anthology

The Roadhouse Chronicles Series

- One More Run
- The Redeemed
- Dead Man's Number

Faded Skies series

- Heir Ascendant
- Ascendant Unrest
- Ascendant Revolution

Temporal Armistice Series

- Nascent Shadow
- The Shadow Collector
- The Gate to Oblivion
- The Queen of Discord

Vampire Innocent series

- A Nighttime of Forever
- A Beginner's Guide to Fangs
- The Artist of Ruin
- The Last Family Road Trip
- The Phantom Oracle
- How Not to Summon Demons
- Ordinary Problems of a College Vampire
- A Vampire's Guide to Surviving Holidays
- An Introduction to Paranormal Diplomacy

Standalones

- Wayfarer: AV494
- Axillon99
- Chiaroscuro: The Mouse and the Candle

- The Spirits of Six Minstrel Run
- Sophie's Light
- The Far Side of Promise anthology
- Operation: Chimera (with Tony Healey)
- The Dysfunctional Conspiracy (with Christopher Veltmann)
- Of Myth and Shadow
- The Girl Who Found the Sun

Winter Solstice series (with J.R. Rain)

- Convergence
- Containment
- Catalyst

Alexis Silver series (with J.R. Rain)

- Silver Light
- Deep Silver
- Silver Quarrel

Samantha Moon Origins series (with J.R. Rain)

- New Moon Rising
- Moon Mourning

Vampire For Hire series (with J.R. Rain)

- Moon Master
- Dead Moon
- Lost Moon

Maddy Wimsey series (with J.R. Rain)

- The Devil's Eye
- The Drifting Gloom
- Dark Mercy

Samantha Moon Case Files series (with J.R. Rain)

- Blood Moon

Immortal Operative series (with J.R. Rain)

- Broken Ice

Four Elements series (with J.R. Rain)

- The Elementalist
- The Black Rose
- The Wakefield Curse

Young Adult Novels

The Eldritch Heart Series

- The Eldritch Heart
- The Cursed Crown

Evergreen Series

- Evergreen
- The World That Remains
- The Lucky Ones
- Nuclear Summer

Standalones

- Caller 107
- The Summer the World Ended
- Nine Candles of Deepest Black
- The Forest Beyond the Earth
- Out of Sight

Middle Grade Novels

The Adventures of Ubergirl series

- My Dad is a Mad Scientist
- Aliens Ate My Homework
- The End of all Halloweens

Tales of Widowswood series

- Emma and the Banderwigh
- Emma and the Silk Thieves
- Emma and the Silverbell Faeries
- Emma and the Elixir of Madness
- Emma and the Weeping Spirit

Standalones

- Citadel: The Concordant Sequence
- The Cursed Codex
- The Menagerie of Jenkins Bailey

www.ingramcontent.com/pod-product-compliance
Lightning Source LLC
Chambersburg PA
CBHW020505260626
47156CB00006B/1864